Julie E. Czerneda

BEHOLDER'S EYE

DAW BOOKS, INC.
DONALD A. WOLLHEIM, FOUNDER
375 Hudson Street, New York, NY 10014

ELIZABETH R. WOLLHEIM
SHEILA E. GILBERT
PUBLISHERS

Cover art by Luis Royo.

DAW Book Collectors No. 1100.

DAW Books are distributed by Penguin Putnam Inc.

First Printing, October, 1998
6 7 8 9

"OUR PROBLEM IS IMMEDIATE. AND NEEDS A DRASTIC SOLUTION."

"Does this mean you are planning to excise me from the Web?"

"Pointless," Ersh responded. "Close the door and lock it."

I didn't see how she did it, but a small rectangular space opened in the rock wall. A puff of mist slipped out and sank. Ersh reached one hand inside the opening, and carefully brought out a well-wrapped object, then resealed the hidden compartment before turning to me.

"Take this."

It was cold, cold and heavy.

"Some might call what you're holding a gift, Esen," Ersh said quite sadly. "You are at least wise enough to know better. Lock the door behind me. We will talk again when you are ready."

I did as she asked. After what Ersh said, I wanted nothing to do with it. But would it do any harm to see what I was refusing?

A smooth, blue drop winked at me, its flawless surface like some fabulous gem. An irresistible hunger surged through me and I snapped up the morsel before I had time to think.

Ersh-taste exploded in my mouth, scalding like acid. I cycled desperately. Web-form. Blind, deaf, and dumb, I huddled as Ersh-memory burned through me. She had been right. *This was no gift.*

I now knew what I had done. It wasn't the Humans Ersh feared.

The Web had mortal enemies. Enemies Ersh had fled by traveling across a galaxy. Enemies she had hidden from for thousands of years. We'd been safe.

Until I'd introduced myself to a Human. . . .

Novels by
JULIE E. CZERNEDA
available from DAW Books:

Web Shifters
BEHOLDER'S EYE
CHANGING VISION

Trade Pact Universe
A THOUSAND WORDS FOR STRANGER
TIES OF POWER

To Aleksander Antoni Maciej Czerneda
There are many people who have faced challenge and change throughout their lives, but I can't imagine anyone who has faced adversity with such grace, adventure with more gallantry, or indeed has experienced all life offers with so much wonder and joy. My love and this book are for you.

Aleksandrowi Antoniemu Maciejowi Czernedzie

Jest wielu ludzi, którzy stawiali czola wyzwaniom i zmianom przez cale swoje życle, ale nie znam nikogo, kto przeclwnośol losu przyjmowalby bez gniewu, szarmanoko pokonywał przeszkody, czy też z entuzjazmem i radością zakosztowal wszystkiego, co życie mu zaoferowało. Moja miłość i ta książka jest dla Ciebie.

ACKNOWLEDGMENTS

My second book! Thank you, Sheila Gilbert, for your belief in me. (And thanks, Debra and Amy, for answering those neophyte questions.) Thank you, Luis Royo, for your wonderful book covers. We have indeed "connected across the kilometers." Thank you, Scott Sellers of Penguin Canada, for putting so much effort into an unknown. The entire Czerneda family would like to thank Marìa Strarz-Kañska for kindly providing the Polish translation of the dedication. And, most importantly, my thanks to all those readers who took a chance on a new author's first book. I hope you had fun with it, too.

I've been overwhelmed by the support I've received this past year from professionals and fans alike. Thank you, Josepha Sherman, for the "Js' Tour," where I learned to spot a bookstore in any language. Thank you, Lois McMaster Bujold, for showing your fans my book during my first pro panel. Thank you, Larry Stewart, artist and friend, for being even more excited than I was. Thanks Allysen Palmer, for my first fan letter, Merilyn Vyse, for offering to be my first fan club president, and to all at Orillia Smithbooks. Thank you, Anne Bishop, Alison Baird, Robert J. Sawyer, Ken Day, Barbara Saxberg, and Marion Hughes for your support. And to Guy Gavriel Kay, for explaining how to graciously handle comments from readers, even related ones.

Thank you, Scott Czerneda, for your help in planning the strategy and weaponry used in the battle scenes. You're hired! And thank you to the rest of my family: Roger, Jennifer, my Dad, Tony, Maureen, Colin, Bryan, Philip, Veronika, and Mum. If it seems a long list, it's because I'm one of those fortunate folk who could never give back as much love as she receives.

CONTENTS

Out There

YOU could die here. Repair shops and the law were a week away, translight. And the hazards of the Fringe arrived in the blink of an eye: a blocked air hose, a cracked panel, a visitor tempted by opportunity.

Of course—flip side of risk—you could strike it rich. You could even live long enough to enjoy it. So you cared for your equipment—and tried for crew that valued their own hides.

The crew of the starship that nestled against the mid-sized asteroid, sharing its skewed orbit around sister stars, knew all this. They lay awake in their bunks, counting on their future, listening to the ship's mauler as it chewed into the metal-rich rock like the teeth of a lamprey into the body of a hapless fish. Few more weeks—the ship's stomach would be full, and they'd all be rich.

Counting on a future in the Fringe was dangerous. That asteroid night, Death came in along the ecliptic, undetected until it cracked the starship's hull and began to hunt.

"Mayday . . . May—" The screams for nonexistent help ceased almost at once.

The mauler didn't pause. It ground its way deeper, the rich ore tumbling into the holds, that growl the only sound echoing in the empty corridors.

The corridors where Death searched, still hungry.

1: Moon Morning

"ESEN-ALIT-QUAR." Those with mouths chanted my name for the third and last time, echoes rattling down the cliff like loose stones.

Welcome home.

I tried to savor the moment, then gave up. There were too many new memories intruding on the familiar. Maybe it was the aftermath of all that had happened, not the least being the return trip from Rigel II. I'd gone from barely escaping with my life to almost being enlisted in a war. About the only good thing had been the relief of being anonymous again.

So now I was home, which to some species meant a birthplace. To me, and those with me, home was wherever the Web gathered. Today's home was Picco's Moon, early morning, and bitterly cold.

Everyone present, except Ersh. I suspected glumly she'd sent the meeting call from her rocky moon the day I'd left on my disastrous mission to Kraos.

"Esen-alit-Quar," intoned the voices again, as if impatient.

"I'm ready," I mumbled, which was technically true.

I stood, tongue loose and panting, and watched the members of my Web take their places around me. Ansky was over to my left. She was agitated enough to be midcycle, more rainbow than flesh, likely radiating heat as she fought to control the energy waiting to be released by her every molecule. *No support there.* Still, I found it reassuring one of my Elders could be in such a state. Whenever we cycled into other forms, it required a sacrifice of our mass into energy to distort and bend our essential structure, energy that in part remained within that structure, a potential like the compression of a spring. Releasing form, like releasing that spring, had its inevitable results. Learning to return to web-form without damaging the neighborhood with pyrotechnics was the first, basic lesson of our kind. *If Ansky was struggling with this,* I decided uncharitably, *maybe my own recent performance wasn't so bad.*

As usual, Mixs had been late, scampering to her place on the six legs of her preferred form. Personally, I found her about as compassionate as the Hive species she lived with most often. *There's one who wouldn't forgive a loss of control.*

The other two, Skalet and Lesy, stopped chanting my name, abruptly in web-form. They looked revoltingly cheerful. *As if none of the others had ever made mistakes,* I thought to myself, making sure the memory remained private.

Where was Ersh?

The wind was damp and stank of sulfur. The Web met where Ersh decided; today's decision did not bode well for me. I avoided the cliff edge, knowing from experience that its jagged plunge made me queasy. There wasn't a scrap of vegetation in sight, not that Picco's Moon was overly life-endowed; what there was huddled in the immense cracklike valleys girdling the equator. The rising bulge of Picco itself on the horizon was its usual eye-straining orange and purple. When fully exposed, the giant gas planet's lurid reflection did truly nauseating things to the local landscape. The distant white sun gave up the struggle to produce color except during the occasional eclipse.

But the place was old with tradition. The footsteps, or whatever, of the Web had worn the path up to this rocky pinnacle smooth during the last millennia. It was remembered by all of us as "the peak where truth is shared." There were other, nastier connotations, but I refused to remember them.

A soft thump and shuffle. Then a wheezing sound. The sequence repeated, growing louder. Louder to me, anyway, since I was the only one currently with ears. I watched the edge where the worn stone stairs led to the top.

First the knobby end of a stick appeared, thump, then the wispy gray-haired head of the very, very old Human female using it as a cane. Her breath wheezed in, fluttered as if stuck, then wheezed out again. Her feet shuffled along the rock as if reluctant to part from it.

There were reassuring gasps, twitters, and color changes around me. *Ersh, in Human form?* She hadn't used it in at least three hundred years—certainly never in front of me. When I was very young, I used to wonder why. When Ersh judged me old enough to share her memory of Humans, I knew.

Ersh's years didn't translate well as a Human. Her steps were as labored as her breathing. She was naked despite the wind, her skin hanging like tatters of cloth on her bones as she made her slow way to the sixth and last place in the Web.

Her bright black eyes found and impaled me. I felt my ears go flat against my head and my tail slip between my legs; I panted as my body temperature soared, an instinctive dump of energy as I fought the urge to cycle. To lose form because of an emotional response would not impress Ersh.

Those eyes were anything but feeble, despite her form. And the other message about Ersh and the Human species was plain before us all, aimed at me, no doubt. Form-memory was unforgiving. Her thin right arm ended halfway above the elbow in a smooth blunt tip—a reminder that as a Human Ersh had sacrificed her flesh rather than cycle before aliens.

No, this wasn't going well. I straightened up. "I'm ready to share, Senior Assimilator," I said as steadily as I could. I released my hold on the molecules of my body with relief, cycling back into my web-form, feeling echoing releases of energy warm the air as Ansky and Mixs did the same. I concentrated on maintaining my outline in the proper flawless teardrop.

No touch, no hearing, no sight, no sense of smell. Yet in my web-form I was exquisitely sensitive to other, rarer things: the complexities of chemical structure, the dizzying spin of stars and atoms, the pervading harmony of electromagnetism. The gravity of the planet was like a deep throbbing heart above me, the moon's a soft counterpoint.

The wonder of it all usually took me a moment to grasp. Today, I almost ignored the change, busy interpreting information about my Web. Skalet and Lesy were struggling to keep their shape integrity, losing it once or twice. Typical—they were easily rattled by Ersh. Then Ersh herself, next to invisible to me as a Human, became clear in all the perfection of her web-form.

I tasted her message in the wind. *Share.*

This was it. I shunted my private memories deeper within. There was no point taking chances with Ersh in this mood. Then I spread, elongating myself from teardrop to five reaching arms, offering one to each of the other web-forms, keeping central only the minimum mass I needed to maintain personal survival. I sensed their mouths form and open wide, tooth ridges sharp and uneven. They closed in and began to feed.

For an instant, I wondered what beings of other species would think if they could see us now, like this. Could those outside the Web possibly understand? We had no equivalents for words like agony or pleasure. In sharing, the giving of mass has more to do with endurance than pain, and certainly is more like duty than ecstasy. Even for us, being consumed is a fundamental threat to life, and the instinct to cycle and survive has to be fought. How could I explain that winning that battle, to offer life in trust, brings a wonderful joy, an intensity of belonging and acceptance? Without this understanding, all that would be seen was the horror of their feasting.

Why had I thought horror? The urge to flee suddenly threatened to overwhelm me. I kept myself whole by remembering the joy and belonging from other times, holding it like a shield against each hungry bite, each slice of tooth through my flesh.

I'd never had so much to share. Their feeding seemed to go on for hours. So, by the end, there was very little of me left. For a time, I sensed extinction and wavered, wondering if this was Ersh's judgment.

Then the command came. *Feed.* I found the strength to form a mouth of my own somehow, but not to move. *Feed.* Substance in my mouth. I bit down and ripped a piece free, chewed. Ersh-taste. Ersh-memory. I felt myself grow, enlarged my mouth, ate faster. Ansky-taste, now Skalet. One after another, my kin gave me their mass in exchange for mine, the transfer precise and totally satisfying.

At some point, they left me. I huddled, alone on the rock, to assimilate what I had been given. It takes a while to weave the threads of five other memories, to take living pieces of five other lives and work them into your own. I struggled to detach information from personality, to hold what was Esen intact and free of the influence of those others, respectfully shedding what I dared not keep as moisture to the air, each evaporating droplet a spark of cold on my surface. Ersh, as Senior Assimilator, had always fed from them first, then given all to me presorted. I supposed, having got myself into so much trouble, Ersh felt I'd grown beyond such pampering.

I wasn't in a hurry anyway. I knew what the others were assimilating in turn. My memories of Kraos. And my adventures with the Humans.

2: Planet Day

KRAOS. My first mission. I had been so proud, so sure of myself. Too sure, as things turned out.

Ersh's warnings, which I in my wisdom ignored, were all variations on the same theme: "It's different on your own, Youngest." *Different? Of course it would be,* I'd said to myself. I'd at last be free of their advice, their decisions, and, most importantly, their belief that as youngest, I was least.

Or did Ersh think I was a fool? I knew how essential it would be to maintain shape on Kraos—to think and be what I appeared. Or did she (and the others) simply expect me to fail? Well, I was confident enough for all the Web. Especially when I learned the camouflage best suited to my mission was the canidlike Lanivarian, my birth shape. It would be no real test of my skill to cycle and hold shape, if that was all I had to be. I suspected Ersh had chosen my assignment in order to give me that advantage—implying I'd need all the help I could get.

Unfortunately, Ersh was right. *I hated that.*

My rude awakening had come the instant the clouds overhead consumed the shuttle, leaving me alone on the Kraosian mountaintop. I'd panicked, releasing my shape integrity so quickly it was a wonder Skalet didn't pick up the heat signature from orbit. I'd quivered and oozed in web-form, tasting the alien wind as it tried to coat me with dust.

My next coherent act was to lodge myself out of sight. Exposing web-form to alien eyes was forbidden. This wasn't difficult, given Skalet's choice of my drop-off site. There was a small, hard-to-find cave nearby for me to hide in, though Skalet had expected me to use it to hold any artifacts I decided to collect.

In the cave's womblike darkness, I argued, pleaded, begged, and threatened myself—to no avail. Every few hours, I would gather my nerve, sacrifice mass into the needed energy, summon form-memory, and cycle into Lanivarian form. I'd set my paws on the path out of the cave, ready to take the road down to the city where the subjects of my work waited.

And I'd revert to web-form in a blaze of exothermic energy. The cave was soon black with soot.

I had nightmares about a curious Kraosian peering in at me. Forget the potential for disaster inherent in my virtually exploding at the beginning of any conversation; I had to worry about the result if the poor creature survived and witnessed my resulting cycle into web-form. Kraos was an untouched world, without even literature to hint at the possibility of extrakraosian life. I could start some.

But Skalet wouldn't be back for another ten planet years. How long could I stay locked up by my own stage fright?

My Lanivarian form began to fray at the thought; I cycled back to web-form just in time to stave off another cataclysm.

I recalled Ersh's advice when I had left her. If I couldn't sustain my form, she'd said—the mere suggestion of which I'd found offensive at the time—go back to basics and retrain myself. Really going back wasn't an option for the next ten solar orbits. I settled in my cave to relearn from my own memories.

The teardrop web-form is the original, root-shape of my kind. Changing shape—cycling—to match our molecular structure to that of our surroundings is an instinctive response to danger. Fortunately, this instinct is so far back in the Web's past that it happens only rarely. As Youngest, I could testify that it is very humiliating to have one's edges trying to match a curtain or floor under stress.

Harnessing this instinct to cycle from one form to another involves learning fine control. Acquiring this control, I'd found, has less to do with being taught than it has to do with being tormented by one's peers. It is like humanoid children who taunt one another to see who can hold their breath longest.

I, of course, am not and have never been a child. I may be Recent, but then, that's our way.

I had a mother. Sort of. When Ansky answered the howls of masculine nature on Lanivar, some five standard centuries ago, she was simply indulging her risky predilection for romance. Fortunately for the inhabitable planets of this galaxy, genetic combinations that result in offspring of Web stock occur perhaps once a millennium—if that. The rest of Ansky's follies lived out normal ephemeral lives as perfectly normal specimens of their father's species.

Ansky herself had the dubious pleasure of innumerable flings, far too many of which ended in a pregnancy which locked her in a steadily enlarging and uncomfortable form for its duration. Not a pretty picture. Still, Ansky enjoyed this vicarious lifestyle enough to succumb on a fairly regular schedule, with one such occasion leading to my arrival. Her surprise for Ersh. But that's another tale.

Oh, yes. Breath holding. Well, imagine you have accepted the challenge and drawn in the biggest breath you can possibly hold. This is like the moment when a fragment of web-mass is converted to energy and spread throughout the web-form, deforming and altering molecular structure to match memory.

At first, the urge to laugh it all out immediately seems irresistible. But you hold on, feeling like you'll burst well before your rival.

Then, as you begin to feel in control, your confidence rises. Nothing to it. You wink at your friends, pleased by the growing respect on their faces.

Seconds drag past, slowing as they go. You hold on. Your ears feel pressure. Nothing painful, but you have to consciously control the urge to breath out, to empty your heavy lungs, and fill them again. Your throat feels swollen, as if the air trying to escape has somehow concentrated itself there, at the gateway. This is how it feels when web-form struggles to release energy, to allow bent, twisted molecules to return to normal.

Still you hold. But it's hard.

The difficulty passes. After a while, you wonder if you've forgotten how to breathe. Your thick head seems to have lightened. Things appear clear to your eyes, yet farther away. You could do this forever. Success is at hand.

Your friends are shaking you. You can't hear their voices over your heart's rhythm, an ocean in your ears. You realize that you are dying, killing yourself, yet the willpower to survive seems lost.

Somehow, a whimper of air slips through your nostrils. It signals the explosion as your abused lungs throw out the stale dead air. You can hardly finish breathing out before every muscle of your body strains to suck in life, fresh air pouring down your throat like a cool drink in summer. Web-form reestablishes itself, radiating energy in wavelengths perceived as relief.

Another, calmer breath, and you grin at your anxious friends. "No problem."

Converting web-mass to energy is a pointless sacrifice unless harnessed to form-memory and used. Cycling is the easy part. Maintaining a different shape confines energy, like the air held in lungs. The pain of it is primal, but then so is the fear of failure. I grew up on stories of Recents exploding rather than losing form before granted leave to cycle.

Although totally accurate memory is my kind's pride and curse, I had my doubts about exploding Recents. I'd never caused anything more traumatic to my surroundings than the odd thermal crater. The trick was to know your limits and push beyond them each time. My first shape change lasted mere seconds, just long enough to experience triumph. Relaxing back to web-form, I felt the loss of mass as an imbalance, a not-unpleasant hunger that proved what I was.

By my second century, I had mastered the techniques necessary to hold an alien form for several minutes, with little or no discomfort. Frustratingly, my Elders in the Web seemed able to exist indefinitely in any form they chose. Some rarely appeared in web-form at all, finding life more convenient in a shape with hands, tentacles, or other digits to handle the local technology.

Driven by their amused contempt (or worse, their "it will come to you" attitude), I gradually learned a finer control of the energy holding my changed body together. There were ways to reduce the strain, some as simple as holding body temperature above species norm, especially on cold nights, draining tiny amounts of excess energy. Another hundred years of practice, and I was rarely driven from form until I was ready.

It was about this time in my life, having worked and suffered for such a worthy goal, that I discovered my omnipotent Elders were actually cycling in closets or when they thought I wasn't around in order to encourage my efforts.

By my fourth century, I'd perfected my art. I could slip in and out of any remembered form and hold it indefinitely. And Ersh, Senior Assimilator of the Web, grudgingly admitted that though I was Most Recent (and she hoped I would stay that way, with Ansky under her watchful eye), I was now qualified to serve the Web. I could have a job.

And so I was on Kraos to do my duty to my Web—to obtain molecular samples of the intelligent species on this world and memorize all matters of its behavior and culture. When my task was done, the information would be assimilated by my Web, adding a new species to our shared memory. Ersh would at last be proud of me.

Given I could pull myself, literally, back together.

Hunger was what finally cured my fright. Each attempt to cycle had, of course, cost me mass. The only way to replace that mass was to assimilate other living matter into web-mass.

A wind-bent shrub grew conveniently into the front of my hiding place. I thinned myself, coating the branches and leaves I could reach easily, and coaxed the plant molecules to reform into more of me.

It was when I used up the last remaining vegetation around the cave that I suddenly realized I was out of options.

I could ignore this particular hunger, as long as I didn't need to cycle into a form of equivalent size. Which was the problem.

The Lanivarian form so necessary to my work on Kraos was my birth form. I knew instinctively when my web-mass was equivalent to it—or when I was too small for that particular change. Given the mass I'd expend to cycle again, I was much too close to the limit I needed to keep. If I couldn't hold the Lanivarian form in my next attempt, I would be forced to abandon that shape until I could locate and convert more living mass somewhere on this mountain.

I did have the choice of staying in web-form—a choice

that included hiding in this cave for the next planet decade, or risk breaking the Web's first and inviolate Rule: never expose the true form to aliens. I shuddered. *Ersh would have a lot to say about that.*

I cycled, gripped form memory more tightly than I ever had before, and found myself panting after a few minutes, panting, but whole.

I stretched one hand out of the darkness to sample the sunlight outside the cave. Warmth, no more. Still, this limited form had excellent scent and vision. I took a tentative step forward, then another. The air was cool and fresh in my lungs. So far, so good.

Now for my disguise. I carefully curled the fingers of both hands, exposing their broad padded knuckles. Every second of stability in this form gave me more confidence. *I can do this,* I thought. I realized, belatedly, that Ersh had not doubted me. I had doubted myself.

I dropped forward, my long front arms easily matching my legs for length. Lanivarians reserved this posture for distance running and the odd theatrical event. I swung my jaw upward and laughed at the wind as it carried news of the unsuspecting city below. *An actor I would be.*

3: Market Morning

I'D licked the problem of holding form. And six hundred days later, I'd accomplished the first half of my task: deciphering the molecular structure of the Kraosians. I'd scrounged hair and nail clippings from several hundred different individuals simply by hanging around the rear of barbershops for a couple of months. That information was safely chewed, swallowed, and incorporated into my biochemical memory. I was a success.

I spat out a flea.

The tricky bit was learning what Kraosians did with their biochemistry. Ersh was right, again. Formal training just hadn't prepared me for Kraos.

"Welcome! Come! Come Here!" the shrill singsong from somewhere over my head was immediately smothered by a multitude of others, each attempting to broadcast its greeting to shoppers first—or at least loudest. You'd have to be deaf to sleep past dawn within earshot of Suddmusal's Marketplace.

Or be comfortably tucked under a thick pile of fabric scraps, which blocked sound as effectively as it kept away the evening's damp. Worming my head through the stiff layers, I peered up at the fading stars. Definitely morning. I'd overslept.

Not the first time either, I thought with a twinge of conscience. I turned the twinge into a stretch, trying to pull the kinks out of my spine. *Ah, that was better.* A little rotation on the left hip eased another tight spot.

A long but worthwhile night, I consoled myself, working free of my warm nest. More dry bits of information discovered and carefully remembered—duty first, everything carefully shunted to the memory core I would share with my Web.

I briefly closed my eyes to better recall last night, easily summoning the images of overlapping circles of streetlight and torch, pavement glistening with dew, figures moving from shadow to puddled light, ramshackle booths unfolding like midnight blossoms. The only sounds had been the occasional muffled word or the snick of a clip to its ring. Even the ongoing game of cheat inches from your neighbors' space had seemed choreographed for my entertainment.

Daydreaming again—the path to a short and inglorious life. Embarrassed, I opened my eyes and began to pay proper attention to my surroundings.

The market was as loud in the brightening daylight as it had been silent at night. Unmindful of the barrage of voices, shoppers struggled good-naturedly with each other to reach the merchant of their choice. Everyone knew the pavement would be bare again in another hour or so, every booth collapsed and swept into its cart as if the market was evaporated daily by the punishing heat of this season. Kraosians were nothing if not sensible folk about weather.

I surveyed today's edition of the market, its confusion already well in place. Scents ranging from delicious to rancid forced their way into my nostrils and stuck on my tongue. "Welcome! Come! Come here!" shrilled that voice again. I flattened my ears against the noise, but it was of little use.

I was surrounded by singers.

The Kraosian version of tourists loved Suddmusal's market—more precisely, they loved its singers. Every booth, regardless of its size or the value of its goods, boasted a living signpost—a hired singer perched precariously atop a makeshift pole; this pole typically a vital support for the booth itself. In the predawn coolness, it was rather charming to listen to the first, fresh voices caroling out their wares: a soprano from the plumbing dealer gateward, a warbling tenor from the pottery shop closer at hand.

Unfortunately, volume was more valuable than tune when singers were rubbing elbows. Once the market was packed, both voices and tempers quickly wore thin. The woman clinging to the pole above me mercifully stopped for a moment, but it was only to swirl water in her mouth from the flask hanging round her neck. She spat accurately at her nearest neighbor, then began to shriek again. "Welcome—"

I launched myself away from the fabric dealer, seeking the safest route among the dust swirls kicked up by heavy feet, dodging through a forest of wool-clad legs. Course, I wasn't the only one down here.

From my chosen vantage point, a meter or so from the ground, the market had a second set of visitors: small, shelled, and multilegged, or larger and sinuous on four legs such as I. I counted and cataloged each automatically, for myself taking special note of the occasional groomed and perfumed beasts. The well-fed pets which accompanied their Kraosian masters and mistresses to market were unpleasantly eager to sink their teeth into the haunches of freer creatures.

Finding a temporary haven beneath the bed of a cart, I sprawled out and amused myself briefly by pulling a mat of spiny seeds from between my longest toes. It was a precise procedure: teeth had to be placed just so, then a gentle squeeze and sharp tug. I chewed the tasteless lump thoughtfully before spitting it out.

I was definitely living my appearance. I permitted myself a grin. Old Ersh would probably have cycled before sinking her teeth into my last meal of fish bones followed by fruit rinds furred with mold. "All in a day's work for those in the field," I dared to mimic her didactic tones to myself. "Field observers must be inconspicuous." I'd learned for myself that being inconspicuous usually translated as uncomfortable and bored.

I stretched again, pulling the last knots out of rangy muscles and feeling lazy pleasure in the suppleness of my spine. A quick glance up at the too-bright sky. I really was late for work. I spent a moment yawning, then flicked my mind into alertness. I was, after all, a professional.

Well, not quite, but I would be one day. I would succeed here and then—well, anything was possible then. I knew this was pride, or at least ambition, and therefore highly improper. However, no one here cared, and I certainly wasn't about to worry.

Why was summoning that pride this morning unexpectedly hard? I found myself wondering. Perhaps it was because today marked my six hundredth day on Kraos. My six hundredth day of talking to myself.

I sneezed dust from my nostrils and tried to twitch that useful pride. *What had I expected?* As youngest, a dubious distinction as I was frequently reminded, I was expected to appreciate my assignment for what it was—a way to keep me out of trouble while I matured.

Well, it didn't matter. I would make the best of this place and my time here. If the path of advancement meant a slow, lonely march up each strand of the Web, so be it. I might suffer from the impatience of youth, but I was determined enough to match anyone's centuries of experience.

I stood, checked my path with practiced care, and stepped back into the dust-filled maze of legs.

Ah. My first destination, reached without incident. I surveyed the area from the shadows behind the strident inventory of a rug merchant's booth before venturing out. The open-air café, although just as short-lived as any of the booths, had a customary spot which boasted the shade of a misshapen, drought-denuded tree. It also had a clientele which often as not included highly placed officials and landowners. The gossip here was frequently worth committing to memory.

It was, of course, completely irrelevant to a professional such as myself that the table scraps were of exceptional quality. I slipped into my own customary spot, safely out of sight of the serving staff, and cocked my over-sized ears wistfully.

"Hey, Cradoc, your friend's shown up after all." This announcement came from the group at the table nearest me. I didn't need my nose to tell me what was available today; I could see the crisp brown tips of fat little sausages overlapping a yellow platter near the table's edge. I let the tip of my tongue hang delicately.

Cradoc, a good-natured if coarse fellow I had singled out for attention several mornings recently, tossed one of the sausages to me with a laugh. I caught it deftly in my teeth, careful as always to keep my betraying front paws covered by a curl of tail. It wouldn't do here to seem different from the curs freely accepted as scavengers in the market and city. *Little risk of such exposure this morning,* I thought, saliva running freely and shamelessly from my open jaws. *What a delightful beginning to my day.*

"—not me . . . nothing he's said makes sense . . . I'll not—" the voice rising from behind and to one side of my benefactor was hotly defensive. It struck a jarring note in the calm bustle of the eatery; some people turned, seeking the source, then went back to their own conversations.

I missed the rest of what was said, occupied with holding the sausage cautiously, if awkwardly, in my jaws. I didn't dare bite down, since its tasty interior was hot enough to scald my tongue. My predicament amused Cradoc, who slapped the back of his neighbor and pointed my way.

The partly overheard conversation was probably an insignificant quarrel, not worthy of my time. I swallowed around the sausage, the taste making me drool even more. But I was curious. Were I totally honest, never a worthwhile pursuit, I would have admitted to restlessness—a worse trait than ambition. I was here to learn the normal, not be distracted by the odd or unusual.

Perhaps because it was the six hundredth day of nothing but normal happenings, I quickly suppressed my guilt, straining to hear more of the unusual conversation, grateful for the huge ears I could imperceptibly shift to center on the sound.

"Invaders. Thieves at best . . . likely worse . . ." I lost the thread then caught it again. ". . . tell you. The Protark has been bewitched to allow them to approach the city!" This was the worried voice again. I slid my gaze in that direction and this time found the man immediately. Absently, I sank my teeth deeper into the still-hot sausage.

The worried voice belonged to a soldier of some kind, wearing a uniform I hadn't seen before. Once bright with typical Kraosian gaudiness, it was currently marred by the dirt and creases of hard use. *Intriguing.* Kraos was free of conflict, at least presently. Such military as existed appeared to be part of the ceremonial trappings of government. So why did this soldier, and his companion, look to have just completed a forced march?

"We have our orders, Ethrem. Here's no place to discuss them." My worrier's companion was only slightly older, but wore a complex insignia of rank high on one shoulder. I spared an instant to memorize its design. He attacked his breakfast with zeal—yet his tablemate sat staring at his plate, turning his implement in small circles.

The other diners seemed to be ignoring them a bit too obviously. *Fascinating.* I made myself as small as possible and, as Cradoc and his group left with a convenient dispute over their bill, I crept closer to the pair.

"Orders," Ethrem echoed with disgust. The food abandoned on his plate somehow caught my eye; camouflage tended to become a habit after six hundred days. He felt my stare and pointed at me with his fork. "Rather than follow such madness, I'd change places with that miserable excuse for a serlet." *Huh,* I thought to myself.

"You'll have the chance soon enough if we don't report back on time."

Ethrem's hands shook visibly. "But I can't go back. You must cover for me, old friend; find some excuse. I can't face those creatures—not again—"

"Get hold of yourself." What was close to a parade ground snap shook the hunch from Ethrem's shoulders if not the wildness from his eyes. Seeing this, his companion took a quick intense glance around, scowling at anyone he caught looking at them. As his eyes fell on me, I let my own gaze idly trace the course of a small insect past my nose.

The officer continued in a low, hurried voice, like someone driven to reveal a secret. I had to strain my ears to pick up his whisper. "There are plans beyond what you know, Ethrem. The Protark can handle the situation."

"How? What plan has he? Openhanded hospitality to those devils?" A sneer. "Next, he'll offer them summer quartering with the Royal Caste—or perhaps a few days at the seaside to enjoy the cool ocean breezes."

The officer glanced about again. "Do you think our current Commander shares strategy with the ranks? He's a close one, this Theerlic, close and fond of power. But I have my sources, Ethrem." He hesitated, then leaned closer. "This is not the first ship Protark Theerlic has handled. These latest invaders were expected—and none of them will leave Kraos. Not if *we* do our job. Know this for the truth, Ethrem. You and I—we'll be among those who save the world."

Leave Kraos? Save the world? Invaders? I bolted down

the meat, ignoring both the taste and the burning in my mouth. *What in Ersh's name did he mean by ships?*

For a moment, I numbly thought about paddleboats and steamers, although there was no open water within several days' travel unless one included the unnavigable torrent moating the city perimeter. Then, I actually looked up, as if watching for a passing air vehicle, though I already knew Kraosians were oddly disinterested in airborne travel, despite a technology that included solar power and the generation of electricity.

My mind fumbled its way to the only possible interpretation—an interpretation which collided violently with the unchewed sausage in my stomach. *Offworlders. Damn.*

This was not going to impress Ersh.

I felt my shape threatening to explode and held it with all I had. My duty was quite clear, made so by explicit and firm standing orders. There were worse penalties for failure to follow the Web's First Rules than losing seniority or rank—much worse.

Fighting a tendency to snarl to myself, I dodged a kick from an alert waitress and walked out boldly behind the two soldiers when they left—judging correctly that they were too preoccupied to notice a small tagalong, especially one that appeared to be a miserable excuse for a serlet.

Following at the Kraosians' heels like a well-trained hunting beast suited me; in a way, I felt almost grateful for something easy to do while my thoughts whirled. I found myself totally self-absorbed for the second time since I arrived. *This couldn't be my fault,* I concluded at last, as if that would help. Skalet had checked this planet. Kraos was supposed to be an untouched world, with the requisite native belief that they were unique in space, a world blissfully secure in its ignorance. Ideal for my first post—or so Ersh had agreed.

Obviously, Skalet's report was old news. I swore to myself. *What was I supposed to do with an impacted culture?* I had no training. At best, I could hope for another and likely bleaker posting. At worst—well, I wouldn't worry about that yet.

Of course, almost immediately things grew worse. The two I trailed paused before a rack of sisni drivers. It would be impossible to keep track of them if they rented one of the small and maneuverable cars. The pause lengthened, punctuated by conversation I couldn't hear over the din of the marketplace. Finally, the officer patted his wallet pouch and shook his head. I breathed again only when they moved away.

They were leaving the market area. I dropped farther back, keeping them in sight with quick glances, and concentrated on weaving a path through the hodgepodge of containers and litter edging the road.

Two irregular blocks passed in this way, putting the boundaries of the market behind us. Just as well it wasn't the midwinter holiday season when merchants outnumbered local citizens and the entire city was paralyzed with shoppers.

Gradually, I grew convinced that Ethrem and his companion were heading for the outskirts of the city, close, in fact, to where I had entered myself two planet years ago. As the current area of pavement where they walked was inconveniently tidy, I took a chance and, turning down a familiar alleyway, began to run with all the fleetness of my long legs.

Athletics was not my strong point. I took a corner too quickly and a twist of pain thrilled through an overstressed tendon. With a grunt, I dismissed it, aware if I lost the chance to intercept my quarry before they reached the multiple city gates, I might never find them again. It was a tempting excuse, however.

Pure luck sent me skittering clear of the wheels of a clattering hand truck, although close enough to feel the air of its movement. I flicked one embarrassed ear at the language flung after me. Fortunately, the rotten fruit missed.

Puffing, I slid to a halt at the alley's end, in view of the second great open area of the city, the elaborately paved and fountained square which gave access to the seven city gates piercing the old city wall. The gates were a particularly Kraosian absurdity.

I'd already noticed that Kraosians seemed to delight in any distinction they could make between themselves, from clothing style to subtleties of accent. It took on the proportions of a cultural need. So, for a Kraosian, it doubtless made sense that each caste of Kraosian society entered and left Suddmusal by its own gate. No one seemed to care that this had meant punching seven huge holes into the city wall and funneling traffic into seven often snarled streams through the city square, just to end up crossing the Jesrith River over one and the same bridge.

I used the claws on my left hind foot to dig at an itch behind my ear, scanning for my quarry. At least I knew they'd have to join the traffic aimed at the second to westmost gate, the one designated for the military. I breathed easier at the sight of the two soldiers walking briskly toward me, their steps unconsciously matched in parade rhythm. I watched, expecting them to wait for their opportunity to cross the line of merchant trucks, but instead they turned in the opposite direction. I soon realized their destination was the series of doors dark-edged into the shadowed east wall.

With a sigh, I selected a parked truck with a crate handily placed at its side and bounded up to its roof in two easy leaps. On this vantage point, curled in a ball, I prepared to wait. I knew where they were going. Another Kraosian custom. Ethrem had undoubtedly convinced his companion to let him seek the services of a licensed soothsayer. The Kraosians were as mystically inclined as they were stubborn about caste. With my luck, the troubled Ethrem would have enough money for a full spirit consultation—the better soothsayers could stretch one of those for hours.

4: Mountain Afternoon

THE soothsayer must have had a virtual treasure trove of wisdom to pass along. As a consequence, or due to other arrangements I wasn't consulted about, we were climbing the road from Suddmusal to the mountain range beyond at a truly ridiculous time of day. Not for the first time, I glared down with disgust at Ethrem and his new companions. He was now an indistinguishable part of a tight, purposeful group of thirty-two, built gradually and with suspicious casualness from other pairs of returning soldiers as they left the city.

As behooved a being of superior intelligence, I was sensibly traveling in the shade of the bordering low shrubs and trees, cutting across the road's ceaseless switchbacks to keep ahead of the troops constrained to its course. Even so, Ethrem and his companions were moving quickly, far too quickly for midsummer at the sun's zenith. There was an urgency to their passage, and no complaints, despite the sweat glistening on every brow.

I had plenty of complaints, but no one to share them with on this planet. My tongue wouldn't fit in my mouth anymore and hung out one side like laundry on a line, too dry to help cool my body despite the hot pulses of air sliding up the mountain from the baking plain below. My footpads and knuckles were already tender from running on rough hookgrass, sand, and rock. *Oh, well,* I thought to myself, waiting for the Kraosians to march around the next switchback, my front feet wide-spaced to hold against the slope, *I'm no longer bored.*

I'd expected to feel excitement. After all, this was becoming an adventure, just like those I'd read when I was too young to appreciate that literature was an ephemeral's way of remembering. What I felt instead was a sense of pressure, as if I were putty being forced into a very small and uncomfortable mold. Problem was, I was an observer, not an action taker. Had things proceeded normally, nothing in my assignment would have required me to actively do anything—in fact, a large portion of my training had dealt with eliminating the urge to react, to participate. I was uneasy, anxious—emotional responses I rather glumly realized were trying to make me cautious—a virtue Ersh had long ago failed to find in me.

I reached the crest of the first mountain ridge well ahead of the Kraosians. I knew this place; up the next rise was the cave where I'd spent weeks building my courage—and exploding. This far slope tumbled to the depths of the jagged gorge still being cut from bedrock by the frothing madness of the Jesrith.

A delicate web of a bridge tossed the road from my feet up to the next ridge, where its pavement disappeared into haze. It was a beautiful, uncanny structure, completely inexplicable by anything I'd learned so far about Kraosians. Only foot traffic could use it; suggesting a short journey to a worthwhile destination. Yet to the best of my knowledge, the road and its air-spanning bridge led to nowhere of significance.

The sound of heavy footsteps snapped the spell of the incredible view. I pressed myself under a berry bush, curling up in its deliciously damp shade. The Kraosians sensibly chose this same moment to rest themselves, wandering off the hot pavement and stretching out wearily wherever they could find level ground among the stones.

An instant later, biting, wingless insects scurried into my fur from what seemed every leaf of my shelter. Frozen, not daring to even twitch, I felt innumerable small pricks as the beasts enjoyed their unexpected feast. I catalogued the species, licking one up to test its molecular structure. *Adventure. Glory.* I added to my mental list: *worry and bugs.*

Ethrem, his companion, and one other officer had remained standing, looking out over the bridge, air, and tumbled rock with eyes that perhaps saw beauty, or perhaps merely an obstacle. It was tricky working out the aesthetics of other species.

"Come," the new officer said, turning with an impatient wave of a hand missing several fingers. He had a beard, the first I'd seen on a Kraosian, currently matted into three sweat-darkened ringlets. "They'll be waiting for us at the Commons House in Grangel. If we're late, the Protark will likely serve our heads as the first course." With understandable alacrity, the men re-formed their column and headed single file across the bridge.

The bridge was narrow, solid despite its fragile appearance, and completely devoid of cover. I could only trust in a trick that had worked before. As they marched, I stepped quietly into the shadow of the endmost soldier, my nose almost on his knee. He blinked down at me wearily and my legs tightened in preparation for a leap away, but then his hand dropped down to scratch behind my ears. I gave him my best tongue-hanging grin and a slow flutter of my tail. "'None of our business what's ahead, friend," he muttered more to himself than to me. "But there's good ale in Grangel's Commons House, and not as dear as some." I nodded wisely, a wasted gesture as my chosen partner returned his attention to the march.

Crossing the great bridge was an experience worth the discomfort of its sunbaked pavement on my unprotected toes. I took delicate mincing steps and savored the fragrant breeze lifting the scents of the mountain forest below up to my nostrils. The same breeze kept the bridge swaying gently from side to side—a movement that the soldiers adjusted to in unison, as if rehearsed, and I had to anticipate in order to avoid falling off. The Jesrith roared far beneath us, a voice of thunder and foreboding. As if in echo, real thunder sounded off to the north where darkening clouds hung against distant white-tipped peaks. I forgot my sore feet and hands.

The farthest reach of the bridge was terraced in huge flexible steps, easing the climb to the greater height of its landing. Five of these: easy steps for the soldiers and comfortably small leaps up for me. After the fifth, we stood on solid rock again. I took a last regretful look back at familiar ground, swallowing my doubts.

At least it was cooler here, a welcome change as a sense of being close to their goal, or thoughts of waiting ale, drastically speeded the soldiers' pace. This improved my chances of remaining unnoticed, given I could keep up—*not a guarantee,* I fussed to myself, panting as I trotted, legs burning. There was no shelter along the roadside through which I could leave my soldier to seek the more prudent cover of rock-clinging evergreens higher up.

Our sudden halt came none too soon as far as I was concerned, standing wide-limbed and shaking as I peered between the legs of the men in front of me. I could make out the rounded shape of a long, low building. It would have been impossible to miss, being painted in cheerful colors and surrounded by a riotously lush garden defying the season. A Commons House: an apt naming since it was one of few places where people of every caste mingled freely, permitted so by the practicalities of roadside hospitality. I was willing to bet it had great parties.

And it was around this haven of peace and welcome the Protark's troops were deploying themselves. Out of backpacks came the first weapons I had seen on this world, nasty-looking tubes with extensions of sharp jagged metal, doubtless for use after their power to fire was exhausted. Each man received one and then, following a plan that must have been dealt with before my arrival, faded into the surrounding bush with unexpected skill. They looked significantly more formidable now.

My own guardian had shouldered his weapon, following none other than Ethrem toward the rear of the House. I chose this moment to back slowly into a shadow and crouch; it could be very complicated to be recognized as the table-beggar of Suddmusal's marketplace.

But follow these two I must. My moment came as the attention of the remaining soldiers was fixed upon the arrival of some travelers approaching the House from the opposite side. Lingering to see who these were was an invitation to be noticed and probably shot. I dashed after Ethrem and my soldier.

They had crept alongside the shelter of a white, dilapidated fence, following it to the back of the House. Most of the effort to maintain the grounds had been spent on the front and sides; here the garden became more weed than flower. A pair of smaller outbuildings leaned against each other in a kind of drunken resignation.

But even so, it was a friendly disorder, ready to welcome a traveler seeking privacy and quiet. There were roughhewn benches under the few trees large enough to cast shade; baskets planted with wildflowers hung in their drought-bare branches. I felt the hair on my neck rise and realized with some surprise that I was angry at the soldiers for threatening this peace.

I couldn't have asked for better guides, though. Ethrem led the way right up to the large rear door of the main building, easing it open with a careless confidence that spoke of prearrangement and well-oiled hinges. I snuck forward, feeling clumsy despite the careful placement of legs and paws slinking on all fours demanded.

At the door, I strained all of my senses to detect what lay within.

Smells of food and of a varied clientele drifted past my twitching nose, but I heard no sound. The hair on the back of my neck rose once more and I took a slow easy step into the shadowed doorway.

"Watch those teeth!" The cry gave me scarcely enough warning to fold back upon my haunches, twisting about desperately in an effort that slipped my head past the heavy net being dropped from the darkness. I panicked, snarling and rolling, but couldn't free my back legs from the net before a burning adhesive stuck it fast to skin, pulling fur. *Fool!* I could hear Ersh now. How many explorers have died by underestimating more primitive cultures? *Was death ahead for me, too?* I felt an overwhelming urge to lose this shape, to cycle into web-form (or better yet into any form with bigger teeth). I panted with the heat energy I released to simply stay as I was.

Hands dragged me inside then, taking my sudden immobility for surrender. I lay on the coolness of a tile floor, the sum of my struggles having succeeded in little more than to wrap the net around me with painful tightness. I rolled my left eye frantically, seeing what I could.

I was in a hall, dim and cluttered with furniture, mostly chairs stacked in rickety columns. It was illuminated only by light escaping through a distant archway, this opening into what must be the main room of the Commons House. Through it, I could see the backs of people seated as if around a table. Details were impossible to distinguish. Reluctantly, I rolled my eye back up to my captors.

The soldier I had accompanied across the bridge held

one end of my imprisoning net; Ethrem held the other, though he looked as if he would prefer to drop it and run. The fear in his eyes drew a new and echoing fear from within me. I essayed my best pitiful whine. *He must not imagine me other than I appeared.*

My second whine softened the face of the soldier. "Poor beast," he said, a reproachful look at Ethrem. "I thought you said we were being followed by some enemy. These ropes are cruel—,"

"Loosen them, and I swear I'll shoot you where you stand, Crawleh." This was a new tone from Ethrem, a barely curbed violence coating the words with ice. "It's no serlet. I don't know what it is—but the soothsayer warned me of great evil on the road today. And this creature has followed me since morning. What beast would do such a thing?"

Crawleh looked tempted to reply, then thought better of it. For at that moment, the sounds of hastily shuffled boots came from the interior of the House, as if numerous people had risen as one to their feet. I tried to see past Ethrem's legs and failed. Crawleh could, however, and I heard him suck in his breath. "That I lived to see this day," the Kraosian said softly.

"They shall not live to see its end," Ethrem said viciously, but so very quietly I believed I was the only one who heard him. He sheathed his weapon, glaring down at me as though he wished he were free to use it. "We must get to our positions. This spawn of darkness will keep."

"We can't leave the beast here to trip someone," Crawleh said reasonably. "I'll take care of it while you go ahead. This door is my post anyway."

"I warn you—"

"Go. Go!" Either Crawleh's urging, or the welling of voices from the hall convinced Ethrem. With a last burning look my way, he walked through the door.

As soon as Ethrem was gone, Crawleh bent down beside me and, using a small can of spray, somehow loosened the tightest bands. I heaved a deep sigh of relief as the one constricting the movement of my head fell free. Crawleh snatched his hands back, perhaps wary of my teeth. I reassured him with a whine and a quick lick of my long tongue, tasting salt and dust as well as Kraosian. "There," he said with a pat, though stopping short of freeing me completely. "I'll see no animal treated cruelly, especially one who has chosen to follow such a miserable master so far from home." Lifting me gently, no minor feat considering my lanky bulk, Crawleh put me against the wall, dropping the can nearby. He left his hands flat against my body for a moment, eyeing me with concern. "You're burning up, poor beast. I'll bring you water when I can."

Of course I was hot. All that energy wanting to be released had to go somewhere, or this doorway would soon be larger. With this amount of stress, I might have to cycle soon, or I wouldn't be able to safely hold this form.

Charity complete, Crawleh went beyond my limited line of sight, presumably to guard the outer door. *Good enough.* With an effort, I wriggled forward ever so slightly, with the utmost care and silence. I drew my front right paw out of the net as far as it would go, unrolling those long, flexible toes so very different from the feet of Kraosian beasts. *There—I had it.* Quickly, I wrapped my toes around the can and used its spray to free myself from the rest of the net's adhesive.

Still panting, I rose to all fours and hesitated, considering my options. The hall continued in both directions from the archway, closed doors at regular intervals along the walls. I went to the right, more to avoid passing in front of the archway than because I had a reason. The tiles were cool on my feet and hands, a sensation I concentrated on to avoid the temptation to whine.

I was confident that the doors along the wall opposite from the main room would lead only to accommodations or storerooms, not to other exits, aware of the irony that my own life might now depend on my less exciting studies of Kraosian architecture. Nearly at the hall's end, a bar of light suggested another entrance into the main room. I went up to it cautiously.

There was just enough clearance for me to fit my head and shoulders under the black metal swinging doors without need to crouch. There was no one close to this end of the room. In fact, I had stumbled upon an ideal view of the proceedings within.

The main hall of the Commons House was a big, cool expanse of carved wood and brickwork, brightened by roof windows of tinted glass. Immense fireplaces made diagonals of each corner, the one next to me full of flowers in this fireless time of year. The floor was crowded with tables of some dark, scarred wood, wheeled for easy movement over the broad yellowed tiles.

The centermost table was the only one occupied. I identified the elaborately coifed Kraosian seated at its head as the current Protark, Theerlic, Appointed Commander of the military caste. Officers in only slightly less brilliant uniforms flanked him, three to a side. At the other end of the rectangular table, hands on their chairs as though awaiting an invitation to sit, stood the three who were causing Ethrem such nightmares.

Offworlders in truth. I felt the hair on my back bristle. Not just any offworlders, but a First Contact Team from the predominantly Human Commonwealth, if I took a well-educated guess. These were all humanoid, most likely pure strain Human, a choice of personnel undoubtedly intended to reassure the humanoid Kraosians. There were two females and, yes, the one standing off to the side closest to me was a male. His yellow-and-orange uniform bore a pair of specialty bars across the front, and he held a recording device discreetly in one hand. His tan features were full of barely restrained excitement.

If the specialist showed excitement, the only emotion I could read in the face and stance of his senior officer was caution. She wore a full dress uniform, dull by Kraosian standards, but still another sign of some good preliminary survey work. "We have complied with your request, Protark Theerlic," she was saying in a polite but firm voice, the accent quite acceptable. "We brought no weapons to this meeting. Our intentions, as stated before to your staff, are peaceful and noninterventionary."

I glanced about. There were only a few soldiers in sight, these all by the doors and corners of the room; none carried obvious weapons. I knew better. All at once I wished desperately I could detach myself from what was happening here. I even spent a useless moment wishing for the sight of Ersh, regardless of how she would peel strips from my hide for incompetence. I was out of my depth and, what was worse, I knew Ersh would completely agree with that assessment.

A voice startled me from my anxiety. It was the Protark. "Captain Simpson," he said, with a smoothness to his deep voice. "We, as representatives of our world, appreciate your courtesy and trust in agreeing to this meeting." I thought his tone remarkably collected and calm. Too calm, for a leader of a people supposedly confronted for the first time with the shattering knowledge of other intelligence in their universe. I thought I saw a flicker in the specialist's eyes, a smoothing of expression from simple excitement to the beginnings of suspicion. "It is important that we begin our mutual understanding of each other away from the, to us, overwhelming evidence of your superior technology. Accept our thanks. Please be seated."

Leaving their ship was a calculated risk, but one which was probably unavoidable, I agreed to myself, readily able to empathize with the Humans. First Contact Teams had to take a position of apparent vulnerability—though I doubted if the Kraosian had the slightest conception of just how immense a civilization the Humans represented.

Captain Simpson nodded to her female companion, and the two of them were seated. The male remained on his feet, with an apologetic gesture to the device in his hand. "With your permission, sir, I would like to record images of the truly outstanding carvings on your fireplaces," he said with appealing enthusiasm. I might have imagined that flicker of suspicion earlier. The Protark waved magnanimously.

This was a signal for more than the specialist, who bustled off happily with his device now at eye level. Serving staff moved forward from their wait behind the Protark's table, bringing forth large pitchers of frothy cold beer and plates of bread. There was a general air of relaxation, and conversations started sporadically among the soldiers, although none left their positions. I could no longer hear what was being said by the Protark and the Human officer, although heads nodded as if in agreement.

More empty assurances, I thought, feeling frustrated and useless trapped in the doorway. I considered my chances of retracing my steps past Crawleh. Somehow, I had to reach the outside of the building, prepare some diversion. The key was to introduce a deviation—something to defuse the Kraosian plot before it could begin. I hadn't exactly studied strategy yet (Skalet wasn't prepared to waste her tactical expertise on someone of my youth), but I'd read what I could find. And I had to try something.

Footsteps approached from behind me, I froze for an instant, then realized there was no choice but to slip out under the doors into the hall itself. Pressing myself to the wall as much as possible, I held my breath, expecting at any moment to be noticed by the servers as they pushed the doors open in order to wheel through a cart loaded with delicacies. Any other time, I might have drooled. Now, I shook and quivered, so frightened, I unwittingly did the best thing I could have done and remained still.

When a hue and cry did not immediately ring about my ears, my mind began to function again. A table blocked my view. It could also hide me. I put one paw ahead of another with painful slowness, reaching the supposed shelter of the table only to find I was not the first to do so.

I was nose-to-nose with the ugliest, most vicious-looking hunting serlet I had yet seen on this world. The monster was grizzled with age, with green, definitely malignant eyes, and horrid black-stained teeth bared in a snarl. Its breath smelled truly remarkable for something still alive. I backed up so quickly that I didn't see the legs behind me until I crashed into them.

"Saa. Don't be afraid." The words were in comspeak, the interspecies' trade language of the Commonwealth. I looked up a yellow uniform until I met the interested gray-eyed gaze of the Human. His recorder dangled from a strap. He made an effortless switch to quite passable Kraosian: "Easy, pup."

From this close, I could read the symbols marking the bars across his chest: linguistics and alien culture specialist. *Perfect.* I put on my best tongue-lolling grin and sat so I could unobtrusively curl my tail over my front paws. He patted my head gently, then said softly in comspeak: "What goes on here? I'd wager you know, don't you." I tensed, then relaxed as I realized the question was for himself, the Human being too distracted by his situation to really have noticed me.

Unfortunately, the same could not be said for the two soldiers rapidly and purposefully approaching us, one of whom I recognized with a sinking feeling as Ethrem. I swallowed and dove back under the table, using the momentum to carry me in a rush over the rightful landlord of the place. Teeth snapped closed a hot breath away from my neck as I scrambled out the other side.

Instantly, pandemonium broke loose. I ran, slipping and panting on the polished tiles, fearing I had done more than I bargained for in arousing the old beast. He was bugling his fury in full voice, a fanged demon given respectfully clear passage by the amused soldiers. I kept my tail firmly between my legs and both ears cocked back to my pursuer. I heard laughter and a confusion of commands, although I was too preoccupied to look around. This was hardly the distraction I had in mind, but it would have to do.

Then a crackle of energy blackened the floor in front of my paws. I slid to a halt, a move that threw the old beast off-balance. As if in slow motion, I watched him skid past me, mouth agape in surprise. In that instant, he unwittingly saved my life; Ethrem's next shot, meant for me, turned him into a charred heap.

There were shouts: angry ones from the officers, and a pitiful shriek from one of the serving staff—perhaps the owner of the ill-mannered and ill-fated beast. I couldn't take my eyes from Ethrem as he moved to stand before me, an involuntary reaction to the death that had nearly been mine. It was a betrayal of my true nature that narrowed Ethrem's eyes in triumph as he raised his weapon yet again. I tensed, preparing for his shot.

The weapon was struck aside by a yellow-clad arm. As if released from a spell, I yelped and dove for the nearest table. There was a flurry of voices and sound. I crouched in the dark, panting. The odor of cooked serlet was sickeningly strong.

What was happening? Had they forgotten me? I wanted desperately to somehow ease through the wall of legs surrounding my shelter and run. If there had been a gap large enough, I might have tried. Time seemed tangible, measured by heartbeats and gasping breaths. I fought to think past my fear and somehow calmed myself. *What had Ersh said?* Beyond courage lay necessity. Necessity meant easing to the table's edge and peering out.

The Human specialist and Ethrem were standing face-to-face—one calm and the other shaking like a leaf. They appeared to me as mirror images, similarities in form far outweighing any differences between them. Perhaps the Human was more slender, his tanned face flattened and more oval than the Kraosian's. The rainbow hues within Ethrem's eyes were locked upon the startling black, gray, and white of the Human's; this was the most striking difference between them, though Kraosian eyes varied to both these extremes.

Ethrem's commanding officer, the one he had called his friend, held a hand weapon ready, but pointed deliberately at the floor. There was no mistaking the direction of Ethrem's aim. The Protark and the remaining Humans were standing. No one moved. "Am I worth your fear?" I heard the specialist say very gently.

Ethrem flinched as though conversation was the last thing he had expected from the alien being. He tightened his grip on his own pistol. I swallowed, aware, as were the others helpless here, that Ethrem was beyond reason. Yet the Human remained still, calm, serene, his voice compelling: "I am as you see me, Kraosian. Nothing more than a man, and nothing less." He didn't quite smile, but the corners of his mouth lifted. "And a rather thirsty man. Join me for a glass of beer?"

It was masterfully done. Ethrem seemed puzzled, confused by so ordinary an enemy. He glanced about for help, his aim losing its rigidity as the weapon's deadly tip dropped slightly. Another moment, and I believe that the Human might have had him calmed and rational again. But I had forgotten that calm rationality was hardly part of the Protark's plans for this day.

"Kill the alien! He's bewitching you!" came a harsh command from someone unseen. Ethrem flinched, then moved faster than even the troops to either side of him. But the Human had been ready, and dropped, rolling, seeking the shelter of a table. Ethrem, thwarted, wheeled.

I howled in terror, leaping out to try and stop him. I was a step away when he fired at a new target. Launching myself into the air, I hit him in the torso before he fired again, but it was too little and much too late.

Captain Simpson and the other Human female were dead before they hit the floor.

Out There

THE dome glittered from within, the sun of this system too distant to be more than a navigation hazard. The Tly mining consortium did its best to counter the lack of a true day for its miners, knowing the importance of a diurnal rhythm to productivity.

So, day cycle, the dome shone with its own radiance like one of the fabled gems from its shafts. A promise of welcome and wealth to travelers.

There were lights, but no life, to welcome the next supply ship. She arrived and docked, automatics receiving the grapples and connecting lines. The bewildered, then anxious, visitors walked the empty domes and shafts; they found no sign of the two dozen who should be there.

Fortunately for the searchers, Death had already left.

5: Moon Afternoon

BOTH wind and memories had taken turns whirling me about, but eventually I cycled from web-form into Lanivarian and went to find Ersh. Her home was actually a cave deep in the rock of this mountainside; Ersh liked to be thought of as living a Spartan life, though her cave contained every modern convenience including a state-of-the-art replicator. I found her with Lesy and Skalet, all three trying the Kraosian form.

Ersh was older than any Kraosian I'd seen on that planet, but her form had good teeth and looked fit, if well-used. She had already ordered clothing from the replicator, and was dressed in the style appropriate to the scholar caste. Skalet could have stepped off a farm truck. Lesy, as usual, looked adorably plump. She was holding up one of a selection of festival dresses. I lifted a lip over one tooth, but didn't comment.

"Don't snarl at Lesy," Ersh said without a glance at me that I caught. "You know she likes clothes; it's her artistic nature. Skalet will return to Kraos and complete your work—including a report on the impact to their culture by your actions."

I winced.

"Despite this, you made a respectable beginning in the time you had, Esen. I'm proud of you."

Proud? If she'd cycled into a moonbeam, I'd have been less surprised. Suspicious was a better word. I snagged an apple from a bowl and pulled a chair from the wall, dropping on it heavily. I watched them posing in front of the mirror as I considered Ersh's comment.

"Where're the others?" I asked finally, still tasting their memories and feelings as if something was missing.

Skalet grinned evilly and winked at me. "You know Mixs won't go humanoid if she can avoid it, tween."

I didn't rise to the nickname—it was an old joke. Anyway, I hadn't been stuck midcycle once in the last hundred years. "So where are she and Ansky?"

Lesy looked unhappy. "Hurried, packed, left," she blurted, not yet comfortable with the Kraosian tongue. She turned back to her dresses. I didn't push the issue, not so much to avoid upsetting Lesy as because I had a pretty good idea myself why the others left so quickly. My shared memory had some very unusual components. My web-mates had left me to Ersh.

I settled back, knowing that Ersh would talk when she was good and ready. At least her kitchen was an improvement over the Kraosian dungeon.

6: Dungeon Night

THEY had taken us—the Human, Ethrem, and I—into Suddmusal late that same evening. The Jesrith was in spate, swollen from the mountain storms that had stretched long pale fingers to blot out the stars and rumble deeply in the distance. Always an intermittent boil of mud and froth, at Suddmusal the Jesrith fought its masters, chewing the edges of the rough channel that bound it to two-thirds of the city's perimeter.

The bridge was stained with rust-colored splatters of mud along its length. I paced in my cage, watching the roiling water as we crossed, permitted this much by virtue of size; in a similar prison, the unfortunate Human was forced to crouch when he stood. I thought it likely that he was in shock. There was no sign that he was aware of what was occurring. Or if he was, he wisely chose not to care. They had taken his clothes, forced him into some threadbare garments suitable for a servant of the rural caste. He looked thoroughly disreputable, and passably Kraosian to eyes that did not measure proportions or matters of grace.

My cage was placed between the Human's and Ethrem's on the back of the truck which had awaited us at the base of the mountain. *An empty precaution,* I thought sadly. Ethrem was unable to bother anyone else. More accurately, what was left of Ethrem was unlikely to do so. I avoided looking into his vacant staring eyes. He had finally found a way to flee his fear.

I had no doubts of our destination, nor the purpose for this hurried, after-dark travel. The Protark had been forced to play his hand openly against the offworlders. Whatever blameless treachery he had planned had been laid waste by Ethrem's public assassination of the Humans. There would be panic-ridden conferences tonight with the heads of the other castes, frantic efforts planned to either appease or eradicate the remaining offworlders—and witness. But first, he needed us securely in his grasp and safely out of sight.

I had been correct in my assessment, but I took no satisfaction from it. The heavy overhanging arch of the prison quarter swallowed the light from the few bulbs that lined its ceiling as we waited permission to pass its gate. The rain was near enough to give a damp chill to the evening air. I felt my fur rise in response and pitied my less protected companions. The door opened at last, letting the truck and its foot escort move inside a paved courtyard, closing behind with a sullen thud. I shook myself before forcing my body to lie down.

Something made me glance up. I met the Human's level gaze. There was pain in his eyes and more—recognition. I considered for a long moment, then eased one of my paws forward, unrolling its slim, *useful,* toes as if in an idle stretch. His eyes blinked slowly, then again. His own hand repeated my gesture before he deliberately turned and watched the advance of a group of four uniformed Kraosians.

Not shock, then, I decided, chilled by more than the weather. The Human had been biding his time, lulling his captors into believing him helpless and defeated. And he recognized the form I held.

That promised to make things interesting.

"Put them below," a voice far too cultured for a jailer ordered softly. "His Excellence wishes them to contemplate the future without disturbance." I yawned as I looked at the officer who had spoken.

"Surely he can't mean the serlet as well, Commander?" his aide asked in disbelief. I wagged my tail, delighted at his perception.

"It is not our job to question His Excellence," the gentle-voiced officer said wearily, pulling his night cloak more tightly about himself with a shiver. "Put the mongrel in with the serving boy. It's probably his anyway." I tried not to show my relief; being imprisoned with Ethrem's husk was more than either of us could have borne.

The long, narrow cell was damp, though its walls possessed no window to allow in the night air. My nose ran with the strength of odors I preferred not to contemplate too deeply. I also preferred not to think too much upon what the next day would bring. To keep my mind occupied, I began memorizing the number of blocks per wall along with their composition and thickness of mortar.

"They've left us for now," my roommate said in perfect mid-Lanivarian, with all the proper overtones of respect and new acquaintance. I curled my lips back from my teeth; he was a fool after all.

Despite this warning, he continued glibly: "I am Specialist Paul Ragem, First Contact Team Seven-Alpha-Six. I formally request your aid as a fellow sapient and member of the Commonwealth—ouch!"

Specialist Paul Ragem held the hand I had just nipped to his chest and was mercifully silent. I grunted with satisfaction and curled into a ball on a portion of floor less moist than the rest. I resisted the impulse to look up at the peephole I was certain was part of the light fixture above us. Let the Human make his own discoveries.

Darkness aroused me. I was pleased that I had rested—I thought it indicated a growing maturity on my part, to sleep when scared half out of my mind. I was also uncomfortably damp and shook out my fur. I rose on two feet, a posture this form managed with an ease certain to startle our captors, and pulled the blanket back up over the one without a naturally warm coat.

The contact woke him, though the Human immediately huddled into the blanket's shelter as he sat up. My eyes could just make out his shape, picked out of the deeper darkness only by the light seeping through cracks along the edges of the door. Insects scurried across the floor. Such dark-loving scavengers lived everywhere; they didn't bother me. This young and likely grief-maddened Human did. "I'm sorry about your shipmates, Specialist Ragem," I whispered, my voice grown unfamiliar from lack of use. I used comspeak; if I was revealing my nature as a cultured, civilized being, it was only polite to use the common tongue of the Commonwealth.

"I saw you try to save them," he responded as quietly, but with an urgent haste. "I can understand how they died—but not why I'm here, imprisoned . . ." he paused.

"And what is your place in all this, Huntress? Forgive my bluntness, but yours is about the last species I'd expect to find so far from home. Everyone knows Lanivarians avoid space travel. How did you come here? Were you shipwrecked?"

My first unmonitored conversation with a non-Web life-form, and I had to get one with curiosity. *The truth was safe,* I decided, *at least some of it.* "I was left behind and chose to hide. Kraos and its government are no strangers to offworlders. But you must have realized this when you met the Protark."

Ragem was silent for a moment, then moved over so I could sit beside him on the dry stone bench. I accepted, though his clothing smelled almost as foul as the cell floor. "I was suspicious—but we were in their midst from the moment we landed. Trust has to be on both sides," he said at last, in a voice so full of controlled pain that it hurt to hear it. "And Luara—my Captain—what could she have done differently? The negotiations had come too far; we'd agreed to make direct contact. Kraos is so vulnerable, so young a world. Who would have expected a madman—to be his target—" another pause.

"But we weren't his first choice of target," Ragem said all at once, a note of conviction firming his voice. "You were."

"We weren't friends," I admitted. "But poor Ethrem wasn't the only danger in that room, Human. The Protark has been against you all along. His talk of trust and aiding mutual communication was a lie. Haven't there been unsuccessful missions here before?"

"Three," his voice was very low. "But they were private expeditions seeking trade. As often as not, those don't report back for their own reasons. Your ship—was it one of them?" When I ignored the semiquestion, he continued. "Captain Simpson and Senior Specialist Kearn expected a routine first meeting. All we hoped to achieve was a mutual interest pact—perhaps an agreement to leave a signaling station on Kraos. A beginning—"

There was an unsteadiness to his voice. To distract him, I pushed my shoulder into his and received an unnecessary but companionable share of the blanket. *No xenophobia in this being,* I decided, impressed. "You speak excellent

Lanivarian," I offered in that language. "It is a gift to hear it again, Ragem; I have been here a while."

"What does the Protark plan for us?" *Not distractable.* Well, perhaps he was right to worry at the main problem immediately.

"We won't have long to wait," I told him bluntly. "Or rather, you won't. They believe I'm a Kraosian animal—a serlet—and just aren't sure about my connection to you. I'll be released." *Or they'll expect me to guard some farm-yard or other,* another part of my mind said. The job sounded very appealing at the moment. "What will your ship do?"

His shrug brushed my shoulder. "Nothing," Ragem said. "What can they do? If the Kraosians don't want us on their world, we—they—must leave." A pause. "And why not? The Protark can spin any tale he wishes. Contact Teams are supposed to lick their wounds and know when to make a hasty exit. The Commonwealth can wait lifetimes if necessary."

I'd been afraid of that. "What about you? Don't you carry any communications devices or signalers?"

"They searched me quite thoroughly, and took all I carried. They knew what they were looking for—" he stopped, sounding offended. "This wasn't supposed to be a high risk world. We were given our shots and standard gear. Implants are expensive as well as uncomfortable."

"Might not have worked under all this rock, anyway," I comforted him, while trying to control my own rising anxiety. There was no rescue for either of us, then—no stellar champions waiting to sweep him back into space where he belonged so I could get back to my now-attractively boring assignment. "How long will your ship wait before it leaves Kraos?"

Silence for a moment. The cell was becoming stuffy as well as damp. I tried not to think of the weight of rock over our heads. "As long as it takes the Protark to convince them that we're all dead, I expect," he said matter-of-factly.

I jumped down, as much to put distance between myself and the sound of doom in his voice as to pace. "I'm without resources, as you know," I confessed, making sure his hopes were not turning in that direction. "It seems we're a good match for each other, Human."

"There must be something we can do. Can we bargain with them?" Ragem asked abruptly. I thought he leaned forward. There were glints of reflections marking his eyes. "You must know this world and its people better than I do. What are their weaknesses, what do they value?"

"You have nothing to offer them that will persuade the Protark to release you," I growled. "You aren't a hostage, Human; you're a threat. Ethrem was more typical than you realize. Kraos is a world of structure, of inborn place and predictability. They simply can't believe in you and keep their pattern of the universe." I kept to myself the logical extension of that thought: *What would they think of me?*

He was quiet for a long time. I respected his need to think, to search for some way out. I had done that already, and disliked the options I saw. When his voice came again out of the dark, I was startled from a preoccupation with scratching a gathering host of passengers. "Then we must escape, Huntress."

"We?" I asked. *Had he forgotten who was in danger here? Beyond the fleas, of course.*

He misunderstood me. "I can't leave you here. You've been incredibly lucky the Kraosians keep an animal in their cities so similar to you in form. That's no protection now that I'm here, close to their own appearance, but alien. You must leave before you are discovered by more than that poor soldier."

His naive concern settled around my neck like a noose. Despite my annoyance, I had to be gracious in return. "Kind of you to think of me, Specialist Ragem. But it's one thing to recognize another humanoid as a threat; it's quite another to suspect a dumb animal. I assure you I'm quite safe. However, you have a problem."

And are a problem, I added to myself. Orders never meant for this set of circumstances, nor my frame of mind, were whirling in my thoughts, contradictory and confusing, and all unhelpful. I was forbidden to act on his behalf; at the same time, the underlying philosophy of my training forbade me to ignore his plight. "Someone's coming," I snapped, backing toward a corner and sitting down.

Lights came on, blinding and overly bright, underscoring the futility of trying to surprise our jailers. Dourly, I lowered my muzzle and watched the cautious entry of two guards, one bearing a tray, the other with a weapon aimed and ready for use. Obviously, their experience in this environment was greater than ours. I pricked up my ears, recognizing the delicious fragrance fighting its way through the stench of our cell. *Sausages!*

"Watch out you don't get another bite," one of the guards cautioned Ragem, an unnecessary confirmation that we were watched at least when the lights were on. The Human remained hunched within his filthy blanket, a figure of abject misery, eyes hot and red-rimmed in a face chalk-white between its smears of dirt. "Those curs know how to steal from a man's plate, they do," the guard continued with relish. "And take a finger or two on the way." I showed a tooth resentfully as I lowered my head even farther; though my stomach was cramped with hunger, I knew there was nothing for me from these two.

"You are kind to warn me. Thank you for the food," the Human said softly in the local Kraosian dialect, exquisitely polite as if to compensate for my failure to demonstrate which were the civilized races here. He took the tray, clinging with one white-knuckled hand to the blanket. It was an awkward, clumsy move born of stiffness and the damp night. Little wonder the plates slid onto the floor with a noisy crash.

Ragem looked down at the mess almost stupidly, somehow still clutching the small jug that had been on the tray. I took my cue and rushed forward, seizing the string of sausage, then wheeled back to my corner, a deep singsong growl advertising my intent to defend this treasure.

The weapon-bearing Kraosian laughed. The other, the one who had spoken, shook his head quite sadly. He gestured at the floor and, picking up the tray and plate, bowed to Ragem. "There'll be no more today." They left.

The betraying light remained, keeping me locked in my role of beast and the Human to his weary silence. Ragem dutifully ignored me, drinking deeply from the contents of the jug before gingerly fishing a piece of bread from the slops on the floor. I ate ravenously and noisily, accepting his gift with the only thanks I dared.

Next followed a long, dreary day, if day it was and not some trickery with the lights meant to exhaust the Human's resources. Ragem refused to play the game, burying his head and sleeping most of the time. I amused myself by ambushing the small multilegged creatures attracted to the spilled food. *Thwump.* I trapped a particularly large specimen under my paw and transferred it to my mouth, chewing thoughtfully as I gazed up at the light. *Quite nutritious,* I decided, *if a shade acid in flavor.*

By nature and training, I thought in terms of survival. The room was cold enough that I could release energy quite steadily, making it easier to hold this form. I decided only water was going to be a problem, should I live long enough. I took advantage of Ragem's rest to stick a long tongue into the jug held in the curl of his arm. The taste made me sneeze—it was some kind of wine and bitter for all it was watered down. I lapped up a bit regardless.

Eventually the lights did go out again, marking a period of time I'm sure the Human hadn't expected to survive. The abrupt blackness made me blink, waiting for my eyes to adjust. Before they did, I felt Ragem's arms go about me to hold tightly, his face buried in the fur of my shoulder.

I had never been hugged before, and tolerated the awkward embrace for Ragem's sake. Still, I found it a strangely comforting gesture. "Thanks for the food, Human," I said to him quietly, pondering how to proceed.

My voice brought Ragem back from his collapse. He rose from his knees and moved away from me. I couldn't see him, but a splash and muttered comment marked when he stepped in the food scraps on his way back to the bench. "I'll ask for water, next," a hoarse promise. So he was also compelled to think of survival.

It seemed unreasonable.

"Confronting the guards is pointless," I said, climbing up beside him, keeping my own voice low. "I can last much longer than you can without water—and while I enjoy food, I don't need to eat as often as you to survive."

"Huntress, what am I surviving for?"

I couldn't answer that; the Human wasn't a fool, after all. I heard him drink some of the wine and refused his offer to share the rest. He finished it. "Are you giving up, then?" I asked his silhouette.

It stung, which was my intention. "As you said, Huntress," he retorted defensively, "the Protark need only produce my dead body in order to convince my ship to leave."

It was unfortunate that I had worse tidings to share, having spent much of my own time in thought. "You are assuming the Protark intends to let your ship leave. Do you believe he does, Human?" I asked him, keeping my tone level.

"What are you saying?" Ragem demanded, alarmed.

"Quietly!" I cautioned him. When I felt his body lose its rigidity, I continued. "From what you've told me, the Kraosians have already stopped three other ships from leaving their world. Why should they release yours? No. I think the Protark plans to move against your ship." *With you or your corpse as bait,* I added to myself.

Silence, then a sudden violent movement as he drove a fist into his other hand. "There's nothing I can do," Ragem said finally, to himself rather than to me. "Kearn will be in command. He has experience—"

"You of all beings should know better than to underestimate this culture, Specialist," I reminded him. "Treachery can strip the most advanced defenses. What if the Protark says that you have become ill? That he fears the ship has brought a disease to his world and insists on a medical team? That kind of excuse could open your air lock, make your starship vulnerable to the weapons of this planet." I paused for effect. "You mustn't be used as a key—you must warn your crewmates."

A short, bitter laugh from my invisible companion. "Huntress, now you demand the impossible. I'm no security tech to overpower the guards and whisk us through the walls of this place. I respect your own courage—and teeth—but how far could those take us before we were recaptured or shot? This is no vid tale. We are helpless." Despair and anger shook his voice. "Let's hope you're wrong. I have friends dearer to me than my own life on the *Rigus.* And there's nothing I can do to help them except pray they leave me behind."

I was tempted to howl. Of course I had known all along that I would be forced into this situation; known but refused to admit it until now. Ragem's death at the hands of the Kraosians was something I would truly regret, but could have accepted. His chosen role on this world included being at risk. I could not accept the destruction of the innocent sapients on board his ship. Which meant he would have to warn them, and I would have to ensure he had the opportunity. *Beyond that,* I promised Ersh in my thoughts, *beyond that I won't go.* I tried not to think of the rules already badly bent, in light of the one I now planned to break entirely.

"I have not been completely honest with you, Specialist Ragem," I announced briskly, almost relieved to have the decision to act made.

"What do you mean?" he asked sharply.

Jumping onto the floor, I tried to compose myself. It wouldn't help matters to lose control of the cycle—the light and sound of an explosion would traumatize Ragem as well as bring back the Kraosians. "I am not actually Lanivarian, as you assumed. I am—of a rather different species.

"Be ready to move quickly, Human," I continued. "In a moment, the door will open and you must overpower any waiting guards—no matter what else you see." He didn't reply, doubtless considering the state of my sanity and possibly starting to believe the sausages had been contaminated with some drug.

Focusing on what was needful, and blocking out the worrisome sense of having company, albeit a safely blind observer given the darkness in the cell, I scanned my memory for my best choice. There were constraints, as always. Environments had to be matched; more importantly, I had to carefully judge web-mass so I could return immediately to the form he knew, hopefully without being observed. *There.*

The process was lightning-swift—it was such a relief to let go of the molecular energy I'd stored holding this shape's integrity so long. I flickered in and out of web-form to my new shape so quickly Ragem might not have been able to detect the intermediate change even if the lights were on. *Just as well.* The thought of exposing my true form to an alien was enough to make me nauseous.

But no time to linger. I glanced at the Human, vividly self-illuminated to my new perceptions—now ranging along a much broader spectrum than mere visible light. He looked perplexed, one hand halted in midmotion as if he had begun to reach for me and suddenly changed his mind. His other hand held the empty jug; as a weapon, it had the virtue of availability if nothing else. It was as well the room was still dark—for his sake as well as mine.

I flowed to the door and began the process of oozing my tissues through its cracks and niches. My lower section traveled fastest, finding clear passage between floor and wood. Then I was out. I excised the taste of grime, oil, and damp wood from my body, creating an amorphous stencil of my base upon the floor. The corridor was empty of life. *Better than I had hoped.* I freed myself from form again, then condensed once more, cycling back to what I had been.

"The keys were outside," I said quickly to Ragem as I opened the door, watching him blink owlishly in the corridor's light and register the absence of a guard with definite relief. To forestall the questions filling his eyes with wonder, I ran ahead—again four-footed and furred. "This way, quickly!"

I didn't bother telling Ragem the door had been the easy part.

7: River Morning, Caravan Afternoon

RAGEM and I moved through silent corridors, each length measured by barred doors that guarded cells empty of all but ghosts. Either there was little need for prisons in Suddmusal, or we had been allotted a remarkably large portion of this one to ourselves. I leaned toward the second explanation. Theerlic wanted word of the alien in his prison to spread no farther than his own control could silence.

"I thought we came this way," Ragem objected, slowing as we passed an intersecting hall.

I growled in my throat and continued to lead the way at the most rapid pace he could sustain, choosing any corridor slanting upward. The Human was right, but there was nothing to be gained by running back to the escort who had brought us here. *Aha,* I thought, finding what I was after. I stopped below a dark rectangle in the ceiling of the hallway, staring up into a square chimneylike structure, its opening marked by dim stars. The older portion of Suddmusal was full of such skylights, predictably open for ventilation during the hot season. This was our exit.

Ragem stood beside me, assessing my selection. "I would have said it was morning," he commented absently.

"It will be all too soon," I murmured, flicking my ears back and forth to listen for pursuit, thinking of the spies above our cell. "Can you climb up?" There were small indentations set into the stone, offering passage to the top. The width was narrow and the steps shallow.

Ragem pulled off the hide boots he had been forced to wear in place of his own offworld footwear. His feet looked sore, toes red from the narrow-tipped Kraosian footwear. "I can if you can," he promised.

"I'll go first, then," I said, rearing to stand erect and flexing my long front toes. It no longer mattered if we were being watched as long as we could reach the open air. Indeed, their shock at my actions could mean the edge on a sniper, a priceless extra second to act. I jumped for the metal rim, usually a convenience for securing a ladder rather than the grasp of fingers, boosted in that effort by Ragem's hands. The Human was athletic enough—or desperate enough—to run and jump to the rim himself once I'd cleared it.

Halfway up—*Ersh, the thing went higher than it looked*—I clung to the stone for a moment to gather my breath, arms and legs shaking violently from a use they had never evolved to perform. Ragem paused, too. I listened to his steady, deeper breathing and drew strength from it. "Not far, Ragem," I panted. "Be ready. They could be waiting."

A calm voice floated up. "May I know your name, Huntress?"

I was surprised enough to look down in a futile attempt to see him. "Esen-alit-Quar," I said. "Esen is better. Es in a hurry."

The Human didn't comment on it being a very non-Lanivarian name. My birth-mother had been feeling particularly poetic at the time of my arrival. "Good Hunting, Esen-alit-Quar," he said formally and rather finally. He knew what would await us above, or so he thought.

"Fair Skies to you, Paul Ragem," I responded to his grim courtesy. Then I drew a breath before I scrabbled under and past the protruding edge of the cover glass to stand on the roof.

I dove behind the pitiful shelter of a wood pile as a warning blast crackled over my head. Things began happening with the jolting clarity of battle. Ragem lunged past me, scattering our shelter to ruins in a glorious berserker rage, yelling his dead captain's name. The experienced Kraosians calmly waited until the Human was close to their line and then pounced. He was immediately in the grip of several soldiers, struggling and kicking like the madman he sounded.

Nothing was ever easy, I thought with disgust. I stood erect, on two feet, not four. There was a deadly and sudden cessation of movement, save for Ragem's private war, as I so pronounced myself to be something totally different from what they knew. There may have been twenty troops with us on this rooftop—not one seemed to even breathe.

Ragem took advantage of their shock to fight free, lurching in the direction I presumed he thought led to escape—at least there was only one row of ensorcelled enemy before him rather than three—calling hoarsely for me to follow. Unfortunately, he presented a target the soldiers could comprehend. Streaks of fire licked toward him.

Somehow, barely in time, Ragem dodged. Others were less agile: one soldier lay screaming, missing an arm and shoulder; his neighbor was reduced to a torso. But between them now lay an opened passage, clear for only as long as it would take the horrified Kraosians to collect themselves.

I saw my chance, accepting the responsibility of explaining all to Ersh—if I could—at some hopefully distant time from now. There were no alternatives anyway.

I lunged for the body of the dead Kraosian, cycling into web-form at the same instant. It was the work of a heartbeat to convert his still-living cells into my own mass. *Barely enough.* I ignored the screaming of those Kraosians who saw.

Meanwhile Ragem had tripped and was trying to get up again to run. I cycled even as I grabbed him tightly, using my momentum to drive us both over the edge of the roof.

More screams, perceived as higher-pitched through the ears I now possessed and fading away rapidly as we dropped below the building's upper level. No time to feel contrite over any nightmares my behavior was sowing behind me.

My takeoff, not really suicide as the poor Human likely judged it, was awkward and labored; with fine irony, it would have killed us both had the building not formed part of the city's outer wall. As it was, I plummeted almost to the damp, heaving crests of the Jesrith before some lift began to slow our fall, in so doing threatening to pull my outstretched wings from their sockets. Ragem helped as best he could, clinging tightly to my underside with both arms and legs, keeping his weight centered and firm. In spite of his self-disparaging remarks during our imprisonment, the Human was proving reassuringly adept at survival.

I had just enough airspeed to begin to circle toward the road into the mountains. Ragem said something I couldn't hear over the wind, then actually risked releasing one hand to point urgently in another direction, toward the pink of the rising sun. I accepted the correction, though less than pleased to be taken along the flat valley plain. This form depended on wind or, better yet, curls of rising air. Over the night-cooled valley, we would be on foot almost immediately, a consequence I couldn't easily debate with my passenger.

The blunt-topped buildings of Suddmusal were still too distinct when I knew I had reached my limit, tilting my head to scan the rapidly approaching ground for some soft landing strip. The view was of a plain of baked-hard clay and thorn bushes in every direction, split into two equal parts by the white, arrow-straight road that led from the city to the lowlands beyond the mountains. The Jesrith, subdued by these dry and level surroundings, was a sullen line of brown meandering to the south.

I shrugged—mentally, of course—and aimed for the water. I felt Regam's hands tighten spasmodically. *What a pity if he couldn't swim, after all this,* I thought, curving my wings to exchange speed for precious extra lift—a difficult task with his additional weight. It would be a rough landing.

The Human let go seconds before I was about to strike the water. Relieved, I cycled in midair, flowing through web-form to my next choice as Ragem hit the water. The small amount of mass I'd needed to shed clung to me as drops of moisture, a donation to the river as I dropped into the water slightly downstream from where Ragem's dark head surfaced.

The river was by no means tamed yet, but its swift current was little more than a convenience to the slim blackness I had become. It was a form I hadn't used since I was very young and Ansky had taken me touring the waterways of Lycorein. For a moment, I daydreamed, exploring memories.

Guiltily, I brought my attention back to the present, turning my nose upstream to search for the much less aquatic shape of my companion. Once more I was pleasantly surprised. Ragem bobbed along the surface of the Jesrith, safely lodged among the branches of some floating debris. I raised a foot so finely webbed as to seem made of water itself to my forehead in salute as he spotted me, then dove. For now at least, the Jesrith would carry us.

And carry us it did for much of that morning. I lazed along, feeding well upon a variety of small agile fish, and keeping a watch on Ragem. He was tiring, the hot sun beginning to take its toll on his unprotected head and body, but stayed alert to the appearance of my snout nearby. The current slowed gradually, grudgingly.

After a while, Ragem's makeshift raft sighed neatly against an undercut bank, twirled once, then ground a firm bed in the washed stone. Ragem took advantage of a confusion of similarly lodged tree trunks and debris, climbing this temporary ladder to the shore.

I kept underwater as I cycled, using up the last of my excess mass in the change. It seemed the least of my worries what form I chose, but I stayed with the one we were both used to. Then I dripped out of the river to follow Ragem.

He found a spot on the bank where shrubs larger than most curved overhead to provide welcome shade and shelter. We had been lucky; I felt my body tremble with reaction and shook water from my fur instead.

Ragem moved forward as if in a dream, reaching a slow hand to touch the soft vulnerable skin along my throat. With him so close, I could only use one eye to see him, and tilted my head to better do so. Then he chirruped a complex sound. If I could have smiled, I would have. *Vain Human, so proud of his knowledge, even now.* "This form has trouble with the language of the skyfolk," I apologized in comspeak. "And, yes, it was a lousy landing."

Ragem's wide mouth curved up in a completely new way, and he began to laugh. I realized this was the first happy sound I had heard from him. It gave me the most peculiar feeling, almost as though I'd done something worthy of Ersh's favor—which I knew couldn't be right. "At least it washed off that stink," he gasped, when once more able to speak. True. Though dripping wet, he did look and smell much better. "The *Rigus* lies behind that peak. My ship," he added unnecessarily and with undisguised longing.

I turned my head to follow his outstretched arm. A full

day's travel at least and, as I squinted at the hot white sun glinting against the mountains, a day sure to have more of the searing heat that kept the native population sensibly indoors. "No problem," I yawned, dropping to all fours. I lay down, putting my chin on my paws and stretching out my back legs to let the sand warm my belly.

Ragem looked affronted and confused. "What are you doing?"

"Getting some rest. You could use a bit yourself, Human," I added kindly. "Sit down!" This more firmly as he showed definite signs of preparing to leave our shelter. "There's no cover past this point, either from our pursuers or from the sun. We must wait."

Ragem's attention settled on me as he obeyed, I thought reluctantly, and sat in the shade. "And what are we waiting for—Huntress?"

I didn't miss the slight hesitation before the name, a new and not surprising wariness in his manner. "We're waiting for the ordinary, Ragem," I explained, sparing a moment to appreciate the irony. "A caravan. Preferably a large one, with lots of people and noise. There should be several today, despite our little fracas in Suddmusal."

"A caravan?" The Human pulled at a stem of grass in a movement that looked idle, but was still tense, even though he eased his back against the curl of a shrub root with a sigh. He half closed his eyes, but I decided it was so he could watch me less noticeably. His attention made the old insect bites under my fur itch and I began scratching at the most annoying of them.

"You have it down pat," Ragem said after a moment.

"What down pat?" I mumbled through a mouthful of skin and fur. The row of small teeth at the front of my jaw was really the only way to ease the irritation on my back. Relieved, I flopped my head around to look at him, prying the odd hair from my teeth with my tongue so I could swallow it.

"If I didn't know better—I'd swear you really were a dog, or the Kraosian version." Ragem seemed to think I'd be offended by this, for he went on with a faint air of discomfort, "I'm sure your acting ability has saved your life here, Huntress." He coughed delicately. "But it really isn't necessary with me."

I stopped swallowing hair and bug bits. "Just staying in character, Specialist Ragem," I said, before I reached over my shoulder again, biting urgently at a spot that hadn't itched a moment ago. *Damn.* I'd picked up something new already.

Ragem was quiet for a while. I could feel his eyes on me, the intensity of his curiosity something I thought I could reach out and touch. It was only luck that had kept him from actually seeing me cycle, or worse, seeing my real form. I wondered suddenly if that mattered. Plainly his imagination was operating full time, conjuring up who knew what outrageous theories about my kind. *Ersh was going to chew me into oblivion.*

Itches subdued, at least for now, I pulled a front paw under my chin and gazed back at him. "Where're you from?" I asked, before he could start questioning me again.

He raised his brows, as though startled. Maybe he'd forgotten what I was already. The thought made me rather smug. "I was born midspace, Huntress. A true Commonwealth citizen."

I shivered with a delicious combination of horror and fascination. Most things the Web stored in shared memory had names which took days to remember fully. Space was short enough. We called it *out there.*

I looked at Ragem with new interest. "Were your parents spaceborn?"

He shook his head. "Just me. My dad's a drive-tech from Senigal III. He met my mom when she was navigator on the merchantship *Thebes.* She pulled a temp-contract for him so they could be together." Ragem grinned. "Didn't last long—turned out Dad gets queasy in free fall—but long enough to have me, anyway. Mom's pure Botharan stock; she can trace fourteen generations." His smile faded, replaced by a thoughtful look at me. "How about you? Where are you from?"

"Not here," I said, doing my best to say it with humor. "Do you enjoy space travel, Specialist Ragem?"

"Depends on the destination, I suppose," he answered willingly enough, then zeroed back on his target with distressing speed. "Somehow I don't see Lanivar as your home, Es."

"The Lanivarians care less for space than your father," I agreed. "Which makes me wonder what he's doing now."

"Who?" he said blankly, thrown off his mark. *As I'd intended.*

"Your father," I repeated.

Ragem shrugged his shoulders. "Couldn't say. He's not much for keeping in touch. But why are you interested in my father?"

"I'm interested in everything."

"Everything." The word came out of his mouth meaning something different. A quiver of caution traveled down my spine and I thumped my tail to end it.

"You find that odd, Paul Ragem?" I asked. "Why? It's been a long time since I could talk to anyone. I've been alone, Paul Ragem. Alone and like this." I stood on four feet, not two. Then I squatted on my haunches, raising my arms to shoulder height. "I do enjoy your company—and stories. Tell me more. We have time."

His intent gaze softened. Perhaps, as a spacer himself, he understood what it was to be alone and lonely, to crave a harmless diversion. "Stories? Hmm. Not much to tell about my life, really. My father always wanted to own a shop—not a big one, mind you. Just something to keep him in touch with other techs and a hand on the newer machines."

Ragem kindly rambled on for another hour or more. I listened, asked questions to encourage him, and remembered. The sound of his voice, his tales, his willingness to share with me made a time that was like the night magic of the merchants. I tucked the memory away in that private part of me. This would not be understood, or forgiven, by my elders. But, by a little bit, my loneliness—which I hadn't felt so keenly before somehow—was eased.

"I've been talking too much," Ragem said at last, his voice sounding well-used. "Your turn, Esen. What about you? I've never heard of a shape-changing species. Where is your world?"

A reasonable and impossible request. I swallowed a growl, but enough of its violence made its way up my throat to roughen the words I spoke. "Don't ask me such things, Ragem."

"I mean you no harm, Esen," the Human said quickly. "I promise."

I dipped my ears in brief apology. "And I mean you none, Human."

"Then—"

"I'll tell you what you need to know to warn your ship and keep both our skins whole," I said, adding somberly, "be satisfied with that." Our eyes met. I don't know what he saw in mine, but it was enough to force his to the ground.

There was a bitter taste in my mouth as I deliberately prepared myself for rest, one ear cocked for the sounds of any travelers on the road beyond our shrub-covered nest. Such sounds could announce both safety or threat. I was reasonably sure I could handle whichever came, though I suspected Ersh would denounce this new confidence as yet another of my youthful mistakes.

Eventually, we did find a caravan willing to accept roadside travelers, although the sun had almost eliminated the shade from our shelter before the first rumble of transports alerted us. A poor, and rather miserable, affair of trucks and quex-pulled open carts, its owners, the Ilpore family, had more reason than usual to be morose. They had passed through a most unusual roadblock before leaving Suddmusal.

"Dreadful business," the old woman repeated numbly. She had introduced herself to Ragem (who had described himself glibly as one Megar Slothe, bound for the Eastern Provinces) as Wetha Ilpore, third daughter of Ankin Ilpore, the caravan's original convener. She was fascinating, with an almost toothless smile and crease-edged eyes that slid politely away from Ragem's to watch her quex negotiate the road whenever he evaded her more pointed inquiries about his past. Those of the merchant caste understood such things.

Ragem eased his bottom on the wooden seat as inconspicuously as he could, ignoring the pungent, musky scent of the sweating team of quex before him with admirable restraint. He should have smelled it from my position. "I heard it was bad for those who were there," he agreed ambiguously. I snorted and knew he understood it was more than the dust beside the cart in my nostrils.

"Doesn't need tethering, eh?" the old woman peered

down at me with renewed interest. "Wish our stock was as mannered. Willing to talk trade, young sir?"

The Human took long enough to reply. I thought darkly of leaving him to his own devices, and abandoning my thankless task of pacing alongside the cart. "A pet, Dame Ilpore, that I would miss." She gave him an uncharacteristically sharp look at this, since my current form, that of a plump, stocky quadruped, was not unlike a meat animal kept by Kraosians on the southern tip of this continent. The Kraosian version, when alive, was definitely without redeeming qualities.

"Suit yourself, young sir. I prefer serlets myself. Now my Sissu is a companion to warm—" her voice failed her, and she sent her whip snapping over the backs of her surprised quex, who had been well into their travel doze. "It was a black day when the Ilpore entered Suddmusal, a black day indeed. My poor Sissu—"

Ragem was not slow in putting things together. "They took your serlet—"

"As they took all the poor beasts, and for what? To be killed! Say it as it was, young Slothe." Wetha then cursed methodically and loudly, as if by doing so she avoided the indignity of tears coursing down her dust-coated cheeks.

"Orders of the Military," she said finally, having exhausted a vocabulary that added much to my own. "Since when has the Military had anything to do with travelers—or their stock! Said they were diseased, a threat to the city, some such nonsense." With a grunt of angry satisfaction, she handed Ragem her whip and pushed a large hand under her heavy shawl, withdrawing two small bundles of white. There was a soft complaint as the sleepy pups blinked their innocent eyes at the light and noise. "Sissu's best," Wetha pronounced very softly, tucking them away again. And she didn't speak until we stopped late in the afternoon to water the draft animals.

I wasn't in the mood for conversation either, and found my formsakes' reputation for a foul temper kept the curious away while I took my own turn drinking and then wallowing briefly in the cooling ooze formed by the broad-footed quex at the river's edge. So Theerlic, or the prison commander, or some more faceless fool had put the blood of all those simple beasts on my hands—including Wetha's beloved Sissu. Sickened, I tried to explain to myself that there was nothing I could have done to prevent their reaction.

But that wasn't true. I could have stayed out of the Human's business; I could have stayed bored in Suddmusal's marketplace; I could have maintained my own cover and not been lured by some ridiculous sense of duty into this mess. So I scowled at Ragem, too, when he made a pretense of calling me to his side.

Wetha pushed a roll of kopi, the trader's staple of dried fruit and meat, as well as a very old pair of boots, into Ragem's hands as he said his thanks. "There is nothing here, young sir," she replied, shaking her gray head at the antics of a fool. "Come with us to M'Ilpore—there is always work wanting strong young men like yourself, and no questions needing answers." The twinkle in her eye belied her age and I thought Ragem's face reddened slightly.

Ragem smiled and bowed over her hand with the courtesy of one of the royal caste. "I have those waiting for me in the hills—hunting companions, good dame. But I will remember your offer and your kindness."

It was little wonder the merchant doubted his sanity. Our way, or rather Ragem's chosen path, led directly away from the road and river, into the trackless mass of dense thorny shrubs that carpeted the plain up to the rising hills. Without comment, I settled into my best traveling pace, several steps behind the Human, my eyes half-closed against the thin, whiplike branches which slid over my tough hide but clung then tore free reluctantly from Ragem's uplifted arms. Sweat covered his face, probably stinging where pinpricks of red marked encounters with overhanging branches. He was not patient with obstacles, I'd noticed.

We reached the beginning of a line of low hills before we chanced upon a packed dirt roadway headed vaguely in our direction. Ragem limped heavily onto it, stopping as though mesmerized. The road was a relief for us both. I didn't want to think about the condition of his feet in their borrowed, ill-fitting boots. I sank down on my haunches gratefully. Ragem stood looking ahead, breathing in great shuddering gasps. I knew he was driven by what might be happening to his ship, if it was still planetside and he wasn't already an exile.

That was not all that plagued him. Ragem swung around abruptly and dropped to one knee in front of me. "A Ganthor can't talk to me without an implant," he said hotly, a strange expression on his face. "Is that why you haven't resumed your—become the Lanivarian? Do you blame me for what the Kraosians did? Is that it?"

I wanted to be childish, and indeed thought fondly of his reaction should I burp up some foul-smelling cud and chew it. But it wasn't right to let Ragem think I blamed him, especially when I was busy blaming myself. I converted mass and cycled. The Ganthor, though quite interesting in their own way, were not my favorite life-form either.

"I don't blame you—" Then, as I looked at the Human more directly, this form being taller at the shoulder, I couldn't believe what I'd just done. My muscles locked and I had to fight the urge to lose shape.

Ragem's eyes were ablaze with an almost fever-bright intensity and intelligence. *When had I reached the point of treating him as a member of my Web?* I thought with alarm. *What had happened to my safeguards—the training meant to keep me from cycling unless either totally hidden or utterly in peril?*

What power did this being have over me?

Or was it simply that Ersh had been right about my inexperience all along—and that thought was the final blow.

"Your ship is close enough, Human," I said flatly. "I wish you luck."

Some emotion flickered in his eyes. "What do you mean?"

Since I had taken a couple of steps back in the direction of the road, this seemed a superfluous question, but I answered anyway. "I've done enough—and you've seen more than enough."

Ragem's outstretched hand dropped limply. "You must realize how fascinating you are, Es," he said with a wry note that pricked up my ears. "Please don't let my curiosity drive you away. I thought we were allies—friends."

Friendship. Was that what made me forget what he was? "Don't patronize me, Human," I warned him. "What you have seen me do—on your behalf, not mine—was never to be shared with aliens. It's past time we parted. Your curiosity is dangerous to my health."

As I turned and trotted away, one flicked-back ear caught his low-pitched voice. "So was Grangel's Commons House, Esen-alit-Quar. Please stay. I promise not to pry any further."

I stopped, bristling with indecision. *True, Ragem had probably saved my life.* And was it his fault that I was thoroughly fracturing the Rules I'd been taught to hold sacred? I knew Ersh's opinion on that one.

On the other hand, what further damage could I do? A few more hours spent with a being I could talk to, who called me friend; compared to what I'd already done, it seemed worth the risk.

"What matters is getting you safely to your ship," I said with resignation, turning back. "I'll see you to within sight of it and that's all, Human. And you'll swear not to reveal me to your kind, or I won't do that much."

Ragem nodded, then smiled a bit wistfully. "A promise I can give you with a clear conscience, Es. Who'd believe me anyway?" He hesitated. "Yet I'd like to ask, for my own sake, so many questions—"

"I can't answer them," I replied as gently as I could. "We're together for this little space, my—friend." I tried the new word and was rewarded by a brightening in his eyes. "It should never have happened and must be forgotten. Let's get you off this world before you complicate my life beyond repair."

I should have realized then it wouldn't be that simple.

8: Valley Night

"QUITE a crowd, Human," I said, stretching one of my slender, clawed toes to indicate the twinkling ring of lights marking the Kraosian encampment about the flood-lit ship. Twilight was deeper within the vast semicircular valley below, emphasized by the concentric circles of artificial illumination lapping at its center.

Here on the hill's upper slope, touched only by the last rays of sunlight, I could see Ragem's grim expression quite plainly. "Clever. To use their own kind to hold the ship here," he said. "But Kearn's not as compassionate as Captain Simpson. If threatened, he'd lift the *Rigus*—even with half the Protark's troops under her jets."

"A less-than-happy thought," I commented, repressing a shudder. *Hadn't enough died already?* I considered the ship, and its surrounding glow of life. "Maybe you should take up farming—and Dame Ilpore's offer."

"I don't count that one of my options, Huntress," Ragem said absently, his attention below. He began to move down the slope. I followed, as I had followed him here in the first place, obliged to see the thing to its end.

To be honest, I knew I had another, less lofty motive. It had been years, after all, since I had talked with another sapient. It would be years before such a chance arose again, granted Ersh let me stay on Kraos. I simply didn't want to be alone again any sooner than I had to be.

We lost sight of the scene below as we entered an area of rubble, deep in shadow and offering extremely treacherous footing. To make it worse, I had begun to smell blood in Ragem's footprints. I winced as the Human slipped, catching himself with his hands. The sound of the pebbles he sent tumbling was almost as loud as his strained breathing.

Step, clamber over raw boulders set in loose soil, jump

logs ripped from the ground to make the slope a nightmare obstacle course. It was as if an earthquake had torn down half of the mountain. Ahead of me, Ragem hesitated before a curiously smooth area, distrustful of its stability perhaps. I came up beside him.

With a muttered curse, the Human dropped to his knees, hands digging furiously in the talus. I stared at him—*had what he'd suffered driven him mad?* There's been no warning of it. Then something definitely not rock or soil reflected the twilight. I added my paws to his labor. Almost instantly, I struck a hard slickness and sat back on my haunches, meeting Ragem's eyes before looking up the slope. We were standing on a tomb.

"They buried the other ships." Ragem sounded numb. "That's why we were told to land here, in this narrow valley, rather than on the plain." He looked up at the opposite side of the valley. I understood what he saw: the slightly overhanging cliff beyond the sleek, living beauty of the *Rigus* was no longer a protection from the weather or camouflage from an innocent populous. It was a weapon ready for use.

"This may be how they have hidden all traces of alien visits to their world," I reasoned, pushing at the Human with my paw to gain his attention. "It can't be how the Protark overpowered the crews of these ships in the first place—nor how he plans to take your own. He can't have mined the entire valley. There must be something else—something more."

"I must get to them—" Even as the words left his mouth, Ragem was moving, running down the slope at a pace sure to break his neck before the Kraosians could shoot him. I snarled and followed, choosing four legs over two for steadier footing.

Ragem's rush took us to the bottom of the hill in a jumble of rock, soil, and noise. I froze, aghast at how close we had come to the area lit by the Kraosian encampment. I could hear voices, smell hundreds of soldiers. At any moment, I expected to be revealed by a searchlight; my flesh quivered at the thought of weapon fire following that betrayal.

Ragem, possessing more courage or less imagination, hadn't stopped. Instead, he was creeping steadily around the edge of the camp, not once looking through it to his ship, so near and so impossible to reach. Shamed, I pulled farther into the shadows and trotted in his wake.

The Kraosian camp was massive, with a chaotic lack of organization that reminded me of Suddmusal's marketplace—*was it only yesterday morning?* But then, why should this camp be more than a collection of tents, lights, casually parked transports, and the odd bonfire? The Kraosian soldiers were not the real threat. They were there to reassure the Humans, a native welcoming committee obviously incapable of harming a starship. As Ragem had perceived, they were also pawns.

Ragem. Where was he now? I stopped, growling to myself which at least sounded better than whining. Then, to my horror, I spotted him among the tents of the camp, zigzagging through shadow and light, taking chances to reach his ship as quickly as possible. I winced as he stumbled over a line and hunched down beside a pile of boxes. In a blink, the Human was gone again.

I was neither as courageous, nor as desperate; I guessed at where he would come out and aimed my own course to meet him, running with the ground-swallowing speed this form could produce over short distances. The pace drove a cramp into my side. I panted, ears pricked to catch the sound I dreaded, twisting to avoid loose rubble. Then it came—just as I had begun to feel some hope—shouts from inside the camp.

The Human had been discovered.

I slid to a halt, trembling in shadows nowhere near as dark as my thoughts. *Now was definitely the time to cut my losses and leave.* But the *Rigus* sat in plain view, vulnerable, ports sealed as a person would hunch over a wound. She was full of unknown and unknowing beings, people worried about their missing companions, but complacent in their technology.

The sense of responsibility crushed me, squeezing out every thought but a kind of dull resentment. All of them, those on the starship as well as the expendable soldiers in the camp, were in my bloodstained and inadequate hands.

Of course, the Humans would listen only to Ragem—in that respect I needed him as much as the Protark. Yet the only shape that could get me inside the camp to find him was forbidden.

Silence, ominous after the uproar of Ragem's discovery, drew me into the shadowed edge of the nearest tent before I thought. *What was I to do?* The rules I had broken so far were trivial compared to assuming a form before it had been assimilated by the Web. I hesitated, then sagged. I could not force myself to make the attempt. Becoming Kraosian, even to preserve intelligent life, was beyond me.

I accepted the dictates of my conscience with some relief. I had begun to wonder if I was still bound by any rules. Helpless and heartsick, I backed slowly into the shadows then continued to circle the camp. At least I could see what the Kraosians planned. Maybe I would find some way to alarm the ship's crew. *And maybe I could fly home,* I thought with disgust.

The *Rigus* towered above the camp, her polished globes and sleek superstructure so complete a statement of technological superiority that I wavered as I gazed at her, doubting for a moment if any of my guesswork about the Protark's intentions was correct. The Kraosians, for all their years of civilization, were barely past caves and firepits compared to the Commonwealth. Yet the evidence beneath the new-formed hillside was a chilling reminder not to underestimate them.

I crawled beneath a parked transport, seeking an unobstructed view back inside the camp. *Good.* By turning my head, I could also watch the cleared area at the base of the *Rigus'* still-deployed ramp. Night made a velvet canopy overhead. It was warm, quiet, and expectant.

I didn't have long to wait. A column of officers, led by the Protark himself, marched from between a pair of larger than average tents, soldiers snapping to attention as the party passed. As they drew closer, I saw in their midst a stretcherlike sled, pulled along by a queu. There was no need for the beast; the camp stank with the fuel and oil consumed by their vehicles.

So the queu was a strategy—a deliberately disarming quaintness. I shook my head. The Humans weren't to be fooled by anything so obvious.

I reluctantly turned my attention to the motionless figure on the stretcher. It was Ragem; I knew him, though he was naked and bound, unconscious or likely worse. My lips curled away from my teeth and I actually considered using them on a leg or two. The cavalcade paused right in front of me, booted feet kicking dust to tickle my nose, as the Protark and some of his officers continued on and shouted up to the ship.

I didn't hear what was said, nor did I care. I could see their plan for myself. A tall Kraosian—head, face, and body wrapped in white—walked quickly up from the end of the column. His hands were gloved. The men around Ragem drew well away as he raised a small vial and sprinkled its contents over Ragem's bare skin.

The queu-drawn cart was sent on its way immediately afterward, Ragem its innocent and deadly passenger. The Protark waved it past, getting no closer than he had to, and began retreating slowly toward his camp. I could see the main port of the starship beginning to open.

I really hated acting on impulse.

I tore past the surprised Kraosians, feeling more than hearing a burst of fire close to my heels as they tried to stop me. I lunged at the head of the queu, snapping my teeth, trying to drive it away from the ship and the people starting to emerge from within it. The stupid beast reared in panic and fell, tipping the sled and rolling Ragem's limp body to the ground.

Sliding to a halt, I looked down at my new friend for a timeless instant, watching his chest rise and fall with light, peaceful, unconscious breaths. I knew beyond anything else Ragem would rather die than carry whatever death was planted on him to his crewmates. As a serlet, I could kill him, but it would be futile; how could I prevent his body and whatever Kraosian poison coated it from being taken on the *Rigus*?

Under the cover of the flipped stretcher and tangled, groaning queu, I gently laid myself on top of the Human's warm limpness and cycled.

The form I chose was the same as that which had released us from the prison cell. In contact with Ragem's skin, the cells of my new body automatically dispersed, coating, entering his every pore. He began to gag as I filled his mouth and nose. I continued, grimly ignoring his convulsions, completing the process of covering but refusing the natural inclination of this form to then begin to feed. Instead, I began absorbing everything my refined sense of taste determined was not Human from Ragem's skin into my own substance. What I gathered, I automatically digested and destroyed.

I sensed movement, hands touching and repelled by what they felt. I knew panic myself then and fought it—I couldn't cycle; the process of cleansing Ragem's skin was not yet complete. Something punctured me, causing intense local pain as it damaged cells. Realizing it was only a breathing tube being thrust into Ragem's mouth, I held on, refusing to defend myself. I would prefer it if he could live.

Then we were lifted and carried—a not unexpected outcome, had I had the time to think through the consequences of my actions. I didn't need the feel of artificial lights, nor the different and metallic taste to the oxygen in the air, to tell me when we entered the bowels of the waiting *Rigus.* The ship was welcoming back her own—along with an unsuspected, and most unwilling, passenger.

How was I going to explain this to Ersh?

9: Starship Morning

QUIET, professional voices consulted, puzzled, reported—there was always a face peering into this enclosed, sealed place. They had put Ragem's unconscious form in quarantine, locked in a clear box, with precautions taken to the extreme of ensuring that even those outside the seal wore the twinkling aura of personal shields. Given warning, the *Rigus'* crew seemed deflatingly capable of protecting themselves after all.

Of course, I was in quarantine, too—which I supposed was at least slightly amusing, since I was the reason they really didn't need to bottle Ragem in the first place.

But hours had worn the irony thin. Long after I finished cleansing Ragem's warm outer surface I was still waiting for an unobserved moment in which to detach myself.

Of course, observers were always too close, and too interested. The med staff were particularly concerned about me, or rather about the opalescent slime coating Ragem's skin. Their concern had meant some rather uncomfortable attempts to remove me. These ceased with Ragem's obvious distress as caustic fluids passed through my tissues to scour his bare skin.

At least no one suspected me of being more than a disease. What I needed was a moment when Ragem and I were left alone; all I wanted was a dark corner somewhere by myself. I needed to do some productive brooding.

The ship had left Kraos. There'd been no mistaking the vibration and surge of acceleration minutes after the outer lock closed behind Ragem's rescue party, let alone the klaxons and flashing lights Humans always felt necessary to mark such a moment. The moment I'd been kidnapped, shanghaied, stolen from my work; it wasn't my fault I was leaving Kraos before I was finished.

Ersh would hardly accept that as an excuse. My planning so far revolved around how to avoid facing Ersh at all. I was sure I could hide somewhere on the *Rigus*. I was pretty sure I could sneak off at her next planetfall. Trouble was, I wasn't the least bit sure how to make my way back to Kraos, now that the Commonwealth had proof visitors were not welcomed by the locals.

Plans come, plans go. I felt the tremors begin in Ragem's flesh; tremors followed by a growing rigidity signaling his return to consciousness. I wasn't the only one to notice. A warning tone from nearby machinery brought a figure to lean over our casing. With a gentle hiss, the lid and side released, floating upward to a resting place against the wall.

"Aiee!" The force of Ragem's scream sent ripples of pain through me. His abdomen heaved, sucking air in through the breathing tube, then another scream tore out of his lungs. Alarms shrilled as Ragem sat up, fingers clawing at me, fighting the restraining hands of the person striving to calm him, to hold him still.

Ragem's terror horrified me. Quickly I gathered my dispersed tissues, pulling free of his skin, even in my desperate haste knowing a tinge of reluctance to leave his warmth. With a shudder, I slid away, plopping onto the floor. *There.* A crack beneath the bed beckoned. Somehow I pushed my tissues through in a rush and huddled inside what must be a drawer or cupboard.

I could hear Ersh now: After all I had done, what was the point of quivering under someone's spare clothes? I was beyond worrying about her opinion, however. It was that held by the two now-ominously silent beings outside which concerned me.

A slit of light appeared. I touched the hard slickness of the material forming the rear of my refuge and knew it would be far more difficult to pass through than the porous door in the Protark's prison cell—even if I knew where I would find myself on the other side. The slit widened. I felt a warm breath, tasted familiar scents.

"Es. Is that you?" No more than a hoarse, incredulous whisper.

I had never been so astonished by anything in the whole of my life, short as it had been by Web standards. *What was this Ragem?* Humans were much more adaptable than

I had appreciated. Or was this acceptance part of Human friendship?

I extruded a filmy pseudopod, firmed it with an effort, and lightly pushed at the cupboard door. More light came through, almost immediately thrust away by shadow as Ragem's face filled the opening. "It's all right, Es," he said very softly, as though not to be overheard. "Please come out."

This form, regardless of its many other talents, couldn't sigh; I contented myself with a mental version. I flowed out into the almost painfully bright light of what I could now recognize as an ordinary ship's cabin—probably Ragem's own. The sleeping bench on this side was overhung by some complex medical apparatus, blinking frantic warnings to itself as if the medic had neglected to inform it that its patient was again on two feet and independent.

Two feet, independent, and pink verging on red, would be a complete description. My somewhat ruthless first aid, combined with the meds' removal tactics, had stripped away several layers of Ragem's skin. Despite this, I thought he looked well, if tired. His companion, obscured within his shield, seemed less relaxed. "Ragem?" he began, voice cracking on the word. "What—?"

"Who," Ragem corrected, never taking his eyes off me. "Her form is unusual, Tomas, but this gentle, intelligent being has saved my life. And," he added very slowly, "I think she may have saved all of our lives." He held out one hand to me.

I excised the harmless residue of the disease-spores as discreetly as possible before extruding a thinner, wavering pseudopod to touch his fingers briefly. Ragem's intent was clearly to establish my harmless nature immediately, before alarm could spread among his crewmates. *Good plan,* I thought, but for both our sakes, I hoped no one on board was better acquainted with the Ycl.

"We're on the *Rigus,*" Ragem said to me with a sigh of relief, as if for him that solved all things. *I supposed it did.* Then he glanced down at his glowing skin. "What did you do to me?" He touched his feet, still red-looking but now free of blisters. "Or do I want to know?"

The man called Tomas laid a gloved hand on Ragem's

shoulder, removing it at Ragem's wince. "Can we talk, Paul?" Tomas ventured cautiously, eyes on me.

Ragem took his friend's hand in both of his own. "Tomas—the Kraosians planned to kill every one of us—they'd planned it all along. Their leader, the Protark, told me—" here Ragem's quick intense delivery faltered. "They caught me, you see, trying to get back, to warn you. The Protark gloated of how he could defeat us despite our technology. He said they were going to infect me with the spores of a native fungus, something we couldn't be vaccinated against, something our devices wouldn't detect in time. Judging by what happened to the other ships' crews, it would have been quite—lethal." Ragem pointed to me. "My friend here must have removed the spores from my skin somehow before you or the others could be infected."

"We thought you were infected by—" Tomas broke off, apparently finding it difficult to complete his sentence. *I could understand that.*

"By my friend?" Ragem laughed, but I could sense a feather of remembered panic in the sound. This second time, I was certain he was avoiding the use of my name. *Such a clever being,* I thought warmly, then chilled as I wondered what he was anticipating in the future. I'd need my name as a Lanivarian; if Ragem expected me to cycle into that form on demand, he was going to be waiting a few lifetimes.

"I'm not surprised," Ragem continued as I fussed to myself. "I was—startled. But my friend has a habit of finding unusual solutions to problems." His attention shifted back to me. "Did you leave me any clean clothes?"

By way of answer, I flowed to one side, allowing him access to the cupboard. Tomas stared from one to the other of us, *unsure who was more alarming,* I decided. Meanwhile, Ragem gingerly eased a loose shirt over his head, following this with a footed pair of sleek red pants similar to those worn by his crewmate but bearing modifying stripes denoting his specialty. His skin seemed to cause him less discomfort than its redness suggested. Ragem caught Tomas' stare and stopped in the midst of wrapping a belt about his lean middle. "Don't look so worried. I'm all right, Tomas. And I want to talk to Senior Specialist Kearn right away."

"It's Acting Captain now. And he's been in and out a dozen times," Tomas said with a wan smile. "Took it as a personal affront that his own second was unconscious when the waves are burning with orders to report. Everyone will be glad to hear you've—recovered." A slide of his eyes in my direction. "I—" Tomas' voice faded. His next words had nothing to do with me.

"Ragem," he said somberly. "The Kraosians brought out two bodies before you—unidentifiable bodies. With no word from you or Captain Simpson, Kearn wouldn't open the ship; policy was clear enough. Once we had you on board, he ordered lift to parking orbit. But we've all been wondering if there was any chance—if we should have stayed grounded—" Tomas' face was pale and agonized.

Ragem flinched but moved to take his friend's shoulders in his hands. "They were both killed," he said awkwardly. "Luara and Shen felt nothing—it was too sudden, too unexpected. There was nothing I, nothing we, could do to save them. Believe me, Tomas."

"I do," Tomas acknowledged sadly. "I'd hoped for the best, the way one has to, until I saw you, alone and like death itself on that stretcher—then I guess we all knew."

I pressed myself into a small sphere, sharing their grief. It had been a useless waste of life—the Humans, the soldiers at the prison, the serlets, any Kraosians caught in this ship's blast. I found myself consumed by longing for the companions of my Web, for the cleansing ceremonies that acknowledged those whose lives were cut short of their natural end. If we had a worship, it was of the struggling brilliance of life—regardless of form or purpose.

If we had a primeval terror, it was of being the cause of ending that brilliance. I went still to my very core, looking up at the suddenly foreign shapes of the Humans. I was unsure which chilled me more: fear for myself, or fear for what they might force me to do.

"Ragem!" This cry of delight announced a new arrival on the scene. *Great,* I thought to myself, *why not invite the whole crew to meet me, Ragem?* "You're better! Thank the—" The joyous smile on the face of the slender woman in the doorway settled into something fixed and unnatural as her eyes fell on me. I waved a pseudopod graciously.

"Thanks to my friend," Ragem announced with an echoing gesture in my direction. Warned by what seemed a note of challenge in his voice, I watched her more closely. "Willify Guire, I'd like you to meet my fellow refugee from the Kraosians. And my rescuer."

Willify recovered her poise with commendable speed. "Welcome to the *Rigus*." To my currently shifted vision, her face registered a marked drop in temperature. I was curious whether this meant Willify was shocked into paleness by my presence, or was merely in a cold sweat.

It was an academic difference. I could no more respond to her greeting, sincere or not, than I could read her thoughts. Being a loose coalition of cells was a distinct disadvantage. Humans simply weren't equipped with the sensory apparatus to comprehend the chemical voice of this form, however beautiful and eloquent.

I was also feeling decidedly weaker. It was hunger: a need I would not be able to satisfy until cycling into some other shaping. The only food my present body could accept came alive, warm-blooded, and tended to scream. I felt sickened by the quick anticipation which accompanied the thought. No need for Ersh to remind me of the trap this otherwise useful form could become.

Without a voice, I certainly couldn't explain. I also wasn't about to cycle in front of any more aliens. Huddled down into an energy-conserving shape, undignified from a Ycl's point of view, but no one here would notice, I focused my attention on the closest of the three Humans. It was Ragem's turn to take action. As a matter of fact, I was going to leave everything to Ragem—I didn't have much of an alternative.

Out There

ALARM over an empty ship here, a deserted mining dome there, did not make the newsmags. Life on the Fringe had its risks as well as rewards. So Death went relatively unnoticed at first.

But the toll mounted. Supplies were disrupted as freighters were found drifting. Blame was passed, refuted, debated. Armed ships began to patrol key routes, watching eagerly for their foe, expecting to face a familiar enemy.

What they faced had no name, appeared on no scans, gave no warning. Death stalked the gleaming corridors of armed ships as easily as the rock-lined mine shafts.

Ships began to cut their losses and pull back. There seemed only one certainty.

Intelligent life was now prey.

10: Starship Afternoon

AS a Human would put it, I've been on the carpet before Ersh (or some web-sister) a few times; *well, maybe more than a few.* Being familiar didn't mean that I cherished the feeling, even secondhand. Mind you, there was somewhat more dignity to Ragem's position, square-footed and at attention before his superior's desk, than my current one.

I was in a box.

It was a nice box, clean enough to have been used for storing food or other perishables, and just now two-thirds full of my present, somewhat condensed, alien form. While I appreciated the relaxation of letting the box determine my shape, and the privilege of watching Ragem's dressing-down from my vantage point on his superior's desk, I was less than enthusiastic about the lid resting near Kearn's elbow.

"I haven't denied Kraos was a disaster, sir," Ragem was saying, still obstinate though his stiff posture was beginning to sag at the edges. *Good,* I thought. The combination of Kraos and disaster made perfect sense to me.

"And Kraos wasn't enough for you, Specialist Ragem?" Senior Specialist and Acting Captain Kearn asked with a voice that could have been heavy with sarcasm if it weren't for its resemblance to a petulant whine.

There wasn't much personality in his office either. Judging by the shelfload of image cubes on the wall behind the desk, each showing a smiling Kearn with some dead aquatic animal, Kearn hadn't taken over the quarters of his dead captain yet, which was a minor point in his favor. A truly desperate-looking plant clung to life and a strip of artificial bark in one corner of the room. *It might have been lush once,* I thought. I wondered why he cherished it enough to bring it on the ship if he couldn't care for it.

Kearn rocked his chair back and forth, sending irregular and annoying vibrations through the desk supports. I oozed up the side of my container, wishing I could glare back at him in a way he'd recognize.

Ragem's superior officer was of average height, indeterminate age, probably male, and looked as though he'd borrowed his current clothing from several different people. To be charitable, I was not seeing Kearn at his best. His being rumpled and irate was partly our fault, I admitted to myself, but this hardly justified his behavior.

Kearn didn't have Ersh's ponderous—and earned—air of authority. *In fact, he was not an impressive creature at all,* I decided. But then, I was inclined to dislike anyone with close-set eyes and a tendency to diminish major problems into personal affronts.

Kearn had been tearing verbal strips off Ragem's hide for almost an hour now. The theme hadn't changed much. This was the second time he'd circled back with peevish persistence to an apparent belief that Ragem had somehow sabotaged the mission in an attempt to ruin Kearn's own career. To my perception, Ragem's face had long since faded from a heated glow to an unhealthy mottled hue.

"What were you thinking when you came on board, Ragem?" Kearn accused. *Not much,* as I recalled events. Kearn fortunately was not privy to my internal commentary. "And what," he demanded darkly, "am I going to do with this—stowaway?" Kearn paused just long enough for Ragem to jump in again.

"My friend saved our lives," he said, not for the first time. I cringed. Being a hero and famous was not turning out well.

"Bah." Kearn then screwed his tiny mouth into an impossible tightness, as if for our sakes he chose to hold in language inappropriate to an acting captain. His stubby, well-manicured fingers were less controlled, drumming compulsively on the desktop.

I waited, expectantly, for the rest of the routine. Sure enough, Kearn seemed to notice his hands all at once, and smoothly folded them together. This lasted about ten seconds before he began running his hands rather violently through the few wisps of hair clinging desperately above his ears. I was quite taken with the notion that Kearn's anxiety of the past few days had already scoured the rest of his hair from his head, or at least was responsible for its shine.

"Okay, Ragem. According to you—" doubt about Ragem's reliability as a witness dripped from Kearn's voice. *I'd heard that tone before.* "You say that without the aid of this creature we'd be all dead by now."

"Yes." I could tell Ragem was becoming stubborn. "Sir," he added.

"Where's your proof?" Kearn chose to ignore Ragem's tone and his voice switched suddenly to calm reason. "Isn't it just as likely we're dealing here with some kind of outcast, maybe even a criminal?" He glanced at me with suspicion. "I read you the report on the Ycl. These creatures eat people! Who knows what this one was up to on Kraos!"

I had to give Ragem credit. He made the switch from stubborn to reasonable smoothly. "What more proof do you need, sir? We shared the same prison cell. Surely if she'd wanted to—feed—she'd hardly have needed to come on board the *Rigus.*"

"I haven't forgotten that," Kearn snapped. "Did it occur to you she might not have been hungry? Yet?"

Good point. Actually, I was a bit peckish. I rose slightly, oozing up in order to taste the air and immediately wished I hadn't. Kearn's choice of perfume did nothing to enhance his basic organics.

Ragem smacked the side of my box, turning some of his frustration into action. I slumped down, letting the resulting wave action slosh me back and forth, wishing I was somewhere else—somewhere boring. *Somewhere with sausages.*

"I'm the alien culture specialist," Ragem insisted, for about the twelfth time since we arrived in Kearn's quarters. "I asked for her help—"

"You *asked* a Ycl for help?" Kearn repeated, eyes wide. If this was an attempt to ridicule Ragem, it was a failure. I'd been ridiculed by experts in my time, and I could tell by the glint in his eye that Ragem's opinion of Kearn's ability was on a par with my own. "And how did you become expert in communicating with a species the Commonwealth considers too alien for contact?" Kearn tapped a red-banded cube in front of him. "A species so obscure that only one report exists in the memory banks?" Kearn drew a deep breath. "Let's forget for the moment that the Survey Team making the 'no contact' recommendation donated several members to the palates of these—these—" words failed him.

I could only compress myself so far. The organized memories of machines were dangerous. Their shared knowledge and its transmission were similar to the assimilation of shape knowledge within the Web. Given time with such machines, and the right questions, Kearn could find out too much about the Ycl—and possibly about me as well.

"She is my friend," Ragem said flatly, and put his hand on the edge of my box again. I overlapped to touch him, reassurance being all I was capable of at the moment. I withdrew from the contact, watching my appetite.

"Med-tech Crandall saved you from choking to death, or did we misunderstand your *friend's* intention in suffocating you?" Before Ragem could protest, Kearn continued. "Your duty is to the crew of the *Rigus.*" He stopped and lowered his voice with an effort. "Your friends are here, Paul." *Very species-centric,* I thought scornfully.

At that moment, the door irised open, letting some of the heat out of the room and admitting a visitor. I studied the creature with professional interest, finding no match in my memory. Its large round eyes flickered from Kearn to Ragem, finally settling on me, or rather my box.

The alien was two-armed and -legged, quite humanoid, in fact. The features of its face were subtly different, the jaw heavier and the nostrils flattened and enlarged. The portion of its skin which showed beyond its uniform jacket was delicately furred. To my broad spectrum sense this fur was dappled by subtle violets of warmth. Human eyes would perceive the being as dirty white.

The nostrils were able to flare, as they were doing now, as if the creature was testing for my scent. Lips parted to reveal weaponry suited to a carnivore. It spoke, a soft snarl and spit rendered into comspeak by a small device almost hidden in the fur of its throat. "Do you know what have you brought on board, Specialist Ragem?"

I froze, which as a Ycl meant dampening kinetic movement at the molecular level. There's a saying in the Web: what's seen depends on the beholder's eye. *Could this being see some inconsistency in my current form?* I fretted to myself. *Did he know?* Ragem's fingers drummed softly, yet I thought in warning, on the side of my box. The vibration distracted me.

"Old news, Sas," Kearn said impatiently, obviously irritated by the interruption. "Liaison's database is every bit as good as Security's."

"Really, Acting Captain Kearn?" Keeping teeth exposed in that carnivore's grin, a sign of nervous tension if nothing more, the new arrival moved past Ragem and me to push a small disk into a slot on the wall across from Kearn's desk. "You must understand that there was no time to check the remotes before lift. I thought to do so before going offshift. What you'll see will startle you, sir. Be prepared."

I tasted salty moisture in the air; Ragem had broken into a sweat. In a tense puddle of my own, I turned my attention to the images on the screen. There was the Kraosian camp as seen through a lens that had to be high atop the ship. The scene played itself out once more: the appearance of the queu-pulled stretcher, the seemingly insane attack of what looked to be a serlet, ending with a crisp and unmistakable image of the beast blurring, melting, pouring itself into a clear, gleaming mass of plasm over Ragem's convulsing form.

Having never watched myself before, I spared an instant to be impressed. Ansky herself, a self-acknowledged expert on the shapeless Ycl, couldn't cycle more smoothly than that.

Thud. Down came the lid.

My box vibrated with the aftershock. Four separate clicks marked the locks on each side being closed.

This was an interesting twist. I could conceivably pass through the crack between the sides and the lid, but I really didn't expect Kearn or Security Officer Sas to watch me ooze forth without taking some even more regrettable action.

Of course, given another few minutes, the lack of oxygen in the box would change matters again. I would not be able to hold form once my life was truly threatened. And my current energy load would ruin Kearn's desk at the very least. On the plus side, I might destroy that damning recording.

Suddenly my world, the box, turned sideways and rose. Someone must have picked up my prison. Before I could be more than a bit dizzy, the locks clicked, the lid vanished from sight, and I was poured out on to the deck.

And on Ragem's boots. I eased myself clear and looked around.

Kearn was behind his desk. Literally. I could only see the shiny top of his head and the knuckles of his hands. Sas was, for who knows what reason, on the desk—snarling and spitting so quickly it wasn't translating into comspeak. Ragem was waving his hands. "It's all right!" he was shouting.

Fanged mouth open on a roar, Sas, leaped at us, scattering what was left of Kearn's careful piles of plas on the floor. Kearn squealed something incomprehensible. Ragem threw up his hands in a futile reflex.

I blew up.

I couldn't help it. Fortunately for Sas, his leap had been somewhat short of me. He wound up back on the desk, where he blinked like an owl through soot-blackened fur.

The smoke and soot also hid my grab for the only nonsapient living mass in the room. I hoped Kearn would forgive me. Need satisfied, I cycled faster than ever before. I turned to Ragem. He was trying to sit up, having been thrown to the carpet near one wall; he rubbed one shoulder absently. "Sorry," I said, going over to him. My tail had a tendency to curl between my legs. "Stress reflex."

Kearn let out a whimper. I twitched my nose, suspecting he'd experienced a reflex of his own.

Things were definitely not going well.

11: Galley Evening

"I HOPE you appreciate your galley techs, Ragem. That was an excellent meal," I said an hour or so later, eyeing the remains on my plate with slightly uncomfortable satisfaction.

"First thing to make a crew grumble is poor food. But you're right—I'll definitely congratulate Max next time I see him. Feels like the first meal I've had in days." Ragem stretched back in his chair and groaned with contentment. "How's the belt? Still fit after all that?"

I dropped my paws to cover the band locked around my middle. I might have mistaken its display of subtle colors for decoration, except I'd been told to wear it next to my skin, concealed under clothing. "You know this is pretty silly."

Ragem sighed. "Be grateful Kearn went for the telltale instead of trying to lock you up in one of the storage holds." He gave me a sudden, suspicious look. "You'll keep it on, won't you? If the alarm goes off, it's my job—"

"Trust me. I have no intention of cycling out of this form. Things are bad enough already." *And having redecorated Kearn's office, I shouldn't feel compelled to release more energy for weeks.* Shame Kearn hadn't taken the disappearance of his plant well, but he hadn't been able to think of a reasonable way to blame me for it.

Ragem seemed about to say something, but instead stood to refill his cup of sombay from the galley dispenser. He took his time, appearing fascinated by the steam coming up from it. I knew stalling when I saw it. "What's on your mind, Specialist?" I said, carefully tucking leftovers in my pocket for later.

"Nothing. Why?" Ragem came back to the table and put down his cup. Liquid slopped over the top. He grabbed a napkin and blotted at the resulting puddle. When he finally sat down and looked at me, I curled my lip to show a tooth.

"You're not a good liar."

He put his hands around the cup, as if to protect it from further loss. "I don't know about that," Ragem said lightly. "The eavesdroppers in the dungeon believed everything I said."

Did I imagine the emphasis on the word "eavesdroppers?" Probably not, judging by the intentness of Ragem's expression. If ever there was a being trying telepathy without success, it was this Human across from me. I glanced around the galley, then realized there was no need to hunt for hidden devices. My paws clenched over the belt locked around me. Ragem nodded once, slowly. *Great.*

I controlled a snarl. Best to take advantage of this time we remained alone. I snatched Ragem's cup from his hands and poured the rest of its contents over the table. Working with one toe, I spread the warm liquid into words. *Audio only?*

He nodded again. I let out the breath I'd unconsciously held. While I licked the taste of sombay from my toe, Ragem smeared the spilled liquid with his hand quickly, then wrote: *fear u.*

I stared at his pale face, seeing the red spots rising on each cheekbone. I pointed at the words, then slowly raised my toe to him. Ragem shook his head vigorously, then took my paw quite gently in his hand. His other hand smeared the evaporating spill, writing: *Kearn.*

I reclaimed my paw and pulled in a deep breath. We were being overheard, so we should be talking. *What would be more suspicious: meaningless conversation or failing to ask what mattered to me most?* I wasn't sure. I reached for the napkin to wipe up our conversation. Ragem put out a hand to stop me and found just enough sombay left to write: *ask wher.*

Ask where, indeed. I locked eye-to-eye with the determined-looking Human. *Let a bit of concern into the voice,* I decided. "Where's the ship heading, Ragem?"

"We're still in orbit about Kraos. The *Rigus* is waiting to take you home, Esen-alit-Quar."

Home? "The southern continent of Kraos—" I started

to suggest, already thinking about the Ganthor and trying to decide if it was safe to travel as a domestic meat animal.

Ragem interrupted me. "Your home. Whatever world or system that may be." He leaned forward, eyes full of warning. "The acting captain is willing to follow any course you provide."

"And what else does he want?" I asked, no longer worrying about secret listeners. In fact, had Kearn shared the table, I would probably have had my paws around his neck.

"No more than you'd expect, Es," Ragem hesitated, eyes dropping to the belt and back to me. "We're curious about you. We've never met an intelligent species with your ability." Ragem leaned forward, his thin face intent and determined. I wondered if he had forgotten our audience, and was now asking for himself. "What were you doing on Kraos? Why did you help us? Were you really marooned? Did you need this ship for transport off-planet?"

I fastened on the easy one, quickly. "Off-planet, no. But life would be easier for me elsewhere on Kraos."

Ragem didn't smile. The hair prickled as it rose on my neck. "The acting captain has received full authorization from the Commonwealth to meet with your people."

Ersh. I couldn't think of a safe, clever response to this, too busy remembering warnings, too late: warnings about involvement with cultures comparable to our own, about the dangers of revealing our abilities to any outside the Web, about the abyss of direct communication with any intelligences as ephemeral as these.

Ersh would excise me from every strand. I would be alone, exiled for as long as my life would stretch. Which now promised to be far too long.

If she found out.

Shaken by the dark turn my thoughts had begun to take, I forced myself back to the here and now.

"There is only me," I said flatly, quite certain I wanted this overheard.

From Ragem's expression, he didn't think this was a clever response. But he didn't argue. "And where is your home?"

"Take me to Hixtar VII, if you won't return me to Kraos."

"Hixtar VII?" Ragem repeated blankly. "I know it—

there's nothing there but a station. It's just a quadrant stop-over for miners and traders. Why there?"

"Did I ask you questions before I saved you from the Kraosians?" I spread those slim-fingered paws flat upon the table, eyeing their calluses with a feeling of nostalgia. It had been so simple when my hands were only feet. "They could have killed all of you," I reminded him, "despite your weapons and ship. Perhaps I should have asked your terms first!"

Ragem stood up so abruptly he knocked his chair over. It made a muffled thump as it bounced on the plas-coated floor. For a moment, I thought he would leave. I pointed down at my belt in warning.

His lips twitched, then he came around to my side of the table and knelt beside me. I realized this gesture was meant to add another layer of meaning to what he said next. "Esen, you know I'm grateful. And I'll do what I can to help you get to wherever you want to go. But I'm not the captain of this ship. And my superiors don't always consult me before they make decisions."

His superiors. I didn't know who else I had to deal with, but I realized that Kearn couldn't be a total idiot—though I had my suspicions—and he was undoubtedly ambitious. The man badly needed to recover something from this disastrous voyage to Kraos. I could understand, if not sympathize. *So.* I searched Ragem's face before I nodded. "I know about orders, Ragem," I admitted grudgingly. "What do your superiors want?" *Besides my home,* I added to myself.

Ragem let out a ragged breath, as though he had been unsure of me after all. "You're unique, Es. Unique and powerful. The Commonwealth has arranged a meeting between you and the Quadrant Minister when we reach Rigel II. They need an assurance that your species—you—poses no threat. You'll be asked to join the Commonwealth itself—or at least to permit an ambassador of ours to accompany you home."

Not for the first or last time, I wished I had left the Humans and their business alone. Ragem was coming close to pushing me into very regrettable action, and I resented that most of all. *Hadn't I'd done enough adventuring for one lengthy lifetime?*

"I'm not interested in meeting officials of your or any other species, Ragem," I said at last.

Righting his chair, Ragem sat back down, this time on my side of the table, and tilted his head to regard me with what appeared to be simple curiosity. "We've been ordered to bring you to our quadrant base, Rigel II, failing an offer to go to your home system."

I reached for a piece of fruit and peeled it, admiring the flexibility of claw tips and paws as I worked, pausing to lick juice from my palm. I wouldn't be ready for polite Lanivarian society for some time—*as if I cared at the moment.*

I broke the peel into smaller and smaller pieces as I spoke. "I find you Humans curious, Ragem."

"In what way?"

"I saved your lives. Now you are taking me with you against my will." I began to arrange the peels on the table. "Being-napping is against most species' laws, is it not?"

"It's only for a conversation, Es," Ragem said, watching my paws. "No one intends any harm to you."

I finished my work. Ragem read it, then closed his eyes tightly for a moment as if considering a variety of unpleasant options. *I'd already done that.*

He placed his hands on my shoulders and bent his head to touch his flatter Human nose to mine. In Lanivarian culture, the gesture meant several things, not the least of which being a promise of loyalty through difficult times. I peered into the alien gray, black, and white of his eyes and hoped for the best.

A sound behind us warned of the end of our privacy. Ragem jumped up and swept the peels from the table.

Erasing the only word I'd written.

Friend.

Out There

"NOTHING on scans."

Officer of the Watch Stagdt dropped one hand on the shoulder of the *Cappella's* com-tech. "Keep on it, Pat," she said in a low voice. Several on the Tly warship's bridge were frankly dozing at their stations, catching a rest while systems ran on auto during shipnight. No one felt like heading to the isolation of a cabin, not after finding yet another empty, drifting ship.

Stagdt paced, her steps and breathing light, feeling the lives sharing the bridge as something fragile, something to be protected. Against what? That was the rub. The *Capella* was well-armed and -crewed. But something in the Fringe no longer respected either. And despite what the Tly government said, no one out here believed they faced their Human rivals from Garson's World or Inhaven.

As the *Capella* searched and waited, Death slowed, considered, then passed. It wasn't hungry.

Still, life was irresistible.

Death turned back.

12: Lounge Evening

THERE was a tingling under my paws, flattened on either side of the port, each time the engines worked to maneuver the starship in the approach lanes. I twisted my head around once in a while, feeling a bit foolish. None of the *Rigus* crew looked my way. I pressed my nose against the port again.

I'd never seen anything like this before. We were suspended over the night side of Rigel II, an intricate beadwork of light marking cities and transport grids on the surface. Most of the curve of the planet was lost, black on black, except for a hint of a glow where her sun was slipping with playful slowness over the top rim. Suddenly, an arc of white gold traced out the edge of the world. With a click, the port closed, shielding me from the full glare of Rigel's sunrise.

I closed my eyes also, remembering every detail, storing the image as well as my feelings. I included self-consciousness as well as rapture; my "grounder" fascination at the port a source of amusement to those playing cards or relaxing in the lounge. Yet how alive that awareness of others made me feel! *Another moment Ersh wouldn't understand,* I reminded myself, carefully shunting the memory to my private storehouse.

I moved away from the viewport and tried to ignore the entrance of a crewmember bearing a tray of sweets. At least she was thoughtful enough not to offer me any. Following my disgraceful eruptions after my first meal aboard, probably everyone now appreciated why Lanivarians hated space travel.

I'd known, but hoped I'd be spared. Spacesickness wasn't enough to make me cycle within range of Kearn again. Looking on the bright side, being sick was a novelty in its way. I'd undoubtedly remember every miserable detail. Something I could share with Ersh. I ran my paw over the faint bulge marking the telltale belt under my clothing. And something I'd definitely shared with any eavesdroppers.

"There you are, Es."

I grinned toothily at Tomas as he made his way past tables full of his fellows, slapping shoulders good-naturedly as he went, pausing only to pilfer a chocolate from the plate of one of his friends. The protest that followed him was a cheerful one. I'd met puppies with the same mischievous, company-loving nature.

"So, Es. What do you think of Rigel II?" he said around bites, peering over my shoulder to look out the port, shrugging without much disappointment I could see when he realized it was closed.

My stomach gave one great threatening lurch at the smell of chocolate. "Beautiful," I said quickly, trying not to breathe through my nose.

"Well, from up here they all look good," Tomas said thoughtfully. "Hate to disillusion you, but this world's a hole—even if it is home."

"You were born there?" Now that the offending food was no longer in evidence, I followed Tomas to the nearest unoccupied couch and curled up comfortably in one corner, wiggling my toes at another new friend, Lawrenk Jen, the redheaded engineering specialist. She waved back and quickly returned her concentration to the cards in her hand, the grin on her broad mouth causing the others at her table to exchange glum glances.

I edged one leg over my tail in an attempt to stop its thumping. The position wasn't comfortable or dignified, but then neither would be the reactions of a true Lanivarian to my behavior. Irresponsible tail-wagging was equivalent to a Human running about naked, except possibly on Hinesburg II.

"Born on Rigel?" Tomas repeated. With the ease of an unconscious mimic, he curled his thin frame into the other corner of the couch. His mouth curled up, too. "Oh, none of us are Rigellian—or at least admits it. Home is what a First Contact Team calls its quadrant base. Helps keep things simple. Our current 'home' happens to be Rigel II." Tomas sighed melodramatically. "You watch. It'll be boring from orbit on down, Esen. Absolutely nothing disgraceful to do."

I pulled a file from a pocket of my coveralls. The clothing actually fit to some extent. I'd had to make some minor adjustments, such as cutting off the sleeves, trimming the collar, and, of course, snipping a hole in the rear to accommodate my tail. Fortunately, when I showed off my tailoring, Willify assured me she hadn't wanted the clothing back anyway.

Being dressed made one feel incredibly civilized. I stretched out the toes of my right paw, inspected the calluses on my knuckles, and resumed the tiresome process of filing away at them. It would take some time to remove the evidence of six hundred days on all fours.

"Lots of important types at this base?" I asked Tomas with what I thought was a properly casual note of interest.

His blue eyes twinkled, their natural state. "Will be once the *Rigus* makes orbit. You'll stay for a while at least, Esen? We could use an excuse for a party." Predictably his mobile mouth drooped. Tomas' face, ever transparent, never failed to show when he was thinking of his murdered crewmates.

"We'll see," I hedged.

"Hey, Tomas—we need a fourth. Lawrenk's deciding to lift her haul while she's ahead." With an apologetic shrug to me, Tomas got up and joined the cardplayers, taking the seat the engineering specialist had vacated.

I watched the bustle contentedly. This had become my favorite place, a combination of refuge and entertainment. During on-duty shift, it was lonely in the room I shared with Tomas and Ragem. But people came and went in the *Rigus'* rest lounge like flotsam on a tide. At some point or other in the shipday, each crewmember would drift in, to socialize or sit alone, eat or just stretch out on a couch to enjoy the sense of activity. Only a few shared my fascination with the viewports. I had begun to suspect that Humans were capable of becoming used to anything.

They'd gotten used to me. There weren't many non-Humans aboard, just Sas, who was a Modoren, and a couple of dozen Quebits floating in the null grav parts of the engine room when they weren't climbing around the exterior of the hull. Sas didn't trust me, and I already knew

Quebits had the conversational abilities of doorknobs. Fortunately, most of the twenty-two Human crewmembers of the *Rigus* were friendly, especially here and off duty.

And here was the source of Ragem's desperate courage on Kraos—the connections between these people, connections as strong in their way as those of my Web. Ragem's sponsorship admitted me to this group, although their welcome was based on a somewhat creative explanation of our relationship.

I appreciated that Ragem and Kearn had to explain my arrival, since I could hardly be hidden for the week-long translight voyage from Kraos to Rigel II. And, since I'd lied to Ragem in the first place, why should I quibble? So I somewhat philosophically accepted my role as a semi-crazed Lanivarian trader foolish enough to land on Kraos. I was even grateful that the secret of my shape-changing was being kept by Sas, Kearn, and, certainly, Ragem, at least on this ship, though I was sure reports had burned the com links. Tomas and Willify, the only other crew to meet me as Ycl, had been told that being was safely hibernating in a stasis box in the hold. The entire fabrication seemed to satisfy all questions.

It was the constantly expanding details of Ragem's heroic rescue of me from the depths of a Kraosian prison I was beginning to detest. *Who had saved whom?*

I replaced the file in my pocket, promising the reddened skin of my knuckles some cream, and scratched discreetly behind one ear. Though I'd left my insect passengers behind on Kraos when I cycled, the habit was soothing. I stroked the sides of my muzzle, pleased at the smoothness of a good trim. *Couldn't pass for a serlet today.*

A shout of dismay from the cardplayers meant that Tomas had inherited a lucky chair. I considered joining the game, sure of my welcome, then changed my mind. Watching our approach to Rigel II had brought to focus my own predicament.

The crew accepted me; knowing more of the truth, Kearn and his superiors did not. My fingers couldn't push between the telltale and my skin, though it was comfortable enough.

I couldn't see the use of it, unless it was to help Kearn avoid facing me. Certainly, we'd never encountered each other since that first day, and it wasn't that big a ship. His suspicion was as valid an indicator of how I would be received on Rigel II as the friendship in the lounge.

"Did you catch the sunrise?" Ragem dropped down beside me with a sigh. He set his cube reader on the floor and shoved it under the couch with one foot, like someone thoroughly avoiding further thought of work.

"Hello." My tail wriggled loose and thumped. "Yes. You were right—it was spectacular. I will remember it."

"Sorry I missed it." Ragem stretched, then rubbed his hand over his eyes. He looked tired.

I didn't want to ask what he'd been doing. If I did, he'd either have to lie or evade the question. Besides, I could guess. This ship carried Survey records on a thousand worlds and hundreds of sapient life-forms. Kearn wouldn't be wasting any time trying to learn about me.

"Want some sombay? There's a fresh pot in the galley."

He shook his head. "I've had my limit today, thanks. What about you? How's the stomach?"

I bared my teeth in a grimace. "Empty and complaining. The med-tech assures me his pills satisfy all my nutritional needs—but believe me, I'm starving to death."

The Human nodded sympathetically.

I wrinkled my nose; his scent wasn't right. "You aren't well, Paul," I decided, concerned. "You should spend more time resting, or with your friends."

"What am I doing now?"

"That's not what I mean."

He glanced around the lounge. The nearest group to us was the card game, still punctuated by howls as Tomas continued his winning ways. "I've been busy, Es," Ragem said with a sudden quiet urgency. He tapped his finger to one ear. *Yes, I never forgot we were being overheard.*

I lowered my ears, then deliberately pricked them up. "Looking for information about me in your records? You won't find any. I'm a private and peaceful being, Ragem." *Kearn could make what he wanted of that.*

"And the only one of your kind. There's just you."

"Yes." Ragem doubted me, but what I said was true, in a technical sense. I was one flesh with the others of my Web. And ours was the only one.

Ragem brought out a pad and stylus from his pocket, with a conspiratorial glance at the others in the room. We were unnoticed. I peered over his arm as he wrote quickly: *Don't know how long we have. Why were you on Kraos?* He hit erase and passed me the implements.

So he wanted a reason to trust me. They must keep at him when we were apart, trying to talk Ragem into a more species-oriented loyalty. I searched his gray and earnest eyes for a moment then wrote: *Studying culture. Civilization is my hobby.* As he read this, I hesitated, then erased and wrote: *Meant no harm. Disguised so I could observe without alarming the Kraosians.* I erased and handed back the pad and stylus. What would he respond to that?

Ragem pressed his lips into a thin, determined line, writing quickly for several seconds after a glance to make sure no one was paying attention to us. He passed the pad to me, saying out loud: "Sombay sounds good after all. Some for you?"

"Water is the only safe drink, thanks," I said, already reading: *I envy you. Must have good stories!* I smiled, then read further and felt my stomach threaten to heave, despite its current empty state.

Kearn pushing idea you are a parasite or predator like the Ycl. Wants tight security. Minister disagrees, plans to meet you as a first contact, diplomacy. Be careful not to give Kearn more to use against you.

Then below, one word I looked at thoughtfully before erasing. *Friend.*

"I heard from the com-tech that the Minister and her staff have arrived ahead of us," Ragem announced as he returned. "Don't worry. Probably the worst you'll have to go through will be a dozen or so boring speeches and tedious dinners."

"Don't you dare mention dinners," I growled, still holding the pad and thinking about our real conversation.

Ragem passed me my drink and sat down, stretching out his legs. "I'll be there."

Unfortunately, so would I. I couldn't see any way to avoid going to Rigel II without playing into Kearn's hands and making matters worse. Famous was bad enough. I couldn't afford to become infamous at the same time. Humans took a depressingly narrow view of what they perceived as a threat.

The lounge was no longer a comfortable refuge. I wanted to go home.

And explain to Ersh?

Maybe wanting to go home wasn't such a great idea.

13: Planet Night

SNOWFLAKES patted the window, tumbling past and catching the light from my room. I squinted, trying to ignore my own reflection and see something in the blackness beyond the fat white flakes. But Rigel II was keeping its scenery to itself tonight.

I sighed, then absently licked the resulting oval of fog from the window. The snow ignored me, too busy trying to fill in the corners of the windowsill. A futile task, since each little pile always reached a crisis and whirled away in a miniature avalanche. The image roused web-memory—Ansky had spent months under a drift of frozen oxygen on Kaleb IX.

Being buried alive was fine if you enjoyed composing poetry while you waited for a thaw. I shoved the unhelpful memory aside and turned away, pacing erratically around the stools, tables, and bed platform of my Rigellian home—wondering which of the ship's crew I'd displaced from his or her planetside quarters.

It was better than worrying about tomorrow, when I would officially become the honored guest of the Commonwealth and start the round of formal dinners and talks.

Honored guest, ha! My door was locked from the outside. Kearn's message had been quite clear: Stay put.

Ordinarily I was good at that. I was even better at passing through locked doors, as Ragem knew all too well. "Promise me you'll stay here at least until tomorrow. You have to meet the Deputy Minister," I snarled out loud, not bothering to mimic Ragem's pleading sincerity. "Kearn's made me responsible for you. It'll be my career if you leave, Esen.

"What about my career, Ragem-the-troublemaker?"

My elbow bumped the corner of the creteng tank, a

bulky ornamental thing stuck in the middle of the floor. The contact stung and I snapped my teeth. It also set the tank's water and inhabitants rocking. "Sorry," I said, then felt as embarrassed as if Ersh had caught me talking to myself. *Pets.* I steadied the tank and found a couple of towels to cover the puddle on the floor. The creteng, finned specks of color too small at this age to be worth eating, refused to stop cowering behind their fake water plants.

The door whistled cheerfully. *As if it wasn't enough to lock me in, they had to pester me in the middle of the night.* It wasn't likely to be a meal, so I ignored it, curling up on the rug beside the bed platform, wrapping my tail over my nose.

A second whistle. I snarled: "All right. Come in."

The door opened to reveal Ragem, dressed in a thick patterned coat with a furred collar. He was carrying a bright red bundle. I glared at him through the wisps of fur on my tail. Snowflakes winked to waterdrops on his hair. His face was rosy-cheeked and split in a wide grin.

"Quit sulking, Es!" Ragem ordered as he marched into the room, his boots tracking snow for the first couple of steps. He bumped the creteng tank and quickly sidestepped the slosh of water that followed. "Time to get out and enjoy life." He shook out his bundle, dropping a pair of boots on the carpet and holding out an enormous red coat.

Trying to keep the tip of my tail from thumping wasn't easy. I sat up and tucked it under my hind paw, swinging my ears back and down in disapproval. I pointed at the belt around my waist. "Kearn does know about this." It wasn't a question.

Ragem's smile was angelic. "I don't think that's a problem. Kearn's busy. Everyone is! Don't you know what day it is?"

In other words, I said to myself, smelling a rather potent whiff on Ragem's breath, *there's a party someplace to welcome the* Rigus *home and my buddy here has become potted enough to reconsider his career plans.* I flicked my ears up, decided not to remind him, and took the coat.

Ragem hadn't quite abandoned all sense, I decided moments later as I followed him out of the building. He had made sure no keen-eyed watcher, mechanical or otherwise, would recognize his companion. The boots hid my paws;

the coat was hooded and draped almost to the ground. He led the way down the slushy ruts of the main driveway. I licked a snowflake off the smooth skin of my muzzle and peered around with interest.

The driveway linked a series of square, two-story buildings, their upper corners hung with baskets of green-and-red lights. I thought it was rather charming and took time to remember. A few windows, mine included, cast beams of light onto the snow-covered trees bordering the roadway. Otherwise, the place seemed deserted. The only sounds were our breathing, the wet smack of our boots, and the sighing of snow down the fabric of our coats.

I was about to grab Ragem's sleeve and find out where he was taking me when the twin headlights of a groundcar shone on us. It moved slowly through the snow, stopping at Ragem's signal. The markings on the vehicle's side reassured me on one point. I doubted I was being kidnapped in one of Big Al's Rent-for-Less, Winter-Ready Specials.

We climbed in the back seat, shaking clumps of wet slush from our feet as best we could. The floor of the car had once been protected by sheets of plas; these now held brown puddles of melted snow that shivered as we seated ourselves.

The driver turned around to greet us. I was somehow not surprised to see Tomas' cheerful face. "Are you fit to drive?" I asked, twitching my nose at his breath, too.

"Absolutely, my dear Fang Face," Tomas replied, doffing his white-trimmed cap. I showed him a fang or two, but kept it friendly. A large silvery bell sewn on the tip of the cap tinkled as he replaced it on his head. "To the festivities!"

"I thought you said this was the dullest planet—"

Ragem chuckled. "All too true, Esen—"

"But not tonight. It's time to howl, Old Hound!" Tomas sang out happily, sending the groundcar forward with reassuring care for the snow.

Fang Face? Old Hound! The Humans were impossible, rude, and just what I'd needed. I found myself tingling with anticipation and suspense. After tucking the feeling into my private memory, I made one final attempt to salve my conscience. "This isn't a good move for either of you. I was supposed to stay in my room."

Ragem took off his mittens and shook them over Tomas' head, spraying drops of melted snow over all three of us. "Do we look worried? You know you were miserable. Well, Tomas and I were miserable. How could we have fun without you?" *Hah,* I said to myself.

"Besides, we know what we're doing. Far as I'm concerned, it should be against the law to miss Rigel's only party," Tomas added, leaning rather alarmingly right into the back seat to grin at me. The groundcar didn't swerve, so its servo brain must have had a good nose too.

They wouldn't tell me anything more, delighted to keep me puzzled. We drove along in Big Al's Rental, blinded on all sides by snow, trusting the machine to find the road. Ragem and Tomas spent the time trying to match their voices around a wide assortment of songs, usually tripping each other on the first few lines.

After a while, I decided the pair of Humans weren't so much drunk as they were unwinding like a pair of released springs. I, though far too professional for a similar display, found myself howling along to one of their more consistent musical efforts.

"Close as we'll get now. Better park it here," Ragem announced some time later. I opened the window on my side, licking up the snow that immediately danced in to land on my face, and looked at our surroundings. It was a parking lot—*well, maybe it was supposed to be a parking lot.* Right now, I was looking at a dense pack of snow-covered mounds each about the same size and shape as our vehicle. An overhead crisscross of lights struck sparks of red and green from the still-falling snow. Following Ragem's advice, Tomas slid to a stop, managing in the process to completely block the exit of at least three other vehicles.

The heavy snowflakes seemed to take their time choosing a landing place. I watched them dance and slip, admiring their unpredictability. "Oh, hurry up, Es," Ragem and Tomas said at once, hauling me out of the car.

I twitched a snowflake from one ear, then swiveled both to catch the faintest of sounds. Music. Hardly had I identified it before each of my crazed companions took one of my arms and hustled me in the direction of the sound. "Hurry! It's almost midnight!" Tomas said breathlessly, his feet slipping and sliding until I thought I was the only thing holding him up as we half ran down an empty street.

Small tidy shops and homes lined the street, each appearing dark inside, but outside ablaze with lights—all red or green. I would have appreciated at least a second or two to search web-memory about them—something was teasing me about the colors and snow. The Humans didn't give me time to concentrate. The music grew louder as we ran toward its source, swelling into recognizable voices and instruments.

We literally burst out into a broad square. Hundreds of people stood around its edges, each so well-bundled against the cold that species was impossible to determine. I hoped Kearn would take that into account tomorrow. Then I looked at the source of the music and finally understood.

"It's Christmas."

" 'Course," Tomas said, leading the way through the crowd around the towering tree ahead. The massed choir changed songs and answering hums throbbed from all sides. "And if you'll move those paws of yours a bit quicker, Puppykins, we won't miss New Year's."

Still linked between them, I could only smile toothily in apology as we nudged, bumped, and basically shoved other spectators out of our way. Fortunately, no one took offense, most calling out a "Merry Christmas, Happy New Year," softly enough not to disturb the carol singing.

Ansky was fond of Christmas, I remembered nostalgically, part of her poetic nature. When not busy on Web business, or studying the Articans, Ansky was a sucker for guided tours. Her last planet-hopping trip had boasted ten consecutive Yuletides.

Although when Christmas fell was a planet matter, and many worlds indulged themselves more than once a planet year, Christmas traditions were amazingly consistent. I was personally convinced this had more to do with traveling salesmen than any Human effort to keep the custom intact. Ansky thought this very cynical of me and insisted I'd appreciate such things better when I was older.

Not inclined to quibble, I howled along with a carol Ansky had learned for me and settled down to enjoy myself.

The Rigellians had sacrificed the traditional evergreen

tree, propping the corpse up with plas supports. *Not bad,* I decided, approving the wide range of edible decorations. Snow frosted the tops of hanging cookies and reflected the surrounding lights. The clock at the top of the tree was star-shaped, and, again traditionally, counted down the minutes to the New Year.

Someone squeezed in between Tomas and me—no mean feat since we were already crushed together. The dwarf, no, child, wiggled ahead purposefully. The crowd around us shook like the surface of a jelly as a veritable army of children pushed through at waist height to cluster at the base of the tree. The adults good-naturedly stepped back to give them room.

"Midnight's coming, Es!" Ragem shouted. I pinned back my ear with a wince, able to hear quite well despite the babble of voices from all sides.

I nodded, watching the clock just like everyone else. The last notes of song hung themselves on silence. Snow whirled above our heads, the tree, the waiting children, and snuck down the neck of my coat again. I shivered with excitement. *One minute to go.* Some worlds claimed they used Terran-standard clocks, but this minute had to be slower than even that myth demanded.

Ten seconds to midnight. A countdown began, shouted from several hundred throats. ". . . Nine, eight, seven . . ."

I found myself shouting with all the rest. "Two, one . . ."

The clock exploded right on midnight, showering our upturned faces with multicolored sparks that melted just overhead with a whiff of cinnamon. The tree split into four, curving apart from its crown, majestically arching its branches and their treasures down to the eager hands of the waiting children.

"Happy New Year!" The adults grabbed, hugged, kissed, and generally acted without restraint or manners. I lost track of Ragem and Tomas. No one seemed to mind that I licked instead of kissing back.

Ansky hadn't shared this, or else I hadn't assimilated her memories properly. I felt an intense belonging, a feeling of welcome almost as strong as that within the Web itself. *Maybe stronger than my future welcome,* I thought glumly. I couldn't stay glum for long. As the crowd quieted, this time with a delightful sense of exhausted release, someone passed me a huge roll of pastry, steaming hot and fragrant. I bit into it, tasting cloves, raisins, and crunchy bits of sugar. *What wonderful people!*

"Es?" Ragem tugged at my sleeve. "Come over here. Tomas found some spurl."

I was game, whatever spurl was. Lanivarians, on the ground at least, had very capable digestive systems—something I'd proved scrounging on Kraos. Anything my omnivorous primate hosts could safely consume, I could. In point of fact, I could safely consume anything, having only to shift to web-form to deal with whatever became disagreeable. Even Ersh had never encountered a poison fast-acting enough to seriously harm a particular form before she could cycle from it. Make it sick, definitely. But nothing permanent.

Which was good, because eating was such a pleasure in almost all forms. I hooked the paw free of pastry under Ragem's bulky sleeve and let him find our way through the expanding eddies in the crowd. I finished my treat, licked each slender toe, and speculatively eyed the cookies being carried by children on all sides of us. *Probably not a Christmas thing to do,* I decided, closing my mouth so I wouldn't drool.

Fortunately, spurl was equally worth drooling over. It was a spiced drink thick as soup, served frothy and hot, and with a sneaky ability to glow along nerve endings by the third cup. The Rigellians, in no hurry to resume their staid reputation, had set up dispensers of the stuff all around the square. The crowd was no smaller, but had become appreciably more mellow. Adults walked around, cup in hand, or sat on benches to watch the children prowl through the remains of the tree. A few groups sang softly to themselves.

Some time ago, unnoticed, the snow had stopped—as if on cue. The sky had cleared to a black arch. It was too bright in the square to make out stars, but without the clouds the air was cooling quickly. Ragem could make rings with his spurl-warmed breath.

Tomas had left us after sharing the first cup or so, spotting some of the *Rigus'* crew. Ragem, I was pleased to see, preferred to stay with me.

Ragem was just drunk enough to be talkative. He was

telling me about Christmas on Botharis, his mother's homeworld. I was just drunk enough to be content to listen and remember. "We give gifts—always to the kids and usually to each other," he said, sounding wistful. "Depending on who's home of course. And we have snow, like this. My favorite part was always the rides we'd take, late at night, under the stars."

He sipped spurl, its steam curling past his wistful eyes. I hazarded a guess. "Horses?"

"Snowspeeders. But when we were young, my brother and I'd pretend we had horses. Kids do that at Christmas. Riding through the snow." Ragem stopped talking for a moment, staring into the steam.

I squinted into my empty cup and thought I'd probably had more than my share. "How long since you've been home?" I asked him.

"Too long."

I felt my ears go down in sympathy. We were both a bit maudlin and sentimental—New Year's does that to beings. Then my ears pricked up as I had a truly fabulous idea. I hadn't seen any horses (or speeders) in the town, but I knew something even better at running through snow. I'd cheer Ragem up by giving him a Christmas present.

Later, I'd remember this moment and realize just how stupid I'd been.

But that was later.

"I want you to wait here, Ragem," I said quickly. "Give me ten minutes. Exactly ten. Then meet me by those trees over there." The trees I pointed to were on the far side of the square.

"What're you up to, Es?" His coat crinkled in the cold as he turned on the bench to look at me suspiciously.

"I've a little Christmas surprise for you," I said, pushing down on his shoulders as I got to my feet. It kept Ragem still and countered an odd tendency for the ground to spin. "Promise to give me a ten-minute start before you come."

"I made you promise to stay," Ragem said with a melancholy sigh, his mind spinning off on an unexpected tangent. "That wasn't fair, was it? Selfish. My asking, I mean, not your staying. Staying would be nice; you're my friend. Shouldn't ask. I'm sorry, Esen, I—"

I cuffed his head gently to shut him up. Too much spurl

and too little time to relax, I decided. "I didn't say I was leaving, Ragem." *Yet.* "I said I have a surprise for you. Now wait here ten minutes, then meet me by the trees. Okay?"

Ragem tried to scowl but failed. "Okay." His wandering gaze fixed on the nearest spurl dispenser.

I found that once I started walking, the ground steadied itself—more or less—although everyone around me had a tendency to weave, making it difficult to move in a straight line through the crowd. The snow was packed, but in the cold it creaked a bit underfoot. I looked cross-eyed at the curls of white frost forming on the tiny hairs of my muzzle—better shave in the morning.

Ah. Finally out from the crowd, out of the lights, and under the stars. I looked for a suitable tree.

Plenty to choose from, I saw with satisfaction. There were two rows, planted in a staggered fashion to mark the edge of town. Their skeletal shadows cut black lines in the glittering fresh snow. Beyond stretched a night-etched rolling plain, likely farm fields in summer, welling up into low hills on the horizon. The spaceport was just past that horizon, but there were no ships moving tonight.

I compared several trees of about the right mass before settling on one I didn't think would be missed in spring—it grew much too close to its neighbors. I took off the jacket and boots Ragem had given me and laid them carefully over a nearby bush. Kearn's telltale belt would just have to drop in the snow. It was hardly my problem if the moisture damaged it.

I took a couple of deep breaths, fur standing up along my back not so much from cold as anticipation. I couldn't wait to see Ragem's face. The tree bark was coated with ice on one side. I moved to the other and pressed myself against its cold roughness as tightly as possible. Ten minutes should be more than enough, but it would spoil my surprise if Ragem's drink-fuddled head couldn't tell time.

I had always been good at enlarging, better than any of my Elders. They said it was because I was barely formed yet myself. In my opinion, it was more likely that Lesy and the others were squeamish about taking in so much nonsapient mass. As for Ersh—I quickly stopped thinking about her.

I loosened my grip on the Lanivarian form, cycling into web-form after one last look around. In that state, almost as amorphous as the Ycl, I inserted my tissues into the contacting tissue of the tree, climbing like sap in spring through every branch and twig. As I became almost-tree for an instant, my thoughts slowed, smothered into a rigid order, consumed by purposes my mind labeled *survival* and *growth.* I clamped down on the familiar sensation of mild panic, knowing it was just the proximity to nonintelligent life.

The rest of the process was automatic. Tree tissue readily re-formed itself into more of my tissue along each of my extended strands, my sense of myself expanding in size with each acquisition, my thoughts quickening again so that I knew the moment when I had gathered the mass I needed. I cycled.

There. I pulled my rear foot out of the frozen soil with only a bit of a struggle. I'd judged it nicely. It wasn't easy to avoid the roots, and embarrassing if not dangerous to wind up half-buried underground.

The spurl no longer affected my system, but I tingled with another kind of exhilaration. I shook myself from head to foot, admiring the cascades of heavy fur that blanketed my rippling muscle. *Wait till Ragem took a ride with me!*

"My God."

Ragem stood about three meters away, absolutely motionless. I'd forgotten how tiny Humans were compared to this form.

"Rag'm," I boomed, having forgotten for a moment that the Crougk had only rudimentary vocal cords and fewer vowels. I loosened my tongue. "L'k g't?" I asked hopefully, bending my head down as far as possible so my faceted eyes could see under his hood, my mouth agape in a fanged grin, breath frosting with each word.

Ragem took a step back, his hand reaching out for support and slipping on the icy trunk of the next tree in the row. Another step, clumsy and urgent; he almost fell in a snowdrift. *What was the matter with him?*

Suddenly, Ragem's face tilted, caught a moonbeam's worth of light. It was enough to show me his lips drawn back from his teeth in a horrible parody of a smile. His eyes were worse. The terror in them tore out my heart.

Whirling on my powerful haunches, I flung myself away, leaping over the snow, heading for the distant hills and the spaceport beyond. My wide feet barely sank into the drifts. Each curl and extension of my legs sent me farther and farther, faster and faster, until the wind in my ears and my heaving breath came close to drowning out any thought.

Merry Christmas, indeed.

14: Spaceport Night

WHEN Thomas had originally referred to Rigel II in less than glowing terms, I'd assumed he was complaining about its lack of amusements for a crew newly in from space, hazardous space at that. I kicked one huge foot pensively in the snow, glaring at the gate in front of me. I now shared his opinion. Any planet without automated credit access was less than a hole in my terms, too.

Some time before Humans traded bits of shell with one another for fish, Ersh had concluded that the ability to change form, especially on civilized planets, was not enough to ensure safety or comfort. She considered the amassing of physical wealth to be a necessary descent into ephemeral concerns, one which she could luckily leave to unusually long-term investments. So, barring an unpredictable collapse of the entire Commonwealth economy—and likely even then—the Web had a credit rating to turn most system governments green with envy, had Ersh ever kept it all in one account or under one name. Suffice it to say, I could travel to any civilized world and access the appropriate currency to allow my form's self to meet the demands of a comfortable life.

Which meant I had more than sufficient funds at my disposal on this particular planet to buy passage on any of those ships, so temptingly near on the other side of this gate. If I wanted to risk Ersh's outrage, I could pick one, buy it outright, and return home in style, a thought I definitely tucked into private memory.

If Rigel II's spaceport had a proper automated access point, that is. What was before me was plainly a gatekeeper's booth, where one would doubtless have to deal directly with some being, a procedure at minimum requiring clothing and other civilized accoutrements: at worst, proof of ID and inconveniences such as a credit chip.

There were other ways. I shed excess mass as water, too shaken by my experience with Ragem to enjoy the effect as the liquid turned to whirling diamonds of frost around me as I shrank during my cycling. My final form bore no resemblance to the Crougk. In fact, it bore no resemblance to anything ever seen on Rigel II before, this species having the misfortune to inhabit a world whose atmosphere shredded to nonexistence during a near-collision with a comet shortly before Humans spread to this part of space.

A revealing choice, should an expert in alien cultures such as Kearn or Ragem see me, but I had no intention of being seen. I was also in no mood to sit here until morning, attempt to argue with the living or servo gatekeeper when it chose to come to work, and likely end up being caught in some search for Esen anyway.

It was a lovely form, however; and I paused a moment to admire myself—an admiration made easier by a neck capable of swinging my head completely out and turning it to face my long, sinuous self. *Elegant,* I thrummed to myself, *glorious. Indeed, beautiful beyond mere words.*

And so incredibly self-centered and vain, I reminded myself, breaking the spell becoming Acepan always cast. I dropped down on to my hundred-and-six tiny legs, scurrying forward with that blinding speed humanoids found so troubling in the multilegged. The snow flew under my clawed feet and the vertical wall of the gate, slippery with hoarfrost, was no obstacle whatsoever.

I ran down the other side of the wall headfirst, racing for convenient shadows, well aware even the most peaceful of planets tended to protect its spaceport with more than walls and a gate. The Acepans had been artful dodgers and hiders, but this form shivered at the mere notion of some guard beast left on patrol. I made myself dash across the open pavement, counting on the flurry of snow my passage caused to hide me from any vids.

There were dozens of ships docked along the roadway, or rather shipway, for the only traffic using this pavement would be the docking tugs as they brought each ship from the landing area to place it on its reserved spot among the others. All appeared abandoned to the night's silence and cold, their crews most likely part of the Christmas revelry beyond the fields at my back. I hurried past them all. Dawn was approaching and I didn't expect Kearn to allow me much time to pick and choose.

Ah! I exclaimed to myself in relief. In the distance, a massive shape loomed up in the center of the shipway, motionless, tied to the ground by sleek drifts of snow: a tug, with what looked to be an intersystem freighter cradled in its ungainly arms. It was facing toward the landing field, first in line for lift tomorrow. *Perfect.*

I blinked ice crystals from my long lashes, attempting with limited results to clear the distortion prisming the view from my central ocular. *Oh, well. It was best for objects within claw reach anyway.* I closed the ocular, relying on the less precise but motion-sensitive outer ring of six.

Beside the tug and its cargo, last ship in line at the field rim, was the *Rigus.* I could never forget her silhouette. More to the point, the *Rigus* had more than enough surveillance equipment, as they'd amply and distressingly demonstrated to me.

Time for some serious sneaking, I decided. I bent my legs until my knees were higher than my spine and the entire length of my belly immediately numbed from contact with the cold pavement. *It was going to get worse.* I took a final look at my target, fixing its direction as best I could, then pushed my head under the snow.

Ersh, it was cold! The planet must be bleeding all of its heat into space tonight. I avoided the temptation to raise my body temperature; that release of energy could well trip the sensors on the *Rigus.* I longed briefly for the triple fur pelt of the Crougk form, if not its conspicuous size. I moved slowly, to prevent any patterning of the thin layer of snow now slipping over my back. The circulation in every third foot shut down involuntarily, preserving my core temperature while adding the resistance of each newly immobile limb to the difficulty of this passage, an unnecessary reminder that this form's survival physiology for extreme cold would eventually shut me down completely in a curl of winter hibernation if I let it.

Made it. My claws drummed like tiny castanets against the metal as I climbed over the lower brace leg of the tug. My Acepan noses, conveniently located in the front third of my feet and two even more sensitive spots near my posterior segment for physiological reasons no longer significant in an extinct species, detected volatile hydrocarbons and a tinge of musk: the tug's protectants against corrosion, I guessed, since it was hardly necessary to grease a starship.

In that I wasn't quite right. One of the hydrocarbon sources moved out of my way. *Ah, yes,* I realized, taking a moment to reprocess what I was seeing through my ring of, by some standards, currently indifferent oculars. *Rats.*

No time for snacks, though I had to admit the wee things smelled tasty. The ship within the tug's grip had a patchwork appearance this close, a shabbiness that made me hesitate, an Acepan-aversion to the less-than-secure temporarily overruling my personal sense of satisfaction at something far easier to break into than I'd expected. All I wanted at this moment was space-ready *(if her crew was willing to gamble, so was I)* and no questions *(given I made the entrance I hoped, that wouldn't be a problem).*

Under a strut, twist between cables, squeeze and barely make it between the clamp and a thoughtlessly-positioned atmospheric maneuvering fin—I did all I could to make my way up to the ship's side without revealing myself to the *Rigus,* so overwhelmingly close. There was a point at which I had to risk showing at least part of myself. I made that part small, and moved it as irregularly as Acepanly possible, judging that while a stealthily moving life-form might be noticed, a quick scurry, pause, and scurry again might not, being mistaken perhaps for a blur of snow caught in an errant breeze and tossed upward in a perverse fling at gravity.

Well, that's what I hoped.

Although the ship would be locked tight, I was reasonably confident of finding one or more of her vents exchanging air. The owner of a ship this decrepit should prefer to take advantage of a port where the atmosphere was free, and Rigel II's wintry air, I inhaled appreciatively, was of excellent quality. Of course, there was the outside chance that the crew weren't oxy-breathers, but I doubted it in a wreck willing to land on a world with rather basic facilities.

Still, the thought gave me pause, which entailed locking thirty-six pairs of legs around a docking clamp, the seventeen numb pairs dangling loose, while I twisted my neck to look for identification. None, unless the recent scarring of what could have been blaster damage along her underside was indicative of where this ship hadn't been lately—anywhere safe.

Better and better. A war zone wasn't in my plans, but this wasn't a warship. Instead, she was looking like a smuggler, or, to be more gracious to beings I hadn't met, an adventurer. Such would head to the Fringe rather than to Inner Systems. The Fringe and closer to home.

And Ersh. I trembled from more than the frigid night and carefully unlocked my grips, one pair at a time. I began climbing over the hull.

Whomp!

I found an air intake. *Or the intake had found me,* I thought, disgusted, my belly plates sucked flat against the grille. Pulling free involved a certain amount of discomfort.

The air intake was not an Esen-intake; even this scow would pass incoming air through biocontamination filters. *Uncomfortable at the least.*

The air vents, however, should be very accessible. There were supposedly regulations about what could and couldn't be vented, but by far older custom, if a ship was permitted to land, its captain expected the planet to be willing to share air. It had long been considered an individual planet's responsibility to maintain its ecosystem, not its visitors. Sensitive worlds—or rich ones—maintained biofilters and scans around their shipcities or ports. Others, such as Rigel II, hoped for the best, recorded arrivals and departures, and kept a cat or its equivalent on spaceport grounds for the odd runaway.

A rank smell of moldy fruit drew me to what I needed. The vents were paired here, running in two parallel slots about a meter in length and almost half that in width. The air rushing out was not only fragrant, but moist. A lumpy chain of ice had already formed, wrapping the edges of the vents in a thick coating that would likely cause some delays in the departure if the space-proof doors couldn't close properly. A suspicious amount of warping around the vents implied the usual method of clearing such deposits consisted of repeatedly slamming the doors against the frame.

I clambered up the side of the ship, positioning myself so that I hung head down over the top of the nearest vent.

The condensing water vapor hid me nicely as I prepared to cycle into something that could fight its way in past the howl of air. I tried to ignore the condensation coating my oculars as I considered the problem.

Ersh was fond of reminding me that a conservative approach was always best. If the current form could manage, use it. I experimented with my first six pairs of claws, flattening myself against the outer slope of the icy buildup and driving each chisellike claw tip deep into the frozen mass for purchase. As I moved into the path of the air, it slid over my smooth back, offering relatively little resistance to my next steps. A false security since if I lost most of my grips even for an instant, I'd be blown off the side of the ship and likely land flat against the *Rigus.* I found the ability to drive my claws in a bit deeper than I'd thought possible.

What a stink. Rigel II would not appreciate this particular donation to its environment. The timing of the venting, in the darkest hours of the one night everyone was away from their post, seemed a bit too convenient. However, I did appreciate the warmth, feeling life restart in the limbs gone cold-dormant. The wind whistled out any chance of detecting the warning sounds of machinery and it was black as the heart of a tax collector inside the vent itself. I counted my successes in centimeters, content to make progress without risking more than a claw tip if I encountered the blades of a turbine or whatever archaic device they were using.

After a few seconds, which oddly passed more like hours, I felt my rearmost claw tips leave the ice rim and meet the metal of the interior of the vent. Relieved to be safe at last from the *Rigus'* vids, I paused, pressed almost flat against the side of the vent both by inclination and the force of the air, the latter a pressure that contrarily sought to lift me away when I incautiously curled any portion of my long spine outward. I settled myself more firmly to wait.

No telling how much deeper the vent extended. The outer walls of the ship would be honeycombed with conduits for biohazardous materials such as fuel and sewage, the inner wall strengthened to hold against vacuum and provide a last hope for the crew in case of a breach. Some species designed their ships so that each interior compartment was actually a separate entity, capable of disassociation once free of atmosphere and the need for a sleek outer hull. But this felt and certainly smelled Human. And Human designs were reasonably straightforward.

My chance would come when the crew shut down the exhaust before launch. I pressed harder against the cold metal, trying to ignore the shrieking of the air as it tore past me, and hoped it wouldn't be long. Much of this and I'd have nightmares for sure.

Have no nightmares of me, friend Ragem, I whispered to myself sadly. An unlikely wish, I thought, remembering the last sight I'd had of his face.

15: Freighter Morning

I'D dozed for a while until startled awake again. The wall under my claws suddenly began to vibrate out of synch with the throbbing of the exhaust motors. I fought panic, Acepans tending to a paranoid flight response to alarm, and tried to figure out what was happening.

The tug was heading for the field at last, I decided almost at once, the abrupt lurching from side to side being another clue. It must be morning, a fact I couldn't verify with my head and all its oculars rammed as far as possible down into the vent. The air rushing over me was as clean as Rigel II's own, which by now it was. I waited for the exhaust motor to stop, readying myself to scurry forward as soon as it did.

That wasn't what happened. Later, when I had time to think, I realized the true sequence of events and knew the ship hadn't really grown teeth, clamped down on the rear five segments of my body, and then sucked the rest of me forward in a pain-filled blur of heat and explosion. But that was later.

Whirrrr, thud. *Pain!* Cycling was involuntary and rapid enough to scorch the inside of the vent. Propelled by my own release of energy, my web-form shot deeper into the vent, my consciousness literally torn as I *knew* I was leaving part of myself behind, imprisoned in the vent doors, part of me too small for independent life, part of me already dying. There was nothing I could do to save it.

The rest of me was in trouble enough. I hit the fans an instant before they shut down, my velocity sufficient (I decided when once again capable of coherent thought) to destroy most of the vanes, permitting me to pass more-or-less intact. *Less,* I cried to myself.

Thwump!

If there was a cosmic figure playing with the lives and fates of sentient beings, it must have chosen to intervene—or else had finished toying with my life and gone on to torment someone else. I found myself floating in a tank of creteng: nice, mature, full-grown creteng. Meal-size creteng. It was the work of an instant to snatch the few dozen finny things I needed to rebuild my essential mass.

Then I let myself sink to the bottom and spread to fill the available area, hoping the crew would assume the water displaced on the deck was due to rough handling by the tug, and the reason the remaining creteng were hysterically clustered at the surface was simply their usual mindless dithering.

I was left alone, as I'd expected, granted much-needed time and solitude to heal myself by the simple practicalities of prepping a ship for lift. Duties multiplied when a ship left port, and the Christmas celebration would undoubtedly impair the efficiency of the crew. This assumed the crew was efficient. Their cavalier treatment of the living beings in their hold certainly left that open to debate. The cretengs decided that the chance of my converting more of them to web-mass was preferable to being sloshed out on to the deck and several grew quite daring in their approach to the bottom of the tank. I tried not to eat too many; they had saved me, after all.

Remembered pain coursed through my entire being, jolting me at unexpected moments, pain mixed with loss no new mass could mend. I felt whole, yet there had been no chance to sort my mass during the split seconds of the accident, no way to ensure the totality of my memories—of me—was saved. It was the nature of my kind that I would never be able to tell. Memory lost was lost. If there had been time before lift, and I was brave enough, perhaps I could have climbed back up the vent and retrieved what was imprisoned between the door edge and its seals.

I quivered, sending a coordinated flash through the school of creteng who once again decided the surface was safer. *What was, was.* Another of Ersh's favorite sayings. One which now meant something.

I hadn't experienced lift from a planet in web-form before. The freighter's internal gravity field alerted me to the moment, kicking in to thrill through my body like a descant soprano aria over the deep pulsing resonance of Rigel II's own heart. The destruction and reformation of atoms within the ship's engines were exquisite in their release and capture of energy. If I had known how to sing along, I would have tried.

The rapture faded as the ship passed effortlessly through the final lines of attraction. Rigel II gave us to space with a reluctance part of me shared. I was leaving something irreplaceable behind.

I shunted all thoughts of Ragem to the deepest core of my memory. There would surely be someone back to check on the tanks and other cargo soon. I'd done enough to the laws of the Web; time to behave.

First I had to choose a form that could hide successfully until the next planetfall, not having the slightest desire to further interact with any Humans for a while. The Lanivarian, comforting as my birth form, was out of the question. I'd had enough of its reaction to spaceflight—let alone the chance of being recognized as Kearn's lost guest.

I pulled myself together and flowed out of the tank. If there was a collective sigh of relief from the creteng, I ignored it. The hold was dark, decidedly damp, and starting to smell of moldy fruit again, in spite of the recent air exchange. I investigated that odor, determined to match it to something I remembered.

Wait! I focused on a trace of something complex, atoms clenched in a protein's erratic curls, barely detectable under the fruit's reek, but instantly identifiable. Without a second thought, I reached back into the tank, converted more creteng mass to mine, and cycled.

As a Ganthor, the darkness was even worse, yet at the same time less relevant. My fine sense of smell located what I needed to know. *I wasn't alone.* With a subdued squeal of delight, I rushed past the crates of ripe cotylmelons—a Ganthorian delicacy—and pressed my snout against the force-field barrier marking the back third of the hold. To a Human, and likely to their sensors, this barrier looked like a wall. To my more sensible nose, it was a fake and my kind were clustered behind it.

They weren't prisoners. The body odors spoke to me of

health and contentment, if tinged with a scent of boredom. *Why were they here?* I wondered. *And why hidden?*

I backed up and ducked behind a crate, hoping they hadn't scented me in return, trying not to reveal my presence. It was so tempting to stay close. Ganthor had an incredibly strong herd instinct, which explained the many other-species' jokes relying on the predicament of Ganthor separated in a crowd of aliens. In this form, I knew its power, felt the need to go to the others of my kind like a hunger. *Not my kind,* I insisted to myself, aware I was responding to the craving for the group with a need that had as much to do with my personal anguish as any instinct, however perfectly appropriate to the Ganthor themselves.

My care was wise. Lights came up in the hold, making me blink my tiny eyes at the sudden glare; the small door inset in the bulkhead opposite to the creteng tank began to open. I peered carefully around the edge of the crate, able to see through the gap between it and the one next to it. They hadn't packed this hold particularly well, which was fine by me.

A head topped with a mass of curly brown hair only partially contained by a net poked through the doorway, the body staying outside as if the person doubted the wisdom of stepping within. It was a female Human, her expression one of complete disgust as she took in the state of the hold, from the water puddled at her feet to the twisted wreckage of the fans overhead.

"Frat!" Her head disappeared but her voice carried quite well through the still-open door. "Lars! Smithers! You idiots get down here now and clean this up!"

I'd expected as much. Even the most slovenly of spacers took proper care of loose objects before going translight. The tendency of unattached objects to keep their momentum and direction if anything went wrong with the ship's drive was not to be trifled with, not if you wanted to maintain the integrity of the hull and continue to breathe. Judging from the conditions in this freighter, her captain didn't worry overmuch about tidiness until hitting space. On the other hoof, the odds on a drive failure in this scow were probably pretty good.

Ganthor weren't foolhardy beings, but they weren't easily worried about the future either: an approach to life I found soothing at the moment. Instincts, drives, and all manner of hardwired behavior were biological constraints I'd been taught to identify and deal with as carefully as I had to consider the pros and cons of a leg joint with only one direction of movement. Other beings had the luxury of disregarding their inner nature, or at least taking it for granted. I did not. The courage I was feeling as I began looking for a secure hiding place was as alien to my true self as the panic of the Acepan had been.

Hiding had been my plan all along, and I'd had a lot of practice under Ansky's tutelage. I moved cautiously among the crates, searching for the ideal spot. My feet and hands were hoofed, allowing travel on all fours as I'd employed for my disguise on Kraos. However, the hooves of my hands were capable of spreading into two very useful digits, opposed by a third, longer one extending from the back of the wrist. The inner surface of each digit was spongelike and sensitive, in contrast to the bony shell that formed the outer shape of the hoof. A charming and remarkably strong hand. Excellent for percussion instruments, I recalled, tapping experimentally on a nearby crate before I stopped myself.

What was I thinking! I shook myself, literally, feeling my heavy hide and its rolls of fat ripple from shoulder to hip. I turned my attention back to weighing the comfort of secreting myself in the crate of delicious cotylmelons against the risk of discovery should that food be needed shortly. The cotylmelons were only the most noticeable of the Ganthor-specific foods I could see all around me.

The Ganthor themselves were a serious distraction. If I kept this sturdy, comforting form, it would mean a constant effort to resist the urge to hide as close to the others as possible, to seek the security of the herd. My present distance of a few meters from the false wall was far enough from the other Ganthor in the hold to trouble me when I let it.

I could join them, and hide in plain sight. Most Humans couldn't distinguish one Ganthor from another. I suspected Ragem might be able to do so, but then he seemed an unusually perceptive being. There was, of course, the opinion of the Ganthor to consider. Depending on the stability of the hierarchy among these Ganthor, I might be accepted without question. Or I might be trampled to death. One was never sure. Theirs was an intelligent, technologically advanced society, but those who dealt with Ganthor in a herd knew to exercise care, including other Ganthor.

No, I decided. *Hiding by myself was the right choice.* During this internal debate, I'd continued searching the vast hold for a place to avoid the coming cleanup crew. Still no sign of them; maybe the woman had had to wake them up from some post-spurl recovery. Couldn't be long before the ship went translight, not if they intended to get anywhere soon.

The walls of the hold were ringed with two layers of deep shelving, the lowermost set at about twice the height of a Human from the deck. Under most circumstances, cargo would be stowed on these shelves by a servo lift. I didn't see one. It could have been in another hold, but I had a feeling this ship was more likely to rely on chains and pulleys. Another advantage to the disorganization in here: a convenient pile of plas bags had been casually dumped in a corner beneath the shelves, forming an easy way up to the first level.

I collected an armful of cotylmelons, shoving an especially ripe one in my mouth, and climbed the pile. Every couple of steps, one or the other of my feet sank in a bit deeper, making a cracking sound as it did. I hoped whatever was in the bags wouldn't rot too quickly.

This crew apparently preferred to fill up the hold deck space before using the shelves; they were far from fully loaded. I checked to see that there were nets attached to the wall that could—and should—be pulled over the containers. They would help hold me in place, too, should there be any problems.

Juice dribbled over my chin, collected on my fine sprout of bristles, then trickled down my round belly to collect in the first of several creases. I'd do a bit of grooming later. Right now I cheerfully made my way behind a series of crates, the gap between them and the wall a far better hiding place than I'd hoped.

"Told you we needed a lid, but no, Mr. Fish Expert, you knew better." The voice, Human male and with an underlying whine to it, carried perfectly. There was a clatter and bang I assumed meant the crewmen had come armed for the struggle with the vast puddle on the deck.

A second voice, another Human male, deeper-pitched. "Help me put them back, Lars," this being urged impatiently. "They're worth a credit apiece to that fish breeder. . . ."

Since by now the sounds of frantic flippers and flopping bodies had stopped, the doomed creteng reduced by this point to futile gasping at best, I doubted he was going to succeed in saving even one credit's worth. Still, the sounds of the two men cursing and splashing about made me wish I had a way to safely peek out at them.

The spongy toes of my Ganthor feet allowed for quite silent movement, as if I needed this ability when the two below were continually shouting at one another. I squeezed behind a crate larger than the rest, *no room to curl up back here,* and quickly walked past a gap in the cargo to duck behind the next group of crates.

All at once I staggered, as if the corrugated surface of the shelf behind my hooves had suddenly heaved. *We couldn't be going translight,* I thought in desperate confusion, half convinced the decrepit ship was going to be my doom after all. Momentum took me forward two quick steps, until I was able to grasp a handful of greasy net and stop myself.

The smell told me what I had done—that and the sudden surge of happiness in my Ganthor heart. I'd burst through the force field. I was standing right above the hidden Ganthor.

And from the tang of changing scents filling the air, they knew it, too.

Out There

THE Tly blockade around Inhaven's agricultural colonies, denounced by both Inhaven and Garson's World as provoking the current state of war with their former ally, caused little more than speculation in the commodities' market and inconvenience to shipping. The Tly may have felt the colonies an unconscionable encroachment on their territory, but patriotism hadn't deterred Tly traders from purchasing fresh produce, especially fine Inhaven hops, at prices the colonists considered quite reasonable. In all, the blockade was civilized; a means to occupy those captains with a military bent without expensive consequences.

Which is why the inexplicable silencing of the five ships guarding the approach to Ag-colony 162, known to its inhabitants as Vineland, sent shock waves through the blockade keepers. Frantic messages went translight: demands for instructions, reinforcements, orders.

The order came to shoot first, and check identities second. A warning went to all inbound freighters and trade ships, comtechs sounding as incredulous as those receiving the news. The colonies prepared for a true blockade and began hiding their treasures. The crews sat and waited.

Death approached its next target with less care than ever before, no longer bothering to use the cover of asteroids or planets in its approach. The gunner on the Tly warship picked up the anomaly on her scans and fired without hesitation.

Pain!

Death veered away, in its flight expending energy with an abandon that suggested an unknown power source to the astonished gunner . . .

But was really the surety of finding another, less wary, supply.

16: Freighter Afternoon and Night

GANTHOR, though incapable of vocal communication without surgical implants—a process endured stoically by their translators, diplomats, and the occasional crime lord—were quite adept at expressing themselves in other ways.

The preferred method between Ganthor encountering one another for the first time involved physical contact. Usually quite firm contact. Contact which tended to leave bruises. Since I had no intention of jumping down from the shelf, and they had no means of climbing up, that level of establishing mutual identity and status was on hold.

The second method was involuntary chemical signaling. Without going into physiological details, I could smell the Ganthor below working their way from an emotional state of alarm, to threat, to puzzlement, and, most recently, concern. My signals were probably stuck on alarm, with an underlying scent of herd-need, making my head swim with the contrary nature of it.

The method closest to what a Human would consider communicating ideas and abstracts was clickspeak. The flexibility and hard outer surface of Ganthor fingers made them perfect instruments for this percussive language. Many other species had adopted clickspeak for use as a convenient nonvocal signal, but few could master its intricacies.

Not that we were into the finer points of grammar at the moment, I thought. Stamping one's hooves was used to add an element of shouting and outrage. So far we'd avoided that. Barely.

Not herd the lead Ganthor below clicked again, an underscent of threat still present and, from its potency, probably hers. *Spy*!!* That was definitely a stamp.

Not herd!! *Not herd* echoed the rest.

Need herd I clicked back, distressed by their rejection and surely revealing it by my aroma. *Pursued*

Danger to the herd!!*!!*

Poor choice of words, I decided, wincing at the racket from below. Alarm scent threatened to make me panic. Certainly the Humans on the other side of the barrier could hear all this. That they could, and weren't reacting, meant they knew the Ganthor were here and they expected the Ganthor to deal with their own problems. *Interesting.*

I came out of hiding, moving to the edge of the shelf to look down at the herd. *No wonder I'd set them off,* I said to myself. *Mercenaries tended to overreact at the best of times.*

Sixteen adult Ganthor looked back up at me, snouts twitching, most with left hand on a weapon of some sort. Each right hand was curled upward just before their chests, frozen in midclick, the customary position for speech when a quick, more physical response might be needed. I was happy to be out of reach. I was less happy about their armament. Ganthor weren't known for their thorough thinking; one blast from even the lightest of the arms they carried would put a significant hole in this ship. I hoped they kept that in mind as a particularly unpleasant side effect of any attempt to end whatever threat they felt I posed.

The largest being below, the Matriarch and so commander of this herd, put down her blaster rifle and beckoned me to come down. *Join us* she clicked. *Identify danger to the herd* Her snout, once handsome and now marred by numerous scars, flared and dripped mucus as she sought clues from my scent. *Now**!!* she clicked and stamped.

Danger to me I clicked back, not believing any quick change of heart from a group obviously used to protecting itself. *Not to the herd*

*Come*Safety in the herd*

The offer couldn't be a lie, not with the scent shift to a more benign cluster of emotions: curiosity, vigilance, welcome. If it hadn't been for the height of the shelf and the Ganthor's definite lack of flight capability, I might have jumped down to be among them, to belong.

Instead, I concentrated on caution, hoping that would work its way through the whirl of fading scents to those madly twitching snouts. *Protect the herd* I clicked suggestively. *Hide me up here*

The concept of leaving one apart raised tension levels. A couple of lower-status males nudged each other emphatically enough to send a third careening away. The Matriarch ignored them. *Wise beyond your years* she clicked, the words intoned with approval. *Protect the herd*!!*

With that, the Ganthor lost interest in the debate, moving off to whatever business had occupied them before my intrusion, revealing the stress I'd caused in the way they deliberately sought to shove past certain key individuals, reaffirming the status within the herd I'd threatened to alter with my arrival. The unlucky trio who looked to be lowest in stature received the brunt of this behavior, but acquiesced without apparent concern. There was comfort in belonging, even to those beneath.

While the Ganthor part of my psyche understood and envied, I found nothing to admire in this herd. I sat down on my haunches to watch them. The Matriarch and two who must be her Seconds bent their heads over a series of diagrams on a crate-turned-table, clicking almost soundlessly among themselves on the tabletop. The rest returned to a variety of tasks, some dismantling what appeared to be artillery pieces and putting these in packs, others making an inventory of energy cubes and other supplies.

Mercenaries. The Web understood warfare as part of the culture—and in a few cases the biology—of a multitude of otherwise intelligent species. Understanding didn't mean approval. Our purpose, the core of our existence, was to preserve the accomplishments of intelligence. War so often achieved the opposite.

Though Ganthor made excellent foot soldiers, I acknowledged to myself. The herd instinct worked in their favor on the battlefield, inciting them to heroics most beings took drugs to emulate. Individual herds, like this one, operated under contract to other species—the Ganthor themselves resolved their conflicts on a more personal level. I wondered who held the contract for this group.

Uneasily, I recalled the scarring on the outside of the freighter. *Where was this ship going?*

More to the point: *where was it taking me?*

* * *

Sometime later, when the dimming of lights beyond those used by the Ganthor indicated the cleanup crew was finished in the hold at least for now, I collected my wits and clicked for the Matriarch's attention. She pushed a shoulder into that of her nearest Second and that worthy looked up at me, a good indication the herd had assigned me some place above least, though I was now too far beneath their leader for her casual notice.

Speak he clicked.

It was an older male, scarred as were most of them, something in his eyes eloquent of conflicts held under distant suns for causes likely even more foreign. I felt both respect and revulsion, emotions he disregarded with a wrinkling of his snout.

Where goes this ship I clicked, adding a tactful "to a superior" flourish at the end.

To battle the aroma rising from all of them echoing satisfaction. I saw their preparations in a new light. The freighter's departure from Rigel II must mark the final leg of this journey for them. *Worse news for me.*

Where I repeated.

Tly System

The Fringe! And a system near enough to the area of space I wanted to sound almost like home. I'd done better than I'd hoped getting on this ship, even if it had cost me dearly. I shivered at the memory, the broadcast of my emotion diffusing downward and causing a rise in anxiety in the Ganthor, distracting several from their tasks.

Calm!!* That emphatic stamp from the Matriarch, who glared up at me. *Hide here*Wait here*Herd will return*

I'd had no intention of participating in their battle anyway, but saw no value in trying to explain that to her. So I could stay hidden on the freighter while they disembarked? Odds were good that would be a quick process, done in the dark and somewhere much less legal than a spaceport. I clicked a gracious acceptance and went back to my spot on the shelf floor to rest, nibbling on a cotylmelon to sooth my nerves. Now all I had to do was think of a way to convince this ship to make a small detour.

An afternoon's nap put me no nearer to a solution than before. I certainly didn't plan to wait here until the

Ganthor finished their "battle" and hopefully survived it. For one thing, I thought the Matriarch hopelessly naïve if she expected the captain of this scow would stay insystem, let alone on the ground, to wait with a potential conflict brewing to endanger his or her ship. Far more likely the ship would agree to return at a specified time. And might even do so, if the price was guaranteed.

Where would it go in the meantime? I felt a wave of loneliness so intense I knew it would spread below. To calm myself, I licked the sticky cotylmelon juice from my skin, something a prehensile tongue was admirably suited to accomplish.

Translight travel still consumed subjective time. I spent the next few days exploring the hold, though it grew more and more disconcerting to leave the proximity of the Ganthor. They would click anxiously whenever I left, something I always announced in advance to prevent them taking alarm if my scent faded without explanation. Not compassion or caring as Ragem would have expressed it; I was warmed by their concern nonetheless.

Lars and Smithers had expended most of their cleaning efforts around the crew entrance to the hold, probably correct in assuming no one would bother coming farther in to check on their work. The smell of ripe cotymelon was something few but the Ganthor and several small insects could relish.

However, the captain of the freighter—*Serendipity's Luck,* Omacron registry (if one were to trust any plas-work attached to this ship)—had braved the odor daily since our departure from the Rigellian System. Her name was Serean Croix, something I thought also subject to change, and she came for reassurance from her passengers: reassurance the Ganthor seemed uninterested in providing.

Croix's last visit had been typical. One of the Matriarch's Seconds had an implant and could produce comprehensible, if heavily accented, comspeak. He translated at a snail's pace, something I could tell from her expression the Human took as an insult. I couldn't very well explain the poor Ganthor vainly sought clues from her scent as to the emotional content of her words. What I could smell of her indicated a fixation with attar of roses and a poor diet. Her own accent was tricky to place; the more I heard it, the more it labeled Croix as someone who'd been well-educated and raised but deliberately let that part of her life go.

"Would thee ask thy Commander if there's been any word from the contact ship?"

The Matriarch's response, carrying an undertone of impatience, was negative. Her clicks translated roughly as: "Call them yourself."

Croix glanced around the hold area, assessing the unloaded crates and well-loaded packs. "The *'Dip* doesn't have a two-way translight com. Surely thee do." The Ganthor translator waited, not taking the statement as a question to pass along. The captain realized her mistake and added: "Would thee ask thy Commander if thee can call the ship? Remind thy Commander that our contract is for transport to this meeting point, not any closer to the Tly blockade."

The Ganthor started clicking, his scent conveying a distinct pride in his ability to so serve the herd. The Human broke in, saying urgently, "I won't wait either. Tell thy Commander that."

Captain Croix turned on her heel and left without waiting for a reply, a rudeness that ignited bouts of stamping and general mayhem in the herd, though precautions weren't neglected. The force field was reinstated and the now-mortified Second completed the translation. *Not bad,* I thought to myself. He conveyed Croix's ultimatum very clearly.

The Matriarch was also impressed. She quickly ordered the message sent, a decision that agreed with my own assessment of both Croix's willingness to strand them somewhere unpleasant and the futility of using this scow to try and pass a military blockade. It also spoke volumes about the funding for the mercenary group. Translight equipment was not cheap.

I settled back into my corner, working on keeping my emotions under my own control; I'd no need to be drawn into the herd's fervor for the battle ahead. Judging from their passion, and state of readiness, the contact ship would take them straight into action. *It would be without me,* I reminded myself firmly.

17: Warship Night; Planet Morning

THE contact ship never arrived, and the *Serendipity's Luck* ran out halfway through shipnight, announced by the ringing shudder of her hull plates, transmuted instantly into a shelf-quake that shook my shelter into chaos. *Had we been rammed?* I used my muscular shoulders to pry myself free of the mass of crates and snapped net, grateful for the Ganthor-instincts insisting I think of the herd's safety before contemplating the vacuum so appallingly near.

Gather!!*Danger to the herd*!!*Gather*!!* came the order from below as the Matriarch and her Seconds reacted to the disaster. The command and need were so strong, I almost threw myself off the shelf. I grabbed the edge instead, looking down at the mass of packs, weapons, and crates now spilled across the deck like so many playthings. But it wasn't play. Briefly, the Ganthor gathered around a split-open container of what looked to be cast metal globes, clicking mournfully as they gave up trying to free the two bodies pinned beneath. *Mines,* I realized, once again torn between the magnetism of the herd and my feelings about mercenaries.

*!!*Down*!!* stamped the Matriarch, her tiny eyes fixed on me. Her scent was overpowering, redolent of concern, determination, and her right to rule. Her Seconds clicked furiously, ordering four other troops to clasp hands, forming a living net. *!!*Down*!!* she repeated.

Jump? I didn't like this one bit. The ship shuddered again, and this time the hull breach klaxon began to shrill. If I didn't jump, they wouldn't leave. I knew it. Even if I cycled into some other form and left, they'd keep waiting for the return of their mysterious comrade. It was their strength and their weakness.

Moving as quickly as possible, I pulled the torn net from the toppled crates and tested its remaining hold on the wall with a hard tug. *Good enough.* I tossed the net over the shelf edge, gripped it tightly in both hands, and swung myself over. The net stretched alarmingly then held firm. I started breathing again and, finding it easier if I kept my hooves away from the net, climbed down as far as possible using only the strength in my arms.

Hands reached up and seized my legs, pulling me down into a mass of warm concern. All of them, including the Matriarch, tried to touch me at once, to make certain I was safe. I closed my eyes for a moment in bliss and inhaled their welcome.

The ship made a sound I'd never heard from metal and plas before. One of the Ganthor clicked *Grapples*!!*

The herd broke away from me to lunge for their weapons. I found myself looking up at the Matriarch; she alone hadn't moved. *Safety* she clicked, her scent adding the overtone that meant I belonged in the herd core, surrounded by those older and stronger—and in this case, armed and capable of herd defense. Her snout flared, mucus dripping as she assessed both my response and the emotional state of her herd.

The lights faltered, going to emergency backup systems, cut in brilliance by half. The force field isolating this section from the rest of the hold dropped at the same time. The door burst open and fourteen weapons hummed like angry insects ready to protect a hive.

I couldn't see past the Ganthor encircling me like a living wall, but since they didn't fire I assumed the intruder belonged to the *'Dip.* In confirmation, a hoarse Human voice rang out. "We're being boarded by the Tly warship *Avenger.* Captain wants you to put down your weapons. The Tly promise immunity to noncombatants. Do you understand me? Put down your weapons!"

The Matriarch clicked and stamped immediately, her Second translating almost simultaneously. *I accept terms for this herd. We disarm*!!*

I wasn't certain if this meant these Ganthor were under contract to the Tly and so had nothing to fear, or if they considered this situation to negate their contract with the Tly's enemies and were confident the Tly would agree—not something I'd assume with Humans. However, judging by the continuing wail of the klaxon and the now-flickering emergency lighting, *Serendipity's Luck* didn't seem worth fighting for anyway. I let out a scent of relief that I didn't care if the other Ganthor shared.

The Matriarch had been right in her assessment. The *Avenger*'s captain was quite willing to confiscate the weapons and other military hardware in the *'Dip's* hold in exchange for safe passage for the Ganthor, myself, and the *'Dip's* crew to the nearest neutral system, Ultari. No one commented on Ultari's myriad worlds and lax laws making its central spaceport, located on Ultari XIV, a logical place for the *Avenger* to sell off the contents of the *'Dip*'s hold without question, turning the flavor of the deed closer to polite piracy than protecting a blockade. But then, Ganthor vastly preferred a barter system, and the *'Dip*'s crew knew not to question the mellow good nature of a captain who could as easily have them charged and executed for transporting mercenaries. Or left them on their cracked-open ship—which would have been just as certain a death.

I wasn't inclined to complain either. Once I knew we'd be dropped on Ultari XIV, the greater part of my problems were solved. I'd be able to access Ersh's account and buy passage direct to Picco's Moon without any difficulty.

Except the one surrounding me. The herd was still anxious, the Ganthor rightly suspicious of any communication with beings who couldn't clarify their meanings by scent. Anxious Ganthor meant stubborn, herd-preoccupied Ganthor.

Just my luck, I thought, when the *Avenger*'s port opened at last, allowing us to exit onto Ultari XIV—all of us: myself jostled into the core position almost involuntarily by the others. I had a great view of Ultari's beige-and-russet morning sky and that was about it.

Fortunately, I had been able to convince the Matriarch I'd been a victim of *herd theft!!* that is, ceremonial kidnapping. It was commonplace among Ganthor to coax or outright steal promising offspring from other herds to join their own. The system was an admirable solution to inbreeding and it was considered an honor to be stolen by a herd of accomplishment. If one was stolen by a lesser herd, one could protest by trying to leave that herd and journey back to one's own—a task so difficult for the average Ganthor as to be almost legendary. I fabricated a tale of suffering and effort so convoluted it convinced them all, my conscience assuaged by the knowledge my entire story was based on one of their own folktales.

As result, this herd was willing to help me return to my home, though there was continuing gentle effort to coax me to change my mind and stay with them. I admitted to temptation, but held firm.

At last. I settled my long spine deeper into the passenger seat—first class, having deserved it by this point—and allowed myself to believe the worst was over. The Ganthor had bid their farewells to me at the spaceport, intent on seeking another merc contract. I'd made the moment of separation quick and in a crowd, so the scents of other beings would immediately disguise my own. Then I ducked into the humanoid section of the restrooms by the gate, cycled in privacy, donned the clothing I'd bought earlier, and stepped out, Lanivarian and independent once more.

At last, I repeated to myself, carefully chewing on the spacesickness lozenges the attendant brought, and holding the bag that came with them nearby. I didn't care if I did get sick. It was a short hop now to Picco's Moon. A short hop with no blockades or suspicious Humans in the way.

My stomach spasmed ominously, but it wasn't the flight.

I'd just remembered it was a short hop until I saw Ersh. And had to explain, somehow, why I was no longer on Kraos performing the duties of my very first mission, but was instead fleeing the attention of the Commonwealth government.

Perhaps I should have taken the longer way home.

Out There

DEATH had passed other dead ships lately. The conflict was wasting life, life Death could have put to better use. Still, it paused at this one, *tasting.* Once there had been a tiny bit of life left, huddled in a life pod, waiting for rescue. The experience had been—*rewarding.*

Hesitation. Some dead ships had traps set; some living ones could cause pain. Death had learned vulnerability and approached this latest quarry with the utmost care.

No energy traces. No traps. No life. Hungry, Death slowed and prepared to follow more promising prey.

Wait!

An irresistible *something.* Death flung itself on the side of the drifting hulk, tearing at the metal, ripping away until it found what it sought.

Blue flesh glistened along the rim of what had been a door.

When Death had consumed all it could find, there was only one desire left.

More!

18: Moon Night

I SHUDDERED myself free of memory. *What was done, was done.* I'd exposed my kind to the dangerous attention of humanity and its allies. And, to my mind far worse, I'd managed to terrify the one Human who could have spoken for us. All that remained was to see if Ersh could come up with a punishment equal to the crime. I doubted it.

The memories I'd eaten and assimilated were quickly becoming mine. Skalet had added another dialect to the language of her favorite avian form. *As if any species needed forty-three hundred and seventeen ways to express itself,* I thought with a mental snort. Lesy-memory contained the pattern for Security Officer Sas' species, the Modoren. A bit late for that to be useful. Ansky had spent the last year composing rather shocking love poetry to a trio of Urgians she'd met. Mixs had mostly gossip and little more. So my accomplishment of the Kraosian form was not shabby at all.

I cycled into the Modoren form. My vision was nicely enhanced, extending well into the ultraviolet. Ersh needed to wash her tablecloth. Unfortunately this form's sense of smell was dead compared to my nose as a Lanivarian. Well, it explained how Sas tolerated Kearn's choice of cologne.

"You look ridiculous," Skalet burst out laughing. "Better wait for that one, 'tween."

I walked over to the mirror and hissed at my reflection. The translation of relative species' age was not in my favor. I was maturing unusually quickly for my kind, but never quickly enough to suit Ersh or myself. Lesy-memory in mine labeled me perfectly. *I was an overgrown kitten.*

"But it works nicely for me," Ersh said from behind. She cycled, her change so rapid that I could barely catch the moment. As a Modoren, Ersh was in her prime: powerful, sleek, with a distinguished peppering of gray on her facial fur. She batted at me playfully. Though we were close to the same size, the blow knocked me off my feet.

I cycled back to the Lanivarian, and found to my dismay that I was furious. It was an effort to get the growl out of my voice. "Why did you do that?"

Ersh cycled, too. It was the ancient Human who cocked her wizened face at me. Skalet and Lesy snatched up their Kraosian clothing and retreated from the room without a word. I stood my ground, having nowhere else to go.

"I said I was proud of what you salvaged from your posting. That has nothing to do with what you did afterward—with the Humans." She took up her cane. "And if you're ready, it's time we discussed the consequences of that."

I nodded reluctantly.

"Come," she said, shuffling to the door that led to her private chamber. I sent off a quick prayer to the Snaggle-Toothed God of my present form and followed.

The chamber had one chair, Ersh's. It had one light, controlled by Ersh's hand. And it had one exit, with Ersh's permission. Duras plants lined the walls, growing under lights in precise measured ranks. Ersh didn't believe in scrounging for mass.

I knew this room, having spent a lot of time in here during my formative years. It was Ersh herself who seemed new and strange, her unfamiliar Human shape out of place. I couldn't read her face at all.

Ersh-memory floated up as I waited. As usual, it was full of gaps and edits. It was one of the reasons Ersh was still the center of the Web—her talent at not-sharing. She'd left in her reaction when I'd arrived unexpectedly on her doorstep. I tried not to wince.

"You've made us famous," she said after a soul-destroying pause that Kearn would have died to achieve.

There wasn't much to say to that, but I met her glittering eyes. "I didn't see any choice in the matter."

"Choice?" she sputtered, tiny flecks of saliva appearing at the corners of her thin lips. "I trained you. We all trained you. When did we say, in this or that situation, the choice will be up to you?" She waved her stump of an arm.

There was a time when I would have lain on the floor and showed my belly then and there. Even crippled, withered by this form, Ersh crowded the room with her age and wisdom. She dominated us all by her position in the Web. Her memories were the oldest we shared; she had been the First.

But I'd been on my own. In a way, I'd formed my own Web, a fragile little web of friendship, even if it had been cut. I spoke quickly, before my brand new courage failed.

"Tell me, Oldest. What would you have done differently? Should I have let Ragem die? Should I have let his crewmates perish instead? To keep our moldy secrets, should I have forgotten the Rules of the Web, to find and preserve *intelligence*?"

Ersh sucked in her cheeks. For a moment I was startled, then realized it was a smile—she didn't have many teeth left. It wasn't a pleasant expression. "You quote rules to me, Youngest?" she said, tiger-soft. Then a spittle-coated roar: "I made up the damn Rules!"

"Don't you believe in them?"

"Don't you talk back to me!"

"Fine," I said, turned, and walked to the door. Inside I shook like jelly and wanted to cycle into something with a lot of body armor.

"Wait." The voice was suddenly the deeper one I was used to, and I stopped. I knew what she was now without looking, the form Ersh used most. "You shared deeply and well, Esen. We are each other's flesh. Let's honor that by not bickering, at least."

I went out to the other room, picked up a kitchen chair, and brought it back. Deliberately, I sat down and looked at Ersh.

The Tumblers were native to this moon, which gave Ersh both cover and company when the strands of the Web were stretched by distance. In Tumbler-form, she was more mineral than meat, looking like a tower of spun plas. Her deep, musical voice emanated from resonating crystals. *A dignified, capable body.* When I'd been very young, I used to sneak up and tap her quickly with a hammer of stone—she'd ring like a bell. Ersh had never been impressed by this habit.

"What do you want me to do, Ersh?" I asked quietly. "The past is done."

"True. A past with a foul, poisonous taste."

"It's not that bad," I protested. "A few Humans with a wild story—a hint of a mysterious life-form. This kind of contact was bound to happen sometime." *But why to me,* I thought with a significant amount of self-pity.

"Some have asked that I excise you, cut you forever from the Web."

Really bad news takes time to sink in, so I didn't bother dwelling on it. "They all shared with me," I countered, bitter. *Mixs and Skalet, no doubt.* At least those two, though I hoped no others.

Ersh chimed, a discordant sound. "They appreciated the necessity of knowing what you'd done."

"What I did was—" I hesitated. "I saw no other way, then or now. Ersh, the Humans don't know anything important about us—you shared my memory of it."

"Your sharing wasn't complete, Esen."

I worked at keeping my ears up. "What do you mean?"

"Did you think to fool me?"

This seemed like a dangerous question to answer so I kept quiet. Ersh made a wind-over-sand sound—a Tumbler sigh. "I know you well enough, Esen, to fill in some of what you didn't share. Ragem, Tomas. These names come with a taste of friendship. This tells me you've forged connections with these ephemerals. They will search for you; you are now of their Web."

I whined my disbelief, deep in my throat. *After Rigel II?* I remembered Ragem's horrified expression.

Ersh, of course, remembered it, too. She said sharply, "You terrified the being—what did you expect? You weren't exactly clear-headed yourself. Ragem's fear won't last. He's your friend." A stress on the last word, or did I imagine it? *Maybe it was only my conscience.*

"The Humans won't find me again," I said, talking as quickly as I could, afraid of what she was trying to tell me. "Their memories fade. They only live a handful of years at best." Ersh sat silent, considering me with a deadly attention. I slowed down. "They made records, Ersh, but of what? Their meds examined me, and found me Lanivarian. All they have is an image of something unusual. Who'll believe in me after a decade or two?"

"Unfortunately, we can't wait. Our problem is immediate. And needs a drastic solution."

How could a being whose life span was longer than most civilizations use the term immediate? I fought back my confusion and growing alarm, focusing on what was familiar. It was my fault—whatever it was. "Does this mean you are planning to excise me from the Web?" I asked numbly.

"Pointless," Ersh chimed a harmony, the key minor and ominous. She tilted forward slowly. I moved my chair out of her way as she gracefully tumbled past me to one wall of the room. "Close the door and lock it."

A lock? Against whom? I obeyed anyway, recognizing with dismay that I was becoming a participant in something unexpected again. Ersh was a far less comfortable partner than Ragem.

I didn't see how she did it, but a small rectangular space opened in the rock wall. A puff of mist slipped out and sank. A Tumbler's hands are quite dexterous, like a set of trowels with joints. Ersh reached one hand inside the opening, and carefully brought out a well-wrapped object about the size and shape of a pear, held in the tips of two fingers. I craned my neck and made out several more of the objects nestled within. Ersh resealed the hidden compartment before turning to me.

"Take this."

It was cold in my paws, cold and heavy. I stared at the wrappings, cataloging them as leather—very old leather.

I looked up at a gentle sound from Ersh. It was a bell tone, the one I used to get when I snuck up on her with my favorite hammer. "Some might call what you're holding a gift, Esen," Ersh said quite sadly. "You are at least wise enough to know better. Lock the door behind me. We will talk again when you are ready."

I did as she asked, without bothering to understand, then curled up in my chair facing Ersh's empty one. I held the thing—her "gift"—in front of me and waited for inspiration. After what Ersh said, I wanted nothing to do with it. *But how to get rid of the thing without causing more trouble?*

The warmth of my paws slowly thawed and softened the leather. I used one slim toe to tease open the top of the wrapping. It wouldn't do any harm to see what I was refusing.

A smooth, blue drop winked back at me, its flawless surface like some fabulous gem—or an eye. An irresistible hunger surged through me and I snapped up the morsel before I had time to think.

Ersh-taste exploded in my mouth, scalding like acid. I cycled desperately, hoping to save my Lanivarian form.

Web-form. Blind, deaf, and dumb, I huddled as Ersh-memory burned through me in a different kind of pain. She had been right. *This was no gift.*

I now knew what I had done. It wasn't the Humans Ersh feared.

The Web had mortal enemies. Enemies Ersh had fled by traveling across a galaxy. Enemies she had hidden from for thousands of years. We'd been safe.

Until I'd introduced myself to a Human and become famous in the process.

19: Moon Night and Day

MYSTERIOUS powerful beings, bent on searching out and destroying all strands of the Web, able to spot us in any form—

Maybe Ersh was senile.

However, believing that could mean worse things than monsters. If Ersh could end, I decided, squirming uncomfortably, then it followed that everything could end. Surely at my age I was entitled to depend on living forever, even if that included forever answering to Ersh.

So I had to believe in monsters, ready-to-pounce ones at that. *Damn.* I picked up more loose stones in my beak, absently swallowing a few smaller ones to comfort my empty gizzard. It was too dark to fly, but I felt better as something that could safely fall off Ersh's mountaintop.

I tossed back too big a stone and almost gagged on it. I flicked it out of my throat and away with a twist of my head, wishing forlornly that Ersh's "gift" was as easy to spit out. I resented having to keep it in my private memory, festering among my treasures.

A subdued thunk came from the shadows below me as the stone I threw hit another. The tiny impact dislodged a second rock from its bed, sending it rolling downhill, clattering, in its turn ousting others from their places.

I peered over the cliff edge and tried to see, but the darkness was complete, a treacherous velvet draped over the cracked landscape. It was easy enough to follow the progress of my little avalanche by its sound, a delightful rushing cascade that quickly grew to a formidable growl.

All at once, the sound included an orchestral accompaniment: multiple bell tones, one or two somewhat flat. *Oops.* I'd hit a Tumbler. *No,* I winced, *more than one.*

Great. Even fate was going out of its way to booby-trap

my life lately. *What were Tumblers doing down there at this time of night?* Tumblers considered traveling without Picco looming overhead to be unsafe.

They had a point, at least with me upslope. 'Course, if these Tumblers were waiting to see Ersh, the hillside might be the logical place to squat; it gave an easy view of departing guests—Tumblers tended to be on the shy side unless annoyed. I shuffled back hastily, in case my silhouette was visible against the starry sky.

I'd come up here to avoid the others. Ersh was supposed to have secrets—not me. Assimilating even one of her secrets twisted my position in the Web from youngest and last to youngest and second. The others would want a chunk out of me if they knew. I wasn't planning to tell them, but I had a creeping suspicion that it would somehow show on my face—whatever face I chose.

I balanced on my right foot as I stretched the tension out of my left foot and wing. Just like Ersh to give me a promotion I couldn't enjoy. *What else did she have in mind?* I was cold, suddenly, inside and out. I fluffed out my feathers to hold more body heat against my skin. *What if Ersh expected me to actually do something about her monsters?*

Time to think of anything else. My present eyes bulged from either side of my head, though aimed forward; the arrangement provided me with a horizon-spanning view of the night sky, dusted with stars as long as Picco was behind its moon. (Tumbler science held tight to the belief that the gas giant circled the moon—as a guest I didn't argue the point.) I firmly pushed Ersh from my thoughts and concentrated on a part of the universe that surely couldn't cause me trouble.

But the brighter stars overhead reminded me of sugar sparkles on a cookie. Ragem and Tomas were out there, their uncomplicated lives continuing without me. I clicked my beak in a sigh.

"May I?"

I almost fell off the cliff, catching myself at the brink with one frantic beat of my wings. Rocks slipped under my talons, dropping into the dark, clattering. I hoped the Tumblers were out of range.

Ersh settled beside me, avoiding my still-flailing wings as I attempted to put my feathers back in order, her body blurring from crystal to skyfolk. There was an irritated tinkling from below. I hummed a bit to cover the sound.

Her great talons gripped a handy boulder as she arranged her own wings into a shelter against the night air. Her head swiveled up. "Ahh. Nice stars tonight, Esen. You've always had a knack for the spectacular."

Actually, a literal translation of what she said in the language of the skyfolk was more like: "oppressive-dark-useless-flickers," and "insane-vision-talent-perverse" but I was reasonably familiar with the skyfolk's doleful expressions and knew what Ersh meant. *I hoped.*

"I never try to be spectacular," I said somewhat morosely, resisting an urge to retract my neck and pull my head down between my shoulder blades.

"It was a compliment, daughter."

In the skyfolk tongue, "daughter" came out as "ultimate-destiny-future-soul." *Ersh was after something.*

I changed my mind about being able to read her meaning through this form's convoluted language. A mistake could land me in serious trouble. I cycled, hoping Ersh wouldn't take offense, and clutched my now-furred knees to my chest for warmth. The mist from my excess mass condensed in fine drops on the night-chilled rocks. "Ansky is my mother," I reminded Ersh through the nervous chattering of my carnivore's teeth. I knew all about sex and babies. I'd snuck some mating pheromones last time I'd been on the Ycl homeworld. Made me dense and dizzy for a while, until Ansky found me and explained that it took a cooperative triad and would I please metabolize the pheromones out of my system.

"You're being overly technical. I am Ansky's parent and so yours, too." Ersh had also cycled, politely keeping form. She occasionally followed her own rules. "We need to talk, *daughter.*" Ersh was also frequently stubborn. I decided to concede her the point.

I moved my tongue carefully around words with more hiss than click to them. It took practice not to spit. "What do you want, Ersh?" I cringed the moment the words were out. Modorens must be rather blunt.

"To further enlighten you."

I forgot the cold and the damp rocks under my behind. The fur along my spine shivered erect from the base of my tail to the top of my head. "I feel enlightened enough, Ersh." This was about as daring as I could get without turning and running.

Ersh might have been one of the statues Humans put in pairs in front of old buildings. She was mainly silhouette; even with the enlarged pupils of this form, I could only collect enough starlight to make out the curved tip of her ear, the flash of teeth as she licked her lips pensively. "Really?" Somehow she managed to impart menace into the single word. "I didn't expect you to be foolish, young Esen."

Privately, I thought about old fools as well as young ones. "I'm not being foolish," I said after a moment. "I don't like knowing secrets. About the Web," I added truthfully; the truth was important after sharing flesh. "I don't see why—"

"The others can't know?" Ersh finished. "I wish they could. But I'm stuck with you, however irresponsible, flighty, and stubborn you are. These are faults you'll grow out of in time, Es," she said with what sounded like dubious hope. "But only you and I have the ability to keep secrets during the sharing of flesh." Her voice deepened with a dangerous snarling undertone. "I will take no chances on what I know being assimilated by those outside my Web."

"The Enemy." Just saying it evoked the Ersh-tasting memory, the words wrapped with dread, fear, and oddly, a wisp of longing. But no form, no details, only emotion. *Not that I wanted to know.* I squirmed a bit, trying to find part of my rocky seat that didn't slope. In my experience, trouble followed those who deserved it. The activities of the Web were downright boring—let alone our tendency to simply outlive everybody else. Something wasn't fitting together at all. "Ersh, why do we have an enemy?"

She didn't answer directly, instead asking in her familiar drillmaster tone, "What is our purpose?"

I recited without thought, "The purpose of the Web is to find and preserve intelligence. To commit to shared memory the culture as well as the form. To be a living repository so no accomplishment of intelligence will be lost."

"Quite a noble purpose, don't you agree?"

I hadn't thought of judging it. The purpose was part of

life, as fundamental to the Web as sharing form. Yet her voice—this form had little subtlety of expression. Ersh's voice had sounded sarcastic, which I knew had to be wrong.

"Other civilizations are ephemeral," I said cautiously, whiskers straight with apprehension, finding my claws had a tendency to poke out. "Without us, they would disappear forever, even their works becoming dust—"

"So ours is a noble purpose." *Couldn't miss the sarcasm this time.* "And you have no doubts?"

I closed my teeth on the quick answer and thought hard. "You gave the Web this purpose," I countered. "If there are doubts, wouldn't you have given them to us, too?"

Ersh gave a soft grunt. Maybe I'd said something clever, but I didn't count on it. "The Human—Kearn—might argue that we're parasites," she said. "He could say we copy other forms for our own benefit, steal their knowledge only to perfect our disguises."

Old ground—this was simple basic training. "Using a form is essential to understanding the species," I repeated, again from rote. Exhaustive details on Kraosian architecture swam up behind my eyes before I could suppress the memory. "We remember a lot more than we'd need for simple camouflage," I complained before I thought.

Ersh sat, attentive but still rigid, a demigod expecting a sacrifice—*an unfortunately apt image,* I decided. Her age wore against me, almost immeasurable even by Web standards. I found myself thinking of *before* and realized with a sick feeling that I hadn't asked the right question at all.

"Why did you give us this purpose, Ersh?" I said, careful to keep my voice low.

"To atone."

Modorens tended to react physically. I didn't notice scrambling backward until the back of my right heel struck a rock. Hopping on the other foot, I hissed and spat for a moment, trying to salvage some composure. *This wasn't fair.* I was the youngest and already in trouble enough. *Why should I have to listen to terrifying revelations after everyone else was sensibly asleep?*

I must have been complaining out loud. Ersh was on me in an instant. Her powerful form knocked me to the hard ground. I froze beneath her weight, stuck between submission and struggle. Her breath was warm and slightly garlic in my face. Then her tongue rasped my nose in a quick kiss.

"You still react like an ephemeral. Excellent! Another reason I need you and not the others," Ersh said, thoroughly confusing me as she stood and then reached down to help me up. My back throbbed in at least a dozen places, each one where my flesh had been ground into the rock.

"We'll continue this in my chambers," she ordered. "There's much more you have to hear and it must be done privately." So she'd heard the Tumblers' grumbling.

"What if I don't want to listen?" But I spoke to empty space. Ersh was already a shadow bounding down the stairs.

Picco was pushing at the horizon, staining the edge of the night sky with orange. I eyed it, then cocked the tiny excuse for a tail this form had and carefully aimed a stream of highly scented urine. It hit the boulder where Ersh had been sitting, spreading with an intensely satisfying splash. *Physical species had their points.*

Rebellion done, I began to walk slowly down from Ersh's mountaintop, taking the stairs in morose little two-footed hops. Ersh would tell me what she wanted to, she would change me into what she needed, and she would undoubtedly send me on some revolting task for the Web's sake.

But I didn't have to like it.

In the morning, the kitchen smelled sour. The sombay had been waiting too long for customers, bubbling to bitterness in its pot. Maybe Skalet and Lesy had left last night. I hoped so. I knew if I looked at any of the others, talked to them, I would feel like a stranger. My Web was gone—I'd been ripped loose from it as surely as if Ersh had excised me. All that remained was one strand, a strand of secrets.

Ersh was somewhere down the slope, in Tumbler-form, talking to her new guests. She wouldn't be back before I left. I wasn't surprised to feel grateful.

My tongue touched the burns inside my mouth, a good enough reason to avoid breakfast. It was a Lanivarian the aircab had delivered; a Lanivarian had to leave. This morning all the old cautions and Rules were hysterically sharp in my mind, the way a drowning person perceives a rope floating just beyond reach.

* * *

Later, in the ground-to-orbit shuttle, I hunched beside a port, sucking on a piece of ice the steward found for me. He'd also brought a disposal bag in case I reacted to space in true Lanivarian fashion. I was too wrapped in my thoughts to be queasy.

Noble purpose. I stared at my companions—a Human, two Poptains, and a cluster of Rands, likely all gem dealers—tasting my utter knowledge of them, from their genetic heritage to their current cultures and languages. Out of habit, I added the new slang phrase the Rands were using to describe the Human to my memory.

I wanted to whine. *Guilt.* Ersh's noble purpose was rooted in it; no, root was the wrong image. Our great and noble purpose was a bubble bursting from a pocket of rot.

I owned Ersh's guilt now, beyond any ability to give it back. She'd shared with me throughout the entire night—if sharing's what it's called when one decides to give and the other is forced to accept. I'd listened, consumed, assimilated over and over until Ersh memory had crowded mine to some outer limit where it clung, barely, to remembering Esen-alit-Quar.

Memories older than I'd thought possible kept washing through me like waves of fever. I moved the ice to another sore spot in my mouth, my mind's eye witnessing the beginnings of a new galaxy. I slipped away from the here and now . . .

. . . becoming part of an organized appetite, *instinct,* rushing through the void, attracted by a cluster of new matter, raw energy, feeding through the millennia.

When sated, fission into two, renewed vigor. Sensing others failing to divide, each growing to a gluttonous mass that slowly died, solidifying into stone, drifting until snagged into orbit around a star.

Then, *self aware,* beginning to chose a path, moving away from the others, drawn from the feast by a different hunger. Call it curiosity.

Almost death, that journey away from the blazing richness of the new galaxy, a journey through space empty of all but wisps of matter, blown by solar winds.

Almost death, but just in time drawn by the energy-rich

glow of gamma radiation marking the edge of another galaxy. Starving, straining to find food, but this galaxy is older, more formed, with less free debris to feast upon. Wait, a pulse of energy approaches, trapped within a shell of concentrated matter. Feeding, a frenzy spurred by the need to survive. The shell cracks. Within is—life . . .

. . . I shifted uneasily, knowing my thoughts were private, but wondering if I now carried some kind of brand to mark me murderer. I popped another piece of ice on my tongue, trying to view Ersh-memory as more myth than heritage. But the memory-borne sensations were too intimate to push away . . .

. . . the shell-full-of-life was delicious, complex, satisfying, the best feeding ever. Hunting for more, insatiable after near-starvation. Another shell, but this one flees too quickly to follow. *Disappointment.* Time passes. Another shell, larger, bristling with sharp protrusions, approaches. Pain as energy from the shell touches . . .

Quicker than any thought, transform into resistant matter, hide in rock form, shudder in fear. The shell leaves. *Assimilated memory surfaces and merges with cunning.* Cycle into the shell-form . . .

Disaster. The form-memory is only of that which lived, not its inert shell. The life-form cannot survive in space. Almost death, almost death, almost . . .

. . . I couldn't breathe. Some being thoughtfully thumped my back, dislodging the ice stuck in my throat with the first blow, continuing until I snarled in protest. I managed not to bite the Human only because I was more concerned with regaining my breath. I gasped out my thanks, waving away the hovering steward.

The cluster of Rands pointedly ignored my convulsion and recovery. They had conceptual trouble with beings that didn't live in groups larger than twenty individuals. They must be regular travelers on this line; the steward knew enough to use a net to hold them together during lift—trying to sort the crawling mass into separate seat belts would have caused an outburst of hysteria. And quite a few stings.

The Poptains, however, regarded me with grave interest, their gloved tentacles tightly wrapped over the cases they'd insisted on carrying to their seats, their green eyes as faceted and beautiful as the crystals they bought from the Tumblers. Every once in a while, an honest Tumbler would try to explain to a Poptain that these particular gems were Tumbler excretions, and wouldn't they prefer something of true value. The Poptain would unfailingly look suspicious, as if the Tumbler was trying to distract them from their treasure. Different worlds.

An ache reminded me to loosen my jaw. I was developing a tendency to grind my back molars together. *Damn Ersh.* The thought of her dredged loose more memory, and I spun helplessly back . . .

. . . Time passing in heavy, hungry waves. But cunning was firmly in place. This space held a wealth of places to go, bodies with surfaces rich with the taste of life, waiting for the eating. Move slowly, watch for shells. Slip within the cloak of an atmosphere. Others would have fed on gases or minerals; others would have been satisfied. This one's appetite was whetted for more.

Night was best, suggested a memory. Here, said another, where the rooted growing things surrounded a rooted version of the shell. Hard to catch. Wonderful tastes everywhere. Hard to eat fast enough to satisfy the hunger. Two, three, four, a dozen, more.

Lights, noises, fear! Cycle instinctively, shed mass, blend with those nearest. Noises becoming soft. The novel sensation of being touched, of being carried by other life. Warmth. A different kind of food, rich in taste. *Satisfaction.* For now . . .

. . . The shuttle docked, jarring me loose from Ersh's memories. I gathered my belongings, numbed as always by the thought of Ersh as a baby.

20: Station Afternoon

"TAKE it or leave it."

I narrowed my eyes at the dealer. He narrowed all six of his eyes back at me, then stuck out a forked tongue for good measure. "Won't find better."

Won't find them at all, was the truth, I thought, staring down at the various hoobits on the counter. It had taken credits enough to persuade the owner of this so-called souvenir shop that it would be worthwhile to show me his private wares. Grave robbing was an offense to most civilized species. Not to this Queeb, obviously. Most of the merchandise crowding the shelves, floor, and even hanging from the ceiling of his back room looked to have spent time underground. My hood collected the mustiness near my nose, and I sneezed periodically.

"How much?" I said, pointing to the cleanest hoobit of the four.

The Queeb named an astronomical amount. *I looked that gullible? Probably.* I weighed the odds on bargaining and sighed. I entered the amount on my credit chip and passed it to him to encode whatever clandestine account would nibble at Ersh's funds.

The being whistled cheerfully to himself as he put my purchase into a senso-screen bag. *As well he might.* "Mind you don't take this out until you're off-station, Customer," he warned. "Gropers don't take kindly to aliens having their sacred objects. They'll shoot you first, then explain to station authority."

I glanced around his storehouse of sacred, forbidden things and wondered if this possible consequence ever bothered the Queeb. *Likely not.* I tucked the hoobit, secure in its bag, under my cloak, peeled my credit chip from a tentacle that was loath to part from it, and gladly left.

* * *

A half hour later, I stuffed my cloak into a recycler. The machine reminded me to insert my chip for a refund, but I didn't intend to leave any further trails, electronic or otherwise. I surveyed the long, pensive lines of my new face in the restroom mirror, satisfied, then went back to washing the hoobit in the sink.

My long supple fingers with their disklike tips deftly removed the bits of lint and dirt caught in the hoobit's many crevices. My hands were the strongest part of this form, quite capable of bending this or many other metals. Fortunately, I didn't need their strength for this task. Three applications of the metal cleaner I'd purchased earlier today had removed the last traces of mourning paint. *There.*

I held the now-gleaming circlet in my hands. Perhaps its previous owner would rest more quietly in that pilfered grave, his or her sacred burden passed safely to another of its kind instead of sold to an alien collector as a curiosity or doorstop.

That I wouldn't stay a Ket forever was a point I'd consider later, soothing my conscience with the intention of couriering the hoobit back to Ket-Prime along with a discreet comment about a certain Queeb.

I strung the leather braid through the hoobit's ring and put it around my neck. The disk hung exactly at the center of my slightly concave chest. *Perfect.* My fingers fluttered over the complex textures embedded on its surface, sending sensual thrills along my arms.

I hadn't explained to the Queeb that it wasn't being caught with a hoobit that worried me—it was being caught without one. No Ket would willingly set foot in public without his or her hoobit sparkling and in plain view.

This tall humanoid form with its outlandishly large hands, body willow-slender and just as supple, was not the least conspicuous choice for my mission, *but it would do nicely,* I assured myself, checking the fall of the skirt I'd also bought around my legs. The plain woven garment was the standard offworld clothing for both sexes, at least where the climate was warm enough. The hoobit was all the ornamentation considered necessary by the greatly misunderstood Ket.

"Gropers," I said to myself, admiring what was a healthy and vigorous body for a Ket. My skin was like the palest of leathers, its fine-grained texture a trait considered quite attractive within the species. I met my new eyes in my reflection, their warm yellow almost glowing in the stall lights. All the while, my hands restlessly explored the quite remarkable smoothness of the sink, then the soothing ridges of the woven skirt. Born with a hand in someone else's pocket was the expression used by other species to refer to Ket. True, it was almost impossible for a Ket to keep its beautiful hands to itself. But that was simply because touch was their favored sense, texture their greatest pleasure.

I fastened my curious fingers on the reassuring curve of the hoobit in the proper dignified manner. Humans were particularly offended by the Ket propensity to fondle whatever was of interest. Of course, this didn't stop them from also being the Kets' best customers. Ket masseuses were in demand everywhere, traveling so frequently in Human space and worlds that one more should scarcely be noticed. A disguise and profession in one.

Now I was ready to leave Hixtar Station and attempt the first task Ersh had set me. To find out what happened after my disappearance from Rigel II.

Hixtar's orbiting station had a reputation as a place where you can eventually buy anything, legal or otherwise. That reputation had suggested, rightly, that I could find what I needed to carry off my form. It also explained why such an inconsequential world was a popular stopover for various ships both from the Commonwealth and the uncommitted systems of the Fringe. I should have had little difficulty finding a ship outbound for Rigel II, or at least that sector of space.

But the glittering script of the posting board was unusually brief. Few ships were due to leave Hixtar in the next couple of days. There were no listings at all destined for the Fringe. *How odd.* Trade usually poured in both directions from the outposts. The miners of the Fringe frequently outnumbered the resident station population.

They were outnumbered at the moment. I'd taken one walk in the noisy expanse of Hixtar's loading arena, bundled against the bitter cold, and been amazed by the activity there. Even more remarkable, those crowding on-station were not the usual Human mining crews and Denebian prospectors. As many beings used the green tubes reserved for non-oxy breathers as rode the climbers to the various entry levels. There were family groups, too many of them for coincidence. And the expressions of those around me had ranged from annoyance to outright fear.

What were they all afraid of? I wondered again as I stared at the unhelpful board. *New taxes?*

"Are you available, Groper?"

I gripped my hoobit and turned to see who the low voice belonged to. *Ah.* An old spacer stood just out of reach, holding a worn-looking credit chip in my direction. His rheumy eyes were wistful as he looked up at me.

Of course I was available, I reminded myself sharply. Kets never refused a chance to touch another species. And, in this form, I was Ket enough to feel a pleased anticipation. Time to find a ship out later.

By the evening meal, I'd soothed enough backs, shoulders, and other body parts to cover half the cost of the hoobit; I'd probably scared the life out of the Queeb by spreading the news that a Ket was on-station—though it was quite incorrect in assuming any Ket would use violence against a grave robber, the species preferring litigation; and I'd missed the only outbound ship traveling remotely in my direction that afternoon.

But my fingers tingled with pleasure. And—given the rumors my clients had shared with me—I was grateful Ersh hadn't sent me any closer to the Fringe.

"War is breaking out," said the Human officer from a survey ship, whose uniform made me remember old friends. "Casualties are mounting. Tensions are rising even faster, fueled by talk of some secret weapon. Things are going to get worse."

"Something's out there," whispered the old spacer, peering around at me through his bushy gray eyebrows. "Something that appears and disappears. Something that consumes whatever lives. First ships, then Fringe mining domes, who knows what might be next? Fools won't listen, but spacers know. Smart captains are keeping their ships bellied-up to Hixtar Station."

There were other versions of both tales. Combined, they

added up to a crisis building in an area of space where species were already close to blaster point over ephemeral issues: ownership, rights, access to supposed wealth.

Which, while fascinating, wasn't helping me find out more about Rigel II. Rumors from that direction hadn't a chance in this place, where ships were being found empty and adrift.

I folded myself to fit into a chair meant for beings with shorter legs and larger hips, quite ready to rest my poor feet. Ket had evolved within a lesser gravity than that operating within the station—doubtless an average suited to no one in particular but bearable by most. It didn't take much exertion to make me grateful to wriggle my long toes in the air and let another part of my anatomy take the strain. Ket rarely used such furnishings, preferring to crouch comfortably with knees and shoulders touching. Under these circumstances, I was content with the chair.

Its other advantage was location. Once I managed to somehow wedge my knees properly under the table, I glanced up to confirm this portion of the food court lay within sight of the main posting board. All I needed now was patience. Eventually, someone would decide even Hixtar was too close to the Fringe and choose to head in the direction I needed.

Three bottles of dle tea later, I was halfway through a Braille book (such a sensuous pleasure, reading), when the public address system announced a ship arrival with a suspiciously relieved tone. Shortly afterward, the posting board flashed on a green-backed and quite lengthy supply request, sending some merchants scurrying from tables to see who could reach their consoles first—not a trading ship then, more likely a transport or government vessel. I moved to another table, more in the shadow of an entrancingly rough-barked tree, and watched the debarkation gate. *What were the odds?*

I should have taken my own bet. Acting Captain Kearn was the third figure through the gate, a handful of forms in one hand, and a definitely anxious look on his face.

21: Station Night

PREVCRACKERS had wonderful crusty bits along their edges. I fondled mine surreptitiously, conscious that most non-Ket considered food-fondling impolite, but I remembered other manners. Quite frankly, the bite, chew, and swallow part of a meal was simple mechanics to me at the moment, especially in a food-service area designated safe for most humanoids and other theta-class beings.

No sign of Ragem, yet. I had checked, and the *Rigus* was loose-docked, ready to move on within hours though its supply list suggested at least one day-cycle at the station. Rumor had the Commonwealth ship here to make long overdue inquiries into the problems along the Fringe.

Maybe, I thought, caressing a fruit peel. But I'd asked Ragem to take me to Hixtar and Kearn would have overheard through the telltale belt.

"Madame Ket?"

I'd been waiting for a *Rigus* crewmember to approach me and was hardly surprised to receive a properly courteous greeting from a member of a first contact ship. *Still,* I sighed to myself, *did it have to be Willify Guire?* I carefully curled my fingers around the hoobit and nodded a greeting to the woman.

She took the seat across the table, promptly holding out a credit chip. More good manners with a Ket. "How may I serve you?" I asked calmly, confident Willify would not connect this form with the Ycl or Lanivarian she'd met on the *Rigus.* Which was just as well, since she'd never warmed to me in either form. Being suspicious of a Ycl was a reasonable survival instinct; her polite dislike of my Lanivarian-self seemed to have started with my quite necessary alteration of what had turned out to be her only spare uniform. *Nobody'd told me,* I thought with a twinge of remembered guilt.

Her nostrils flared delicately, in what I took as pleased anticipation rather than a comment on the remains of my lunch. "Not only myself, madame. There are several on my ship who would appreciate your service. We've had a—difficult—mission recently. Word that a Ket was on-station and practicing her profession caused quite a stir, especially among those like myself who've experienced the wonderful work of your people."

Too perfect? I dismissed my doubts, having deliberately chosen this form to attract Human contact. "This Ket is yours," I replied, after touching my credit chip to hers to verify it. We Gropers were always careful about new clients.

The *Rigus* was subtly different to my Ket senses, textured, curved, altogether more sensuous. The ceiling was definitely lower. I remembered scents, machine and living, but they were irrelevant to this form, as were certain colors. Willify left me alone in the lounge to wait, giving me time to stroke the cool metal walls, and investigate the upholstery of the couches and seats. There was already a pad with a sheet covering it on the floor. I settled myself in a glorious chair of flecked mock-velvet and reluctantly settled my hands around the hoobit.

My first client was the Modoren. If the security officer was checking my credentials on behalf of the crew, he left convinced. Having been a Modoren myself recently, I soon had him relaxed into a limp pile of fur, utterly a throaty, almost soundless purr. I needed time to suck my poor fingers before my next client—that lovely fur was as coarse as wire.

Two female Humans came in next, together. I waited more or less patiently for them to sort out who would be first, using that uniquely Human affectation of each insisting on the other.

When they left, smiling contentedly, I rearranged the sheet then stretched, arching until the back of my head lightly touched my heels. Bidirectional hip joints were not a bonus in this gravity—much more standing around and I'd trade this form's lovely flexibility for a locking pelvis in an instant. I rolled myself upright, then turned my neck gently around from side to side, hearing little clicks of strain as my overtaxed spine moved through its full range to allow me to gaze pensively over each shoulder. *No luck with conversation yet.* The Modoren had puffed and purred, while the Humans had talked to each other.

"Are you still taking clients, Madame Ket?" said a soft voice from behind me.

I was barely able to keep from whirling around, which would not have been a Ketlike response. Instead, I grasped my hoobit, very tightly, and turned with dignified grace. "This Ket is available," I replied.

Ragem could use a good massage, was my first reaction to his hunched, raised shoulders and strained-looking face. Here was one of the costs of my visit with humanity: Ragem wore the plain blue coveralls of an ensign, without specialty bars or rank to be seen.

"Madame?"

I released my death grip on the hoobit and waved at the pad by my feet. "Please make yourself ready, sir."

He unfastened the upper half of his uniform and shrugged it off his shoulders, before stretching out on the pad with a sigh. Most Humans preferred a full body massage, but it wasn't my place to argue.

I stood over Ragem before relaxing into the balanced crouch that brought my knees up to my shoulders and my hands to the floor, feeling oddly like a spectator until my long supple fingers began lightly testing the knotted muscles of his neck and shoulders. Then pleasure that was more than my Ket nature surged up my arms. I pressed my fingers deep into the warm skin of my friend, content to have this uncomplicated moment to free him from pain, if only temporarily.

I worked down the sides of his spine, knowing exactly where to find the pressure points to relax and soothe his tension. He groaned with astonished relief, his eyes closed as my Ket hands worked their magic. *A shame Ragem hadn't opted for full body.* I pushed suggestively downward on the fabric of his uniform, then froze as my fingers touched the hard slickness of the belt locked against his skin.

Ragem rolled like a fish, and I had to hop to avoid being

knocked over. He lay on his back and looked up at me. "Just the waist up, please, Madame Ket."

They'd put a telltale on him. This man who had tried to save all their lives was being treated like some criminal.

Did this mean all his friendships were lost? Had I ripped him from his Human web in my flawed efforts to be his friend, too?

The Human misunderstood my hesitation. His cheeks reddened and he began to rise.

I placed my hand, fingers spread, on the warm hardness where bone protected his heart. "Wait," I said, trying to keep my voice cool and professional. "This Ket is not finished."

Ragem settled again as I stroked the tightness from his chest and shoulders, but I no longer took any pleasure in my task. His ribs were too close to the skin. His unhappy state, though my fault, was beyond my ability to repair.

"What is your use-name, madame?"

I kept my hands moving over his arm; there was nothing significant in his low voice—this was typically when clients began conversations, sensing their time was almost up and hoping to prolong the pleasure of a Ket massage.

Still, only Ragem would ask something inconvenient. I glanced down at the hoobit to check my name, knowing it would be foolhardy to assume he couldn't read the Ket script. "Nimal-Ket, sir."

"Any news from the Fringe, Nimal-Ket?"

Gossip was another Ket stock-in-trade. "There is fear, sir," I replied, moving to his other arm. "Talk of danger to those in ships and even to those planetborn."

Ragem's muscles tensed, and I pursed my lips in a Ket frown. "This Ket suggests another topic if this news will undo the good I have done, sir."

"No, no. This is important." Ragem tugged his wrist from my fingers and sat up. "Can we talk more about what you've heard about this? Please, Nimal-Ket?"

As a Ket, I should be annoyed by having my client end the session, so I scowled ferociously at him and soothed my rejected fingers on the hoobit. As myself, I was reassured by the spark in his eyes, so dull before. "If it is talk you wish, sir," I said grudgingly, eyeing the door to the lounge. "But this Ket has other clients."

"A moment only." Ragem courteously offered me his hand. "Sit with me."

His good manners eased my Ket nature. So invited, I let my fingers explore the palm of his hand as I echoed his cross-legged position on the pad. Ragem extended his other hand, stopping just short of the hoobit swinging from my chest. Quite overcome by his excellent understanding of Ket ways, I nodded. Ragem closed his eyes and ran his fingers lightly over the textured pendant. Since liberties were to be exchanged, I fluttered my fingers over his face, enjoying the bristle of his chin almost as much as the fine lashes of his eyes.

"Such exquisite politeness," I said warmly, once the moment of sharing passed. "I am honored by your knowledge of my kind. This Ket would know your use-name, Human, so I may share it."

Ragem almost smiled. "Paul," he said. "Paul-Human," he corrected himself. "And I am honored, too, Nimal-Ket."

"You wish to know more about the Fringe and its rumors, Paul-Human," I shook my head. "This Ket has heard nothing pleasant."

"We know about the ships found without their crews—and the miners and others missing. The official story up till now is that it's escalation of the conflict between Garson's World, Inhaven, and the Tly System. Those governments have denied it, as you'd expect." His pause was ominous. "But, this time, we believe the protest—there's more going on. What have you heard?"

"Beings on this station talk of something evil, a thing that seeks out intelligent life and consumes it," I said, then temporized. "Many races explain disasters with such tales."

"Perhaps with good reason, Nimal-Ket. Do they say where this evil comes from?"

"No one knows. But one captain told me it first appeared at a distant point in the Fringe, passed through a Tly mining cluster, and most recently affected ships near Garson's World." I wriggled my fingers dismissively. "There have been battles between those of Tly and Garson. This Ket sees no reason to invoke some mysterious monster," I finished, then found myself abruptly wondering.

Ragem sighed. "It's been kept quiet so far, Nimal-Ket, but you'll see it on the screens today. Inhaven's colonies and Garson's World have been heavily blockaded by the Tly. It's gone on for months. Things have changed for the worse," Ragem's voice was somber. "The Tly have sent warships to Garson's World in response to what they've called attacks on the blockade. The Commonwealth experts fear they are going to strike at the planet itself."

"Murder!"

"The Tly media prefers the word resolution," Ragem corrected, holding my eyes with his.

The hoobit gave little comfort as I closed my eyes and rocked in place, humming to myself. *Foolish destructive beings—were their lives not short enough?* This was why the purpose of the Web was so essential. The pattern of extinction at each other's hands was too common. If Garson's World fell, the Web alone would remember the folktales of its people. We would remember the raw exuberance of its settlements, the smell of hops and syrups at harvest, the . . .

"Madame?"

With a shudder, I came back to myself, this form, and this place. I looked at Ragem, recognizing that sharp look of his with dismay. *Now I was his focus.* A true Ket would hardly blink at such news, being a very self-absorbed race. "It has been a long day for this Ket, Paul-Human," I said quickly but steadily. "And your news does upset me. Garson's World contains many—valued clients."

Ragem rubbed one hand over his face, then nodded. "My apologies for being so abrupt, Nimal-Ket. I realize how important your clients are to you. We must prevent any more loss of life, whether by war or this evil you speak of."

"Yes." Keeping one hand on my hoobit, I placed the other over his heart, feeling its beat through my palm, my six supple fingers spanning the whole of his chest. Its warmth was unexpectedly comforting. "If this Ket can help, you need only ask, Paul-Human."

Again Ragem's eyes narrowed slightly. Before he could react further, I said firmly, "This Ket will explain why I am so eager to take up this challenge, Paul-Human, since you know enough of our ways to find this unexpected. Ket-Prime is not far enough from the Fringe to ignore this danger moving through it. As one whose pouch is not yet ready to fill with life, this Ket must take action against any threat to those blessed." *Too true,* I thought, aware of the terrible vulnerability of a species whose reproduction was limited to one planet. The Ket ensured their traditions and privacy by becoming fertile only when old enough to retire to their homeworld.

If the image of my less-than-powerful form as a protector of the innocent amused Ragem, he was far too tactful to show it. Instead he touched my hoobit with two fingers and bowed his head slightly. "As must we all, Nimal-Ket," he said quietly.

We stood. I didn't want him to leave, but what could I say? Perhaps Ragem felt the same way, for he smiled up at me and said: "If we stay docked long enough, I hope you are available again, Nimal-Ket."

I fluttered my long fingers to show amusement. "Your ship's credit is adequate, Paul-Human. This Ket is gratified to serve."

Once the door closed behind Ragem, my aloneness returned like the cold whisper of wind over skin. I increased my body temperature but still shivered. The cold was inside; for all my years and Ersh's training, I had no idea how to warm myself again.

Out There

DEATH paused near a system full of life, tempted. The nearest planet was ringed with starships. No obstacle to its hunger. Still it hesitated.

Suddenly, flares and bursts of soundless explosions dotted the cloud-swirled planet like rot on a fruit. White clouds turned black and red; the dark side of the world blazed with the light of a thousand fires.

Starships wheeled away in formation, then blinked from view as they engaged translight drives.

Death soared over the dying world. *Nothing left.* It tasted the trail left by the fleeing destroyers. Death turned and followed.

22: Station Morning

"—A Lanivarian, no less!" Station Chief of Administration Griffin laughed so hard after this that I suspended my hands in midair for a moment to let his generous flesh stop shaking.

"This Ket was surprised to see the notices, sir," I made the understatement quietly, continuing my work on a back that would have made two of Ragem's. "And you say this being is the danger that has so frightened the people of the Fringe systems?"

Griffin almost choked. "I say nothing of the kind. This man Kearn is out of his mind, that's what I say. We're up against a military uprising less than two days' translight from here, and they send us a nut. You know, this is the third time he's docked here in the last week. I swear he's worse each time!"

I had to rework the tension from his upper shoulders, wishing I could do the same for myself. *Ersh had been right,* I thought. *She'd just underestimated how quickly my little escapade would produce further disaster.* "And this Lanivarian he seeks?" I asked.

"Esen Quat something," he grunted. "It's all nonsense. There's never been a Lanivarian with the stomach to travel this far. And look at the pictures Kearn's had his crew spread over my posting boards! Explain to me how this, this pup! could be responsible for gutting ships in the most miserable area of space ever explored!"

"This Ket has seen the image, sir. I must agree, the being appears unlikely to be the villain they say. But surely this Kearn brought proof?"

I struck a particularly tight muscle and he sighed gustily. "Wonderful hands, you Gropers. Sorry. Ket."

"A name is but a name," I said politely, thinking, as all

Ket, that a name was everything—which was why only our use-names were shared with the always untrustworthy non-Ket. It was an attitude I valued highly, given my present situation. "Is there any evidence concerning this Esen?"

"Classified, he says. Secrets. Eyes only. This Kearn is buried in some vid-fantasy and wants us all to play. Well, I put up his signs; maybe that will shut him up. We have bigger problems. A little more on that side, please. Ummmm."

Although rooms were at a premium, due to the number of ships scurrying to the protection of the station, I'd had no trouble trading my services for a simple cabin. I peeled the Ket symbol from the door of my rented room after Griffin left, having enough to think about for the moment.

So Kearn had labeled me as the probable cause behind the deaths occurring in the Fringe. Whether others took him seriously or not, my name was literally up in lights in every hallway. It was pure luck that I'd confronted him as a member of the one species no one in their right mind would believe a threat to other worlds. I'd been quite happy to reinforce the opinion of stationfolk and spacers alike: the man was crazy. The resultant undercurrent of resentment against the Commonwealth ship was something I was less happy about, but could live with.

I ordered a lunch to be delivered. Four walls felt safer, for the moment. Then I pulled out the station newsmag and studied the chart plastered across most of the front page. Missing ships, unconfirmed attacks, all parts of destruction on a growing scale. Unfortunately, some markings were in colors that barely registered to my current vision. But the headline was clear enough. *Mystery Death On Course to Panacia—Hixtar Spared!*

Panacia. A system barely touched during the settlement of the adjacent Fringe by Human and other mining concerns. Three planets of the fifteen circling its swollen star buzzed with life, beginning with Panacia's Hiveworld, the heavily populated D'Dsel, birthplace of Panacia's insectoid intelligence.

It was Mixs' chosen home.

It could be coincidence. There were always new and strange discoveries when species first met or unfamiliar areas of space were explored. The Humans might simply have troubled something better left alone. Or it could be war, better disguised than most. Or . . .

Or it could be my fault.

I crushed the newsmag in my hand slowly. *Had Ersh's Enemy been lurking in the Fringe, intercepting signals, waiting for betrayal? Had it somehow caught Kearn's messages about a shape-changing being discovered on Kraos?*

I straightened it out again, turning once more to the chart, folding and unfolding the newsmag's sharp, delicate edges. *I had to go to Panacia.* Ersh hadn't shared with me the form or strategy of our Enemy—only that its goal was the destruction of the Web. If this evil ripping through the Fringe was that Enemy, I had to warn Mixs.

If I was wrong, I still had to do something, I decided. Ragem and his fragile ship were prepared to hunt whatever it was in order to save lives. Even misbegotten Kearn had the right motives in labeling me the monster and pursuing me. Something was destroying intelligent life, and all that I was demanded it be stopped.

My lunch arrived. I looked up at the grinning being who stood beside the delivery servo and snaked my long arm out to grab his sleeve and drag him inside.

"What are you doing here, Paul-Human?" I said sternly.

He put the bowl of salad on the table near the door and looked apologetic. "I need to talk to you, Nimal-Ket."

"If you still wear that belt," I said bluntly, "this Ket hopes you have permission to be here. I cannot afford to lose clients by spending time in your ship's brig."

As I spoke, Ragem's hands dropped self-consciously to his waist. *So. No reason to doubt we were being overheard. Ragem's gift for inconvenience continued.*

But he was already shaking his head. "Acting Captain Kearn sent me."

"Here?"

"He wants me walking around the station. Looking for someone. I thought you could help me."

At the resigned note to his voice, I reached for my hoobit rather than comfort him as my Ket nature would have preferred. "Have you had lunch, Paul-Human?"

The answer to that being no, as I'd expected, we shared my salad—Ragem wisely heeding my advice and leaving the rostra sprouts for me. I crunched the last of these between my blunt teeth with satisfaction, enjoying the nut-sweet cyanide tang. It took a lot to stimulate the few taste buds of this form.

And it seemed, it would take a lot to stimulate Ragem out of his current slump. *A conversationalist he wasn't.* Then again, if the device he wore carried all conversation to his superior officer, Ragem probably didn't feel much like talking. Out of habit, I slid my fingers around the empty bowl, even though I knew Human dishes were sadly unornamented. "So, Paul-Human. Who is this someone you are looking for? Would this Ket know this being?"

"I doubt it. But you've probably seen her image on the postings around the station, Nimal-Ket."

"Ah. The vile and dangerous puppy," I said in a suitably hushed voice.

Ragem's eyes hadn't lost all their fire. "Esen is not vile or dangerous—" he began angrily, then stopped as if remembering where he was or at least who might be listening. "The Captain believes Esen may know something about the problems in this area. We just want to talk to her." This in a voice quite without hope.

I clenched my hoobit, holding in my delight at the same time. *Ragem still believed in me.* I hadn't destroyed our friendship with my foolish display on Rigel II—or my flight. "You sound as if you know this Esen well, Paul-Human," I commented as I folded a napkin around my fingers.

He spread his hands and let them fall again to his knees. "Enough to want to be the one who finds her first, Nimal-Ket."

The moment hung between us, an innocent pause on the part of the melancholy Human, a poignant eternity to me. *How easy to reveal myself; how wonderful to reconnect with my Human Web; how potentially disastrous.*

As long as Ragem wore the telltale, my lips—and form—were sealed. But there were other ways to answer the bond between us. "This Ket knows the station and many who live here well, Paul-Human," I said. "I will help you look for this Esen."

A smile lit his too-thin face. "Any help you could give me would be wonderful, Nimal-Ket. Thank you."

I stood and pointed to the pad behind me on the floor.

"First, this Ket would appreciate being permitted to finish your massage, Paul-Human. It does my reputation little good to be seen with a being as tight as a week-old Crenosian water gourd."

Ragem looked inclined to argue, but I tapped my fingers on the hoobit and kept my face carefully stern. Now was no time to let any personality show but that of a true Ket. And never would a Ket ignore the opportunity to practice her craft.

And while I worked, it would give me time to think of how to search convincingly for myself.

23: Subfloor Night

"ASK about any Ganthor."

I turned my head to stare down at Ragem where he stood impatiently behind me. "Ganthor, Paul-Human? This Ket has seen none on Hixtar Station."

"A good friend of Esen's," he lied glibly. "She might know—just ask, please, Nimal-Ket."

While I was beginning to find all this rather entertaining, I was less sure about the attitude of the Human waiting behind the claims desk. *Nothing ventured,* I thought. "This Ket has also a claim against a Ganthor, Official," I said firmly. "Are there any of these beings on-station?"

"Are there any other Gropers as credit-careless as you, madame? If so, I've been using the wrong ones!" I sighed inwardly and let the woman enjoy her chuckle. "Nope. No Ganthor has made a transaction through us during the last month. But Ganthor prefer exchange to credits anyway, so who knows? Any more bad debts to check?"

I shook my head, bowed, and backed away, having to push Ragem to move him out of the path of the next being in line. One of the advantages to Hixtar Station was its lack of air tags or other monitoring devices. Beings came and went here as freely as out in the Fringe. While this wasn't helping Ragem's or Kearn's search, it had definitely helped cover my tracks.

Ragem walked beside me down the hall leading to the central corridor, scrutinizing the floor as if it would hold footprints he could read. This was slightly risky, giving the constant flow of pedestrian traffic moving to and from the station Claims and Credit Office, but no one ran into him.

"It was worth a try, Paul-Human," I said soothingly. "But we are running out of reasonable avenues. Perhaps your friend is not on the station, after all?"

The murmur of voices and footsteps almost covered his whisper, as I was sure he intended. "What makes you think Esen is my friend, Nimal-Ket?"

I bumped shoulder to carapace with a hurrying Carasian—who should have known better than to try and squeeze its bulk between smaller beings in the first place—and mentally reviewed our conversations. *Damn.* Ragem had never referred to friendship. "Then this Ket is mistaken, Paul-Human." To distract him, I turned down a side corridor, thankful it had a bit less traffic. My shoulder felt bruised. "Let us try another contact of mine."

Of course, that person, however willing, knew nothing of any Lanivarian or Ganthor. And if they had, they would have claimed the reward.

"When did your captain add a reward to the posting?" I said a moment later, glad to stop and catch my breath. We watched the image and text play itself out in twenty languages, the message in some leaving a great deal to the imagination. The station needed to upgrade its translation programs. All were adequately, if distressingly clear about the substantial number of credits offered for information about the fugitive Lanivarian. I caught my Ketself, always conscious of the value of currency, wondering idly how to collect. *Stop that,* I scolded myself.

"There was another attack this afternoon," Ragem said by way of explanation. "A ship was found empty in Sector 12."

"Then it's true. This thing is going to Panacia," I said numbly. "It must be stopped! Why are you wasting time here, Paul-Human? Why isn't your ship hunting in space instead of this station?"

Ragem looked past me and seemed to find the bustle of activity in front of the posting board not to his liking. "Over there," he ordered, leading the way down yet another side corridor, Hixtar Station being more prone to haphazard additions than planning. This corridor was lined with less-than-high-class storefronts that looked very familiar. We stopped about thirty paces from the artifact dealer where I'd bought the hoobit now clutched between my fingers. *Ragem had a positive gift for being awkward.*

"This isn't a good neighborhood, Paul-Human." I

glanced at the passersby who looked to be taking morbid interest in us. "The clients are poor credit risks. And there have been instances of theft! This Ket recommends we go someplace else—" *Anyplace else.*

Ragem ignored my good advice. Instead, he stretched up on his toes to bring his lips almost to my ear cavity and whispered urgently, "Why do you care about Panacia? And why are you helping me, Nimal-Ket? Is that even your right name?"

Trouble arrived at that instant in more than the warm breath of Ragem's dangerous questions. We were both grabbed and held for the inspection of a hooded figure that looked distressingly familiar. Passersby were suddenly in a great hurry to leave our vicinity. I didn't blame them. I didn't like the looks of this either.

"Let go!"

I shook my head, fixing my gaze on the dusty treasures hanging from the ceiling. The Queeb's back room must be well insulated. I could hear no sounds but our breathing.

Crack.

It didn't help being ready this time. I almost lost consciousness as the Queeb efficiently broke my second finger. Only ten to go, and the hoobit would be lost again. The strength of a Ket's grip was proverbial. As a Ket, I was quite prepared to put up with both pain and death to hold what was mine.

But I wasn't a Ket. I'd never experienced helpless agony like this in my five hundred years of life—nor in any of my shared memories. Yet I remained firmly in control of this form. *What a time to at last triumph over the instinct of self-preservation.*

Ragem was tied up beside me; his telltale, which could have finally been useful and brought help, rendered useless by some illegal device of the Queeb's accomplices. Ragem was as loud as I was silent, cursing the Queeb in its own tongue, taunting it, trying every thing he could to prevent—

Crack.

Ersh, I thought, as air escaped my lips in a moan, *is this what you wanted from me?*

"There's a customer out front." A deep voice uttered words that made no sense.

Ragem's cursing stopped. I realized through a fog that we were now alone. *That should mean something,* I wondered, dazed. *But what?*

An urgent whisper. "Nimal. Nimal-Ket."

I licked my lips and focused my eyes on Ragem. He was unharmed, except for the certain discomfort of the Queeb's ropes wrapped tightly around his bare arms. My own arms persisted in their famed Ket sensitivity, transferring every pulse of fire from my fingers to my brain. There were tears on Ragem's cheeks and blood dripped from where he'd driven his teeth through a bottom lip. *Dear Human,* I thought fuzzily. *And he doesn't even know who I am.*

And before the Queeb tried my resolve too far, it was time to leave. I unlocked my literal death grip on the hoobit, feeling the bones grind in my abused fingers as a pale echo of the Queeb's torment. A Ket couldn't let go, not in the face of a threat to its identity. Death defending one's hoobit was a matter of honor.

I had other priorities.

They had tied my legs to the bench. I spared my broken fingers as best I could, making fairly quick work of the knots.

As I rushed to Ragem's side, my footsteps echoed in the room, no matter how quietly I tried to move. *How long before the Queeb came back? Was there someone guarding the door?* I refused to worry about the near future and crouched to reach the knots behind Ragem's back. They were much tighter than mine; he had struggled as well as shouted.

And he struggled now, in a well-meant effort to help me. "Please keep still," I hissed through clenched teeth, not needing the additional pain as the rope shifted unpredictably through my fingers.

"Good enough," he grunted. I took a step back as Ragem furiously pulled himself free of his bonds, throwing them to the floor. Immediately he came over to me and tried to see my hands.

"The best first aid will be getting out of here, Paul-Human," I objected.

"No argument from me," he said, shrugging his arms back into the sleeves of his coverall. The useless telltale received an absent kick out of his way as Ragem searched the room.

"What are you looking for?" I whispered, having found my hands ached less when wrapped around the hoobit. Most of the Queeb's illegal stock had been packed, with more speed than care, into boxes labeled medical supplies. The hoobits I'd inspected yesterday were gone.

I had little doubt that my appearance on the station, combined with the arrival and search efforts of the *Rigus* crew, had been enough to panic the Queeb into flight. The irony of my being a welcome target for the grave robber's revenge was not lost on me, but I was more interested in Ragem as he dug into a half-filled box.

"This will do nicely." He brandished a swordlike object, its tip curved into a set of vicious hooks.

Assimilated memory painted a vivid picture of how the weapon worked in flesh, soft or scaled. I opened my mouth to protest, then met Ragem's eyes.

Deliberately, he glanced down at my hands, then up again. "I'm not a violent person, Nimal-Ket," he said slowly, his voice with an edge to it I'd never heard before. "I don't want to become one. But I won't sit by again."

The Human gave me no time to argue. He made me crouch to one side of the only door to the room. I watched with interest as he shoved boxes here and there. *Ah.* Ragem now had a pile below the cluster of lights in the ceiling. He climbed it with primate agility and, with one wild swing, used his weapon to smash the cluster. The room plunged into darkness. I winced at the subsequent crash, hoping the fall of Ragem's boxes was part of his plan. *They had to have heard that!*

They did. The door burst open. The Queeb, possibly frantic at the sounds of damage to its trove, was first through. In the bar of light from the other room, I saw the glint of the sword as Ragem wrapped its hooked tip around the Queeb's stubby neck.

Two other figures poured into the room, stumbling past Ragem and his hostage into the dark. Ragem moved fully into the light, blinding himself in order to make it obvious what the stakes were. And, given the white-knuckled force he was using to hold the Queeb and its death in contact, I thought he should be taken quite seriously indeed.

The darkness filling the rest of the room was a gift I didn't hesitate to use. I cycled, freeing myself of pain and gaining teeth at the same instant. My keener nose located our hidden captors at once; it helped that most Humans sweat during a crisis. I sank my teeth into the soft muscle of one leg, then used my first victim's shrieks to cover my assault on his comrade. This one wore high boots, so I wasted no time on legs. I wasn't proud to enjoy the crunch of his wrist bone as I snapped it and jumped away.

All this screaming in the dark was unnerving both Ragem and his captive. "Nimal!" he shouted. "Leave her alone, or I'll—"

I cycled, then gasped and almost went to my knees as form-memory exactly reproduced the broken fingers on each hand. Somehow I called out something that reassured Ragem. Avoiding the panic-stricken Humans, who sounded like they were climbing on boxes to avoid the teeth-filled darkness, I located my skirt and hoobit, hung both in their respective proper locations, and headed for Ragem.

The moment I reached the bar of light, he reversed his weapon and used its hilt to tap the Queeb briskly on the back. As the being dropped, obviously unconscious, to the floor, I said admiringly, "You have a fine grasp of anatomy, Paul-Human."

"Enough to know you need a med, Nimal-Ket. Now."

24: Starship Morning

I COULD almost believe the mystics who confidently explained all matters, varying in importance from mundane to galactic, in terms of cosmic patterns preset from the beginnings of time.

I was in a box.

Again.

Not just any box. I now rested, for the second time in one life, within the same clear med box where I'd spent my first hours on board the *Rigus.*

Of course, this time I was an honored guest, not a disease. *That did tend to improve matters.* I sipped nutrients from the straw thoughtfully left near my lips and settled back, relaxing in the reduced gravity the med-tech had programmed in for my comfort.

The Ket, while not everyone's favorite life-form, were so widely known to be inoffensive and sensitive beings that the Humans on the *Rigus* had been quite affected by Ragem's tale of my torture at the tentacles of the Queeb. Kearn himself had come to the station's med center, insisting that I be transferred to the *Rigus.* While the station meds had grumbled, they couldn't deny that I would heal more quickly in the ship's state-of-the-art facilities.

I flexed my fingers, wincing only a little. It made sense for a ship engaged in the risky business of exploration and first contact to carry the latest in healing acceleration technology. I was properly grateful. At this rate, I would soon be able to cycle back to this form without dreading the pain.

Though I would never forget it. I traced the curve of my trouble-causing hoobit with an intact finger, finding its texture doing little to soothe my emotions. For the first time

I truly understood why ephemeral authors so often referred to a perfect memory as a curse.

Tap. Tap.

I squinted up past the lights and saw Ragem's grin. The ship's med had assured me I could safely lift the lid for visitors. Having had none till now, I hadn't tried it. Fortunately, Ragem could see my hand fumbling for the control and did something outside that lifted the box with a soft whoosh of air. I sank deeper into the mattress as the gravity climbed back to Human-norm.

"How are you feeling, Nimal-Ket?" he asked as I sat up, carefully unfolding my limbs. It had taken a fair amount of contortion to fit me into this too short, too wide space. I'd been comfortable, but had no wish to crack a knee or elbow against any solid objects on my way out.

I also used this time to carefully examine this new, improved version of my first friend.

Gone were the blue ensign coveralls. Ragem was back in uniform, complete with an upgrade to his alien specialist bars. The tunic was snug enough to prove he no longer wore a telltale underneath. Still too thin, his face was much more like the one I remembered, with a familiar glint of curiosity and interest in his eyes.

Ket were typically unaware of the significance of clothing or rank to other beings, so instead of commenting directly, I reached my hand, very carefully, toward his face. Ragem moved closer so I could travel my intact fingers over his cheeks and brow. "Your life has improved, Paul-Human," I announced with satisfaction after this examination. "Is it because of your brave action to save this Ket?"

Ragem ever-so-lightly touched the hoobit, then perched on the cot across from mine. "If a Ket calls me brave, I consider that a great honor."

I laughed, which as a Ket entailed a painful amount of finger fluttering, so I stopped almost at once. "Every being knows we are not brave, Paul-Human. How does the expression go? 'Gropers are afraid of everything, but most especially bad credit?' "

"I know better, Madame Ket."

"Perhaps." I paused. "Or perhaps you simply witnessed that point beyond which I, as a Ket, was unable to go. Every species has its limit, Paul-Human, including yours."

I took a moment to curl most of my fingers around the hoobit for comfort. The three broken ones were artificially stiffened to encourage correct healing, but I did what I could to achieve the proper positioning.

"True. But I reserve the right to my own opinion, Nimal-Ket. And I have only once met someone with your courage."

Ragem's lips tightened briefly, then he went on, his voice oddly flat, eyes intent on me. "Her name is Esen-alit-Quar."

"The one you denied was a friend?" I countered, suddenly unable to avoid temptation.

"Esen was and is my friend. A good friend."

"Then why do you hunt her with this ship?"

His hands curled into fists on his knees. "I don't command the *Rigus.*"

"Yet you hunt her, too," I pointed out.

"I have something to tell her, Nimal-Ket. That's all."

Tell me what? All I wanted in that moment was to ask him. I could feel my double hearts pounding a confused beat as my Ket body did its best to interpret my turmoil.

And, suddenly, I knew. *Ragem suspected.* How or why, I didn't know, but I could see it in his eyes, in the way he leaned slightly toward me, the tilt of his head. He suspected, but wasn't sure. I couldn't allow his suspicion to become anything more.

Concentrating on being no more or less than a true Ket, I pulled a plas cube from under my pillow and showed it to him. "Has the station located the Queeb and his accomplices yet, Paul-Human? This Ket would like to file suit against their property as soon as possible."

"No. There's no sign of them beyond some traces of Human blood in the room where we were held. They must have had some bolt-hole ready we didn't notice." He took the cube. "I'll see if Station Claims will look after this for you. After all, they should be responsible for your safety."

"This Ket is grateful, Paul-Human. Between my own suffering and inability to service my clients, you can imagine my state of mind."

Ragem wrapped his hands around one knee, rocking back in a deceptively easier position. "Do you remember any more about what happened?"

Tenacity was one of Ragem's less useful virtues. "The Humans in the pay of the coarse Queeb tried to capture this Ket, no doubt to force you to release their benefactor," I repeated what I'd said earlier to authorities, as well as once already to Ragem. "They must have collided with sharp objects in the pile you left."

He wasn't satisfied. "Nimal-Ket," Ragem said earnestly, leaning forward again. "I really need to talk to my friend."

"We Ket value friendships, Paul-Human. I consider you and I to share that. Do you?"

He nodded, eyes gleaming as though he believed I was about to confess.

"Then let me advise you, Paul-Human," I said evenly. "There is a wise saying among Ket, 'To chase friendship is to lose it.' If your friend Esen prefers not to be found, you risk much by this pursuit."

He bowed his head, hiding his face from me. Then he said in a low, intense voice. "You spoke of a point, the limit beyond which none of us can go because of our very natures. Have I pushed Esen to that point already?"

"I am Ket, Paul-Human. I know only my limit."

"Answer me!" He flung up his head and I was stunned by the frustration in his face. "I've driven Es away once. I won't do it again."

"I have no answer for you."

"Yes, you do!" he almost shouted. "Why won't you give it?"

I stroked the hoobit. "Are you this difficult with all your friends, Paul-Human?"

"The ones I care about."

It was my turn to bow my head, to collect my thoughts and emotions before I made another mistake with this being. Then I looked at him. "Perhaps you should try trusting, as well as caring, Paul-Human."

Ragem stood, and gazed down at me. His eyes were troubled. "If I'm wrong in what I believe, someday I'll explain all this to you, Nimal-Ket."

I fluttered one hand in a careful chuckle. "This Ket would appreciate that, Paul-Human."

He touched the side of my long face gently. "But if I'm not wrong, my friend, please think about what I've said. It's a sad and dangerous thing to be alone."

Ragem left.

I repeated his words to myself as I lay back in my healing bed: "A sad and dangerous thing." *He was right.*

Which didn't change a thing.

25: Starship Evening

THOUGH we were no longer roommates—as a guest I rated my own cabin, particularly so I could ply my trade among the crew once my hands healed sufficiently—Tomas considered me his responsibility. His attachment didn't surprise me, knowing his kindly nature. He wasn't the only one to attempt to lure me into friendship. I'd noticed the tendency of this tightly-knit crew to rapidly engulf newcomers into their social life. My Ketself was considerably discomfited by so much affection, and I often found it necessary to retreat to this private space.

Tonight, Tomas had thoughtfully supplied me with the latest station newsmag along with my supper. The headline read: *Mysterious Disappearances Haunt Panacia; Government Refuses to Name Cause.* I read the article below, wincing at the number of missing, and nodded to myself. Unlike the Panacian Hive Government, I had no doubts about the cause. And neither did the reporter. *"The monster from the Fringe has not left or been destroyed,"* the article continued with the appropriate note of barely concealed panic. *"It is now a killer right in our midst. And it will continue taking lives unless the Commonwealth acts!"*

So, the Enemy was becoming almost subtle. "Not reassuring at all," I muttered to myself. A quieter carnage implied a need for concealment, perhaps even secrecy. *Why?* I had a uncomfortable certainty it was to allow the thing time to search for specific prey. I worried even more about Mixs. If this thing was Ersh's Enemy, as I was beginning to suspect, it was distressingly adaptable.

Ersh memory bubbled up through my consciousness of this room, the paper I read, and myself. . . .

* * *

Pain.

Need.

Too large. Too slow. Too much of me.

I writhed in remembered agony, facing with Ersh her first crisis. She hadn't known to control her appetite, to leave those she lived with in peace. She sensed the distinction between nonsentient tissue and that which thought, but didn't yet care . . .

. . . *Murderer,* I thought, feeling again the guilt Ersh gave me as well as the exquisite taste of the deed. *Parasite.* Such names had no meaning to the life I shared through memory . . .

. . . *Appetite.* I felt sick and excited by the hunger. *Something's wrong!* Can't cycle any more into the safe form. *Fear.* Too much of me. *Hide!*

Wise in the ways of her hosts, if not her own body, Ersh disappeared from their view, hiding in web-form, lurking in out-of-the-way places: feeding, growing, feeding, hoarding her mass like treasure. And finally, growing too large to survive.

Too much!

Pain. Fear. What is happening? The body demands a choice; the mind must loosen its hold and permit the escape of mass, or accept the death which beckons. Divide, or become solid, thoughtless, a rock: death by density as web-mass collapses permanently into itself.

I must live! Survival is all that matters. Selection begins on a microscopic scale. I shudder, reliving the battle of flesh against flesh, consciously experiencing reproduction for the first time both as Ersh and as myself. How much stays to maintain the parent? What escapes to a life of its own? Which will have the advantage . . .

. . . I found myself Ket again, a species whose reproduction seemed uncommonly civilized after the self-centered passion of Ersh. Relaxing my grip on the hoobit, I kept my lips pursed in a frown. *Why that memory?* Ersh's gifts to me resurfaced at the oddest moments, but I had no doubt there was a reason here, if only I was clever enough to spot it.

Deliberately, I closed my eyes and sought out that disturbing past, thousands of years older than my own . . .

. . . keep what's mine! Preserve self-awareness. Grasp and hold form memory. The battle wages, tormenting at every point.

It's done.

Tremble. Learn the new size. Perfection.

Not alone. Another web-form, smaller still, trembles nearby, sending confusing messages into the wind, troubling.

And incredibly appetizing . . .

I jerked myself free of the memory. Too late. Saliva made a cold runnel down my chin.

Ersh had remembered for me. The sweetest taste of all was torn from web-flesh.

Had Ersh-memory just shown me the true nature of our Enemy?

26: Hiveworld Twilight

"LOOK OUT!"

I didn't blink at Tomas' alarmed cry. A blur of speed, the hoverbot raised itself just in time, and just enough, to clear my head without so much as a breeze on my bare scalp. The personal transports were everywhere on D'Dsel, the Panacian Hiveworld; I hoped the Humans would hurry up and learn that they were more likely to collide with the local shrubbery.

"Glad to have such an experienced guide, Nimal-Ket," Ragem commented. The three of us had been sent out to sample the opinions of the local population, Acting Captain Kearn unconvinced by the assurances of staff from the ambassador caste, the only group authorized to contact other governments, that nothing was wrong and why didn't his crew simply enjoy a shore leave?

I wore a cloak here, sufficient to keep the, to a Ket, chill evening air from my bare shoulders and upper body. "This Ket's experience here, Paul-Human, is simply due to the fact that D'Dsel is worthy of several visits," I answered calmly. "Given the civilized and gentle nature of its inhabitants." Ragem rarely missed any chance to question me, to probe for something hidden behind whatever I said or did. Even Tomas, otherwise totally oblivious to anything subtle, was beginning to notice something odd in Ragem's manner toward me. Secure in my disguise of flesh, I found myself enjoying the game.

"Incoming!" Tomas seemed unlikely to appreciate the precision avoidance controls of the hoverbots either. His latest unnecessary lunge to the pavement left his normally pink complexion rather pale. "Don't they see me?" he complained, dusting off his knees and glaring at the receding globe.

"You assume the occupant is looking outside," Ragem chuckled. "The 'bots are automatics. I've heard the Panacians use their travel time to catch up on correspondence and other reading. They're busy folks. Speculation is that's why they came up with the hoverbots in the first place, so they can keep working while they move from place to place."

I gazed into Hiveworld's amber sky, already settling itself into night, decorated with hundreds of speeding globes of light dancing here and there, some tiny and distant as stars. I could explain more to Ragem. I could tell him how it felt to fly that way, to swarm with your kind in the still air of dusk, to be haunted by an evolutionary past left behind with wings and instinct.

However, that kind of insight could definitely fuel his suspicions further. I would tell him another day, perhaps. For now, we needed to find some grounded locals to talk to about the headlines. And specifically about their missing neighbors.

"Let's try the mineral baths on the next street," I suggested.

The baths were a reliable place to find Panacians interested in gossip. They were, in general, a reticent species—polite and reserved with others, especially the messier sorts such as mammals. Tucked into their favorite cubbyholes at the community spa, however, most adults succumbed to an urge to chat. We found a pair of older drones, well into their soak by the limp look of their appendages floating on the steaming water. I let Ragem and Tomas strip and gingerly join them. The attendant was unlikely to let the Humans overdo the pleasure. Still, I made note of the time.

I wandered as nonchalantly as I could over to the public vidphone on one wall. Mixs had passed me her most recent memories of this world in our last sharing, so I knew exactly where she was, or at least how to reach her. She was still using the last identity I remembered, Sec-ag Mixs C'Cklet, master architect and neuter of the planning caste, and business head of her chosen kin-group. She was so fond of this life that Ersh had reprimanded her for preying on the suggestibility of the Panacians with regard to reincarnation. I did admire Mixs' persistence. She'd convinced the bureaucrats of her favorite city to declare her dead, then acknowledge her reincarnation three times in a row. It had to be a record. Fortunately for the security of the Web, whether one believed in reincarnation or not, it was not uncommon for newly morphed Panacians to present themselves as a famous ancestor.

Ersh was not amused, but she chose to humor Mixs. Mixs' weakness was architecture. To her, this world, coated with willing builders, was a canvas on which to satisfy her wildest imaginings. Permanent buildings were unknown throughout the Panacian System. Panacians built, but always with the intention of rebuilding as soon as a better idea came along. They favored any construction technique that allowed them to disassemble as readily as build in the first place. In a species which disdained clothing or personal adornment, buildings blossomed overnight into ardent expressions of current fashion, roads and parkways were defined by the traffic of the previous month, and living space was never static.

And how they loved new technology. Traders from a thousand other worlds brought in cargoes of hardware, gadgetry, and new materials. The smart ones also brought ideas to sell, for the Panacians were very sensitive to the criticisms of others, and especially loved being thought of as up-to-date by other species.

The vidphone accepted my credit. There was no public access to any of the Sec-ag rank; they were by custom approached through intermediaries of low and trivial accomplishment. I keyed in the code Mixs kept for her own use, still cautious of using my newly-healed fingers, and requested a voice-only connection; I kept an eye on my companions in the bath.

"Who is this?"

The voice on the other end of the link was not Mixs'. It was also decidedly officious. Another reason I'd chosen the Ket form was its facility with pronunciation. The Panacian whirs and soft clicks were no challenge to this tongue and palate. It helped that Mixs maintained an ongoing fiction to pass any of her real kin through the social barriers raised by her multilevel and extremely protective family. "This is Nimal-Ket, a servant in the employ of Her Glory-D'Dsellan, Sec-ag Mixs C'Cklet-D'Dsellan. This Ket has the information Her Glory-D'Dsellan requested concerning the wondrous new roofing material developed on Epsilon XX."

"We have instructions from Her Glory to accept your communications with joy and anticipation, Madame Ket," the voice responded with appreciable enthusiasm. The arrival of a favored off-world contact was always an event for the entire family, since who knew what new construction technology would arrive at the same time. The incredibly strong and delicate modular framing struts of the Skenrans had inspired the total reconstruction of at least 50,000 buildings. The fad lasted an unprecedented three years, long enough to establish the family fortunes of Mixs' chosen kin-group and its Queen.

". . . please wait only a moment, Madame Ket. I delight to personally bring Her Glory's attention to you."

I stroked the cool casing of the vidphone, then the rough texture of the wall behind it, trying not to look obvious as I checked on Ragem and Tomas. They were still deep in conversation and steam.

"Nimal-Ket? How unexpected."

I clutched my hoobit in relief at the sound of that coldly precise and familiar voice. *When had my fear for her reached that level?* "Your Glory-D'Dsellan. This Ket has news of great urgency to give you."

"Give it." No questions, no revelations. Mixs was one of the best at protecting her cover. I'd always envied that about her.

"This Ket is on a public vid. I regret the need, but we must meet in private, Your Glory-D'Dsellan."

There was a series of clicks and a snap. Mixs wasn't happy; I hadn't thought she would be. She didn't like the unexpected. Actually, she didn't like me much either, despite our molecular-deep bond through the Web. But by any measurement that mattered, we were essential to each other. She wouldn't refuse.

And she didn't. A meeting place and time arranged, I stepped away from the vidphone and surveyed my remaining problem: how to move independently of my companions, without rousing Ragem's suspicions further?

As if he could hear my thoughts, Ragem's head turned to look at me. I fluttered fingers, the intact ones at least, at him and saw his answering grin. I hoped they'd learned something worthwhile; what I could see of their skin appeared unusually wrinkled and verging on red.

"Madame Ket?" I turned to the polite voice at my side. Panacians varied widely in their body form, and I was pleased to see the voice belonged to one of the ambassador caste. This slender, multlimbed, and graceful shape, rising almost to my shoulder, was a duplicate of the one I would wear as a Panacian. She was too young to be reproductive, but her shimmering blue carapace signaled her likely maturation as a producer—possibly even a future Queen within her family.

Of course, as a Ket I should show no sign that I recognized her beauty or rank. "How may I help you, young-D'Dsellan?" I replied in her language.

"My use name is P'Lka-D'Dsellan, Madame Ket." She offered one shapely, triple-hinged claw for my touch. It was cool and slick under my fingertips, like fine, polished marble. "I have been assigned as guide and liaison to your ship's complement. As you are the first crewmembers to disembark, I was notified of your location. Please let me know how I can help you enjoy our home." P'Lka bowed.

Liaison or spy. *Likely both,* I reasoned without disapproval. It was typical Hive thinking. P'Lka was also the perfect ally. It was inconceivable she would place any Human concerns or questions above the merest whim of her own kind. "I do require your assistance, P'Lka-D'Dsellan," I began, keeping an eye on my companions to be sure they stayed out of earshot. "I need some help arranging a private meeting."

"And she gave us these seats. Just like that."

I let my fingers race lightly over Ragem's coat sleeve, a delightful woven garment I suspected he'd chosen to attract my attention. "Her task is to please visitors, Paul-Human. Are you not pleased?"

"I'd be pleased if I knew why."

"Don't listen to him, Nimal-Ket," Willify said cheerfully from her seat in the row behind us. "Ragem's becoming much too glum for his own good. I swear he'll see a conspiracy in his next pay raise—if he gets one!"

There was a chorus of agreement from the dozen other crewmembers around us. P'Lka had been as good as her word, delivering this block of seats to one of the truly memorable spectacles on Panacia. The crew, and Ragem, appreciated the rare honor they were being granted.

We were at one end of the newly constructed amphitheater, its roof open to the night air. Rows of seats curved away from us on both sides to almost touch at the other side of the oval. There were easily a hundred rows above us, and as many below. Every seat was filled, most with Panacians of every caste, but a considerable number with aliens such as ourselves. I'd managed to wedge my long legs and arms between my Human companions with a minimal amount of good-natured collision.

There was the usual provision for the presence of Queens in a crowd: certain seats were set within barriers of living B'Bklar plants. I'd overheard Ragem explaining to Tomas how the plants were chosen both for their lovely flowers and their ability to absorb airborne organics, helping to neutralize the impact of each Queen's pheromones on her hapless neighbors.

The amphitheater itself had been constructed with great care around the event we were to see. It was a magnificent structure, curving back at its height as if encouraging the witness of the stars blazing in the cloudless night sky. Yet the amphitheater was merely a frame for what it cradled between its walls of spectators. It was the Spring Emergence.

The floor of the amphitheater was patterned in a mosaic of color and pattern that at first bewildered the eye. There were spirals and other curved forms. There were areas that seemed abstract, then resolved into meaning which slid away again as your eyes tried to encompass it. Panacians believed that aspects of the future could be predicted from analysis of the patterns. Already, those in the audience who had not seen the mosaic until tonight were entering their speculations on notepads or dictating memos. The result was a low roar of sound, more like the rise and fall of waves on an ocean shore than conversation.

The mosaic was composed of all the pupae ready to emerge this season, many from the surrounding countryside as well as the city itself. The timing was precise, predictable to the hour. The whitish-gray pupae were brought to this place months in advance, arranged in plain straight lines by neuters of every caste until the reed-strewn floor of the amphitheater-to-be was covered completely. Then, as construction of the viewing stand went on around the sleeping offspring, the color of each pupal case began to change. Some darkened to the purple of the builder caste, and enlarged to accommodate the last growth spurt to produce the requisite size and shape. Others took on the gold of harvesters, or the russet of rememberers. The proportion within each caste—and indeed the number of castes themselves—would be known only when all the pupae were mature.

There was one tear in the brilliant pattern below, a harshly angled hole revealing dull brown reeds below. I could hear the Humans around me asking about its significance. They were not answered. I could have told them the gap would have contained a cluster of pupae that had turned the warning orange of the warrior caste. The Panacians were capable of a coordinated ruthlessness beyond what Humans would find comfortable. Fifteen generations ago, the Hive had come to a simultaneous and largely unconscious decision, reinforced by the Queens' pheromones, that the warrior caste was no longer necessary in a peaceful, multispecies universe. In one day, not only had any warrior pupae been killed, but neighbor had turned on neighbor until all warriors were gone, on the colony worlds and ships, as well as on Hiveworld itself. The bloodshed was minimized solely by the fact that the warriors also accepted this decision and died willingly.

Although I deplored loss of life, nothing in me found this act of genocide offensive. It was the way of the Hive, to cull what wasn't necessary to the whole. It was equally their way to nurture the new, as witnessed by the evolution of the newest caste, the ambassadors, small enough to be comfortable in a starship, with mouthparts more capable of foreign speech, and a nature at once secretive and friendly. This development was quite deliberate, the Hive being as expert in engineering themselves as their buildings. It worked for them.

As the current spectacle worked for my purpose. A quiver, like the twitch of a dreaming child, started in the middle of the pupael cluster. There was a hint of movement suddenly across the floor of the entire amphitheater. The audience stopped its chatter and speculation, instead starting up an involuntary trilling sound, something all castes were capable of producing with an organ on their thorax; multiplied by hundreds of thousands the trill made speech quite impossible.

I tugged at Ragem's sleeve. When I had his attention, I made a grimace and held my hands against the sides of my head. The trill was pleasantly pitched to Human ears, but I was counting on Ragem not knowing my expression of discomfort wasn't real. I gestured that I was leaving. He cast a longing look at the now-incredible view of the thousands of pupael cases starting to crack in unison, then got up as if to accompany me. I smiled and pushed him firmly back in his seat, before making my awkward exit across laps, knees, and far too many feet.

When I glanced back, Ragem and his crewmates were gazing with rapture at the simultaneous birth of forty thousand adult Panacians.

P'Lka met me at the end of the row, her trill noticeable, but so automatic that she didn't seem to notice the music under her words. "A programmed hoverbot is waiting for you at the end of this corridor, Madame Ket. When you are finished your meeting with Sec-ag C'Cklet, it will return you directly to the shopping concourse. It is only a brief walk from there to your ship. Do you need directions?"

"No. This Ket is familiar with the area. Thank you again, P'Lka-D'Dsellan. Her Glory-D'Dsellan will hear of how you expedited the mission of this Ket on her behalf."

"I serve the Hive in all things," she murmured with obvious pleasure.

Out There

DEATH was still primitive, running on instincts from a lifetime between stars, but it was capable of learning. Caution had been the first lesson. *Avoid pain.* Ambush was a safer technique than pursuit, so Death began taking its pleasures in dark corners and lonely places.

Pleasure had been another lesson. Death no longer simply fed. Now it savored, relished, took its satiation with the attention it deserved. A pity its prey didn't appreciate the honor.

Most importantly, Death had learned to have a goal. The new prey it had tasted once, briefly, so tantalizingly, *must* be found again.

And, on one of the worlds in a system called Panacia, Death had at last come across a hint of what it wanted, a trace of seductive flavor on the wind, a direction to hunt.

Death moved stealthily across the planet's surface, determined not to miss this opportunity, only consuming those unfortunate enough to fall in its path, following the trail, almost blinded by wanting.

27: Hiveworld Night

RAGEM and Tomas had been able to coax some disquieting information from the drones at the mineral bath. I considered what they told me as my hoverbot danced and jigged its way among dozens of others, the D'Dsellan version of waiting to land. The deaths, or rather disappearances, had originally occurred on the other continent, then stopped. They'd suddenly begun again on this side of the freshwater ocean, but with less frequency. The most recent disappearances had been in this city, which was why Kearn had chosen this spaceport for the *Rigus* out of the seven on D'Dsel. Tomas and others of the crew speculated it was most likely some criminal, perhaps a crazed xenophobe of sorts: somebody a planetary authority could catch.

I looked down at the warmly lit globes below that marked the outer ring of homes of Mixs' kin and really hoped Tomas was right. And I was wrong.

Abruptly, the hoverbot dropped to within a handsbreath of the ground and halted. The antigrav inside completely dampened both the acceleration and stop; nonetheless, I gulped. As a Ket, I wasn't the best at high-speed maneuvering. There was no time to collect my thoughts as the door opened and the seat in the 'bot urged me upright.

"Madame Ket."

Something's wrong. I felt my hearts pounding as I took in the somber expressions on the two Panacians standing before me on the landing platform. The surrounding garden was beautifully lit, a lush display of living architecture I'd otherwise have enjoyed examining. "Where is Her Glory-D'Dsellan?" I whispered.

The younger of the two seemed to crumble into herself, her four upper appendages wrapped tightly around her thorax in an expression of grief and despair.

I didn't hesitate. Mixs' memory in mine contained the most recent plan of the entire complex. I knew where she would have met me. They called out as I hurried past them, but didn't otherwise object.

No one did. Every member of Mixs' family I passed in the convoluted hallways acted oblivious to my presence and my urgency, caught in the paralysis the D'Dsellans felt in the presence of tragedy. I might have been invisible, except that in my haste I bumped into an older drone, then almost tripped over the tools of a builder left abandoned in a doorway, sending them sliding across the polished floor to crash into a wall.

Mixs' room. It was a huge expanse, with tables covered in scale models and benches festooned with bits and pieces of construction materials. There wasn't a chair to be seen—typical of Mixs. This was where she worked, not rested.

I stepped inside very slowly, careful where I placed my bare feet, unsure if what was left of the ceiling would stay in place. No wonder the other D'Dsellans were in a horrified daze.

Titans had battled here.

Trembling, on the verge of losing form, I screamed "Mixs! Mixs!" only to have my voice lock itself somewhere inside. Slipping on broken bits of dreams, I searched the room, hurrying as much as I could without the risk of losing some clue. Then, like a nightmare, I saw it.

A hint of blue glistened along the spiked edge of a shard of glass. I gripped my hoobit like an anchor, resisting the urge to consume and learn. Impulse overcome, for the moment at least, I wrapped the glass in a piece of fabric and tucked it into the carrysack I wore around my waist. The web-flesh would spoil and lose whatever it could tell me within minutes, but I couldn't cycle here. Already, groups of silent Panacians were gathering in the doorways to this shattered place, watching me between awed glances at the scorched hole that had replaced the ornate raised ceiling.

"Madame Ket, the Queen will speak to you."

My grip on the hoobit became an absolute clench. But I nodded graciously at whomever spoke and followed without protest. The Queen of any family here was the final law; a comfortable enough arrangement to one raised by Ersh.

* * *

The Queen of Mixs' family was old enough to keep her successor close at hand where she could learn the family business and understand its management, and young enough to insist her beloved heir sit on the floor, two steps below the ring of drones that never left their Queen's side. I bowed as I passed through the tingle of the force field that concentrated the Queen's pheromones for transport to all of her diffuse family, and waited for her to speak. It was a singular honor, if one I could have done without as Mixs' fate continued to rot in my pouch.

"Madame Ket." The Queen's voice was feather-soft yet clear. "You come to us on a night of terror. I remember dear Mixs telling us to trust her courier. Can you explain the events here?"

"Tell me what happened, and I will try, Queen-D'Dsellan," I said as quietly, my own passions subdued by the calm in this place, a calm reinforced by the absence of corners or edges, by the complex, subtle patterning of the walls.

The Queen raised a claw. One of the four drones attending her spoke from his place at her feet. "There were terrible cries from Her Glory's workroom, the sounds of furniture being broken. We rushed to Her aid, only to be thrown from our feet by a tremendous explosion. The harvester in the garden saw a projectile, like a streak of light, break through the roof and head into space. The house watchers have found no evidence. They have not found Her Glory either."

I must control myself. Fiercely I shot up my temperature to the limit this form could tolerate and remain conscious in an effort to keep form integrity. *Mixs gone?* I had to deal with this part of her family before I could deal with my own loss or its cause.

"This Ket does not know what has happened, Queen-D'Dsellan," I admitted. "But I feel certain that Her Glory has been murdered." I paused while the audience and the Queen trilled their distress. "The vessel which brought this Ket to D'Dsel is searching for a creature that—" I stumbled over the word, "—hunts this way. We feared it had reached your world."

The Queen curled herself into a posture of despair. Almost instantly, all of the other Panacians followed suit, helplessly obedient to the emotional signals she released into the air. I took a step backward, then halted as she raised her head and gazed at me with her glowing eyes. "There will be cooperation with the Commonwealth ship, Madame Ket. We wish this creature eliminated as a threat." She made a gesture of dismissal. "Mixs' business with you is not of their concern. I expect your discretion as you may ours." She straightened, gesturing gracefully with one slender limb. "We shall await the next incarnation of our beloved Mixs."

How could I explain? I hesitated, torn between the truth and comfort. Perhaps there was no need. In the way of the D'Dsellans, Mixs' name could well rise again in the next generation. That it wouldn't *be* Mixs this time mattered only to me and mine.

I bowed and left.

There was only one chance to find out what had happened. Once inside the hoverbot, I disabled its interior sensors, cycling into web-form almost instantly. I consumed both pouch and glass in my haste, but what mattered was the trace of Mixs and what it might tell me.

An instant later, I cycled back to Ket, replaced the hoobit and pulled on my skirt in a breathless contorted struggle that would have been amusing under other circumstances, and reactivated the sensors.

All I'd tasted was surprise.

Out There

DEATH writhed in ecstasy and confusion, careening through space like a comet, shedding excess mass in a spree of self-destruction that ended far short of pain.

Self-awareness.

Assimilation.

All she knew, *I know.*

All she was, *I am.*

Death, confident and full of purpose, took note of the stars and distances.

That way. My next feast is there!

28: Starship Morning

"THERE'S been another disappearance," Ragem announced, not bothering with politeness. At least he'd pitched his voice for my ears only before dropping into the seat opposite mine in the galley. The engineering shift from last night was busy cleaning up from their supper and preparing to play some game or other. The officers from the day shift were filing in for breakfast and discussing protocols. There seemed a surprising amount of activity for a ship on the ground. "A Sec-ag of the planning caste. Right out of her home."

I looked up from my plate. "Not an auspicious beginning to the day, Paul-Human."

Ragem accepted a cup of sombay from Lawrenk Jen as she passed with a trayful, nodding an absent thanks. His gray eyes focused on the fragrant steam curling upward, then lifted to mine. "It happened last night. During the Spring Emergence." He took a larger than normal swallow and grimaced. "Where were you, Nimal-Ket?"

I fluttered my fingers in a deliberate chuckle. "This Ket sought peace and quiet, Paul-Human, as you know."

"Where?"

So. I gazed at his face, noting its deliberately mild expression. *Ragem should never play cards with Lawrenk Jen's crew,* I thought. His eyes always betrayed him. Right now they were quite alarmingly suspicious.

I picked up a piece of toasted bread and enjoyed the sensation of pulling it into bite-sized pieces. The outer surfaces were prickly in delectable counterpoint to the soft interior. Many Human foods were this contradictory. *Shame they had no perceptible taste to this form.* But I'd procured some Ket sauces in the market on my way back to the ship and I tapped one of the small jars with a finger before I dipped the toast into my favorite. It had a standard poison warning on it—Panacians were no more capable of ingesting Ket delicacies than Humans. "This Ket enjoyed the market, Paul-Human. I do not understand your curiosity about the doings of this Ket when such a tragedy has taken place." I let my voice grow stern.

Ragem picked up one of the jars, his relief as transparent to me as his suspicion. I'd bought them because I knew perfectly well he would check what time I'd arrived at the ship, and would demand an explanation for why it took me so long after leaving the ceremony. *How much simpler to arrange to tell the truth.*

Thinking of the truth cost me my appetite. I'd had a difficult night, trying to make myself believe Mixs could be dead when everything I knew said we couldn't die. Worse was my suspicion, almost certainty, that she had been consumed against her will. I could imagine the terror and pain of that ending all too well.

She should have ended by her choice, some unimaginable millennia from now. She should have become solid, a monument to her life, perhaps a small moon orbiting this world she loved. What I carried in my substance of her memory was all there would ever be now.

"Kearn has been sent the sensor records for the area where the disappearance occurred," Ragem had continued, oblivious to my distress or attributing it to the topic. "The Panacians are finally taking our investigation seriously. Guess it took the loss of someone of sufficient rank."

The loss of part of me. "What do these records show, Paul-Human?" I asked, not hoping for much.

"Whatever it was—and right now there's no agreement whether the records show a vessel of unknown design, a projectile launched from the room, or even a life-form—it's left the Hiveworld. The orbital sensors lost it almost immediately, but the Panacian techs are certain it's also left their system."

The Enemy was gone. I was safe. Guilt ran up the heels of that treacherous relief. If the monster was a web-being, a conclusion I no longer doubted, within hours it could have assimilated some or even all of Mixs' memories. It would know I was on D'Dsel. *I'd tried not to think about that.* The explosion that ripped open the roof—Mixs' death throes or last effort at defense—must have sent the being into space, inadvertently saving me from being detected immediately. I'd been that close to sharing Mixs' fate. I couldn't help moaning and grabbed my hoobit to gain some self-control.

"Don't worry, Nimal-Ket," Ragem said immediately, concerned at my reaction, if misunderstanding it. "We do have a trajectory to follow and several tracker probes have been launched."

"Where is it going, Paul-Human?" I asked, holding my voice steady. *And how?*

Ragem frowned, but not at me. "That's the puzzle, Nimal-Ket. If it holds a direct course, the thing will pass through the major arm of the Jeopardy Nebula. There are no inhabited planets along that route at all. Not even a regular shipping lane."

No planets, I thought numbly. Ersh's unforgiven past was close enough to my consciousness now that I did know one taste of web-flesh would never be enough. And planets weren't the only source of life. "There is an artist colony just outside this nebula, Paul-Human," I said. "It's very small. Very private."

And Lesy lived there, painting rather badly, singing rather well, as she waited for Ersh to give her another culture to remember for us all.

Needless to say, Kearn wasn't thrilled by my urging him to take his ship to protect a colony of perhaps forty beings. Artists, no less. At least he had no trouble accepting that I knew its location; Ket could be depended upon to have contacts in the most obscure places. There was less difficulty arranging to stay on the ship. Most of the crew, including Kearn, visited me regularly and were distraught at the mere thought I might leave, even though I was thoroughly Ketlike in my bookkeeping and the ship's debt was climbing nicely.

"We haven't completed our investigation here, Madame Ket," Kearn said, plainly trying to find a way to say no without dismissing me too abruptly. He continued happily, "I've been granted an appointment this afternoon with Secag P'Clor of the rememberer caste to discuss the pattern of disappearances—"

"We have all of the D'Dsellan's pertinent data. sir." This from my unexpected ally, Sas, the Modoren security officer. Sas twitched constantly as if the instinct to chase was literally painful to control. "I must agree with Madame Ket that our time is better spent in pursuit."

"The local patrol has offered to forward any new information they collect to us, sir. After all, we aren't investigators," Ragem added unwisely.

Kearn's happy mood evaporated and he began stroking his head—not a good sign, as I remembered well. But he really had no good reason to keep the *Rigus* rooted to the ground, beyond his ambition to personally visit every high official on Panacia's Hiveworld. Not that I suspected him of such shallow motivation. No, Kearn had taken to the role of detective with an enthusiasm I found disquieting.

"Well, the main thing is not to lose this Esen character," he said ponderously, needlessly confirming my worst fears. *He still believed I was the monster.* "We don't know what the capabilities of her vessel may be."

I made my fingers flutter. "You remain convinced these disappearances are being caused by this pup, Captain? This Ket does not understand."

Kearn gave me a warm smile. "There are many things about Esen that you do not know, Madame Ket, and I am not at liberty to reveal. Trust me when I say she is more than capable of these actions. All the remains is to uncover her motive—then we'll be able to predict her actions and capture her at last."

I bowed my head in acceptance; Kearn was, oddly enough, right in a way. As a web-being I was capable of almost all that had happened. With one exception.

Of all that Ersh had shared with us, she had never taught us how to fly.

Later, I went in search of Ragem. He was in the nexus room, where he shared a research console with the ship's protocol officer, Willify. I found them both deep in concentration over one of the screens; I chose to wait for them to notice me rather than interrupt, finding a quiet spot near a wall to crouch in comfort.

The nexus was one level below the operations bridge, where the astrogator and other officers controlled the ship's movements. In many ways, the nexus was more important to the *Rigus'* function, since it contained the information on which any first contact would be based, from communications monitoring to linguistics, biosensors to defense. The room was easily three times as large as the bridge, yet seemed crowded. This perhaps had more to do with the casual attitude of those in it than numbers, since at the moment at least five conversations were going on, most across the entire room. Several hands and other appendages were waved at me. *Such excellent customers,* my Ketself preened.

As I moved my long-toed feet out of the way of a preoccupied Quebit, Ragem waved me over. "Hello, Nimal-Ket. I've got the pattern of disappearances on D'Dsel laid out now. Did you want to see for yourself?"

I allowed him to see my shudder. Besides, there was nothing there that would help their hunting or mine. I stood. "This Ket has come with a request, Paul-Human. If I may have your attention for a moment?"

"Of course." Ragem nodded toward an area near the door which was marginally quieter.

"What can I do for you, Nimal-Ket?"

My toes found an imperceptible flaw in the flooring and rubbed at it. I made the rest of myself be still. This hadn't been an easy decision, but I was wild with impatience. "I wish to send a message."

"You are certainly welcome, Nimal-Ket, as long as our equipment is capable. To whom?" Ragem's eyes had that disturbing keenness. I almost balked. But it was Lesy's life.

"This Ket has a valued client in the artists' colony."

One eyebrow lifted. "Near the Jeopardy Nebula."

I nodded. "May I send a message, Paul-Human? Your captain rightly has concerns about alarming the public before we are certain of danger. Yet this Ket has an obligation. You may see the contents of this message first."

"Nimal-Ket—" he began, his head starting to shake.

"This Ket will pay any cost," I added hurriedly, my fingers restless at the seams of my skirt, finally composing themselves in the hoobit's comforting curve.

"It's not necessary, Nimal-Ket. We've sent a general warning translight, recommending caution with unidentified vessels requesting dock, stepping up security, requests for reports of unusual activities."

"Has Portula Colony responded to this message, Paul-Human?"

He hesitated, then shrugged. "No. But depending on their funding and tech, they could send their mail and com using scheduled bursts or even probes. We might not hear anything until we're within a day of the outpost. You know the saying: *Only bad news travels translight.*"

I stooped, dropping my chin to my hoobit to put my eyes in line with his. "How long until we reach the Nebula, Paul-Human?"

Willify, who was passing by at that moment, sang out: "If we push her, five standard days, Madame Ket." She kept on going.

"So long," I whispered. "So much could happen by then."

The Human didn't answer for a moment. His eyes searched my face. "Nimal-Ket, my friend," he said ever-so-softly. "How long until you tell me the truth?"

He wouldn't have liked my answer to that.

Out There

THE tracker probe was inorganic. This did not mean it was without limited awareness. So when the moving dot of energy locked within its sophisticated sensors slowed and came about, the tracker hesitated. Its programming included remaining inconspicuous. It did not include defending itself against boarders.

Death tasted the knowledge of *construction* and *technology* that floated up within its consciousness as it touched the cold exterior of the probe. No life. No food. But opportunity. The one it hungered for would accept a message from such a machine.

And Mixs-memory supplied the words.

29: Nebula Midnight

LIFT. Three days translight. Once convinced, Kearn was apparently pushing the *Rigus* to her limit. The engines howled between decks as if they knew their complaint would be unheard in space and were determined their effort be appreciated.

It didn't matter. I was going to be too late. I knew it. Lesy was going to die in the jaws of that thing. Another piece rent from my life without my being able to do a thing about it.

Damn Ersh.

My cabin door was locked. I could no longer marshal the proper calm detachment to let me service my clients. I'd probably leave bruises in even the Modoren's tough hide.

I'd tried to think like the monster. It had been too easy. The nightmare returned just at the remembrance . . .

. . . forming jaws, jagged teeth, for one purpose.

Web-flesh in my jaws. A thrill of pain from every molecule of the other. An explosion of taste far beyond mere appetite. I conquered. I seized.

Assimilation.

Disappointment. This was my flesh, shed for a purpose I only dimly remembered. Distraction. What was left fled, but I knew it was too little to survive. Disassociation would follow . . .

Ersh had tried to consume her first offspring and almost succeeded, despite the reason she'd fissioned. The instinct to consume and assimilate was that strong. No recollections had surfaced concerning the fission that had produced my sister beings. I hoped this meant Ersh had learned to control this particular taste; just as likely. Ersh thought it was none of my business. She had very specific things for me to learn from her memories.

If what I had learned was terrifying, what I suspected was worse. The monster would have some of Mixs' memories, perhaps all. The explosion on Panacia was due to the transformation of web-matter into energy, but whose matter? And why? I didn't know how one web-being might fight another, with the exception of cutting remarks and the odd fit of pique.

Running in the opposite direction could be my best move, and I was afraid enough to wish it were possible at least once an hour. But I was too angry at the loss of Mixs and the stalking of Lesy to do more than acknowledge it. It was a moot point anyway, given I was on a ship doing its utmost to gain on my Enemy.

A rhythmic humming sound brought me back to the here and now. The vibrations seem to emanate from the door. *This was a new tactic.* I'd refused to answer the polite chimes and com buzzes since yesterday, a not-unusual Ket tendency when seeking a respite from other species.

Curious in spite of myself, I placed my long fingers delicately on the door's cool metal. The humming was quite melodic to my Ket tastes, the feel of what was truly music soothing to my hands. I allowed myself a few seconds to enjoy the sensation, then realized there was likely only one person on board who would use this method to get my attention.

Maybe he could take my mind off useless speculation. Either we would be in time to save Lesy, she would escape herself, or— I stopped thinking and cued the door to iris open.

"You sang, Paul-Human?"

Ragem looked around for somewhere safe to deposit the formidable-looking sonic wrench he was unsuccessfully hiding behind his back, then gave up. "Good evening, Nimal-Ket."

I reached out my hands. He passed me the tool somewhat sheepishly. It was warm from his grip and from its recent use. "You weren't answering your door. I was worried."

My Ket hands were more than strong enough to heft the truly amazing tool. I would have to share this with Ansky;

she knew several Ket musicians who were always looking for innovative instruments. The molding process had deposited some intriguing surface details on the wrench I explored while I considered what to do with Ragem. "Where on a ship like this do you use such a tool, Paul-Human—besides on the door of this Ket?"

"No idea," he grinned. "Lawrenk had it in her locker."

I stood to one side of the doorway, tacit invitation. "And what is so important you had to resort to this method of gaining my attention, Paul-Human?"

Ragem looked over his shoulder before entering, then closed and relocked the door. I didn't need his sudden air of secrecy to know he was planning to grill me again on my true nature. I wrapped my fingers more firmly around Lawrenk's pilfered tool and rather fondly calculated the range to his head. *What was it going to take to convince Ragem to leave me as a Ket?*

"You look like one who could benefit from the services of this humble Ket, Paul-Human." I offered, sure I was correctly gauging the tension in the set of his shoulders and neck.

"I wasn't sure I'd find you here, Nimal-Ket." Ragem's hands were restless. As if uncomfortable in my presence, the Human paced the small room, making me turn my head almost fully around to keep watching him.

"And where else would I be, Paul-Human?"

He threw up his hands in an odd, angry motion. "In a drawer. Out there, chasing whatever we're chasing. Invisible. How should I know?"

The wrench was too much temptation. I laid it gently on a shelf intended for personal possessions. As Ket, I had none but the hoobit. As Web, I had only my flesh and my link to those of my flesh—and this Human, difficult as he could be. I made my voice and posture as unruffled as his was barely controlled. "Paul-Human, if you have something to say to this Ket which will make sense, I would gladly hear it. Otherwise, I would appreciate returning to my contemplations."

"Always the Ket." Thankfully, he stopped his prowling about and sat on one of the two chairs in the room.

I didn't even bother asking what else I could be—it would only give him an opening. "As you are always the

Human," I responded instead, fluttering the fingers of both hands as I crouched politely near him, though there was nothing funny at all about our continued fencing around the truth. "Have you heard anything further about the object of our pursuit, Paul-Human?"

"Bits and pieces from Panacia. Nothing we hadn't surmised from the data on our own by now. But we've received a list of the artists and staff on Portula Colony." Ragem passed me a slip of plas from his pocket. I took the slim thing between two fingers and glanced down at the names. *Lesy.* Her name on the list was Riosolesy-ki, her species' Dokecian, something she had in common with about a third of the other artists. The Dokeci form had many advantages to her art, including a rare breadth of visual acuity and a brain capable of controlling the independent action of five extraordinarily mobile arms. Few Dokecians retained this mobility as adults, their strength fading at middleage, too weary to do more than languish on pillows, cared for by their smaller, stronger offspring while they themselves discussed the adventures of their own youth. Lesy, like other mature adults who wished to continue an un-Dokecian active lifestyle, sought out null or low gee environments.

Such as provided by the luxurious surroundings of Portula Colony. I'd visited her there several times, sent not so much because Ersh felt I could learn from Lesy as to get me out of Ersh's way when I'd been particularly obtuse. The exile never bothered me; I loved null-gee swimming, and Lesy's pool was bathed in the rainbow glow of the seething Jeopardy Nebula. And the food!

In her favorite form, I'd seen Lesy paint three different views of the Nebula, while simultaneously sculpting in clay and using a fine laser to etch crystal. She was so productive—and her work so consistently unremarkable—her fellow artists had convinced her to store her masterpieces for safety in pods tethered to the colony. They were kind, Lesy was happy, and the colony was a model of harmony.

Was, I thought numbly, not believing in the throbbing engines or the mercies of fate.

"Is your client on the list?"

I shook off my sense of doom. "Yes, Paul-Human. There." I pointed to a name three below Lesy's on the list.

No sense giving this bright-eyed searcher any more than he needed.

"I asked Captain Kearn about sending your message. While he didn't agree to that—as I warned you—" this when I looked up hopefully, "he did try to contact the colony himself. There's been no reply yet." Ragem paused and considered the way his fingers were folded around each other on his knee. "Which could easily be explained by the type of equipment they have—or its condition. Techs are scarce out here; breakdowns are common," a tightness to Ragem's lips belied the reassuring tone of his voice.

"What you say is true. But this Ket is not optimistic, Paul-Human."

Ragem studied my face. I bore the scrutiny, confident that my somber Ket features would tell him nothing useful. *How could a disguise be flawed that was genetically perfect to the last cell? Cut me and I would bleed Ket.*

"This being you know in the colony, Nimal-Ket. Martha Smith. She's more than a client, isn't she?"

I drummed my finger on the hoobit, a welcome distraction. "This Ket does not specify her relationships to others."

"No?" For the first time, I saw a glint of something truly hostile in Ragem's eyes. "Yet you expect us to take this ship and crew in the direction of your choice, into a danger you may understand and we do not. Is that correct, Madame Ket?"

I hadn't put it to myself quite that way, but I couldn't argue the point. "You asked me for my help, Paul-Human," I countered. "Perhaps I should have asked under what terms you were accepting it."

"What did you say?" he whispered, hostility forgotten, leaning forward and staring at me, eyes wide.

What did I say? I wondered as urgently, knowing I'd somehow given everything away to him. Then I remembered, and watched the echoing recollection slide across his face at the same time. As Esen-alit-Quar, I'd asked Ragem almost that exact question when confronted with Kearn's plans for me.

It was always the little things, I thought with complete disgust. *Ersh.*

"What did you say?" Ragem asked again, louder, rising

to his feet as though pulled by strings on his shoulders. I rose too, towering over him, bewildered to still feel dwarfed. "Who are you?"

The room was too small. My options certainly were. "Don't—" I clenched the hoobit, letting my body temperature soar. "Please don't ask these questions, Paul-Human."

His expression softened, softened but remained committed. His left hand brushed the curve of the hoobit and over my fingers, then reached up to touch the side of my face lightly. His fingertips were ice cold on my skin. "You're burning up. But it's not a fever, is it?" he asked, amazed. "Is this how you maintain control?" I had little doubt he was thinking back to the time I'd lost control so dramatically in Kearn's office. *Damn his curiosity.*

I closed my eyes. "You are crazy even for a Human. Go away," I said faintly. "I have no wish to continue this conversation, Paul-Human."

"Es—"

The shrill peeping of an incoming message was so well-timed I thought Ragem would explode himself with questions and emotions. I dodged around him to touch the companel. "This Ket answers," I said, somewhat breathlessly.

"Madame Ket, this is Tomas. We've received a translight signal from Portula Colony. Captain Kearn thought you should be notified."

I must have said something affirmative, for Tomas continued: "It was their automated distress beacon. I'm sorry. There's been nothing else."

I shut off the com. *Lesy.*

"Es?"

Another piece of me stolen.

"Esen? Is this you?"

Without looking at him, I waved one hand at the door, sharply enough to rouse a hot little spurt of pain from my recently-healed fingers. "Go."

The door closed before I could act on the impulse to reach for the comfort of my friend and finally betray what I was.

30: Nebula Afternoon; Colony Night

ERSH-MEMORY had given me something new about my kind—something Ersh had neglected to share with the others or include in my normal education.

Web-flesh did quite well *out there.*

While I hadn't yet proved that to my own satisfaction nor, until now, contemplated doing so, the web-flesh I could see streaked along the outside of Sas' helmet looked unaffected, its lush blue gleaming and perfect despite its passage within the exposed shards and twisted wreckage of what had been Portula's beautiful spheres. My fingers ran restlessly around the port's rim as I fought the urge to somehow rush to the tiny bit of mass and learn whose it was, confirm who had been lost.

Other things had certainly died. There was sufficient gore adrift outside the *Rigus* to have silenced all conversation within the ship's galley. I was dimly surprised no one had suggested closing off the view.

A helpless place, peopled by introspective beings who paid handsomely for their peace and this setting. I couldn't take my eyes from the blue-tainted helmet, now making its inevitable way toward the ship, but on some level I was aware of the vast Nebula as it pulsed and blossomed beyond what was left of the colony.

"They'll check everywhere," Ragem said in a low voice. He hadn't been one of the handful of the crew qualified to take part in the search, hazardous in the extreme as they clambered over and sometimes cut their way through twisted, broken plas and metal; like those gathered here, he'd been a mute observer. "There are storage pods linked to the colony along its spinward axis," he continued. "Maybe—"

"No, Paul-Human," I explored his face, tracing out the creases of his despair. "Please warn your searchers that those pods contain finished art by the colonists. I believe the pods contain preservative gases and some works may be sensitive to a loss of pressure. This Ket suggests you take care; the pods' contents are the legacy of those who have been lost."

Ragem moved away to pass along my warning to someone, then came back to keep vigil with me. There had been no further questions or innuendoes. Whether he now believed he knew the truth or was merely sensitive to my grief, I couldn't tell. Nor did I, at the moment, care. *I had other priorities, starting with that web-stained helmet.*

"This Ket may be able to give some comfort to your crewmates, Paul-Human. Surely this task of hunting among the dead is distressing."

Ragem touched my hoobit graciously. "You are kind, Nimal-Ket, to think of them."

"They are my clients," I said, as if he were foolish to remark on it. Ket, while not truly compassionate, were capable of a deep sensitivity to other species' emotional states. It was good business as well as their nature. "So this Ket can be ready, please tell me what procedures will be followed to bring your crewmates safely within this ship, Paul-Human. Will there be any delays?"

What Ragem described was worse than I thought. No remnant of Lesy—or the Enemy—would remain on the helmet if Sas followed the full decontamination protocols. Knowing the Modoren's fastidiousness, I had little doubt it would.

I rubbed one finger in a tiny circle on the plas, over and over, as if to somehow taste the black emptiness so close. Web-form could survive out there.

Maybe.

The *Rigus* observed Commonwealth standard time, a diurnal pattern based on the spin of a planet orbiting a sun so far back in Human history it was now legend. I thought idly I should spend more time recalling Ersh-memories of what Terra had been like, gain more understanding of Ragem's kind, since I seemed to be spending most of my time surrounded by Humans. In the meantime, I appreciated the convenience of a lengthy span of dimmed lighting and skeleton crew. The *Rigus* watched for the Enemy with her automatics and a few sleepless beings at their posts. I knew the enemy was gone, having found and taken what it sought.

But where?

There was only one way I could find out. I moved as quietly as possible down the crew corridor, something my Ket preference for barefoot travel made easier, slipping past the solitary bar of brighter light marking where those still seeing the nightmare of the shattered colony behind their eyelids had gathered for comfort in the galley. It was highly unlikely anyone, including Ragem, would approve of my intentions. *Better they never even know,* I'd decided.

The *Rigus* had two main locks, one for personnel and the other capable of swallowing immense crates of supplies. Both had ample warning systems against unauthorized exit or entry.

But the Quebits, dear little doorknobs that they were, had their own set of air locks, several on each level. The tiny beings needed access to all areas of the ship, inside and out, in order to carry out their assigned tasks of maintenance and repair. I'd overheard Lawrenk Jen complaining that off-duty Quebits liked suiting up, plastering themselves to the outside of the ship, and admiring the display caused by venting pressurized plasma. Since her staff were responsible for the plasma stores, she was understandably less than impressed by this evidence that Quebits weren't quite as dull as everyone believed.

Having been a Quebit on one less-than-memorable occasion, I could reassure Lawrenk that they really were the most boring of species. One day in that form and I'd felt as though my brain was solidifying. Ersh hadn't thought much of my reaction. She'd wanted the Quebit form to teach me patience and devotion to duty.

There. I spotted a pair of Quebits in a branching corridor and started following them. They softly whistled and popped in conversation, oblivious to my presence. *Typical.* Well, I didn't need their form; I needed their door.

The two I'd followed met a third, this one already half-stuffed into an evac-suit. The suit made the little creature even more closely resemble an animated sausage topped with a bouquet of budding flowers. The suited Quebit exchanged some whistles with its crewmates before expressing a second pair of foot appendages, the suit material stretching easily, and trotting away.

Our mutual destination wasn't far. The portal was ergonomically designed, for Quebits, consisting of a circular entrance about the diameter of my hoobit, located slightly above the floor. The crew being hesitated just as it was to enter, then gave an exasperated whistle and continued down the corridor. "Wrong door?" I said, but to myself. *Perfect.* I checked the corridor in both directions again. *No one.*

Beside the portal was a stow-it, one of the small cupboards set at intervals into the bulkheads of most ships in order to allow crew to quickly secure loose objects in case of gravity failure. This one was empty.

I checked one final time to make sure I was alone and unobserved. The corridor was too short to warrant a scanner box. One would have recorded my passing this way from the larger corridor, but I should be unseen here.

I pulled off the hoobit and skirt, shoving them into the stow-it, letting go of the circlet with the reluctance of my Ketself. *I'd been in this form too long.* Then I cycled.

I flowed into the Quebit portal as quickly as I could, anxious at the exposure of my true self. I'd never stayed in web-form so near aliens. The tubelike entrance was barely long enough to hold all of my mass, yet I didn't dare shed any, not if I was going to become Nimal-Ket again.

I paused, comforted beyond words by my own shape, in spite of being packed into a tube. Gravity hummed its symphony within the structure of the *Rigus;* I could sense the interplay of tension and stress restraining the ship against the invitation of vacuum.

Vacuum. I tasted the mechanisms responsible for the doors to seal this cylinder from the interior of the ship, then open it to space. The inner door operated automatically, opening and closing to allow passage as long as there was air on both sides. The outer door was the problem. It wouldn't release unless the air within had been evacuated—a most annoying and typically Human safety feature. Without appendages, I couldn't manipulate the evacuation controls, but I thought I could fool the device.

I absorbed every molecule of gas from within the cylinder. The tricky bit was keeping my own mass tightly compressed so that the space around me would register as airless. The process generated an uncomfortable amount of heat. *Hurry up,* I urged the sensors. *How much vacuum do you need?*

A faint vibration signaled the release of the outer lock. *Success.* Pushing I could do, so it was a simple matter to open the door to space.

The instant I did so was the same instant I realized I had no proof this wouldn't kill me. *Fine time to think of that,* I chided myself. After a few ominous seconds, I didn't feel any discomfort. *So far, so good.*

I'd planned how to prevent the lock from sealing behind me; it required a temporary sacrifice, not cleverness. I used the door itself to help me cut off a portion of my body, after shunting all memory from the piece to be abandoned. The piece, looking inexpressibly dear and forlorn for a bit of blue jelly, would force open the outer door until I returned and rejoined it.

Thus I became the only member of my Web besides Ersh to see the universe without the blur of atmosphere.

I clung to the ship's hull like a Quebit waiting to vent plasma, spellbound by the limitless spectacle in front of me. To my web senses, space wasn't a black void, it spread before me like a surging ocean, tossed by solar wind, lit by radiations, and rich with spinning hydrogen. *A perfect place.* I couldn't understand why Ersh had hidden this from us.

I longed to soar through that golden darkness, to taste it against my outer surface, to feel its harmonies in my soul. It was a longing I resisted only because I had no idea of the kind of wings to use. *Something to definitely ask Ersh,* I decided firmly. This was an advantage all to my enemy's benefit; it was a lack in me I felt as physical pain. Then my attention fixed on the colony.

The *Rigus* was tethered to the grapelike cluster of broken spheres by several cables, including a set of three the crew used to travel back and forth. Those cables were my route to the colony as well, given I could avoid the attention of the sensors and whoever was currently monitoring them.

Web-flesh wasn't quite as amorphous as that of the Ycl, but I had no trouble thinning at one end until I was partially a cable myself. It took innumerable attempts, but at last I was able to hook one end of myself around a real cable. Grabbing it for an anchor, I spun myself out and away from the ship. Anyone looking out could see one of the cables growing oddly thicker than the others for a moment, but I doubted they'd notice. *I hardly believed what I was doing—how could one of the crew imagine it?*

Then I was on the colony's shattered structure, feeling lost away from the ship in spite of my growing confidence in my abilities. I had a completely new perspective on the courage it took for true air-breathers to don a suit and step out here.

Maybe it was easier when your destination wasn't an open grave, loosely held together by the tatters of what had been the ultimate in modern technology. The crew did its best on every shift to collect the former inhabitants of Portula Colony, catching and bagging anything that appeared organic for later identification. In web-form I could taste what they'd missed. There wasn't true vacuum within the colony. Its gravity generator, tucked into the core sphere, no longer functioned, but there was sufficient mass here to lure homeward the scattered molecules of sculptors, painters, and musicians.

I oozed my way among the debris, so angry I felt my outer surface throbbing. All of this had been incidental. The Enemy had destroyed the colony and its life in its search for Lesy. I had no proof of this; I had no doubt either.

But had it found her? I had several advantages over the *Rigus* in examining the wreckage for clues. I knew the former structure of the place. And I knew where Lesy would run.

Think of it as a puzzle to solve, a game, I calmed myself, at all times aware of the direction of the hum of gravity and life that was the ship. It was hide and seek with the Rigus' sensors, just as it must have been hide and seek for Lesy during the colony's destruction. I could play both.

It didn't take long to find Lesy's quarters, or what remained of them. The pillows she draped herself over when the colony upped the gravity for visitors were gone, perhaps lingering in orbit around the wreckage, but the patterned carpeting with its whimsical motif of feather and scales looked brand new. *Here.* I detected the first traces of web-flesh. Again I thinned myself to a cord's width to ease across the opening, preferring to be paranoid than be detected by the *Rigus.*

There. A lump of life, stuck half within a door panel. I rushed to it, forming a mouth and consuming the flesh before even thinking the intention. I should have.

It wasn't Lesy.

. . . *Seething appetite.* How dare you lock me out! I am what matters. Give me your flesh . . .

I flung myself out of memory, finding myself huddled against the comforting mass of splintered bulkhead. I hastily excised every molecule of my Enemy from me, but the memories of its flesh were impossible to vomit. I was only grateful they weren't worse.

Pouring my way past what remained of the door, I navigated through the apartment suites and studios of this portion of the main sphere, keeping my mass as tightly to myself as possible. At least I was out of sight of the *Rigus'* sensors now and could move freely. *Move freely?* I was alive and comfortable in an environment that welcomed nothing else to my knowledge. *Why had Ersh named space "out there" and "no life" to us? Why had she kept us from this?*

I ducked under the swollen torso of a Dokecian, its lovely arms stretched to their maximum length as if to beg some meaning from the cold, ever-changing Nebula overhead, my thoughts traveling down so many paths at once I hardly noticed the poor creature. Ersh hadn't shared our abilities in a vacuum, a selfishness that suddenly seemed a great deal more reasonable to me than most of Ersh's Rules. It kept us to ships, to travel no faster and no more conveniently than ephemerals. It kept us under control.

I sighed mentally. Now, it left us at the mercy of the Enemy, a web-being completely at home in space and capable of translight.

I humped my way down an exposed conduit pipe. Not much time left before I'd have to be back on the *Rigus,* not having my Enemy's independence.

There. Another sparkle of blue, this time a broad smear along a wall with an unhealthy tinge to the edges. There were streaks missing from the middle section. I could imagine Sas banging his helmet against it. I settled myself near enough to touch the smear with a pseudopod if I chose, and tried to decide what to do. It could be more of the Enemy. *Or it could be,* I shuddered, *all I had of Lesy.*

The surrounding wreckage showed no signs of scorching. Whatever strategy Mixs had used to defend herself, Lesy hadn't had the time to try. Or maybe not the will, since such an explosion could have shattered any remaining integrity of the sphere. Had Lesy hesitated, knowing the kind of damage and death the Enemy had inflicted on the colony in its rampant searching, aware that her defense might take the last hope from any survivors? *I'd never know.*

Unless I tasted for myself.

I had no tongue or its equivalent. To ingest the web-flesh from the bulkhead, I had to enlarge my mouth and consume the nonliving metal as well. I took an instant to worry if the teeth marks on the wall would be detected by the next shift of searchers. Then . . .

. . . *Fear. Resignation.*

This was Lesy. I relaxed my guard, assimilating memory as quickly as possible, excising the metal from my form at the same moment.

. . . Under the emotion, a last sequence of clear thought. *It knows my name. Mixs and not Mixs. It* hungers *for more. Ansky and Skalet. Esen. Ersh, save us . . .*

The names were wails of despair, the plea a hopeless one. *Lesy.* I opened my senses to the pulse of the Nebula, concentrating on the wild flavor of its energy, feeling suitably the smallest and least in a universe conspiring against all that was mine.

I made my way wearily back through the lock, ingesting the flesh I'd left behind automatically. The outer door whooshed closed and locked, its safety mechanism fooled by the apparent loss of vacuum as I expanded to fill the interior. The inner door irised open as I moved toward it, air from the ship's corridor rushing in, tasting of living things and warmth.

The lights were still night-dim in the hall. I cycled into Ket as I poured myself through the Quebit's' portal.

"Here," said Ragem, holding out my hoobit and skirt.

Out There

OVERLAPPING memories warred with those distinct to each. Death fought to keep its self-awareness under the deluge of ideas and information. Languages, form-memories, customs, histories—these things meant nothing to its purpose. Personality was a threat it burned away first.

Death hurtled through space, spending energy with abandon, assimilating furiously. More. There must be more.

Ah.

Death slowed, recognized star patterns from Lesy-knowledge, *knew* where it was in relation to those it sought.

Not the *Oldest*. Not yet.

Death would save the best until last.

31: Nebula Morning

RAGEM almost died in that instant. My grief and fear overwhelmed me. I wanted to cycle into something capable of violence, to shred flesh and spray blood until I could find nothing left to destroy. The need was so great, so impossible to ignore, I smacked my newly healed hands against the wall until the agony roaring up my arms drove away the rage.

Ragem, perhaps belatedly aware of his risk, had stayed absolutely still during my tantrum. When I stopped, finally, settling into stillness myself, he reached out as if to touch my hand. I flinched, feeling my sanity and sense returning from wherever they'd fled, grateful to have won the battle. *And so tired.*

"You don't give up, do you, Ragem?" I said, drained of all anger, aware on some level of relief. Whether it was because I hadn't killed him or because I could stop pretending, I wasn't sure.

A shrug lifted his shoulders. "It hadn't occurred to me." I noticed he was dressed only in a robe. He smiled and held out the hoobit. "Welcome back."

Welcome back? "You are crazy," I concluded, letting him help me tie on the skirt. From the feel of my hands, I'd rebroken at least one finger and possibly cracked a bone in the palm. At least there was no blood on the wall. Neither of us had come equipped to clean it.

"I'm crazy?" Ragem echoed mildly enough. "I suggest we debate relative mental states after you've been back in the med unit for those hands."

He was right. I could feel this body shaking, both from what I'd done to it and with it. In fact, unless I cycled, I wasn't certain I could walk that far. "Agreed. Ragem?"

At his nod, I continued: "I think I'll need your help to get there."

Ragem wrapped one arm around my waist and I gratefully, if somewhat awkwardly, leaned over him until I could put my arm over his shoulder and let him share some of my battle with gravity. As Ket, I wasn't heavy, but I certainly wasn't strong either; I could do little more to help Ragem support me. I could tell he had to strain to hold me, and my hand throbbed intolerably where it dangled against his chest, but this was a distinct improvement over collapsing on the deck. Until I realized how we might appear to anyone we met, my Ketself draped languidly over the compact Human like some drought-stricken tree, and my fingers twitched involuntarily.

"What's so funny?" Ragem wheezed between slow steps forward.

"I hope you've got a story to satisfy anyone we encounter on the way, because I certainly don't." *A typical Human fantasy wouldn't do,* I thought to myself with even more amusement. It was common knowledge that Ket away from their homeworld were completely uninterested in sex with their own kind or any other—a biological quirk that occasionally disconcerted those new to the sensuous pleasures of a Ket massage.

"I'll think of something," he said, then made a warm, oddly contented sound like a sigh. "But at least I don't have to worry I'm losing my mind any longer. You came close to convincing me, Madame Ket."

Better if I had, I thought, grateful for the transportation if not the responsibility.

Ragem's inventiveness did not need to be tested; we met only Quebits on the way back to his and Tomas' cabin. Once there, he helped me on the med unit and activated the box before sitting on the other bed and rubbing his shoulders. His voice carried easily through the clear walls. "You're a pretty substantial ghost, Es," he complained good-naturedly.

I sighed, but otherwise remained motionless to allow the unit's sensors to diagnose the latest damage I'd dealt this perfectly healthy body of mine. I could almost hear the machine's disapproval. I disagreed. *Far better a sore hand than having to wash off Ragem's blood.* "Please don't surprise me again, Ragem," I said firmly. "I'm not always—safe."

Ragem tilted his head, his gray eyes shadowed in the night lighting of the room. "Noted."

"How did you find me?" *Ah.* The unit did something to relax my nerves and stop the jangling pain from shooting from finger to shoulder.

"I saw your face when we were watching the crew outside. I knew you wanted to go to the colony—to look for yourself. So I followed you."

So much for my skills at espionage, I thought wryly, more amused than dismayed by how little all my precautions had mattered.

"I won't ask how you managed it," he went on. "But did you find any sign of Martha?"

Martha? I remembered the name I'd given instead of revealing Lesy's. Ignoring the objection of my hands, I pushed up the box lid to better see him. "Come here, Paul," I said, suddenly desperate. "Please."

Ragem stood and then knelt beside the bed so I could look directly into his face. It held the expression I remembered best: calm, accepting, the face of my first ephemeral friend, lit by concern and never-ending curiosity. "Be sure of me, Esen," he said gently, before I could speak. "I know why you ran from me on Rigel II. I've cursed myself every day since. I thought I was too well-trained, too experienced to react on a purely instinctive level. I was wrong. And I understand how I hurt you."

I touched his face with one of my better fingers. "Well, to be fair, I'm supposedly too well-trained to have put you in that situation." *Not necessarily too experienced,* I added to myself. I traced a cheekbone, too near the surface of his skin. "You paid for my mistake, Paul." I encountered a hint of beard and my Ket senses were pleased by the texture. But it was the not-Ket part of me that said: "Remind me never to drink spurl again, Christmas or no Christmas."

I surprised a chuckle from him. "Done," the Human said emphatically. "It's off my list, too." He tilted his head, his smile fading, eyes intent on mine, "Do you trust me now, Esen-alit-Quar?"

"That depends on how much of my trust you wish,

Ragem," I came back as bluntly, folding my aching hands over the hoobit. "I warn you. There's more at stake than your keeping the secret of what I am outside this room."

He nodded slowly, not surprised. *I hadn't expected him to be.* "You spoke of limits, once. Respect mine. That's all I ask. I won't endanger my crewmates or any innocent lives. I don't believe you would," he added quickly, as though sensing my protest before I uttered it. "Beyond that," he continued, "you can trust me as far as you need to. We're friends, Es." This last on a lighter note, as though some joy came with the commitment.

I thought grimly of the Enemy, of the innocent already dead, including Mixs and Lesy. "That's all you ask? Take care, Ragem. I came very close to killing you tonight. I can't promise it won't happen again."

"You didn't. And you've warned me."

He made it all seem uncomplicated. We were friends. To this Human, it seemed a binding as soul-deep as any I had with those of my Web. On another day, I might not have perceived the exact moment in which Ragem gained that stature in my life, but today I'd tasted the last thoughts of my web-kin. It left an agonizing emptiness Ragem's offered friendship somehow helped to fill.

Ersh? She could have a problem with my adopting Ragem into the Web. I decided it was simplest not to tell her about it.

"Get comfortable, my friend," I suggested. "I've a lot to tell you, starting with poor Martha Smith."

There wasn't enough time before the day period began on the *Rigus,* with its growing activity—including Tomas sure to arrive shortly afterward to seek his turn in bed—to share everything I wanted to share with Ragem; as it was, I could tell by his somewhat glazed eyes that he'd enough to think about for a while.

But the quick-witted Human did grasp our current dilemma. "So we have no way of knowing which of your kin this Enemy will go after next."

"None," I admitted. "But Lesy's last thoughts were of Skalet and Ansky." *And me. And Ersh.*

"And you've no idea what it looks like."

Not at the moment, I comforted myself as I lied: "No.

Our Eldest passed on stories about a predator—a solitary, deadly being—that might one day come to hunt us through space. The thing was supposedly mindless, yet implacable and dangerous. I'd believed it was only a legend, the kind of thing you Humans tell your children to make them behave."

"Legends have their roots in the truth," Ragem noted.

"So it seems."

"Can you find it?"

I was tired, too, but the med unit was helping, and it was important to chase down every idea. Ragem's thought processes were subtly different; his assumptions about my abilities, as now, made me question my own. "If I can see or touch another of my kind, I know them for what they are," I thought out loud. "This Enemy found Mixs, but I don't know how. Yet. But when I was out there," simply thinking of the experience brought an involuntary longing to my voice, "I didn't sense anything that could be followed."

Something else to ask Ersh, I decided. I hadn't told Ragem about Ersh, for his own protection. Ersh had made the Rules. I sincerely doubted she'd bother to obey them if Ragem became a threat to her privacy.

Ragem stretched, glancing at the chrono on one wall. "Day shift's about to start," he observed as he rose to his feet. "Back in a minute."

While he was in the 'fresher stall, substituting being deluged with water for a night's sleep, I kept trying to think of some action to take, something we could do. Running home to Ersh's protection was beginning to assume an unexpected charm. At the same time, I knew I couldn't risk drawing the Enemy to her.

I was as helpless as the Ket form I inhabited.

Fortunately, Ragem's thought processes were more productive. I'd noticed this about Humans in showers. He jumped out, looking remarkably refreshed for a being who'd had a night like ours, grabbing clothing as he spoke rapidly. "Kearn will be sending reports out this shipday, Es. I think I can slip a couple of other messages translight within the same courier signal."

I couldn't help saying bitterly: "As I tried to send to Lesy."

Ragem paused midway through pulling on a pant leg. "I know. I'm sorry, Es. But perhaps these will be in time."

I wanted nothing more than to pull down the lid of the med unit and let it put me to sleep. But Ragem was right. I couldn't ignore any possibility. "I'll dictate."

I stayed in the med unit the next day. Ragem and I had concocted some story about my overexerting myself and needing the relief of some lower gravity therapy. The untruth came back to haunt me; many of the crew left messages of condolence and remorse for having caused me to harm myself.

Tomas snored. He'd offered to sleep elsewhere while I used the med unit, but I demurred, content to rest. Ket hearing wasn't as keen as Lanivarian; I'd tolerated his snoring in that form without trouble, now finding it only a peaceful, background kind of sound.

Anything peaceful was welcome, short of the med unit deciding to administer more tranks to put me under. I'd been able to keep my Ket body calm enough to forestall that waste of my time. *Where was the Enemy going next?* Every minute we waited here was a minute closer to the loss of someone else. *But who?*

It helped that Ragem was doing something when I couldn't. I'd given him the latest code words and locations to reach both Skalet and Ansky, as well as a warning message blunt enough to get a response from a stone: *Mixs and Lesy murdered. You may be next.*

Skalet might have already left for Kraos to finish my task. No chance to reach her there, but Kraos was, I thought, safely distant. What I knew of its craving suggested my Enemy would seek the nearest source of web-flesh. I shuddered. It was the ultimate perversion, to take flesh without offering yours in return. If I allowed myself to dwell on that fate, both my hearts hammered until the med unit threatened to put me out.

I'd almost identified the Enemy in the message to Ansky and Skalet, but stopped myself in time. Putting such dangerous information in a concrete form risked some ephemeral less open-minded than my friend Ragem starting to ask the wrong questions. *Ersh would not be amused. At all.*

I'd felt a twinge of guilt at not telling Ragem the truth,

that our Enemy was web-being. But it was, I found, an easy guilt to bear, much easier than imagining his likely response. *Bad enough Kearn believed I was such a monster than seeing the same realization on Ragem's face.*

Where would my Enemy go? What was it capable of? Tomas stopped snoring for a moment, then resumed with a startling moan. I could have echoed it. Lesy-memory surfaced, "Mixs, not Mixs . . ." *What did it mean?*

Had she been fooled, just for a moment, by some imposture by the Enemy? It couldn't have been in person. We couldn't disguise ourselves as any other individual. *How else?* I caught my breath. Was it possible the Enemy had assimilated enough from Mixs to know the contact codes, to be able to send its own messages, messages that could trick one of us into a trap?

And would it try the same trick on Ansky or Skalet? I could only hope Ragem's carefully hidden signals would reach them first.

But how could it send a message at all? If Ersh could contact us without using technology, surely she would do so. For a semi-immortal being, she was incredibly impatient with communication delays.

I felt as though I should be hiding in the med unit, not healing. *Was this alien web-being capable of more than Ersh?*

This last thought was too much for my Ket physiology. The room and my problems became less distinct as the med unit quite firmly took control of my distress and chose to end it. For now.

Out There

JOEL Largas dimmed the lights in the children's cabin, automatically counting each of the five tousled heads as he would bags of freight. He was brusque with them when they were awake—not used to encountering toddlers and toys in translight and at any given moment certain the whole scheme would spiral to disaster at the curious push of a tiny finger on some panel never remotely made childproof.

He closed the door, flattening one space-dark palm against it. There'd been no problems; he devotedly hoped that between himself and the rest of them, Char and the older sibs, they'd keep the ship and its contents safe till planetfall. You couldn't keep young ones cooped up—not when they'd grown up used to a sky overhead instead of strip lighting.

For a moment, grief welled up, grief for the amber-hued sky none of them would see again. The Largas' family was luckier than most, he knew. Unlike some other ships in the convoy, his boasted experienced crew and well-maintained equipment. When the attack came, anything space-capable had been filled with life and tossed upward. His cousin Lyra's ship hadn't lasted through the atmosphere, tanks bursting along hastily repaired seams, those crammed inside her hull sharing the fate of the rest of their world.

He expected at any moment to hear that they'd lost another ship in the convoy, its engines failing even as they fled to safety at the fastest pace the slowest could manage. Another delay and another risky passage between ships, transferring those who'd never imagined being in space before. It was enough to scar the soul. Thank goodness for the laughter of children and their toys underfoot.

Alone in the corridor, Largas allowed himself to press his

forehead against the bulkhead protecting those he'd saved, and wept for those he couldn't.

Never knowing how Death slowed, *hungry,* considering the tiny chain of ships.

Choosing its next prey.

32: Starship Afternoon

"I DON'T care much for our options, Nimal-Ket." Ragem and I were alone, but we'd agreed it was wiser for him to treat me and, even better, think of me as Ket.

For this reason, the Human lay facedown as I stood over him, digging the fingers of my better hand into the by now loose muscles of his shoulder. "They are as they are, Paul-Human," I said with a remarkable amount of contentment, considering the subject of our conversation. "We can't change where my kin have chosen to live. Skalet studies strategy within the Kraal Confederacy. It is her specialty."

"Strategy? Kraal V's currently pounding the life out of Kraal VII, with the timely assistance of armaments supplied by Kraal Prime and some Denebian smugglers the Commonwealth would love to catch. Oh, a lovely system to drop in and visit."

I fluttered my fingers against his skin, a Ket grin. "Ansky's home is much more—peaceful, Paul-Human."

Ragem shuddered. "Artos? It's been recommended for the banned list for good reason, my friend. The Articans are xenophobic fanatics who'd rather sacrifice an innocent visitor to their God of Bones than feed their own offspring. Have you ever seen the list of taboos they send to any approaching ship? They change them faster than you can print out a copy."

"We each have our own beliefs, Paul-Human. Are you a religious being?" I asked. He didn't answer, so I went on: "Ansky has seen something that calls to her sense of belonging among these beings."

"I'd like to ask her what that could be," he muttered darkly.

Ask her? The instantaneous darkness of my answering thought kept me silent. *Who did this Human think he was talking about?* I pressed the heel of my healthy palm with unnecessary force into his back. *Entirely bad enough he knew of me.* I hadn't planned to introduce him to the family. *Ever!*

Ragem is my friend, came another, better thought. Before he could complain about the sudden vigor of the massage, I softened my touch, then reached for a cream I knew Humans enjoyed. "You've had no response to the warning messages," I continued with what I felt was commendable patience. "We may be forced to simply pick one—"

"And convince Kearn to go there," Ragem sighed. "Easier to face your monster, Nimal-Ket. I can tell you right now, he's not going to—"

Three things happened simultaneously. A warning klaxon wailed through the ship, I dropped the container on Ragem's head as he lunged up in response—fragrant white cream coating his hair and ears—and the door whooshed open. "Paul!" shouted Tomas, hurtling through it, his voice barely audible over the alarm. "Kearn wants everyone at their stations."

I climbed quickly up on a bunk, tucking my feet out of the way of both Humans as they sought bits and pieces of uniform from the drawers beneath. I was puzzled at first, then recognized what they were donning as the coveralls worn under space suits, complete with the fittings that bonded to the life-support gear. If I had been true Ket, this might have alarmed me, but I now found the threat of vacuum of much less concern.

The klaxon stopped as abruptly as it had begun, its dying echo ringing in my skull. While it was entertaining watching the Humans sort arms into sleeves in the limited space, I no longer enjoyed being an observer, especially to potentially dangerous events. "What's going on, Tomas-Human?" I asked, feeling the ship come alive in a deeper vibration through the wall. I'd thought we were staying attached to the ruined station for another shipday.

Ragem, ready first despite having to wipe his hair, paused for Tomas' answer. The redhead's face was pale, freckles prominent. "There's a refugee convoy under attack," he answered. "We're the nearest Commonwealth ship."

Ragem's gray eyes darted to me. "Refugees from where?" he demanded. "Who's attacking them?"

"There'll be a briefing. Come on!" Impatiently. Tomas shoved him toward the door.

"This Ket fears, Tomas-Human," I protested their leaving in a way I knew would slow the kind-hearted crewman. "What refugees? Where are we going?"

"Kraal System."

It's after Skalet. I cringed at the traitorous relief coloring the thought. *All web-flesh was shared,* I scolded myself. Ersh would say my youth was at fault; ephemerals sorted their kin into more-or-less-loved, not us. But I couldn't help worrying most about Ansky.

"Stay here," Ragem ordered over his shoulder to me, meaning, perhaps, more than for my safety's sake.

Numbly, I waved him on, watching the door close behind them, listening to the ship taking me to meet my Enemy at last.

33: Galley Night

THE *Rigus* screamed through the night, leaping to translight with a deep trembling even more pronounced than during our journey to the Nebula. Either something was about to break down, or the Commonwealth had secrets of its own tucked in the engineering of her engines and hull. Skalet, with her passion for military hardware, would definitely be interested in sharing this with me.

If she still lived.

I'd had an unexpected visit from the Modoren, Sas. After hissing a curt query after my health—which probably had more to do with my availability in the future than any other concern—he told me about the current situation, a courtesy I also attributed more to Kearn's anxiety over the possible reactions of a passenger I'm sure he no longer wanted on board.

Sas explained the *Rigus* was monitoring a series of distress calls originating from a small group of ships traveling outsystem from Kraal only to find themselves trapped before reaching translight by an ambush. Although the Commonwealth was neutral in the struggle for control of the immense Kraal holdings and the string of lesser systems that made up the so-called Kraal Confederacy, its policy of rendering humanitarian aid to any side of a conflict was well-known.

Imagining Kearn's probable reaction should the ambusher prove to be, as I believed, a web-being of unknown powers and definite malevolence wasn't good for my health. He already had that damning vistape of my cycling on Kraos, not to mention what he'd had opportunity to observe for himself at regrettably close range. My Enemy could provide all the proof Kearn needed to convince his government, and most others, that my kind was a danger to be hunted down and perhaps even destroyed.

"You will be safe in this cabin, Madame Ket, if you choose to remain here," Sas concluded cheerfully, at total odds to my own train of thought. "Seek the protection of the med unit in the event of a hull breach alarm. If you prefer, go to the lounge or galley areas, where you can easily reach one of the life pods. Someone will be there at all times to assist."

Sas seemed to positively quiver with delight as he intoned my choices for self-preservation should the ship see action. I'd known the hardwiring myself in that form: Modorens vastly preferred attack to stealth, bluntness to tact. Ket were not so forward in their approach to life.

"Sas-Modoren," I said, hands wrapped around the comfort of my hoobit. "This Ket trusts there will be no untoward or hazardous procedures taken by your ship. This is not a combat vessel, is it?"

His broad nose twitched once, likely a hint of disdain for my anxiety at this glorious turn of events, but answered politely enough. "We will only offer medical aid, Madame Ket. Unless attacked first." A subvocal growl. "Then, you may be assured that the *Rigus* is capable of self-defense."

I fixed a look of complete disapproval on my face, in case he could read it. "And how long until we reach this place of hazard?"

"Six hours, Madame Ket. As I have advised, please keep to an area of safety."

Maybe it was the Modoren's pleasure at the prospect of battle, or maybe I was finally shaking off the shock of discovering both Mixs and Lesy gone, but the longer I stayed in the cabin, braiding socks to keep my healing hands busy, the more I began to think of waging war myself. While I thought it likely the *Rigus* would fight my Enemy, I also doubted it could. Web-flesh wasn't invulnerable. I could swear to that. But I believed I could probably survive a blast from an energy-based weapon in web-form, especially out in space where I could absorb and release energy as rapidly as necessary. *Not something I planned to test,* I promised myself firmly.

What I expected was a chase, with only my Enemy knowing the course. Tracking it. *That ability would be handy to have.* I deliberately forced my thoughts from my other, greater need: to be able to pursue it on my own, without pulling these fragile non-Web beings into a risk they couldn't imagine—and I couldn't explain.

Certainly the pattern of its attacks suggested my Enemy knew better than to stay where it might be discovered. Perhaps we shared that urge to secrecy. *That was all,* I said grimly to myself, involuntarily remembering what I'd assimilated from the Enemy's flesh. *Appetite become gluttony. Living chaos, without law or conscience.* It was a glimpse, I realized numbly, at what Ersh had been eons ago.

At what I could be if unrestrained, had I grown without the Web, without assimilating the First Rules into my very flesh. It was a sobering thought; another to add to the nightmares Ersh's memories had already given me.

Understanding the nature of my Enemy was all well and good, but it didn't help me do more than realize how woefully unprepared the Humans were to deal with one of my kind. Any encounter between them was likely to have only one long-lasting result: becoming humanity's worst nightmare. An unnecessary reminder of how wise I'd been to keep the identify of our Enemy from Ragem.

An hour before our projected arrival at the outskirts of Kraal space, I grew tired of my own company. As Sas had promised, there were crew in the galley, their presence and noise reassuring, if the ready-to-suit clothing wasn't. It definitely fit some of them far better than others. I sincerely hoped Lawrenk Jen, for one, never needed to don her space suit. Her arms protruded from the ends of too-short sleeves and she'd given up even trying to fasten the ankle clips. I had the impression most of the crew hadn't worn these outfits before, nor been in such a situation. Crises for First Contact ships must generally occur on planets, not in space.

Ongoing conversation rose and fell, most of it speculation, some of which I sampled. I knew as much or more than any here, whether posted to assist with the life pods or simply taking a spell away from duty. Tomas showed up for a snack, then disappeared again with an uncharacteristic somberness to his usually cheerful face. I hadn't seen

Ragem yet, but Willify, who'd appointed herself my personal entertainment, explained that Ragem, as their best Kraal linguist, was needed in the nexus room to handle the messages coming to the ship.

It was all I could do to stay and make idle conversation when any one of those messages might be from my kin. I stroked the flecked surface of the chair and tried to keep my expression pleasantly attentive.

"—so you see, Nimal-Ket, that's why I've had trouble convincing my sister to—" I lost the train of Willify's story again, but this time as the one I'd been waiting for finally appeared in the galley doorway. Our eyes met across the crowded room. Ragem nodded once and left.

"This Ket asks your pardon, Willify-Human, but I have recalled an appointment. May we continue this conversation about your family at a later time?"

I hardly waited for her bemused nod before getting up with most un-Ketlike haste and going to the door in search of the Human.

"Nimal-Ket!" the urgent whisper came from beside the door. Ragem's eyes gleamed as he held out a message cube.

"What is it?" I demanded, staring at the cube as though it could talk immediately.

"A message from someone who identifies herself as S'kal-ru, Diplomatic Courier for the Kraal Confederacy."

The name and title were right. *Skalet.* I glanced around quickly. We were alone for the moment, the buzz of voices from the galley more than sufficient to cover our own. To play the cube for myself, I'd have to return to my cabin. I wasn't prepared to be patient. "Tell me what it says, Paul-Human. Is she all right?"

One side of his mouth quirked upward. "Well, she's all right until Kearn finds out this refugee convoy is nothing of the sort."

I clutched my hoobit. "What do you mean?"

It was his turn to glance around. *A fine pair of inconspicuous conspirators we made.* "After S'kal-ru received your message, she up-shipped from Kraal Prime with an escort of Confederacy heavy cruisers. The refugee distress calls were apparently her way of getting the *Rigus* to bring you to her, rather than risking her fleet beyond Kraal borders."

Typical, I thought with disgust. Skalet preferred manipulation over any other type of interaction between beings. "I take it this clarification isn't in the messages Kearn has been receiving."

"No. This arrived secretly, under the same protocol as ours went out—tucked within the regular signal stream. Kearn is still receiving a distress call. In fact, it's getting even more desperate." The Human waggled his eyebrows suggestively and lowered his voice. "Pirates have been mentioned."

"Pirates?" My fingers fluttered weakly. "We're trying to save her life and prevent catastrophe and she's playing games?"

"Is this something you'd expect?" Ragem frowned, suddenly grim. "Or is there a possibility this message is from your Enemy? Is it intelligent enough to use technology?"

I crouched, dangling my hands to the floor so I could tickle my toes: a childish gesture, but soothing. "I'll listen to the message myself to be sure, but it's exactly what Skalet's capable of doing. It must be her. Unless—" I rose with a new thought, straightening to step closer to him, placing one long-fingered hand on his chest. *Had it assimilated that knowledge from Lesy and Mixs? Should I warn him?* "Ragem, I haven't told you this, but—"

"There you are, Madame Ket!"

"Acting Captain Kearn," I acknowledged, surreptitiously taking the message cube from Ragem and tucking it into the waist of my skirt. It poked into my skin, cold and comforting. *Skalet was alive. So far.*

Kearn hurried toward us, his hands suspended in midair as though he wanted to rub them over his gleaming head but knew the moment wasn't quite right. Equally unfortunately, from the point of view of command presence, his suit coveralls fit even less well than Lawrenk's, being far too long in both sleeve and leg. He'd had to roll them up, completely obscuring the vital connectors on wrist and ankle. I perceived conspiracy and barely kept my fingers from fluttering in appreciation.

"Just the being I wanted to see," he paused and peered up at Ragem, pouting as if in thought. "Aren't you supposed to be in the nexus, Specialist Ragem?"

"Just down for a drink, sir."

"Then get one and take it back to station with you,"

Kearn snapped. "There's a stack of new messages just arrived. You know I can't waste my time translating. I've a ship to prepare for possible combat!"

Ragem touched his fingers to my hoobit courteously, then walked away.

"This Ket is troubled by your talk of hostilities, Captain," I said sternly, deliberately avoiding his use-name to stress my Ket disapproval of hazard. *Not to mention my personal dislike of this Human,* I added to myself, only partially ashamed of this descent into ephemeral behavior. "Is this not an errand of mercy?"

Kearn sighed theatrically. "We must be prepared for any eventuality, Madame Ket. Which is why I wanted to check on your safety personally. You are our only passenger, you know. Quite a responsibility. I wanted to ask you for next-of-kin information—just a precaution, but things could get dangerous."

Next of kin? My mind went blank as my hands gave a painful clench on the hoobit that belonged to a very dead, hopefully still very buried Nimal-Ket.

"I'm sure you mean you'd like Madame Ket to prepare a sealed data file, to be opened only in the event of the worst, sir," corrected a quiet voice from behind me. "Given the cultural imperative against revealing true names to non-Ket."

Kearn's face worked its way through several possible expressions before deciding on pompous. I maintained a dignified stillness with an effort. "Naturally, Specialist Ragem. I'm fully aware of the culture of our distinguished guest. I intended no discourtesy, Madame Ket."

I bowed. "This Ket felt none. Perhaps you would honor me with a visit shortly, Captain. Your increasingly great responsibilities must cause you tension," I suggested with lips pursed in a frown and carefully still hands. Ragem had to pretend to cough. "These surely need to be eased for full health."

Kearn bowed, too. "I assure you I will come to you, my dear Madame Ket, the instant those responsibilities allow me a moment of my own. In the meantime," he glared at Ragem, "I must ensure that my subordinates fulfill their duties properly."

"On my way, sir, Madame Ket," Ragem gave a hint of

a salute and left, unable to restrain the occasional cough as he strode down the corridor. Kearn rubbed his head, uttering another deep sigh.

"My apologies, Madame Ket, but I must get back to my own duties," he said, distractedly. "There's so much to do. There may be wounded personnel to transfer to the ship. We don't have the space for more than a few without total disruption to quarters. Then the forms to be completed . . ." The acting captain of the *Rigus* wandered away in the opposite direction, taking a turn into an adjacent corridor, his muttered list of tasks and complaints trailing behind. "I wasn't supposed to have to deal with this . . ."

"Behold our Great Leader."

I turned to peer down at Lawrenk Jen, taking her raised eyebrows for an invitation to confidence. "You miss your former captain, Lawrenk-Human? This Ket has been told you lost her just before I came on your ship."

"Aye," she agreed, chewing on a bottom lip, her hazel eyes almost green in the hall lights. Her strong features were resigned. "Kearn's a capable officer, don't get me wrong, Madame Ket, but Captain Simpson, well, I served under her in a few scrapes. Until you've been this close to vacuum," she pinched together her thumb and forefinger, "sucking smoke while crewmates bleed to death at your feet—well, that's when you know what decisions a captain is capable of making—and sticking to."

"And this crew doesn't yet know these things about Acting Captain Kearn."

The engineer lifted one shoulder. "Know? Maybe not." Her eyes hardened. "Regs say we should have picked up a qualified captain before lifting from Rigel II, but this crazy chase of Kearn's after that Lanivarian grabbed support from way up. So he's in the captain's chair. I just hope we don't end up paying for his obsession."

"This Ket agrees, Lawrenk-Human," I said softly. *Completely.*

34: Shuttle Morning; Cruiser Morning

"WHY? Give me one good reason!"

I wrapped a pilfered sock around the half-empty jar of sauce remaining from my shopping trip on D'Dsell. I didn't have any spare clothing to keep the fragile container safe within my bag among my accumulation of creams and ointments, many farewell gifts from the crew. "My thanks, Paul-Human. For all you've done—"

Ragem gripped my arm below the elbow, pulling me around to face him with quite unnecessary force. The jar tumbled from the sock before I could catch it, but bounced safely to rest on the floor near our feet. *So much for being fragile.* Ragem didn't let go. "I don't want your thanks," he said with what seemed real anger. "I want to know why you're suddenly leaving the *Rigus*. I thought you wanted to track down this killer; I thought I was to help you reach Ansky as well."

His fingers dug in, a further sign of emotion, I concluded, rather than any intention to cause me pain. Still, I winced and Ragem released his grip, the skin of his face going from pale to a warm flush. His expression remained furious. "Skalet arranged for me to come on her ship—" I began, only to be interrupted.

"That's another thing. Who knows what story she concocted to get on Kearn's good side? You don't. But it must have been something. None of us can believe the *Trium Set*'s captain isn't at least going to be questioned for misuse of an emergency distress call." He took a deep breath and said in a more reasonable tone, "I don't like this, Esen. I don't trust it."

To be truthful, I was quite curious myself how Skalet had managed to turn Kearn's outrage at her deception into what amounted to slavish cooperation. The result, however, was all that mattered. She wanted me with her. *And I had to go.* "This Ket," I stressed the word, "has been invited to serve an old and favored client, Paul-Human. That is all you or I need to know. There is nothing mysterious in my wanting to leave your ship to seek a more profitable opportunity. It is our way."

"Be Ket with Kearn, not me, Esen," Ragem gritted out between clenched teeth. "You've warned me your enemy has the ability to take information from the memories of your kind as it kills them. What if it learned enough to impersonate Skalet's Kraal personality, S'kal-ru? The Kraal Confederacy is in chaos. Who would question anyone of her rank?"

"Portula Colony wasn't torn apart by a subtle being, Paul-Human," I reminded him. "Why should it try such an elaborate process now to lure me into a trap? From what we've seen, this being could rip its way through the ship faster than you could sound your breach alarms."

We glared at each other.

"Let me come with you," Ragem said after a long pause.

I reached out to cup his face with both hands, fingertips overlapping the top of his head, and shook him gently. "Paul-Human. Friend. It's impossible."

He stepped out of my hold, eyes brimming with the recklessness I remembered all too well from Kraos. "It's not. Ask S'kal-ru to request my presence as a—as a Commonwealth observer to the current crisis. There're hundreds throughout the system. The Confederacy is always kicking them out on some pretext or other; they assign new ones all the time."

Of the myriad objections immediately coming to mind, I picked the most obvious. "How could she justify picking you from those on the *Rigus*?"

"My mother's homeworld—Botharis. It's in the Confederacy. Most of the time," he hedged.

"Which makes you unlikely to be neutral."

"Which makes me the only person on this ship fluent in the Kraal diplomatic language and up-to-date on Confederacy customs."

I felt my body temperature rising. "No."

"Why?" *Back to that.*

"I don't want you to come."

"I'm not going to desert you!"

Enough was enough. I held form with an effort, fondly thinking of cycling into something more convincing than the passive Ket, something with muscle to lift his slender form into the air and gently thump it into a wall once or twice. It was a reaction the Human persisted in inspiring. "You are not deserting me, Ragem," I explained instead. "I am leaving you. If you want to help me, divert Kearn's attention. You won't be able to stop his pursuit of me altogether, but perhaps you can misdirect his efforts."

He raised one hand, a look of abrupt and unhappy enlightenment crossing his face. "You don't want me to meet Skalet. Or anyone else of your kind. Why?"

"I—"

"Is it because of how they'd react to me?" He paused. "Or to your friendship with a Human?"

Or how you would react to them? I thought with a shudder, thinking of sharing flesh, of Ersh's past, of all the other aspects of Web biology, any one of which was more than likely to restore that look of horror on his face. I'd never felt the difference between us so utterly as now.

"Paul-Human," I took a long step to reach the room's one table and waved him into the chair across from where I chose to crouch. I spread my hands over the table's smooth surface, trying for a similar serenity. "Tomorrow morning, a shuttle from the *Trium Set* is going to clamp on the hull of the *Rigus*. This Ket must leave on that shuttle. Skalet could not refuse to respond to my message. I cannot refuse to go to her.

"My kin and I are as one. All of us. The loss of Mixs and Lesy has diminished the whole of what we are. This is also how," I put out one hand to take his, "I view our friendship. You are part of what I am. But not part of what connects me with the others. They could not understand." *An understatement if ever there was one.*

"Then don't tell Skalet about me," Ragem argued reasonably, determination in every line of his face as well as in the firm pressure of his smaller hands over mine. "Esen, I don't like any of this. Call it Human intuition, but it stinks to me like Grangel's Commons House: all honey and smiles on the surface, and who knows what lurking below. Just let me come with you."

I'd said no. I'd meant no. So it was with no surprise at all that I took my seat in the *Trium Set*'s shuttle the next morning, breakfast and good-byes heavy on my stomach, and nodded a mute greeting to Ragem as he and his baggage dropped on the facing bench a moment later.

Typical of the Confederacy, the interior of the shuttle gleamed with polished wood trim and gilt. Probably the captain's personal craft, I decided, sneaking a quick drift of my fingers along silky paneling. There were three crew: tall, slender Humans, with ornate tattoos marking family affiliations and business alliances running over each cheek. I could read them, if I took the time or saw the need. The pilot concentrated on her task after a courteous greeting. The other two, supposedly in charge of our comfort, spent most of the short trip to the *Trium Set* staring at Ragem as if different politics made the Human more alien than I.

To me, Ragem appeared entirely too smug. I'd adamantly refused to contact Skalet and arrange for his invitation. After storming out of my cabin, a decidedly unpleasant way to say good-bye, the Human must have taken matters successfully into his own hands, with the result that he leaned back against the bench's cushioned back as if without a care in the universe. He even wore casual clothes instead of his uniform, his favorite jacket open over what looked to be a woven shirt and pants.

He couldn't have . . . I narrowed my eyes at him, suddenly suspicious. Ragem smiled back. If he'd left the *Rigus* without Kearn's permission, I hoped he'd covered his tracks with some plausible story, though I couldn't imagine what that could be. Otherwise, either Kearn would immediately contact the *Trium Set* and demand Ragem's return, an event sure to perturb the security-conscious Kraal, or worse, Kearn might just start putting the clues together and figure out why Ragem was so devoted to a Ket encountered by chance on Hixtar Station. What Kearn lacked in cleverness he more than compensated for in sheer paranoia.

"We are docking, Madame Ket," the pilot announced,

swiveling in her seat to face me. "S'kal-ru wishes to see you at once."

If anything, Ragem's smile widened.

"S'kal-ru awaits you, Madame Ket," the guard said tonelessly, looking completely past me; his bearing implied, falsely, that this member of Skalet's military force hadn't thoroughly analyzed the likely threat level I poised—none—and the chance of his getting access to a fabled Ket massage—none.

My Ketself approved of the *Trium Set.* If the shuttle had been luxurious, her immense base ship was opulent. In this section, officers' quarters, the doors were works of art, carved in bas-relief down to ornate handles my hands ached to explore. Skalet-memory reminded me of other doors, space-sturdy and plain, ready to instantly replace these ornamental ones should the ship be at risk. Expensive, but then the Kraal Confederacy had never fought its civil wars over mere wealth.

I pulled open the door, trailing one long wistful finger over its intricate surface, and stepped into what had to be one of the better cabins on the *Trium Set.* Skalet had carelessly shoved its tapestried couches and chairs into a confused mess along one wall, leaving the center of the room free for three tables overflowing with maps. An image projector squatted on the floor nearby. I avoided the gashes in the hand-woven carpeting left by her rough redecorating.

"Ket?!" The word came from the dark, all lights in the room being trained on the tables and their tactical displays. "Couldn't you have picked something more—useful?" Skalet's rich tenor voice always struck me as incongruous in this form and manner, a combination reminiscent of the juicy lure held out for unsuspecting fish by the Denebian spiny shark.

I fluttered my fingers, now thankfully free of pain, willing to trust that Skalet would have ensured her own quarters were safe from eavesdroppers. "It has its advantages. Subterfuge for one."

A figure moved into the wash of light surrounding the image projector. In Human form, Skalet, known in this place and body as S'kal-ru, was as tall as my Ketself, her slender body whipcord rather than elegant. The tattoos on her cheeks proclaimed her as one entitled to the unquestioning support of the three oldest and most powerful family Clans of Kraal Prime. She'd chosen to shave her head, a style preferred by soldiers who fought in null-gee battle suits, and one that purged any vestige of softness from her strong features. I'd never been so happy to see anyone in my life.

"So—?" She lifted one pale eyebrow at me.

"My use-name is Nimal-Ket."

"So, Nimal-Ket," she said. "Come and sit. Tell me what you left out of your message. And I will tell you what I have planned in advance of your arrival."

Instead of taking the chair she pushed forward with one foot before dropping into its neighbor, I slid my fingers under the hoobit and lifted it tenderly over my head. I put it on the top of a map of Kraal V, marked with red as if Skalet had spent the day totaling casualties. The skirt followed.

I lost her protest—"Esen, wait!"—as I released form and settled into web-flesh, gaining an awareness of her molecular structure as I lost the ability to hear. I extruded the memories she should have, holding back my secrets, ruthlessly aware I gave her no choice in that sharing. *Ersh had given me none.*

"Space . . ." Skalet's marvelous voice embodied the word with all the wonder I'd experienced, and she now shared.

"Mixs and Lesy," I said, my Ket voice harsh in contrast.

"Yes," she agreed, switching on the image projector. A star field shimmered between us in the dark room, hiding the tables and maps that marked the simplicity of Human war. She worked with controls for a moment, adding a series of flashing nodes to the display whose meaning I understood only too well: the known locations of the Enemy's attacks, including those against our kin.

Skalet's plan lay within my memory, assimilated from the flesh she'd returned to me in exchange. I also contained her outrage at my tactics, an outrage mixed with a hint of approval. She'd always thought there could be sharing between two, something Ersh had forbidden until breaking that Rule herself.

"You weren't surprised by the nature of our Enemy," I commented.

"I always thought it preposterous we'd be the only Web in the universe," Skalet replied absently, still adjusting her machine. "Where did Ersh come from, if that was the case?"

Since Ersh's origin was among those items I hadn't chosen to share with Skalet, I could hardly answer. But I did have questions of my own. "This plan of yours. Setting a trap for it using the Kraal ships. Do you really think the Humans can harm it?" *And what does that mean for the rest of us?* I added to myself.

"Don't worry, 'tween. I've a few tricks up my sleeves."

I tasted the echo of her confidence, but remained unconvinced. "Shouldn't we contact Ersh before—"

Skalet whirled around, her eyes reflecting the star field, her fist slamming down on an invisible table. "No! We must protect Ersh from it at all costs. I can handle this situation, Esen," she went on in a quieter voice. "We will share our victory with Ersh, not our fears."

"Victory? Mixs and Lesy are dead. We're planning to murder one of our own kind. Your plan means risking dozens of Humans and their ships. What victory can you possibly see in any of this?"

"You've never lived out here, Esen," she said in a tone that suggested I was being predictably unreasonable. "You never had to adjust your thinking to fit another species' culture, to accommodate different ways of doing things. Your head is still full of Ersh's idealism. Well, it doesn't always work in the real universe."

Ersh, an idealist? I wondered if Skalet would say that if she owned the Ersh-memories I'd been forced to consume. "And what of our purpose, Skalet?" I asked, refusing to be dismissed. "To preserve intelligent life and its accomplishments. How does risking lives—wasting lives—accomplish this?"

Skalet paused before answering, a pause that gave me time to remember who I was scolding: one of my Elders, the one who had never been satisfied with my progress as long as I could remember. My grip on the hoobit could have bent the metal, had it been made of weaker stuff. My hearts pounded slightly out of synch.

"We shared flesh, Esen-alit-Quar," came her unexpectedly gentle reply. "From your taste, I know you are more than you were; how much more I cannot be sure. You've always been different from the rest of us, thanks to Ansky's dereliction, but Ersh was right to tell me you would one day exceed my expectations—something I found hard to believe until now."

Ersh said that? I kept my surprise to myself. "But you are going ahead."

"There are costs in any conflict. Our purpose is best served by destroying our Enemy, by whatever means." A blue cluster appeared in one segment of the star field, its glow catching her cheekbones and firmly set chin. "Admiral Mocktap will deploy her fleet there. She stands ready to spring my trap on the monster." A tiny yellow spark winked into life within the cluster, began moving outward, splitting suddenly into two, then four, then eight, sixteen; the course of the multiple sparks forming a fan. "There is my bait."

"Drones, ready to release your location the moment they are attacked by a web-being," I said. That location would be on a lifeless moon in a system near the edge of the Kraal Confederacy, in line with where our Enemy should come. I knew the details. *I just didn't like them.* "It wants to survive, Skalet. It must have assimilated at least part of Lesy as well as Mixs. I wouldn't underestimate it."

"I don't." The tiny yellow fan spread farther, along a track leading back to Jeopardy Nebula from Kraal: Skalet's assessment of the probable path of our Enemy, how it traveled still a mystery to us both. "Your assumption it will seek Ansky or me next is valid." Without warning, her calm shattered for an instant. "I don't appreciate sharing its *hunger* for us, Esen."

"What about Ansky?" There'd been no reply to Ragem's message before I left the *Rigus*. Fortunately for my peace of mind, my birth-parent had been in contact with Skalet in the meantime. Ansky had been warned and there had been no sign of the Enemy on Artos.

Skalet shut down the projector, ordering on the lights at the same time. I blinked owlishly in the sudden glare. "Of us all, Ansky is the least able to defend herself," she stated without condemnation. I couldn't argue. *Ansky was, well, she was herself.* "I want you to go and get her."

"Pardon?" I blurted.

"I will give you a ship, Esen, and a crew," Skalet went on as if she hadn't heard. "I'd suggest a change from this cowering Ket of yours, but I want you to take the Human, Paul Ragem, and it's the form he knows."

This was the first mention of Ragem by either of us. I'd kept almost all trace of him from the memories I'd shared, beyond events Skalet had to see in order to understand our situation. She knew him from me as helpful and capable, but safely gullible rather than perceptive.

Ragem, however, had leaped ahead of me.

Skalet-memory held the totally implausible story he'd sent directly to her under my codes. "You didn't believe he was my assistant for an instant, Skalet," I dared. "Even before we shared and you knew. Why did you let him on your shuttle without checking with the *Rigus* or me?"

"The Human obviously expects you will support this imposture. If you have enlisted his commitment to this extent, he could be useful. Unlike Ersh, I fully appreciate the value of ephemerals in a conflict."

Had I made some mistake in sorting my memories? I grew cautious, feeling a coldness settle around my hearts. Skalet was a master tactician. Her ability to slice through a knot of misinformation and complexity was respected by Ersh herself. As was her ruthlessness. Skalct rarcly had conflicts of conscience—convinced that other species sacrificed one another as part of their nature, behavior she observed with clinical detachment. I suspected she was also capable of it. *She mustn't suspect Ragem knew of us.*

"Don't mistake his attempt to accompany me as something personal, Skalet," I said slowly. "You know how ephemerals can become obsessed. The destruction of Portula Colony must have had a deeper impact on this one than I thought. He's determined to hunt down whatever's responsible and may believe I can lead him to the cause." I made my fingers move lightly, easily over the hoobit. "I don't need that kind of help. You should send him back to his ship."

I hadn't fooled her. *I should have known I couldn't.* "There was none of this in your sharing." Lovely or not, Skalet's voice could still project the bite I remembered all too well. I controlled the temptation to snap to attention. "You stink of secrets, youngest and least of us," she continued. "An inappropriate odor I will question when we again stand before Ersh." Before I could respond, she said with total finality: "Take this curious, this obsessed Human with you. Keep him within reach."

"Why?" I whispered, fearing the answer.

"Use him as long as he is willing and unaware, whatever his reasons. If his curiosity grows, inform me. I will deal with him."

I stared at the black-and-red scrollwork of the tattoos under the fine texture of her skin, permanent record of the Web I realized Skalet had formed within this society. The war maps on her tables showed the value she placed on that web. I had been right not to reveal my connection to Ragem—more right than I'd known.

She had taken my silence for squeamishness. "Don't worry so, Esen. Just let me known if this Human becomes any threat to us and I'll take care of the matter."

Ragem, I said to myself, *you've done it now.*

Out There

DEATH replenished itself. Only the contents of one of the small, fragile shells had been necessary.

Satiated, it nestled against the hull of another in the convoy, undetected by the low-capacity sensors of the freighter, content to be carried as long as these shells were traveling its chosen course. It relished the sensation of indulgence.

Lesy-memory had given it the concept of *"saving for later."*

35: Cruiser Afternoon; Scout Ship Night

THE chandeliers, paired and connected by gleaming silver chains, were a nice touch. Perhaps arguably out-of-place in a warship's bridge, but to each culture its own symbols, I'd been taught.

Not that any others of the present company appeared to find anything unusual in a setting that lacked only a small orchestra to turn itself into a ballroom for royalty. *Trium Set*'s officers and crew sat at their stations with nary a look our way, while the five of us were embraced by armchairs which took their profession far too seriously for me. I knew from the moment I sat down—and sank down—I'd likely need help to get out again. Disappointingly, the chairs were all made from some cured animal hide. Soft enough, but with hardly any texture left for my pleasure.

The chairs, set on a dais overlooking the business area of the bridge, formed a semicircle around a low table at definite risk of collapse under the mass of wines, ices, and what the Kraal called "essentials," ornate finger foods having in common a deliberate attempt to disguise their components.

We'd been here for only a few minutes and, to the Kraal, that meant no serious discussion could occur for a while yet, although Skalet had quaffed her second ceremonial glass of serpitay with quite unceremonial haste. The two Kraal captains with us—Longins of the *Trium Set* and his counterpart, Hubbar-ro, from what was proposed to be my ship, the scout class *Quartos Ank*—also indulged in less than the requisite lingering over flavor and hue, obviously used to the courier's impatience. Skalet's status among the

Kraal military was an interesting one. As courier for her sponsors, she could commandeer any assistance she required, no questions asked. I knew she had to account for her actions to the heads of the affiliated family Clans; however, this event apparently occurred only if she lost whatever gamble she took. Which had yet, Skalet-memory assured me, to happen in her illustrious career. *I could believe that.*

Ragem sat with us instead of on the low stool beside my chair, the protocol officer having scrambled to repair the social damage caused by her assumption he was my servant rather than business associate. Despite this clarification, which I announced without a blink and Ragem acknowledged with a gracious bow, the Kraal were not happy. Ragem, whether due to his first contact training or because he did know these people better than most from the Commonwealth, acted oblivious to the sidelong looks he was constantly given by the captains on either side of him as well as members of the crew. I, with my almost naked body, knees almost in my face because of the depth of padding in the chair and hands that could lie on that same floor if I let them, was rarely noticed. *Humans.*

Skalet put down her glass, snapping a long finger against its rim to make a ringing sound. "Our guests will forgive some unseemly haste, Captains. I wish to get to business."

Captain Hubbar-ro swallowed the last of his beverage with a look of regret at the amount left in the bottle on the table. Discretion won. "As you say, S'kal-ru. The *Quartos Ank* is ready for your disposition. How may she serve you?"

I shifted a bit in the chair, trying to straighten up and match the erect posture of the Kraal. It would have been nice to rest my elbows on the chairarms without having to raise them higher than my shoulders. Skalet eyed me, but responded to the Kraal's question: "You and your ship are to serve the wishes of my honored guest, Madame Ket, as the *Trium Set* and I prepare for our—visitor."

Hubbar-ro, quite handsome as Kraal went, young for his command position though an explanation for that might be read in his impressive array of affiliation tattoos, showed no expression beyond polite attention. But his hand snaked for the bottle and he poured himself a very full glass. "As you wish," he said somewhat numbly. The other captain grinned.

Poor man, I thought. *Probably thinks he's giving S'kal-ru's masseuse a ride home when he could be seeking a glorious death in battle.* "This Ket is grateful for your assistance in my very important and potentially hazardous mission for S'kal-ru-Kraal," I said, there being no harm in saving face.

His eyes lost their fixation on the wine to send me a grateful look. "It is my privilege to serve."

"Of course it is," Skalet said warmly, and I witnessed firsthand the power of her incredible voice, when she chose to employ it. Both captains, and Ragem, flushed almost immediately. Backs straightened throughout the control room. I let two fingers wriggle in a restrained laugh Skalet returned with a quirk of her own thin lips. This was, I realized with some astonishment, the first time in my life I'd interacted freely with ephemerals and one of my Web without coaching or practicing for weeks beforehand. The spontaneity was quite exhilarating.

But the reason wasn't, I corrected, stilling my fingers and looking with purpose at Skalet. "This Ket is prepared to leave immediately, Captain. By your wish, S'kal-ru-Kraal?"

"I didn't unpack," Ragem put in, unasked but wisely maintaining his right to the same status Skalet had accorded me.

"Just so," Skalet said with approval. "As you can see, Captains, the Confederacy has willing allies in the most—unexpected areas. I charge you in particular with their safety, Hubbar-ro. Do not fail."

He fairly glowed with pride and indeed leaped to his feet, as if forgetting the glassful of wine in his hand and ready to board ship that instant. Ragem and I exchanged a glance. "This Ket knows what you wish accomplished, S'kal-ru-Kraal," I began to say, then had to stop as I wrestled myself free of the amorous chair. *There.* I stood, flustered, but straightened my body as much as possible before bowing. "We will return as soon as possible."

Skalet had remained seated, as had Captain Longins of the *Trium Set.* "See that you do, Madame Ket," she said quietly. "See that you do."

Out There

CHAR'S calm voice penetrated the din like a force blade into ice. "The *Kenji* should have been scrapped a decade ago and you know it, Feve. Your brothers held her together with thread and lucky charms at best."

"No!" Feve Talkan shook his arm free of the well-meant restraint of his cousin, crowding forward in the already packed room as if this somehow made his point clearer to the group seated around the Largas' galley table. Joel Largas, as captain and head of what remained of the Largas' extended family and their kin, waved away his would-be protectors, judging Talkan no threat. The man simply pushed ahead until he could press both hands on the table and glare around at the fourteen seated there, captains and family heads all, gathered at some risk from the convoy ships to confront what seemed a cruel new punishment being inflicted on them from the dark on the eve of their escape. Talkan's rage and fear was something they all felt now.

"The *Kenji* was old, right enough," the trader grated, his heavy white brows meeting in a scowl over his haunted eyes. "If it was only her, fair enough. But Spence's ship, the *Pulse*? She was in better shape than this flagship of yours, Char Largas, new off the docks and setting records with her first translight cargo. How do you explain that?"

Out of the corner of his eye, Joel watched his oldest daughter settle back in her chair, deliberately pausing until the murmur following Talkan's furious questions died down. "I can't," she said firmly. "But neither can you, with your stories of space monsters—" Voices rose and drowned out the rest. There were over thirty adults crammed in a room meant for a dozen at best, the ventilators already maxed out, Joel decided, leaving too much carbon dioxide in an atmosphere filled with enough verbal hot air and panic.

He stood, slamming his cup as an improvised gavel to reclaim everyone's attention. "We're down to fourteen ships, nine of them towing life pods and barges. Our thanks to Captains Pary and Josh for saving the barges being towed by the *Pulse* before she blew."

A solemn mutter of agreement brought up the heads of the two named. Joel knew them both: not heroes, simply capable pilots who acted on instinct to save lives. As they all were trying to do. He continued: "It's going to take us nine days minimum translight before we reach sanctuary at Inhaven. Whether what's dogging us now is bad equipment, bad luck, or Feve's monster," his hand shot up to halt the round of nervous laughter, "we'll get there together. You know the alternative—"

"None of us want to risk Artos," Feve Talkan said heavily. "I don't care how close we pass to their system. There's enough of us shipped cargoes through there to know there'll be no welcome for us."

"Then we're agreed—" Char began.

Talkan wasn't done. His grim voice reached every corner of the room: "But I'm warning you all. We've got something with us on this journey. Something that is ripping the life out of our ships one by one. And if we don't do anything to stop it, it may be none of us will see Inhaven or any other world again."

36: Scout Ship Night

"WHAT did you say to Kearn?"

Ragem delayed answering to take another bite of boiled rast egg, a delicacy from Botharis he'd been delighted to find on the *Quartos Ank's* menu. Having a first-class chef on a scout ship with a crew of only eight was an extravagance I definitely owed to Skalet. The chef had even managed to produce a platter of arsenic-laced noodles, following a Ket-recipe she'd brought with her from the *Trium Set.* I wasn't entirely sure she appreciated my well-meant suggestion that leftovers were excellent for pest control.

The noodles sent a welcome fire through my taste buds, a sense I'd resigned myself to keeping numb while Ket among Humans. Skalet was ready to take on our Enemy in combat. Every minute took us closer to Artos, where we were to pick up Ansky and keep her out of harm's way. My mood would have been downright mellow, if Ragem weren't avoiding my reasonable questions.

"We can talk freely here, you know," I said, wondering if he suspected the crew of eavesdropping or of the compact yet gorgeous dining room being rigged with the latest recording devices. "This is S'kal-ru's ship. It's a hand-picked crew."

"I'll take your word for it, Es."

I pointed my fork at him. "It's no reason to get careless, my friend. Nimal-Ket, if you don't mind."

Ragem nodded, mouth full again.

"So, my friend. What did you tell Kearn?" I repeated. "He can't have just said: 'Off you go, Ragem. Keep the Ket company. I know we're in a crisis, but the crew and I can handle it without you.' "

"Not quite," Ragem agreed maddeningly. Then he steepled his long fingers before him and launched into a far better imitation of Kearn than I'd managed: " 'Ragem, these Kraal are up to no good. Faking a distress call. Claiming it was so we could meet without their opponents catching on. Trying to bribe this ship!' " He dropped the whine from his voice for his own reply. "How dare they, sir! You must have been outraged!" Ragem's voice rose again, adding a touch of Kearn-smugness I remembered well enough to make my fingers flutter. " 'Well, we had run up quite the debt with Madame Ket, you know, Ragem. Wonderful creature—very few ships can claim to have one on board as long as we did. If you'd seen her bill, you'd understand why. Worth every credit, but not the easiest thing to explain on the ship's budget.' "

"Kearn let Skalet pay my bill," I said, shaking my head for Ragem's benefit. I'd known how Skalet enlisted the cooperation of the *Rigus* from our sharing, but saw no need to remind the Human of such Web abilities. Besides, I was enjoying his performance. "There goes this Ket's profit margin," I quipped.

Grinning broadly, Ragem kept going in his Kearn-voice. " 'Quite understand the Kraal wanting to hire Madame Ket. Most Ket avoid Kraal space—too much conflict all the time. Having a Ket in the entourage is good for status as well as the, ahem, back.' " I almost choked as Ragem flawlessly reproduced Kearn's chuckle at his own humor.

"Explaining his less-than-grief-stricken reaction to my departure," I interjected. "And why Kearn didn't press charges against the *Trium Set*." Now we came to what neither Skalet nor I knew. "How did you—"

Ragem interrupted me, mercifully in his own voice this time. "I suggested to the Acting Captain that there was something suspicious about all this and that it might be prudent to put an observer on the *Trium Set* to find out what the Confederacy really wanted with you. I was the logical choice, as I tried to tell you before. Hence, my presence as your assistant."

"You're Kearn's spy," I said numbly.

He locked both hands behind his head and grinned. "At your service, Nimal-Ket."

Clever being, I thought to myself. *Entirely too clever for his own good.* "Even Kearn realizes a spy is only as good as his reports."

Ragem looked hurt. "What do you think I plan to tell him?"

"Not that." I closed my eyes for a moment, then opened them. "What worries me, Paul-Human, is *how* you're to make those reports." My mouth kept threatening to tighten into a frown.

He pulled the sleeve up his left arm, revealing tanned skin with a dusting of dark hair. A line of paler skin, already almost imperceptible, ran along the blue tinge of a blood vessel. I crooked one finger. Ragem stretched his arm across the table so I could run my sensitive fingertips over the mark, tracing the device under the skin without difficulty.

"Before your temperature jumps, my paranoid friend," he said quickly, "I had Lawrenk do some mods on the implant. There's no record function. It has the emergency homing beacon—we couldn't remove that—but I control it. No signal goes out. Unless my vital signs hit critical, of course."

Would it activate if you're eaten? I wondered, feeling a kind of devil-may-care lightness in my head I suspected was contamination from Ragem. "How long will it take Kearn to realize your implant isn't sending positional information or anything else for that matter? How long before he starts chasing after you, too?"

"That's the beauty of it," he began with enthusiasm. "I planted a matching signaler on the *Trium Set*. Kearn will back out of Kraal space, receiving exactly what he expects and no more. He'll be convinced I'm where he left me. In a few days, I'll need a way to feed him a report, but this ship should have the equipment for it. You see, Nimal-Ket," Ragem tapped himself on the chest, "I've thought of everything."

"You left a Commonwealth signaling device on Skalet's ship," I echoed.

Some of his self-satisfaction faded, replaced by wariness. Perhaps it was the icy tone I used. "To be technical, it's under the bench in the shuttle."

One wall of the dining room—to call the elegant little space a galley did it no justice—was lined with a hydroponic garden. *Skalet's innovation, without doubt.* I stalked over to it, grabbed a nicely lush duras plant, and cycled.

I hadn't needed all its mass. I tossed what was left of the plant onto the table: let the crew make of it what they would; they most likely expected Ket eating habits to be interesting. Then I surveyed my foolish Human friend over a muzzle that wrinkled in rage very nicely. I could put up with the corresponding upset in my space-tender stomach long enough to make my point.

"Have you forgotten what Kearn is really after, Ragem?" I growled into his startled face. "Me. The shape-changer who blew up in his office. As far as he's concerned I'm some kind of monster—maybe even the one he's chased from Panacia. Well, now you've left a tracking device in Skalet's ship. And what kind of being do you think she is?"

"He'd never suspect—"

"Probably not," I agreed, then answered the dictates of my stomach and cycled back to Ket, wiping moisture from my skin before picking up the hoobit and skirt. While I'd cycled to remind Ragem what we were, it had been a relief to shed energy, an opportunity that might not come again soon. *I hoped.*

"But Kearn isn't the immediate problem," I continued in my higher-pitched, yet softer voice. "Skalet will find your device, Ragem. Don't doubt that for a moment. She'll find it and I'm sure will assume you left it there to track *her* movements. The obvious conclusion is that you are her enemy and possibly mine as well."

His face was ashen; his voice so low I found it hard to hear in this form. "She doesn't know I know what you are—what she is."

Had I ever been that young? At the moment, I felt every one of the decades I'd lived before this Human's birth. "Skalet is a leading tactician of a race who treat war as a parlor game, Paul-Human. You don't have to threaten her true nature to be a threat."

I went around the table to where he sat, frozen in place, and wrapped one long Ket arm around both his shoulders. They were stiff, whether from some offense he'd taken at my reaction to his wonderful scheme or a more rational alarm at what I was trying to tell him. *I couldn't guess.*

"Ragem, this is me as a Ket. I borrowed a name to use, but this body is the only Ket I can be. When Skalet is in Human form, she is that Kraal military noble you met. And she can be very dangerous to other Humans—especially you."

Ragem patted my arm. "Then," he said lightly, "I suggest we defuse the problem before it arises. The *Rigus* should be well out of Kraal space by now. Call Skalet. Tell her I discovered the device in my bag and removed it in the shuttle. Say I hid it there in order not to arouse Kearn's suspicions. This was my first chance to let you know. Tell Skalet I urge her to destroy it if she hasn't already."

Not bad, I decided, mulling over the idea. There didn't seem to be any flaws, which didn't mean they weren't there. I hadn't even started my training in subterfuge or strategy, unless this practical experience would count with Ersh. I wrapped my other arm around him and hugged tightly. "Skalet won't be easy to convince, Paul-Human," I warned. "But it's a distinct improvement over what will happen if she finds it first. I'll send the message right now."

I went to the doorway. *Snap.* The sound made me look over my shoulder as I was about to open the door.

Ragem sat looking at the broken stem of the glass in his hand; blood, not wine, dripped from the cut end. I'd seen that bleak despair on his face only once before, when we'd been prisoners of the Queeb and he'd been forced to watch my torture.

Now what? I wondered, close to losing track of which emotion I was supposed to feel next. "Now what?" I asked him.

The Human's face, while not classically handsome, possessed a pleasing symmetry of bone structure I thought would age well. The proof was before me now, as his expression added years. "I lied to you, Esen."

When he pressed his lips tightly together, as if to hold in some further outburst, I decided to give Ragem time to gather himself, since this was definitely the beginning of some confession I wasn't sure I wanted to hear, but I was about to regardless. So I left the door, despite the urgency of contacting Skalet, and returned to the table where I calmly poured us both sombay, spicing mine with a spoonful of leftover sauce from the noodles, careful not to put the spoon into his cup and thereby end his confession before it started. As I fussed over this process, Ragem silently wrapped a napkin around his hand and watched the red stain slowly stop spreading across its white surface.

"Drink," I insisted, taking a large swallow of the hot stuff myself. "Now. What lie, Paul-Human?"

"Kearn doesn't care about the Confederacy. He doesn't care about distress calls and regulations."

"So . . ." I prompted, able to guess where this was leading, but also guessing it was part of Human friendship to let him bare it all.

"The only thing he cares about is tracking down Esen-alit-Quar. You were right. Nothing will convince him you aren't responsible for the murders and disappearances. Nothing is likely to stop him hunting you either." He stared glumly into his cup. "I gave up trying to talk him out of it. We all did."

"I know about Kearn. You are not surprising me, Paul-Human," I said very quietly, as if he were some feral creature I could scare away with a louder or harsher voice. "There are always those who fear the unknown. And what am I but all of the unknowns rolled into one?"

"Don't try to justify him." Ragem flung up his head and glared at me as if I were the enemy. "He doesn't represent my kind. Believe that, Esen."

"Of course," I made a soothing gesture. "But you are distressed by more than Kearn."

He took a deep breath, one that shuddered near its end. "After we spoke on the *Rigus* that last time, when you refused to help me come with you on the *Trium Set,* Sas came to my quarters. He'd found the hidden messages I'd sent for you. The ones to Skalet and Ansky. Turns out Kearn had him doing a random check on com traffic, and our security officer pursued the job like a cat after—well, you get the picture. It was my terminal, my shift. I couldn't deny the logs."

Ersh. "Did he read them?"

"No. I'd erased the content right after sending. He couldn't even be sure of the final destination, but it wasn't hard to figure out when we started getting the refugee calls from Kraal."

"So Skalet didn't fool Kearn at all," despite the seriousness of the moment, I waggled my fingers. *A blow to an immense ego.*

Ragem didn't appear to find this as amusing. "While you finished packing, Sas took me to see Kearn. We had a—conversation. One in which my options were made very clear."

"Poor Paul-Human," I said with true sympathy, able to imagine every detail of that one-way shouting match. "What happened next?"

"I said you convinced me you'd had enough of chasing his monster and had begged me to send a secret message to an old client in the Kraal Confederacy. The message was to take you off the *Rigus*."

"And he fell for that?" I asked, astonished. I knew Kearn's weaknesses better than I wanted to, but it was a stretch even for him to believe a Ket would feel safer in a war zone.

"No."

Ersh, save me from Humans. "You thought of something better, I take it."

"I didn't have to," he confessed. "Kearn had figured out everything."

"What!?" I rose to my feet, knees knocking the table, feeling as though Kearn would burst through the door of the room at any minute and ready to run the other way. Illogical, but that was the way of any instinctive fight/ flight response. In this form, as in the Acepan, the response was predominantly flight, the Ket species having matured into a sensible preference to avoid danger whenever possible. *I had to start choosing braver forms.*

"Relax, Esen," Ragem ordered, rubbing a hand over his face wearily as he gazed up at me. "This is Kearn, remember? He hadn't figured out the truth. He'd come up with some convoluted plot in which you were a spy for Esen's people, sent to keep tabs on him. You were leaving the *Rigus* to rendezvous with her or another of her kind." Ragem's voice slipped into his mockery of Kearn's whine again: " 'She played on your sympathy and used you to send the coded message. Ragem, you really should pick your friends more carefully.' "

"Sound advice, Paul-Human. I've tried to give it to you

in the past," I said primly, settling down in my chair again with only a residual trembling.

Ragem's lips twitched, almost a smile. I supposed he'd been certain I'd react badly. In truth, I wasn't sure how I felt about it, beyond a fatalistic conviction I wouldn't be appearing as Ket on the *Rigus* anytime soon, and so would certainly miss my chance to find out more about Willify's tangled family. With the Lanivarian, that made two of my favorite forms under Kearn's wild-eyed scrutiny. *A tally Ersh didn't need to know,* I concluded.

"Why didn't he assume I was, well, me?"

Ragem drained the last of his sombay from his cup. "Kearn wants to believe you—the real you—are the monster we've chased from Hixtar. Once we found Portula already destroyed, with you safely on the *Rigus,* he couldn't very well have you in both places at once." He raised one brow. "You can't do that, can you?"

"No. I can get into enough trouble in one place at a time, thanks. So Kearn doesn't suspect I'm who I am." I was beginning to wonder who was who in all this myself.

"Right. Luckily for us both, he sees you as someone hired to do a job, likely not even aware of the details. And he wants a lead in this chase of his—any lead. He needs it sooner than later, too, or the Deputy Minister is going to yank him off the bridge of the *Rigus* and put the ship back on the frontier where it belongs."

"So—"

"Set a spy on a spy. Kearn thinks you trust me. He expected you to believe that I was to ferret out some anti-Commonwealth conspiracy among the Kraal."

"With the implant. And your story about the signal device on the shuttle—"

"Too true."

The *Quartos Ank*'s engines kept their noise to themselves, but I knew from Skalet's sharing the engine enhancements of the *Rigus* were familiar stuff to the Kraal. We should reach Artos in another day. The *Rigus* might be haunting the *Trium Set,* or might be who knows where. A Commonwealth ship dedicated to hunting down my kind, not just after a mysterious killer. *Life had been simpler on Kraos.*

"That's why I decided to lie to you, Esen," Ragem said

softly, reading my distress too accurately. He reached for my hand. "I didn't want to tell you, not so soon anyway, how the situation was on the *Rigus,* with Kearn. But I couldn't stick to it. It didn't feel right to keep secrets from you."

You stink of secrets, echoed Skalet's accusation in my memory. "I value your honesty, Paul-Human," I said, while reserving to myself the obligation to keep my own honesty flexible for his sake and mine. "And while your news distresses me, it could be worse."

I stood, tired of the room, the rich food, and secrets. "Let's send our message to Skalet and then get some rest. Captain Hubbar-ro is nothing if not dedicated to seeing us break some records getting to Artos."

Ragem looked grim. "I can't wait."

37: Spaceport Afternoon; Shrine Sunset

WHEN I'd first starting learning about other species, an education begun by my first bite of Ansky—an interesting memory in itself—I'd rapidly concluded that biology dictated the tendency of certain species to remain planet-bound. The inability of Lanivarians, my birth-form, to keep their food down even in orbital shuttles seemed to support this conclusion.

After I'd experienced another hundred years of life or so, Ersh introduced me to the other great glue holding species to their worlds: belief. For every five species casting their eyes, or whatever organs suited them, out there, there was at least one whose beliefs either kept those eyes or whatevers downward or eventually drew them back to an ancestral home to stay.

It was not our way to believe we belonged on any one hunk of orbital rock over another, so I'd found this concept particularly hard to grasp. Ersh-memory of space, coupled with my own experiences, now explained my difficulty. The Web had not evolved at the base of a gravity well. We had never needed to commit resources and time to leave a mother world. This was a fundamental difference between Web and any other species I thought could prove even more profound than our lifespans.

Ansky came closest to understanding the emotional attachment of species to their homes and to one another. She was the romantic of us; the heart, a Human might say. Her experiences, filtered through Ersh for me save for that initial nip and my penalty after Kraos, carried flavors of passion, of underlying forces owing nothing to rational thought. Sharing with Ansky had a bit in common with receiving a mild electric shock.

Ansky's present home, Artos, offered much the same combination of pleasure, discomfort, and outright peril. Ragem and I stepped out of the air lock of the *Quartos Ank* with her captain, our faces immediately warmed by the afternoon blush of rosy sunlight, and as quickly surrounded by the requisite armed escort of Articans prepared to safeguard their lovely world from unbelievers.

Captain Hubbar-ro and Ragem were at more of a disadvantage than I, as Ket. Articans were strangely Human-similar, beautiful in their way, though I knew their biology was thoroughly unhuman. The resemblance had made the Articans uneasy from the day of first contact between the species; the Church of Bones routinely argued that Humans were Articans who had offended the God of Bones and been exiled from the blessed homeworld. They had much less trouble with visitors who were obviously not Artican, such as myself, believing—if Ansky's latest memories were sufficiently up to date on the constantly pliable orthodoxy—aliens were pre-Articans striving to be worthy of reincarnation as true Articans on the blessed homeworld. This vast improvement over the previous canon that aliens were demons had, Ansky concluded, a great deal to do with the increasing value of interstellar trade.

We marched among six-plus-one guards, the six armed and the odd one unarmed for some reason I didn't know. They were all female, and definitely pregnant judging by the bulges around each waist; another change in procedure from my last information. Keeping up with Articans was a headache; of course, not keeping up was foolhardy.

I could see Ragem was itching to talk, but kept his comments to himself. Offworlders speaking before being introduced to the Keeper of the Spaceport Shrine was Number Fifty-one on the list of current taboos the *Quartos Ank* had received while in orbit.

A considerable number and variety of starships had braved the taboos and strictures to do business on Artos. I could see other sets of Artican guards waiting or moving near several of the parked vessels. I refused to speculate how the Articans arranged for so many female guards in the same condition, though I would ask Ansky when I had the opportunity.

The Kraal captain, in full dress uniform with the exception of an empty sword scabbard and vacant blaster holster, was having trouble keeping his eyes straight ahead. I didn't blame him; the Kraal had a pronounced love of aesthetics and our guards were all exceptionally attractive individuals. I doubted he could tell their condition, but I knew Ragem was aware of it and would want to discuss the oddity later. If we succeeded in not offending the Keeper. *No point worrying about that,* I decided, focusing instead on the pleasure of walking barefoot on the prickly golden turf the Articans felt pleased their God more than pavement.

It was a short walk from the *Quartos Ank* to the Spaceport Shrine, but our destination was light-years distant from the Kraal shuttle in form and purpose. A pile of broken rubble, stuck through with scorched timbers, marked the previous shrine I had in Ansky-memory. It looked to have met a violent end. A purge of ideology, no doubt. Such events were not uncommon here.

The new Shrine stood close enough to the ruin of the old to share one wall. The new construction had been thrown together from woven animal hides and smelled as though several of those hides had not been properly cured beforehand. Thankfully, we were third in line and our escort herded us into a position more-or-less downwind of the worst of it.

The clear menace of the place enforced the silence taboo more effectively than the attentive guards and their bristling collection of sharp objects and incongruously modern hand weapons. Denebian biodisrupters, I observed in an idle moment, taking comfort in cataloguing the cultural detail as opposed to imagining the efficient handarms used on our flesh. Trade wasn't always in food or luxuries. I found myself wondering how the Ganthor Matriarch and her mercenary herd had fared on Ultari. I couldn't say I wished them a profitable war.

We shuffled ahead as another cluster of guards and offworld traders entered the Shrine, ducking under a raised tent flap that dripped something truly repulsive-looking on their heads. No curses or complaints. The taboo held. I actually found myself fighting an urge to chuckle; the Articans had found a way to turn bureaucracy literally into a horrific experience.

A group of Denebians—*know what you're here to sell*—exited at the same time. Not their first visit, I concluded from the hoods they'd chosen to wear despite the clear sky overhead.

Our turn came after a tedious amount of waiting. The well-disciplined guards had stood perfectly still, beyond eyeing me as I rocked from foot to foot; I wasn't worried, not having seen any prohibitions in the list against that. My Human companions might have fallen into a doze for all I could tell. The Artican sun was well down on the horizon by the time we were allowed in to meet the Keeper, casting a charming pink glow over the sides of the starships and a somewhat nasty red stain on the Shrine walls.

I shuffled under the dripping tent flap as quickly as I could, successfully missing the oozing liquid by a hairsbreadth. Hubbar-ro was less adroit; I hoped the dark stain would come out of his light green cape. From his hunched shoulders and rolling eyes, he likely assumed the worst about the source of the liquid. I would reassure him back at the ship. I suspected the Articans kept a bucket of stale beer at the tent peak. Their deity was of bone, not blood.

A distinction which strongly influenced the decoration within the Shrine. The Keeper sat behind a desklike altar made entirely of bone, mostly hips and thighs from a large domesticated meat animal but the offworlders were doubtless encouraged to believe otherwise. The Keeper himself wore an animal hide around his shoulders, the head, or rather skull, attached in some manner to appear to be whispering secrets into the Keeper's right ear. As the Keeper was himself gaunt to the point of parody, the combination was doubtless intended to be unnerving.

And was to some, I realized. Captain Hubbar-ro was supposed to step up to that intimidating display to insert his clearance disk into the reader in front of the Keeper's folded, beringed hands. That device, the guards' weapons, and the lighting within the odorous tent were the only offworld tech items in evidence. The Kraal hesitated, however, the delay growing a frown on the Keeper's stern features. I calculated various possibilities then used my toes to pinch

Hubbar-ro's ankle. He hastily shoved in the disk, at the same time depositing the bag of currency gems required for processing our docking clearance. His step backward put the Kraal military officer slightly behind me. I certainly wasn't broad enough to hide him. *Hope you're braver in battle,* I thought, but didn't plan to offer him one to find out.

"You are here to see an Artican?" This utterance, in comspeak, came from one of the Keeper's attendants, a healthier-looking individual standing to the skull-free side of the Keeper. I didn't mistake the question as any less a warning than the weapons close enough to touch with either hand, despite its friendly tone.

Since he looked directly at Ragem, purple eyes wide and guileless, no one else could answer. I settled my fingers around my hoobit and tried to see if there were any exits besides the one behind us. *The well-guarded one behind us.*

"Yes, Keeper," Ragem replied in the same language, correctly addressing his attention to the silent Keeper and not his mouthpiece; I also approved his avoiding the trap of using the Artican tongue with its multiple levels of potential insult or praise depending on the ever-present and ever-changing taboos.

"This Artican is?"

Ragem's answer was firm and again correct. *I hoped.* "My mouth is too impure to hold a blessed name. It has been inscribed within our disk." He nodded at the reader in front of the Keeper. If this was no longer the right protocol, we were all likely to feed the God of Bones. Ragem would just be first.

The Keeper's face tilted, the skull wagging with the motion as if in agreement, its prominent teeth and ridged forehead sinister without flesh and feather. I recognized it as that of a sweet-natured pet animal favored by young Articans. "You have the Keeper's leave to dock your starship for three days," the attendant said in his warm voice. "You have the Keeper's leave to seek this Artican." The effect was spoiled when he added, in the same friendly tone: "By accepting the Keeper's authority in this Blessed Place, you accept the righteous wrath of the God of Bones, should you transgress against our people."

* * *

"You're both crazy."

The young captain of the *Quartos Ank* had expressed this opinion with varying degrees of emphasis throughout our preparations, sipping on a seemingly endless flagon of beer. Ragem flipped closed the top of his carrysack and nodded. "Oh, I agree, Captain. Which doesn't change anything."

I fondled the yellow, red, and white flower petals making up the necklace now drooping over my hoobit. *Pleasing to the touch, if not in meaning,* I thought. Ragem and I each wore such necklaces, the petals being the badge permitting us to travel on Artos. They'd been treated with a compound that would keep them fresh for three Artican days; on the fourth, we'd been warned, the petals would rot, falling off the string to brand us breakers of the taboo.

"Keep your ship launch-ready, Captain-Kraal," I advised him. "This Ket will take responsibility if the spaceport objects. We don't plan to be here long. S'kal-ru-Kraal will hear of your service in her name."

He shook his head doubtfully. "I hope so, Madame Ket."

38: Valley Morning

THE *Quartos Ank* possessed an atmosphere-capable flyer, a small, rugged machine completely stripped of the gauds and decorations found elsewhere in the scoutship. Ragem and I had the blessing of the Keeper to fly it on Artos, as long as our trips followed a straight line between Ansky's home and the spaceport, and as long as we traveled before the sacred hour of noon.

"Was noon sacred before?" Ragem asked, checking over the controls with a confidence casual enough to be reassuring. I hadn't piloted very often before—if I'd wanted to fly in an atmosphere, there were other forms—and never in a Kraal machine. Skalet-memory was available if I wanted to search for it, but there was no guarantee she'd ever been her own pilot either.

"Noon? No," I answered. "My last information put the sacred meeting an hour later, after lunch."

Ragem nodded, as if filing away the detail. Then: "Ready?" At my wave, he activated the grav unit within the tiny airship, the result much less vigorous than I'd endured in the D'Dsellan hoverbot. We rose until clear of the *Quartos Ank*'s nose, then Ragem set in the course I'd provided. A smooth bank to the right, and we were off, heading, as far as my Ket eyes could tell, straight for a black line of mountains.

"Are you staying in this form, as a Ket?" Ragem asked before I could relax. I peered over at him. He looked mildly curious, an expression I'd grown very accustomed to seeing. "Do you get tired of one form?"

"Do you ever stop wondering about things, Ragem?" I shot back.

His mobile mouth stretched in a smile. "Why else did I up-ship and join a first contact team?"

He had me there. "I'll stay Ket on Artos," I said, trying to find a compromise between dangling my arms in the way of the controls or curling myself into a ball. On the other hand, my feet were half again too long for the floor space in front of this seat. "I'd rather not," I confessed after squirming for a moment. "I could use a rest from it." My hands were no longer sore, thanks to the healing technology of the *Rigus,* but they ached at night if I overused them—which Ket had to do.

The landscape flashing beneath us was pastoral, charming in fact. The Articans were predominantly farmers, most in this region growing the flowers used in the many ceremonies and rituals that governed their days. The result was a patchwork of color counterpointed with the green/golds of pasture. The occasional small village clustered around its church.

The churches were no longer so charming. The last few phases of the God of Bones had been dark ones, and the churches, now called shrines, had been rebuilt to reflect that darkness. The buildings were the mottled color of bone left to rot in swampwater, their surrounding grounds a black gravel against which the gray walls seemed to crouch, about to spring. From the air they looked like sores amidst the brilliant blues, yellows, and pinks roofing the other structures in each village.

To each its own, I reminded myself firmly, somewhat shocked to feel such an emotional response. *Must be due to associating with ephemerals so much.*

"How long until we reach the valley?" I asked Ragem, more to distract myself than from impatience. Though I would be very glad to see Ansky and know for myself she was safe.

He checked an indicator. "Well before its Boniness says we have to land." Ragem tugged at his floral necklace. "Itches."

"Keep it on," I advised him for at least the third time. "All the time, too. And I don't think you should take their God lightly, Ragem."

He sighed, looking out the screen on his side. "I don't, Es. How could I? Let's get your Ansky and get off this planet translight, okay?"

* * *

Ansky went by her own name on Artos, a rare convenience of language. She hadn't been on this world very long, by ephemeral or Web standards, yet had managed to carve out a niche for her form's sake.

She'd opened a bar.

To be precise, she bought and now operated an inn, the Sleepy Uncle, nestled in a village lovely even by Artican standards, tucked at the front of a valley Lesy had despaired of capturing in paint. *Lesy.*

The Sleepy Uncle seldom functioned as a inn, I'd explained to Ragem as we wrestled our carrysacks up the building's narrow stairs to the second, and topmost floor. The road its broad front windows watched over so closely saw traffic once or twice a week, less after harvest. Ansky maintained only two guest rooms, primarily for those fools who drank a bit more than was wise and were unlikely to make it home before the evening curfew. Being outdoors after midnight was, of course, an offense to the God of Bones and taboo.

Ansky could care less that her inn's bedrooms were usually empty. She'd bought the place because the Sleepy Uncle boasted a huge dining room, used by most of the villagers on a daily basis. Skalet's passion for strategy and war was matched among our web-kin by Ansky's strangely similar devotion to the study of relationships and more personal conflicts. Last I'd heard, Ansky'd convinced the village council priests to hold their daily meetings in her dining room, a guaranteed window on Artican conflicts if ever there was one.

However, when Ragem and I had arrived, the inn had been virtually deserted, an emptiness occasioned, we were informed, by the urgency of taking off the magitteri flowers before the sacred hour. Every able-bodied villager was in the fields, explained the child behind the counter, a polite being who could have passed for an eight-year-old Human male, if it hadn't been for the juvenile Artican hairlessness of his head and the lingering nictitating membranes in both eyes.

He'd given us room keys, being charged with running the inn in Ansky's absence, and, after a moment's deep thought about the proper ceremony with aliens, had decided not to take chances with his God and given Ragem and me blessing candles to take up with us.

Ansky would be back shortly, the child had promised, clutching his apron, his eyes blinking rapidly. I hoped "shortly" was well before the child could run to the priests and report on Ansky's latest, and most unusual, guests.

"Nice place," Ragem commented, putting down his carrysack and trying the softness of the large mattress. As he sat, he suddenly tilted to one side and made a quick grab for the nearest bedpost to save himself, a comic look of dismay on his face. "How's your room?"

"The same. It will do for the night," I said, noncommittal. I wasn't fond of the combination of country charm and bone-strewn corner altars. No missing where our candles were to be placed: the skulls were coated with runnels of once-melted wax. "We must leave first thing in the morning, Ragem."

"First thing in the morning it is," he agreed.

"First thing in the morning? I don't think so."

We'd found Ansky, or rather a thunderous knocking on Ragem's door had announced her finding us. Articans hugged, so I'd endured the intimacy for a moment before rescuing my poor Ket toes from under her well-shod and heavy feet.

After introducing Ragem, I'd gone straight to Skalet's plan, deciding not to wait and share in private. I was in a hurry.

Ansky wasn't. The harvest wasn't complete.

"Others can pick flowers, Ansky," I said forcefully, hands almost blue on the hoobit. "You must come with us as soon as possible."

"Now, Nimal-Ket, I don't see how one more day makes any difference to you, S'kal-ru, or this fine young man here. But it finishes the harvest. Maybe you'll like to chip in and help?"

I glowered at her. Ragem, her fine young man, hid a smile. It wasn't easy glowering at Ansky. She was imperturbable, a charming rock against which others' haste simply crashed and slipped away unnoticed. Admirable in a being living among those I frankly considered intelligence's lunatic fringe, but completely frustrating now. Actually, it had been frustrating in the past, too.

"Come with me," I growled, wrapping my long Ket fingers around hers and tugging toward the nearest door. "We need to talk. Excuse us, Paul-Human."

Ansky didn't resist, saving me the indignity of trying to pull her significantly greater mass into motion. She nodded graciously at the Human, then sailed out of the room, trailing a scent of crushed flowers behind her.

Her round features only accentuated the owlish look she gave me as Ansky paused from gathering up her clothing. "I don't believe Ersh would approve, youngest," she said breathlessly. "I'm not sure I do. Dear Gods old and new. Lesy gone. Mixs. What has happened to us?"

Her words were mere vibrations in air. I huddled on the floor in a corner of the bedroom, aghast after assimilating Ansky-memory. Bad enough her latest adventures with several paramours. *How had she found time for so much, and so many?* Most of this I was sure Ersh would have filtered at least in part for me.

Worse was the appalling list of newly taboo activities on this world and the punishments now dictated by the God of Bones. How could any intelligent race turn on itself?

"Are you all right, Esen?"

I looked up, remembering the perfection of her web-form, my mind trying to overlap the Ansky I knew as part of me over the Artican's generous curves. "How can you live here, Ansky?" I said, my voice hoarse to my own ears. "They're getting worse."

"Oh, yes." She finished wriggling into the dress discarded during her cycle to web-form. "I'd predicted it."

"You did?"

"Of course. This is hardly the first such society I've watched implode, youngest. The Ompu were definitely similar."

"The Ompu are extinct," I countered.

She shrugged, running her hands through her hair in a futile attempt to arrange its mass of red curls. "Exactly."

"How long do you give the Articans?"

Toiletry complete, Ansky threw herself down in a chair and looked at me. Her Artican eyes were a sky-blue, usually twinkling, now their expression was as grim as I'd ever seen. "If the Commonwealth bans trade with this world, which they should really, I'd say no more than a decade—two at most—before their society collapses to pre-tech. The next stage is almost here. They won't tolerate offworlders much longer. You were lucky to come when you did."

"You know luck had nothing to do with it." I pulled myself to my feet, feeling more Esen than Ansky at last.

"The monster." her teeth caught at her lower lip to stop its trembling; her hands folded themselves in a tight knot. "Why would it come here?"

"You shared. You know how it found Lesy. You know its hunger is for us."

"The Articans—"

"Can't stop it. Besides," I added more gently. "It is after us, not them. You have to leave before it gets here and kills other beings."

She closed her eyes, and blue teardrops slid down her rosy cheeks. I didn't know what to do. Ansky was older, my birth-mother. Uncertain, I obeyed Ket instincts and went to her side, pressing my long fingers into the locked muscle of her shoulders. "Ragem will help, Ansky," I said, running one sensitive finger along her cheek, following a tear's trail. "And don't forget—Skalet has a plan." *I hoped.*

Ansky's eyes flashed open and she turned to me. "Skalet's a fool," she said, the harshness of this condemnation a surprise from my usually complacent birth-mother. "We must go to Ersh; our place is by her side, not in some trumped-up excuse for a battle in space. Skalet would shed blood just to watch the drops explode in vacuum."

"No," I said sharply. "Ersh is where we can't go. Not until it's destroyed." *How much to reveal? How much to hide?* Ersh's past threatened to bubble into my present and I fought it away with an effort. I saw Ansky's bewilderment fading into something closer to suspicion. "It hunts us for what we are, Ansky," my words hurtling out as if to hold her. "Ersh is our center. It will want her most of all."

"Esen, listen to sense. Even if you're right, Ersh can defeat it," she argued. "She is Eldest."

"We don't know she can. We can't risk her, Ansky," I

said, shaking my head sadly. "I wish we had some way to be sure, but we don't."

"You truly believe this—thing—could threaten Ersh."

I felt oddly older, unsure if it was my own feeling or the burden of Ersh-memory. "I know it."

Out There

DEATH wasn't hungry. Without expending energy to travel, it had no immediate need to hunt. There was satisfaction in having others serve. The little convoy of ships moved steadfastly in the direction leading to what Death truly wanted.

More.

Death spread itself thinner against the hull, taking pleasure from the feel of life so very close.

It might be hungry soon.

39: Inn Evening

"NOW don't you try and tell me one serving was enough. Young men have their appetites." Ansky's assertion and subsequent overloading of poor Ragem's plate should have brought at least an understanding chuckle from our neighbors, given the Ártican sense of humor.

Instead, the crowd gathered tonight in the Sleepy Uncle's dining hall remained as silent as the bones of their God's altars. If I didn't know better, I'd have thought there was a taboo against talking indoors. The final tap tap of Ansky's spoon on Ragem's plate rang in the silence.

"Maybe we should eat in our rooms, Ansky," I whispered as she flounced behind me, the immense bowl of chilled vegetable stew under one arm, hand brandishing the spoon as if ready to dole out more.

"Too late for regrets," she said loudly, boldly eyeing her other customers until they found their own tabletops of engrossing interest. "You eat what you've ordered. Besides, my spedinni is the specialty of the house, Madame Ket."

We wore our floral badges giving us the blessing of their God—or at least the permission of their planet's gatekeeper—to be here. We'd sat in a corner far from the area Ansky kept for the locals. We'd been so unremarkable as to be invisible.

But we weren't. The dining hall had filled steadily, by ones and twos, since we'd come down for our evening meal. Ansky's cheery greetings to her regulars had been ignored. No one else had ordered food or drink. The Articans merely came in the door, looked to see if we were there, then took a seat. They were waiting. *I didn't like it.*

"We're in trouble," Ragem mumbled around a mouthful of stew, his eyes measuring and wary.

"Ansky knows these people," I said, more for myself than him.

He dropped his voice a shade lower. "This is a mob waiting for something to happen, Es. I've seen it before."

I looked around casually, and knew Ragem was right. There had to be over forty adults here now, three more just walking in the door, outwardly a normal-enough sampling of the local population. They were a bit too well dressed for farmers taking their ease after a hard harvest. And, despite our low conversation, none had uttered a word.

A necklace of preserved flower petals hardly seemed sufficient protection. "This mob will have to keep waiting, then," I decided. "Because we're leaving. Now."

In hindsight, I should have paid more attention to everything in the room. I should have seen which of us the eyes followed most: I should have known who was really at risk. Instead, I worried about keeping myself between Ragem and the crowd, believing if the worst happened and they attacked us, I had the best chance at protecting him. But Ragem wasn't the target.

We stood, putting down our napkins and pushing in our chairs as if leaving normally. I brushed my long fingers against the soothing grain of the wood, trying to keep outwardly calm. Every sense seemed keener. I looked around, catching Ansky's eyes as she reappeared in the doorway to the kitchen, carrying out a carafe of some steaming liquid. I noticed the steam, the bone altar to the left of the doorway, the way light from the kitchen spilled around her feet and ran into the main hall, brighter than that provided by the purple candles on every table.

I noticed everything but the way every Artican's attention riveted on *her*.

Ragem did. His arm swept me to one side as he walked straight into the middle of the room, passing between tables crowded with silent, brooding Articans as if in his own lounge on the *Rigus*. "Barkeep," his voice sailed out, cheery and loud, his pronunciation of the Artican trade tongue not bad under the circumstances. "I wonder if you've any of that fine stew left in your kitchen."

I froze, finally alert to the anger in the room and its

focus. *Ragem, you fool!* I thought. *She can look after herself.*

Ansky smiled at Ragem as if the two of them were alone and he were her next consort. "As I promised, good guest," she said. "There're no empty bellies in my house."

"A House of Sin!"

I twisted to see the latest arrivals at the inn: a pair of priests who strode in through the main doors as if taking ownership. Both wore the red-rimmed vests of black animal hide signifying they were Seekers, engaged in the lawful hunt to find and punish those who violated their God's taboos. Behind them were guards, male this time, more than I could count through the doors, their weapons' glint about all I could see clearly.

"My inn, Seeker Preador?" Ansky asked just as bluntly, putting the carafe down on the nearest table. "What sin do you expect to find here, among my good and pious neighbors?"

"This!" The Seekers stepped farther in, moving one to each side of the opening. Between them, the guards pushed in a hunched little figure, so curled up and busy moaning its distress I had trouble identifying it for a moment. But that voice wasn't Artican, or anything else remotely humanoid.

"Deny you kept this hidden, Innkeeper!"

Ansky, Ragem staying at her side, cruised across the room like a battleship across an ocean. The guards backed away as she tenderly bent down and helped the creature straighten up. When its face caught the candlelight, there were gasps from around the room.

It had to be an Urgian, I thought in despair. Ansky-memory surfaced promptly, giving me its name (I'd need different vocal cords), far too many details about its sexual prowress, and even this poor being's fondness for fried sausage on toast. I hadn't paid attention during assimilation to *where* Ansky's been writing Urgian love poems. I'd assumed on Urgia, not in her basement.

The being clung to Ansky, its head barely up to her waist, its present morph state dimale-sisfemale from what little I could see within the blankets bundling it against the night's chill and the rough handling of the guards. Ansky's arm was firmly around it, likely the only thing keeping the delicate being standing.

"Why have these aliens come to our village, to your house? Because you encourage these demons to walk among us! Did you not keep this one hidden here, in full knowledge it does not have the Keeper's permission?" the hitherto speechless Seeker announced, pulling at the blankets so we could all see the creature had no petal necklace such as Ragem and I wore for safety. "You have given it comfort and shelter so it can continue to heresy against the One God."

"It can't understand you, Seeker, so don't shout at it," Ansky said sternly. "As for permission, the petals of the Keepers' sign gave it a rash. I have it stored in the blessed corner of my own room if you'd care to see. I deny there has been any heresy. Listen," she turned slowly to look at all those gathered in the room. Many ducked their heads to avoid her gaze. "You people know me. We harvested together this day. I am a true believer and I tell you there is no wrong in this gentle being. He is a guest, like any other here, and has obeyed all of the strictures of our God."

They won't support you, I said, but to myself. *Can't you see that, Ansky?*

The first Seeker laughed without humor. "All? Then explain this, good and God-fearing innkeeper." He gestured to one of the guards nearby, a big, roughhewn male. This Artican moved forward smoothly, obviously coached in what his leader would want done. He pulled the Urgian out of Ansky's grasp, ripping away its blanket.

"Careful," Ragem warned, his hands becoming fists. "It's not as strong as you are." His accent and the words were insulting, a choice I suspected was deliberate rather than a mistake. I wished, of course futilely, for him to be less brave and more sensible. The Urgian moaned to itself, now exposed to the draft whistling through the door. The cool night air was a welcome relief from the overheated room to the rest of us but I could see shivers coursing under its fine scales, as though an iridescent liquid poured over its body.

"We know its weakness," said the Seeker, peering down at Ragem as if disappointed to see still-fresh petals encircling the Human's neck, "And we know its life is a blasphemy against the One God. Show us!"

The guard took one of the Urgian's four slender arms and folded it almost in half. The being didn't appear to notice. The guard bent the arm the other way again, himself looking a tad green as he did so. Again the Urgian didn't react. I heard a retching noise from somewhere behind me. *What did they expect from a species without a calcified skeleton?* I wondered. Which was, of course, the problem.

"This being should not be punished for its nature," Ansky protested, picking up one of the blankets to wrap around the alien. Its one weepy eye regarded her gratefully before closing again in misery. "The God of Bones asks us to care for those living things without its blessing."

"The God of Bones rightly has us care for such beings until they are harvested for the benefit of God's Blessed. Are you suggesting we do so with this?"

Ansky's face tightened ever-so-slightly, its skin reddening—I thought she likely raised her temperature and controlled my own urge to cycle in the same way. But her voice remained polite and level, that famous calm of hers in full force. "What do you suggest, Seeker?"

"We wish this being removed from Artos," the other priest answered. He pointed at me with a burnished fingerbone, its surface carved in some script or other. *Instructions on how to intimidate the masses,* I thought, not ready to be as forgiving with these beings as my birth-mother appeared. "These other aliens have the Keeper's permission to travel among us. They can take this one to the spaceport."

"Of course, Seeker," I said quickly, relieved if astonished at this sign they could be reasonable. I stepped forward to take the Urgian in my own grasp, pulling it gently but firmly away from those in the doorway. The poor thing was icy to my fingers, and I tried to bundle it tighter in the blanket as we moved. *The sooner it was out of the Articans' sight the better,* I thought.

We'd taken only a few slow steps when the Urgian twisted sinuously in my hold, looking back to Ansky. It chirruped something frantic, impossible for me to understand in this form as the sound soared octaves above Ket hearing. I didn't need the content. The Urgian was far from the only being to love Ansky.

Ansky smiled and whistled, a reassurance that drooped the Urgian against me. The poor being must be close to phasing out from stress. *Not now,* I urged it silently. I needed it to stay stable at least long enough to reach the temporary safety of our room.

My preoccupation with it stopped me from being able to act when two guards marched forward in obedience to the Seeker's gesture and took Ansky by the arms. "What is this?" she said, not moving. As she out-massed the guards in total, I could see they were nonplussed what to do next.

"You must be judged, woman," the Seeker intoned. "You will come to the Shrine and face your God."

There was a sound at last from the crowd in the room, a shocking low growl reverberating upward to the flower-hung ceiling and trembling the candle flames. I hurried the Urgian to the doorway leading to the stairs, thrusting it through and pointing upward to the light coming from the rooms on the next floor. It seemed to understand, squirming toward what safety I could provide with admirable speed. I closed the door behind it, turning back to the main room.

The Articans were on their feet now, lips closed, but still making that bestial noise. Their faces were far less Human-similar. *Human!* Where was Ragem?

Oh no. He had stayed with Ansky, actually shoving away one of the guards from the look of it. Before I could do more than gasp, Ragem was grabbed by others and swept out the doors with Ansky, the crowd around me surging forward to follow. Ignored, I shuffled behind the last of them, Ansky-memory supplying horrifying samples of what might be about to occur. *Ersh, this can't be happening,* I found myself repeating inanely to myself. *Ansky knows this culture better than I do. She knows what she's doing. Right?* But Ersh wasn't there to reassure me.

40: Shrine Night

THE Shrine rose in the center of the village, splitting the main road in two to carry its traffic by on either side, the result being that you couldn't travel anywhere without passing the living eyes of the God of Bones—and paying a road tax to the owners of those eyes. As in the other shrines Ragem and I had seen from the air, this building had been altered over time to reflect the rapid evolution of the Artican religion. Its tallest spire had been removed, replaced by the black globe currently popular as a sign of worship. The former warm brick of its construction had been painted an assortment of grays, the effect meant to suggest the building was made of sacred bone, but succeeding only in making the solid structure look leprous and ready to collapse.

Our feet crunched over black gravel, sharp nasty stones my famed Ket tactile sense insisted on telegraphing to my brain as hot sparks shooting up both legs. I had a most un-Ketlike longing for shoes.

I could have used inspiration as well. The crowd was well-behaved, so far; all that had happened being an orderly march from the Sleepy Uncle to the village Shrine. Along the way, we collected what might be every other Artican in the place until more were behind me than in front. I hadn't been able yet to push all the way up to where the guard escorted Ansky and Ragem, but with some adroit dodging I could now see them just ahead, illuminated by the streetlights on either side. They were no longer being held. On the other hand, where could they go?

This was not good, I decided, Ket hearts pounding, my sore feet persisting in distracting me as I made and then discarded plan after plan, considered form after form. *Trust Ansky,* I concluded, helplessly. *Trust her to know what she's doing.* It wasn't a plan, but it seemed the only thing I could safely do for now.

The priests, Ansky and Ragem, and several guards entered the Shrine. Not everyone was being allowed to follow. I took my turn before the guards stationed outside, prepared to be adamant—or at least truly obnoxious—but they took one look at the petals around my neck and stood aside to let me enter without question.

Inside, the building retained its original loveliness, there being not much you could do to alter the grace of wooden beams and arches without bringing down the roof. The airiness of its massive hall was welcome on my overheated form. The Shrine was almost filled to capacity already. Many villagers had gathered beforehand from the looks of it; the benches were packed and more stood along the sides. I made my way to an aisle seat, the Artican female closest to me moving as far away as flesh allowed. At this moment, I was beyond insult, too busy craning my neck to try and see what was happening at the front.

Both Ansky and Ragem were taller than most Articans. I could just see the backs of their heads, Ansky's crowned in its unlikely flurry of red-gold and Ragem's usually neat black locks tousled as if he'd struggled somewhere in the journey. A forest of slender gray staffs—bone, of course—marked where the village council priests must be standing to confront the two.

I stood and climbed up on the bench, using my sternest Ket glare to subdue the immediate objection of the Artican behind me. *At last.* Now I could see and hear what was going on.

I wished I couldn't.

Ansky, alone of all in the now-silent crowd, appeared at ease; I could see the side of her face and thought I caught a small smile on her lips, as though she had just invited those before her to relax and chat. She and Ragem were still gripped by guards, one holding the Human, two holding her.

From the somber black robes of those facing them, I knew we were about to witness a sentencing by the God of Bones' Chosen, not a trial or hearing. Nothing in my shared memories listed harboring a boneless individual as a taboo—*Ansky would have to invent her own crime,* I thought with disgust, trying to subdue my fear. *What would she do?*

It appeared the answer was to throw herself on their mercy. *Not my first choice.* I held my breath and listened. "Seeker Prador has informed me of my transgression," Ansky's voice rang out like a bell, the ideal blend of contrition and humility in every word. "Please believe it was unknowing. I ask your grace to perform my penance to our God."

Heads nodded. There was an approving murmur through the gathering: *a vast improvement over growling,* I reasoned. I hoped Ansky knew what she was doing; the priests would have the final say in what her penance would be and there were some deplorable options on their list of choices.

"Hear us, Blessed of our God," intoned the centermost priest. "Let us pray for guidance."

As those around me closed their eyes and began to loudly exhort their God for advice, I slipped off the bench and padded toward the front. I'd moved to within two rows when a low gong stopped the prayers as abruptly as they'd started. No choice but to step close to the next bench in line and hope to be unnoticed. My new neighbor frowned at me briefly, then decided the events up front were more interesting.

The cluster of priests stepped to one side, allowing Ansky and Ragem, and the rest of us, to see the altar. Aside from being four times the size, it resembled the one in the Spaceport Keeper's Shrine down to the relative number of thighbones used as uprights. But this altar was not made from animal bones alone and its surface glittered in the harsh lights streaming down from above it. *Not the surface,* I observed numbly, *the blades lying on it.*

"Your penance," intoned the priest, "is to be forever blessed to the service of the God of Bones."

There was a collective sigh from the audience, a sound like an orgasmic release of pleasure. It was all very well for them to anticipate a quick trip to Artican heaven as a result of having their bones removed and added to those decorating the Shrine. Ansky-memory did not hold that as one of her dreams.

Nor, of course, was it Ragem's. "What of my assistant, Your Worship?" I dared to call out, thoroughly shocking those around me. "He bears the Keeper's sign. I know he has meant no disrespect to your ways or God." *Much as I'd like to show some,* a notion I shunted deep inside.

"I don't know this alien, Seeker Prador," Ansky added in a quiet, respectful tone. "I believe he was only concerned for my well-being."

"Humans are the Cast Outs!" came a hoarse shout from the back.

"Kill them both!" came another, regrettably repeated several times and at increasing volume.

I'd need more mass to be anything useful, I realized, searching the room with my eyes, unwilling even in my fury at these fanatics to consider taking one of them as a donor.

"The Human will not be harmed," the priest shouted, making me sag with relief. "It is enough that he shall never know the Blessing and must leave our beautiful world forever."

However much I approved of this declaration, it didn't satisfy the blood lust quite thoroughly possessing the crowd in the Shrine. Articans began leaping up, pushing each other in their eagerness to get closer to the front. I let myself be carried along with them.

The priests stood fast for a moment, staffs raised in futile gestures of authority, then seized their prisoners and scurried to one side of the hall, disappearing from view. Cheated, the crowd began that bestial growl, this time loud enough to be perceived as a vibration through the floor under my feet. I took advantage of my long legs and flexible body to speed through the first disorganized ranks—barely restrained by the Shrine's guards who were thus too preoccupied to bother with me—and followed the priests who'd taken Ragem and Ansky.

There! I spotted the door just as it closed. Somehow I eluded the grasp of the one guard who noticed me, flinging myself right over a basket of fresh cut magitteri flowers, their famous perfume something this form couldn't appreciate, even if I'd been in the mood.

The door wasn't locked. It led outside, to a roofless corridor that paralleled the main building, walled by a latticework fence and at the moment more than half-filled with a jumble of empty baskets, staffs, and moaning or unconscious priests. I skidded to a halt, blinking in the near darkness, trying to figure out what could have happened.

"Es! This way!"

"Ragem?" I started picking my way through the confusion to the voice.

"Hurry up!" he urged. Judging by the sounds from behind me, there was good reason to be less careful where I put my feet, though I winced when I stepped on at least one set of fingers. Hopefully their owner hadn't noticed.

"Will you come?" This from Ansky. I could see them both at last, standing at the end of the little corridor, silhouetted by the streetlights beyond. I slipped as I forced my way through the last pile of baskets and found myself in Ansky's firm grasp. "Let's go," she said immediately, pulling me along with her.

"What did you—?"

Ragem's voice had a feather of laughter to it: *equal parts triumph and panic,* I decided. "Let's say I'd never start a brawl in the Sleepy Uncle—or in any establishment run by this sweet lady."

"I should hope not. You seem like a nice young man," Ansky said serenely. She was leading us down the main street, away from the Shrine, but also away from the inn and our borrowed aircar.

"The aircar?" I objected, attempting, in vain, to resist moving with them. I could hear Ersh now. *As well try to stop an avalanche as Ansky at full throttle.*

"That's where they expect us to go," Ragem said from behind me.

"That's where we need to go," I countered, still struggling to undo Anksy's grip on my poor arm.

She released me after a stern tug in the direction of her choice. "We'll go through the orchard and come around from behind, youngest," she said pleasantly, as though we were out for an evening stroll. "Ah."

Ansky's "Ah" turned out to mark a narrow footpath between two homes, one she urged us along. It was dark once we were a few strides past the range of the nearest streetlight, a plus given the rising clamor of voices behind us as the crowd spilled out and discovered their priests. The footing was again the soft turf, balm to my feet.

"I don't remember a taboo against attacking the clergy," I commented.

"I'm sure that will be rectified at the next meeting,"

Ansky returned. "Sssh. They might have left someone at the drying shed to turn the flowers."

We had already passed between three tall rows of houses, all apparently empty of their inhabitants. *One advantage to the mass meeting,* I thought, keeping the hand that wasn't clenched around my hoobit outstretched in case I needed to feel my way around some unseen obstacle in the dark. It was instinctive, Ket night-sight being less trustworthy than touch.

The shed, a mammoth building much longer than it was wide, lay just beyond the hind yards of the last row of homes. Its darker bulk loomed against the rising mountainside, small lights from its high windows confirming Ansky's caution. Ragem stifled a sneeze. Even my Ket sense of smell was affected by the sheer volume of scent oozing from its walls. I heard Ansky draw in a deep breath beside me. "Marvelous crop this season," she whispered matter-of-factly as we passed the building. "The Shrine will offer exceptional blessings this festival." *I won't ask,* I decided, not having an Ansky-memory rise in explanation and quite sure I didn't want to know any more about the Articans—an ephemeral attitude sure to infuriate Ersh. *I don't care,* I told myself, then added the truth: *much.*

We reached the hedge surrounding the orchard, and all of my doubts about Ansky's chosen path came crashing back as I looked ahead. Skalet had considered my birth-mother the least able of us to defend herself. *Here was proof.* "You expect us to hide in there?" I demanded incredulously.

"It's the largest orchard in the valley," Ansky answered in a shaken voice, perhaps feeling her own dismay.

No doubt the orchard was large. By the light of the rising moons I could see its ranks of fruit trees marching to the start of the mountain forest and down again to surround this entire side of the village.

But the feathery tips of the tallest of those young trees would barely reach my chin. Most would be under my elbows.

"We don't have a choice, Fems," Ragem said bluntly, hurrying from where he walked back a few paces to check on our pursuers. "They're coming. Enough of them to cause trouble, at any rate." His arms swept both of us forward through the orchard gate. "Let's not make it any easier."

Out There

DEATH made up a new game. It slipped from shell to shell, exploring their differences, relishing the sense of life so vulnerable and close, imagining the result of cracking open this one *here,* or that one *there.*

Such fun.

The possibilities of pleasure were so great, Death almost forgot where it wanted to go and why.

Almost.

41: Orchard Night; Forest Night

I WAS soon convinced this would be one of those nights I'd replay in my thoughts for centuries to come, forced to remember each painful moment with the acute and vivid accuracy of my heritage. I envied Ragem his fallible Human memory. If we could trade, the first thing I'd choose to forget was running for my life as a Ket through this Artican orchard.

I was young, strong, and healthy. I was also working under several disadvantages. The orchard was carpeted, not in turf, but in a spiked, curling, detestable undergrowth Ansky-memory told me helped discourage small wild herbivores. It was discouraging me; with every step my bare feet translated each tiny thorn's grip-and-release as a needle through my skin. To make me even more miserable, Artos' gravity, while close to Ket-norm, was sufficiently greater to steal whatever excess energy sheer terror lent me.

In a final insult, the warm caressing air had turned chill (to a Ket) and thin, due to the late evening slide of air down the mountain. I gasped, shivered, stumbled, and otherwise made a miserable show of keeping up with Ragem's tireless strides and Ansky's ponderous grace.

I'd have given anything to cycle out of this form.

But, thanks to my web-kin's inspired selection of escape routes, there was no hope of doing that without being seen. I couldn't keep up if I crouched below the tops of the tiny trees. And I wouldn't cycle in sight of the pack climbing steadily behind us. There may have been only three Articans giving chase, but they were three witnesses too many.

Ersh, I hope you appreciate this, I grumbled to myself,

yanking my foot free of a more amorous clump of foliage than most, surely leaving skin behind in the bargain.

"How far up?" Ragem's panting had a reassuringly desperate quality.

"To the tree line," Ansky's voice floated back, still as calm as though we were engaged in evening revels instead of running for our lives. "We'll split up there—confuse them a bit—then meet back at the inn when things quiet down."

She continued to plow ahead, aiming at the knife's edge of shadows marking the verge of the natural forest. From Ansky's memories, I knew it to be an old, overgrown, and wild community, filled with a labyrinth of game trails only a hunter used to this area could safely travel. Surely some of those behind us qualified. Likely Ansky did. Ragem didn't.

My toes snagged again and this time I allowed myself to stop, breathing in the light quick pants that delivered air to my lungs in the Ket equivalent of the Human's heaving gasps as he halted beside me. "What's wrong?" he asked in a whisper, looking behind us at those now gaining with every step.

"Ansky," I called quietly, almost shaking with an anger deeper than anything I'd ever felt before. My birth-mother, my web-kin, turned to look at me, her face in the moons' light showing little more than impatience before she stepped farther into the protection of the shadows.

"This is no place to rest, youngest," she chided. "Safety lies ahead."

"Not for Ragem," I disagreed, knowing what she planned. I dared her to admit that once separated in the forest, she intended the two of us to cycle and escape, leaving Ragem to fend for himself. It was classic web-thinking. Skalet would approve, though doubtless be surprised to find it coming from the usually less than rational Ansky.

I wouldn't allow it.

It wasn't easy making out details on a face half-concealed by the shadow of the trees, but I thought I saw a glint on her cheek—a tear, perhaps. "Individual survival is not one of the First Rules, youngest," Ansky reminded me in her soft, kind voice. I gripped my hoobit tightly, not needing a lecture on rules I'd already broken, not that Ansky would know. Keeping the secrets of the Web seemed highly unimportant at the moment, though I had little chance of convincing Ansky before the Articans reached us.

"We go together," I insisted. "We can lose them."

"We separate. The Clepf River flows from the forest and crosses through the village beside the inn. Follow its banks and keep to cover. You'll both be fine."

A stronger breeze than most rushed through the great branches of the trees ahead, softening to a mere fluttering of leaves as it met the tiny legions of the orchard, as if careful not to harm anything so small and helpless. I couldn't bring myself to take another step after Ansky, even when she made an exasperated sound and turned to go. Ragem hesitated with me.

"What's wrong, Es?" he whispered. "I agree with Ansky—we're safer out of sight. And you can cycle there."

"And what will you do, Human?" I asked. "How will you avoid them?"

Ragem looked over his shoulders at the three Articans climbing toward us. They'd ceased their shouts and curses, perhaps finding the pace Ansky set as difficult as I had. But there was no sign they planned to stop. "I grew up on a world much like this. I know how to make my way through the bush," he assured me. "I'll meet you at the inn. Don't worry."

"I'm not leaving you—" I began to argue. Just then, Ansky came back, perhaps to urge us into the forest. Instead, she froze at my side, looking down the slope at the Articans as they moved through the shoulder-high trees like swimmers through waves.

"Iterold?" she breathed. Then, regrettably at the full extent of her formidable lung capacity: "Iterold!" The word tumbled down the mountainside before echoing from the other side of the valley. *So much for stealth,* I thought glumly.

One of the figures slowed, raising his head to look up. he was too far for my Ket eyes to see clearly, but Ansky didn't have that problem. "Dear God," she said. "It is him."

I didn't know the name, but I knew that tone from Ansky. This must be one of the partners Ersh had filtered from Ansky-memory for me. "Let's go," I said, my turn to urge my web-kin toward safety.

The face she turned to me was wild-eyed and confused. "You don't understand, youngest. We've known each other for years. Iterold taught me how to cook spedinni—among other things. He must be trying to help me. We must wait for him." *This was the Ansky Skalet worried about,* I thought, *with good reason.*

"No, Ansky—" I protested.

"You want me to trust this Human," she countered with the accuracy of desperation. "I tell you, we can trust Iterold!"

Regem added his voice to mine, saying urgently: "They're carrying weapons, Ansky. I'm sorry, but we can't trust any Artican tonight."

"No. You don't—" She broke off and actually began to run back down the hill. It took both of us to stop her, a feat we barely managed.

"For Ersh's sake, Ansky!" I shouted in her ear, my toes digging into the soil as I tried to keep her in place. *An avalanche was right.* "Have some sense! If this Iterold loves you, what do you think he's going to do about the penance? Refuse to send you to his heaven? He's your worst enemy now."

Finally, Ansky listened. I could tell because Ragem and I lurched forward in comic unison, clinging to her for support as she gave up the effort to push past us. "Iterold?" she whispered, still looking over my shoulder. I didn't bother. Footsteps and heavy breathing were all the clues I needed as to what this delay had cost us.

"The forest. Now!"

Somehow the three of us scrambled out of the revealing moons' light into the shelter of the trees and brush before our pursuers caught up. Ansky, either now convinced or so grief-stricken she was beyond argument, didn't suggest we separate but led the way up a narrow trail I barely saw in the almost stygian darkness. I kept both hands outstretched—certain I was going to collide with a branch or Ansky's broad back at any moment, if I didn't trip over my long feet first. Ragem brought up the rear.

Where were they? The silence behind us seemed ominous. I knew the Articans wouldn't give up the chase, not when they had come so close. They could know this trail well enough to move more quietly than we did.

Or they could know another way to go—a way that would cut us off. I suggested as much to Ansky when she slowed to duck under a partially fallen tree.

"There's no other path," she said shortly. "Watch your head."

I turned to pass on this advice to Ragem, only to find he wasn't there. "Paul-Human," I hissed as loudly as I dared, hearts pounding. "Paul—!"

"Here." His voice materialized before he did, proof if I needed any that his woodcraft was superior to mine. *In this form,* I thought wistfully to myself. "Just checking on our friends back there. No sign of them." He sounded as worried as I felt. I thought he was also wondering why Ansky and I hadn't cycled into something capable of escaping. I couldn't imagine how Ansky would react if I told her she was risking her life to keep our secret from the one non-Web being who knew almost everything about us.

I could force the issue, I thought, pursing my lips in a frown, and would if Ragem were in danger or if we had no other options. But given that Ansky's hard-won identity on this world had collapsed, at least two of her current loves were much less than happy, and I'd brought her news of our murdered kin, it hardly seemed the right time to force her from the security of Ersh's Rules.

Besides, I reminded myself with certainly misplaced amusement, *that kind of thing took practice.*

By my estimation, we reached the point at which I expected to meet Ansky's guiding river at about the same time I noticed our path was now a dry streambed. Given my state of near-exhaustion, I appreciated the soothing distraction of the cool, rounded rock. The lack of signs of pursuit was less comforting. *Where were they?*

"Hold up," Ragem said from behind me.

I could make out the pale oval of Ansky's face as she turned to find out what he wanted. It was significantly lighter here, more of the moons' brightness reaching the forest floor as the trees began thinning out. "What is it?" she asked. "We're almost to the Clepf."

"I thought I heard something."

"There's wildlife—" Ansky stopped and I strained to hear what the others were listening to over the pounding of my hearts. *Amazing how the body responded to new levels of fear,* I thought, feeling my Ketself definitely ready to run.

Crash! The sound of the tree falling beside the path was loud enough, especially when it followed the *thwomp* of an explosion. A Denebian mid-range grenade, Skalet-memory provided unhelpfully. There was shouting from behind even as branches continued to slide and crack their way to the ground, one narrowly missing us.

"Cycle!" I hissed to Ansky, grabbing at her shoulder. "Now!"

"No!" she exclaimed in horror. "The Human!" She tried to pull free, but my Ket grip held through my lighter body moved with her. "We must leave him first."

"He knows—" I tried to explain, but my voice was drowned out by another explosion, close enough to spray us with gravel and debris. I froze, still holding Ansky, locked in Ket-panic and a frustrated need for my Elder to make a decision.

Ragem didn't hesitate an instant. His shoulder struck me just above my hips in a violent tackle that drove both Ansky and me forward to the streambed. The scream of ripped wood overlapped a closer, more intimate cry of pain. Both sounds died into silence.

"Ragem!" I cried out, struggling to free myself from the tight grip of his arms—*no,* I discovered with horror, not his arms, but the branches of the tree that had fallen on us all.

I exploded into web-form, immediately sensing Ansky's perfection moving away. She was safe. *Ragem.* I tasted his organics among the dying molecules of the tree floating past my surface. *Too concentrated.* He must be bleeding. *Not dead.* I could feel the impulses driving his heart, running through his nerves. And suddenly, with a force I registered as pain, a new rhythm burst through my senses, played in resonances that said *machine,* a signal blasting past me, past this atmosphere, and doubtless much farther than I could follow.

Ragem's implant had activated.

I didn't care what this meant about Kearn or his plots.

What mattered was that the device detected Ragem's vital signs going critical. *Ersh, was he dying?*

Being surrounded by mass made my choice simpler. I assimilated tree molecules, changing them into more of me with frantic haste, then cycled . . .

Having dozens of eyes certainly helped make the most of the dim light, but I'd chosen the Carasian form for its other attribute—the brute strength of its handling arms. I used my new claws to snip and tear away branches, clearing my view of the main trunk. Ragem wasn't under it.

Voices. I compressed myself into as small a space as I could among the ruined wood, hoping the Articans would miss my black leaf-bedecked mass among the shadows, even closing the upper and lower valves of my head to hide any reflection from my eyes.

The sounds of searching came closer and closer, then began to fade again into distance. *Ansky,* I thought, suddenly torn between duties.

A nearby moan settled my priorities. The Carasian form was a pitiful climber, its spongy footpads and bulky body adapted nicely for existence on rocky tidal flats, but somehow I forced myself through the tangle of limbs on top of the tree trunk and climbed down the other side. I went as carefully as possible, afraid of landing on Ragem if any of the thinner branches gave way under my weight.

"Ragem?" I called softly, hoping he accepted the change in vocal cords. "Paul?"

Another moan, softer. *There.* I clipped and pulled until I could see the Human's body, motionless under a trio of thicker branches.

The bulk of the tree had missed him. At first, I couldn't tell why he lay so still. Then, I saw the reason and shuddered so hard my armored skin rang like thunder. One narrow branch disappeared into his back, pinning him to the gravel bed. *Another memory to haunt me forever.*

I made myself think of it as a test, something Ersh might have devised to assess my ingenuity. The body trapped so helplessly below me wasn't my dearest friend, it was only a problem to solve. *As if I believed that,* I whimpered to myself. Blood darkened most of his jacket, but mercifully no longer poured from the wound. The first thing was to free him without making matters worse.

Clearing away the surrounding limbs was tricky. Some I had to leave so the massive tree trunk didn't roll over on us both, something it threatened each time a *crack* announced a branch farther along had broken under the strain. *Well enough,* I thought, and opened one large claw to encompass the piece of wood spearing Ragem's flesh. My other claw I'd worked underneath him and clamped around the protruding end where it entered the ground. *At least I hoped that's what I felt.* My two, smaller claws were fixed on his near leg and shoulder.

Fast would be best.

"Paul?" I said. "I'm going to free you now. Hold still if you can."

There was no answer, which I hoped meant he was unconscious and wouldn't feel what I was about to do.

I snapped both large claws shut, the most powerful muscles of this form driving their bladelike edges through the wood as though it was a rival's flesh. Simultaneously, I pulled Ragem toward me with my other claws, scrambling back as the trunk groaned and settled, punching the cut end of its branch into the pool of blood where Ragem had been a breath ago.

"Too close," I commented to the being cradled in my arms, trying not to shake him as I continued to back away.

"Ansky?" the faintest whisper caught my hearing, fortunately an organ located near my second elbow joint and so near Ragem's face.

"You pushed us clear, Paul," I told him, only now recognizing what he'd done. "You'd better not die on me," I added, hunting and finding a likely spot. I didn't hear him answer as I gently laid him on his side in the soft moss.

Then I stood and stared at him while checking our surroundings for any sign of the Articans, something easy to do with independently mobile eyes. We appeared to be alone.

Ersh, what do I do now?

The answer was as simple as it was unpleasant. To save Ragem, I needed the aircar to take him to the med on the *Quartos Ank*. To save Ansky, I again needed the aircar and the Kraal ship. "I have to leave, Paul," I said. The higher, soft pitch of my voice surprised me. At some point during my agonized decision-making, I'd slipped back into

Ket, a terrifying thoughtlessness. *Or perhaps instinct,* I admitted, since this was the form I must use with the Kraal—though I found I no longer cared about the opinion of the Articans.

I left Ragem, climbing much more easily as Ket through the wreckage of the tree to look for my things. My skirt had shredded beyond repair and my flower petal necklace was gone, but I found the hoobit, its leather thong broken but serviceable, the metal of the pendant itself blackened with soot. I tied it around my neck, rubbing at the dirt with already dirty fingers.

Back to Ragem. I piled moss up against him for warmth, then used soil and finally small twigs to brace his body so he couldn't roll over and jar the ends of the branch protruding from his chest and back. It had missed his major organs by all the signs I could see, but was a serious injury nonetheless. His face was pale and beaded with sweat despite the cool night air. *Shock,* I fussed to myself. That and blood loss could kill him before the sun came up.

Ragem woke up during this handling, his gray eyes fixed on me, deep lines around his mouth ample sign of the pain he was feeling. "What are you doing here, Es?" he said after taking a couple of shallow breaths; *testing his lungs,* I thought. "Go!"

"Yes," I agreed, crouching so I could run my fingers lightly over his face. "But I'll be back. And soon."

"Bad idea," he murmured, closing his eyes. I stroked the petal-soft skin of their lids. They squeezed together tightly, and I caught the moisture escaping from their edges. "You get out of here," Ragem ordered in a weak but firm voice. "You get yourself and Ansky off this dirtball—promise me, Es!"

"We're all leaving—" I began.

From somewhere he found the strength to grab my wrist; his eyes flashed open, their gray almost black. "I can feel the implant sending. You know what that means."

"We'll be gone before Kearn—"

"It means I'm dying, you fool. Leave me. Get away while you can."

Strangely, Ragem's declaration convinced me he was nothing of the sort. "You're exaggerating to gain my sympathy, Human," I said, fluttering my fingers against his wrist so he could feel my smile. "Just stay put and don't get eaten by the wildlife until I return." I gently freed my arm from his cold fingers and reached up to pull off my hoobit, pressing it into his free hand. "Mind this for me, my friend."

Our eyes met. "Esen," he gasped, as if a last argument.

"I'll have to come back for it, won't I?" I said, ignoring his protest as I straightened from my crouch and stepped away. It literally hurt to leave him like this, though I knew it was necessary., My rough work to make him a bed should also hide him from anyone walking by. I stood precisely where Ragem could see me and cycled into the Lanivaarian. *To Ersh with Ansky's love of the Rules.*

"No dying," I growled, before spinning away on all fours to chase other prey.

Now I could seriously worry about my web-kin.

42: Valley Dawn; Spaceport Morning

THIS form loved everything about the forest: jumping over logs, stirring up damp moldy smells with each step, feeling the cool evening air through my coat, hearing the myriad sounds of living things disturbed and otherwise. On one level, I enjoyed these sensations, relieved of the automatic dread Ket-form attached to new and unusual places. On quite another level, I panted with terror as I ran, the scent of Anksy's pursuers as full in my nostrils as her own.

So it wasn't surprising that I bolted right into the icy waters of the Clepf, tumbling down its bank before noticing the drop, rolling along the narrow gravel shoreline until stopping myself with all four feet in the thankfully shallow river. I had thought we were close to the river; *just not this close*. There was no sign of Ansky or the Articans upstream, but the Clepf made an abrupt bend as it continued down to the village. I couldn't see past the rockstrewn bank.

Otherwise, I could see quite a bit, I realized, moving carefully into the shadow cast by the nearest bank, shaking out my damp paws one at a time as I cautiously followed the river's flow. The Articans called this time of day "first morning," as the light from all four moons added to that of the sun about to rise. It was bright enough away from the trees to see the reds and pinks of the stones standing sentinel amid the white froth of the river. This was considered a lucky time of day to harvest mushrooms. On the other hand, it was also believed to be a lucky time of day to die. I refused to think about Ragem, lying in trust. *I won't fail you,* I promised him in my thoughts.

I lapped up a bit of the glacier-fresh water as I went, ears pricked forward to catch any sound ahead. My nose wasn't as helpful; the body scents I'd been tracking now merged and were too fresh to give me distance. Then I slowed, catching a low rumble of voices. I was close.

Rather than continue alongside the river, I bounded up the bank, using my nose to quietly push an opening in the shrubs at its top, pressing through one paw after the other, creeping forward with all the care this sinuous body could manage. I only had to travel this way about ten paces before I could see the river again. And Ansky.

Ersh.

There she was, stubbornly Artican, and as definitely and ardently being embraced by an Artican. The pair of them appeared oblivious to the others standing nearby on the gravel shoreline below me. Those two stood at ease, one with a grenade launcher looped over his shoulder, the second with no obvious weapons at hand.

Now what should I do? I wondered, hiding in the bushes, tongue hanging sideways as I panted. *Had Ansky built a strong enough web with these individuals, as I had with Ragem, to trust them to act against the will of their own kind?* I began to glimpse the quandary I posed to my web-kin. *How to trust those you don't know?*

Should I accept Ansky's judgment of these beings? I meant no disrespect to Ansky, but I knew as certainly as I knew how to cycle that I couldn't share her trust. Her relationships with other species were based on her imposture as one of them, not, as mine with Ragem, on the truth. *At least a significant amount of it,* I amended honestly. For this reason alone, any trust between Ansky and others was flawed; any web she created was false.

So Ansky, despite this affectionate and prolonged physical reunion with her Artican, Iterold, was in danger.

A shame I came to this brilliant conclusion too late.

At that same moment, Iterold drew back, holding Ansky by the shoulders as if to gaze into her eyes. He spoke—something I couldn't hear over the babbling waters of the Clepf. She answered, a smile on her face. He bent forward as if to kiss her again, a gesture the Articans shared with many humanoid species.

As if in slow motion, I watched knives appear in the

hands of the other two, their polished blades taking fire from the increasing light of moons and sun, thrusting forward as if propelled by their God's will rather than simple bone and muscle. Both plunged into Ansky's back as I leaped from my hiding place, landing in a spray of gravel.

Iterold tried to cradle her as she fell, then screamed—lurching away as what he held *changed* in his arms. *I'd seen that look on Ragem's face,* I recalled with a shudder.

I could understand why. I was shocked myself to see Ansky cycle as she died, her web-flesh flowing over her betrayer's feet, melting into a pool of lush blue on the stones.

There was more screaming, some of it could have been from my throat. I think the Articans ran, but I was too busy backing away from that spreading pool as quickly as I could. Then I lost both sound and the ability to make it as I cycled involuntarily.

Ersh-memory overwhelmed me, tainted by that of my Enemy . . .

Feed. Consume.

. . . somehow I dragged my consciousness out of the morass of grief, rage, and sickening appetite, becoming aware of my surroundings again, web senses immediately occupied in sorting the chaos of molecular information all about, from Ansky's dying web-mass to the tastes of more organized collections marking the living, fleeing Articans. There was a distant, familiar resonance: Ragem's implant.

Gathering all of the control I had, I formed a mouth then tenderly nipped a tiny morsel from the nearest mass of what remained of my birth-mother.

From it came a wash of calm, of caring—somehow she had contained the moment of death closer to her core. I huddled for a moment, assimilating, refusing to take any more than this respectful taste.

Ersh-memory troubled my resolve, telling me how to consume all, to grow in size and rage until I became something large enough, something deadly enough, to kill them all.

But Ansky's flesh, now mine, sang with her love for these people, for all those she had known, for the Urgian huddled back at the inn, for me. Harming anyone would be the last thing she would wish.

I had to leave her and save Ragem. *I'd promised.*

First, I had to ensure what she had been was safe from interference. The grenade launcher lay nearby, dropped in panic. I felt my tail curl between my legs as I thought of what the Articans would tell the rest of their kind.

With nothing to guide me, and no wish to taste any more of what was truly now dead matter, I stood on two legs and, using one of the knives floating on the blue pool of web-mass, dug a trench in the stones to the river. The fresh mountain stream danced behind the blade, flooding into the depression to soften the blue collected there, then, slowly, wash it away to clarity.

It wasn't far to the Sleepy Uncle, especially on four legs, downhill, and at a full-out run. Ansky had almost made it home. Actually, each time I snatched a drink from the waters of the Clepf running beside me, I found the thought of her within it oddly comforting.

I slowed only to make a final cautious approach, sneaking through the culvert channeling the Clepf River under the roadway. The entire village appeared deserted. Maybe they were all gathered in the Shrine to hear about the Boneless Ones. *Maybe,* I thought without bitterness, *they were harvesting Ansky's flowers.* All that concerned me now was getting back to Ragem as quickly as possible.

I honored Ansky, but no longer cared what taboos I shattered or what customs I offended. There was nothing I could to do to erase or explain away the sight of Ansky's body melting from those who had been there, let alone my settling into the same substance. In one instant, we had confirmed the Artican priesthood's worst fears about their God and the presence of aliens on their world. *It was true. We were boneless.*

Without a doubt, the result would be an immediate backlash against any alien beings on Artos.

I made my way to the back of the inn as Ket. As I expected, the aircar appeared untouched—off-worlder property being taboo without special permission from the priesthood. The com system in the aircar let me prepare Captain Hubbar-ro, and through him the other offworlders at the spaceport, for what might be to come.

I didn't have to hunt for the Urgian. The being had been

watching for us to return, and slithered neatly down the outside wall of the inn as I made my call to the spaceport. When I let it in the aircar, it immediately began wailing as it had when forced to leave Ansky. I grabbed a notepad and stylus from a compartment in the aircar and quickly, if somewhat brutally, explained what had happened.

Beyond a shiver as it read, the being showed no reaction, nor did it try and respond in kind when I offered it the stylus and pad. I respected its privacy. I'd planned to fly us out, but the Urgian slid into the pilot's seat with the air of one totally convinced of its right to that action. So I stayed in the passenger's seat, drawing a quick map to Ragem's location.

The machine made the return trip in mere minutes. There was no need for me to point—once we reached where the river left the forest, the clearing left by the fallen trees was clearly visible. The Urgian proved to be a master pilot, setting us down in the narrow space without hesitation, though forced to hover rather than land.

I'd imagined any number of dreadful sights that might greet my eyes, but hadn't actually been prepared for Ragem to raise his arm and wave my hoobit at us feebly. Something tight inside me eased.

By the time I'd climbed out of the aircar and run to him, his eyes were shut again, the hand with the hoobit limp at his side. I took it and placed it around my neck, the metal still warm from his grip. From the steadiness of his breathing, Ragem was unconscious. *Well enough,* I thought, estimating the effort and jostling it was going to take for an Urgian and a Ket to lever a wounded Human into the hovering craft.

It was as difficult as I'd feared, and Ragem's wounds oozed blood again. *A wonder he had any left.* We propped him sideways on pillows in the passenger's seat to protect him against any further jarring of the wood through his body. The Urgian sent the aircar upward with a sickening and welcome burst of power.

The air above the village was fragrant with flowers waiting for harvest. Three of Artos' quartet of tiny moons still hung over the shoulders of the nearest ridge; the rising sun traced the silhouettes of trees and rooftops with its rosy light, reflecting sudden silver from the narrow ribbon of the

Clepf. *And Ansky.* The beauty of the place was enough to gag me.

I tapped the Urgian on what could be loosely called a shoulder. *Time to go.*

"It's definite. The spaceport's closed to incoming traffic. We won't be allowed back, Madame Ket," Captain Hubbar-ro announced with what amounted to relief. "I don't imagine anyone wants to return anyway. 'Cept the Denebians, maybe, but they can look after themselves. The Urgian sent its regards before leaving on the Inhaven freighter. We think it was regards," he corrected himself. "The translator in the com wasn't quite sure. There was some poetry—and what might be an invoice."

I nodded, too tired to do more. I was even too exhausted to have felt more than a dull relief when the *Quartos Ank* had lifted from Artos—Hubbar-ro quite delighted to disobey the Keeper of the Spaceport Shrine and leave without clearance.

Now, however, the Kraal officer hesitated, looking uncomfortable. "You don't need to keep this vigil, Madame Ket. I assure you my med officer Carota-ro is quite qualified," this with what I thought could be a touch of abused pride. "He is certain your associate will make a full and rapid recovery. As he is certain the implant has been safely removed and destroyed." I didn't take the bait offered by this last. I'd already assured the Kraal that Ragem could explain the presence of the device to his satisfaction once the Human awoke. I hoped Ragem would feel inventive.

And I wasn't about to explain that I clung to Ragem's limp hand because I'd lost so much else. It wasn't for Ragem's sake I haunted his bedside. It was for my own.

"This Ket has full confidence in your crew, Hubbar-ro-Kraal," I managed to say steadily, looking up at him. "Please accept my thanks. What is our position now?"

"We are, as you requested, translight on a course to rejoin S'kal-ru and Admiral Mocktap's fleet." He frowned slightly. "Are you certain you don't want me to send a message to S'kal-ru? Surely you wish to notify her about the failure of our mission here."

"It can wait," I assured him, closing my eyes. "Bad news can always wait."

* * *

Ragem, on the other hand, would not wait. "Ansky?" was the first word uttered by his lips when he awoke later that shipday, his voice so dry and cracked it startled me from my own doze.

"Drink this," I said instead of answering, putting a cup to his mouth and watching him swallow the liquid. Over the cup, his eyes met mine, read what was there, and squeezed tightly closed for an instant.

"I'm so sorry, Esen," he said, shaking his head.

I hadn't slept since arriving on Artos; the strain was beginning to tell on my Ketself. "Do you know how close you came to dying, too?" I hissed at him, my hand up as if to strike.

"How— No. Don't tell me now. Come here, Esen." Ragem, with only a slight wince, pulled me down so my long Ket face could hide against his shoulder.

Our anatomies didn't match very well. Certainly it wasn't Ket to seek physical comfort from a non-Ket. Yet I found a strange peace in those moments within the Human's arms, an irrational sense of being protected from harm.

It would have been nice to believe.

Out There

"CAPTAIN. Captain Largas." He pushed his head deeper into the protective curl of his arms, grunting something irritable. This was the first bit of sleep he'd been able to grab in two-and-a-half days.

"Dad! Wake up." His daughter yanked his head up by his hair, a tactic Joel couldn't well ignore. The pain, and the alarm in her voice, shattered the last bit of grogginess. He rubbed his sleep-rimmed eyes and blinked at her, his neck thoroughly stiff from his choice of bed. At least this time he hadn't dropped face-first into his supper—the plate was safely pushed aside.

"What's wrong?"

Char switched her grip from his hair to his upper arm, tugging violently. "There's something on one of the life pods in tow to *Anna's Best*. You can see it."

Joel Largas found himself hurrying out of the galley behind her, definitely awake now. "What d'you mean, something?"

Char didn't answer, moving now at a run down the narrow corridor, those she passed in the crowded ship obligingly flattening themselves against bulkheads to get out of the way as the senior officers of the *Largas Loyal* went by, several with caustic comments about using a chrono in the future.

"In here." She stopped before the doorway into what had been the *Loyal*'s aft passenger quarters and was now the children's playroom. The door was sealed closed, and Char's oldest and largest son stood in front of it, obviously on guard. His normally good-natured face was set in grim lines; his eyes as they met those of his grandfather and captain were haunted. "It's still there," he said, letting them by.

"What's still—"

"Come on," Char said, pushing the door closed behind them.

The lights were off in the room. Joel tripped on a toy he

couldn't see and fondly thought of the days when Char had been spankable age. Then he joined her beside the viewport and caught his breath.

The convoy traveled as a cluster, a dangerous intimacy as ships traded the risk of collision for the risk of losing anyone to drive failure while translight. Largas could easily see the globes and struts of *Anna's Best* through the surrounding pearllike strings of the barges and pods she towed. They were lit by the glows encircling the *Best,* the powerful lights usually reserved for exterior work and kept on now as a more meaningful symbol of safety than the cabling connecting the starship to those huddled in the frail pods. In those crisscrosses of light, the pods and barges gleamed silver against the black void—all except one.

That one was half-coated in brilliant blue, a color richer than any gem Joel Largas had seen in all his years as a traveling merchant, and as out of place here. A blue that abruptly shifted, incredibly moving of its own volition, before becoming still again against the pod's hull.

"What is it?" he whispered.

Char's voice held no doubt at all. "Death."

43: Galley Evening

"LET me do that," I offered.

Ragem shook his head, at the same time performing an awkward yet successful twist with his fork to bring most of a scoop of meat into his mouth. "Broke my collarbone skiing few years ago," he confessed after chewing and swallowing. "This," he chinned the sling locking his right arm and hand to his chest, "is about the same."

I would have preferred to help. The wound hampering him he'd taken to save Ansky and me—the gesture no less meaningful for being unnecessary. I'd never felt such gratitude to another being before, not even within my Web, and wasn't completely sure how to dispose of the emotion. *A remarkable being,* I reminded myself, *if a bit too impulsive to be a survivor.*

We ate in companionable silence for a while, my own appetite far too great to be normal for a Ket. I felt unsettled when I considered it, and longed for a good long stretch as myself. *Out there,* added some new craving inside, remembering the vast clean sweep of space. Life did seem simpler in vacuum.

But what actions I could take had to be here and now. "Skalet's trap isn't going to work," I said flatly, watching for Ragem's reaction. He merely chased a playful vegetable around his plate for a moment. "I don't care how confident she is. We need another plan."

His eyes flicked up to me, their gray darkened by the low lighting in the dining room. The *Quartos Ank*'s cook believed in atomosphere. "We're going to need a great deal more than that, Es."

"What do you mean?" I studied his thin face.

Ragem put down his fork, then startled me by using his teeth to pull up the sleeve covering his arm. He spat out the fabric and shoved his exposed wrist toward me. It was coated in medplas. *Of course,* I realized, staring up at his now-set features. *The implant.* I'd forgotten.

"I was groggy after waking up," Ragem went on, shaking his head in disgust. "It took me a while to remember. The emergency beacon must have activated when that tree tried to go through me."

"I felt it. At least you weren't dead," I added, the memory of that relief crystal clear.

His mouth twisted and he shook the sleeve back down. "You could have fooled me," he said a bit too lightly, as if to shrug away the discomfort of his own experience. I could have told him it wasn't that easy. "The med removed it, but it broadcast from the last night in the valley until the ship left the system. That signal will be passed along by any Commonwealth ship that picks it up. They'll be able to get a triangulation."

"So Kearn knows where we've been—maybe even where we are."

"It's not as though I had a choice about it—"

I silenced him by touching his hand with my fingertips. "I wasn't accusing, Paul-Human." My fingers fluttered involuntarily. "I wonder what Skalet did with your signaling device on the *Trium Set;* if she hasn't destroyed it yet, Kearn could be receiving some very confusing information about now."

Ragem didn't share my amusement. "Minimum damage," he recited, as if making a report. "Kearn will contact Artos. He'll find out what happened there. The Captain tells me ships were leaving the spaceport like leaves before a hurricane even before we were back on board."

"Those ships only know that the Church of Bones was likely to ban non-Articans," I thought out loud. "Hardly a surprise. If the story of what happened to Ansky spreads, why would they make anything more from it than some local, possibly mythic event?"

"Kearn knows the questions to ask," he disagreed. "How long before he puts it all together? How long before he realizes Nimal-Ket was not what she seemed?" He hesitated, then went on with the air of someone burning bridges behind him. "As for me? Kearn's going to figure my connection out pretty fast. I can handle that." He toyed with his food for a moment, as though reluctant to speak, but before I could say anything, he looked up at me with a suspicious brightness to his eyes and added: "The hard part's my friends and family. They'll believe I'm dead." Ragem raised his arm. "What else could they think, with the emergency beacon ending all at once?"

The Human was right, I thought mournfully, though he didn't have my own dark addition to the list: *How was Ersh going to take this news?* At least Ragem had the prospect of returning to his life and Web once this was over. "Let's just hope my Enemy hasn't been busy lately. Kearn doesn't need any more fuel for his paranoia about me." I stood. "I think I'd better send a message to Skalet."

Before I could take a step, the door opened and two Kraal marched into the room, weapons drawn and aimed directly at Ragem. "Our pardon for interrupting your meal, Madame Ket, Hom Ragem. The Captain would like to see you both," one of them said politely. "Now."

Neither Ragem nor I had an easy time explaining to Captain Hubbar-ro why Ragem had had a Commonwealth implant in the first place, let alone convincing the overprotective Kraal he shouldn't lock my friend in the *Quartos Ank*'s brig. *Of course Skalet would have to give me a ship that had one,* I thought with disgust. Skalet-memory conveniently reminded me that all Confederacy ships were so equipped.

I had to give the Kraal credit; he listened willingly enough. "Paul-Human did inform S'kal-ru about the signaling device on the *Trium Set,* didn't he?" I argued. *Again.*

"He could have told us about the implant at the same time and had it removed before coming on my ship," Hubbar-ro said reasonably. "I am still unclear as to why your associate would require a Commonwealth emergency beacon in the first place. More serpitay, Madame Ket?"

As typical for Kraal leadership, this meeting—no matter that it was tense and involved fundamental issues of ship's security—had to be held in a civilized manner. So Ragem and I sat in chairs almost as overwhelmingly comfortable as those on the *Trium Set* and sipped our second glass of ceremonial wine. Unfortunately, we were both too full from dinner to appreciate the plate of essentials. Hubbar-ro, on the other hand, must have either missed the meal or be a nervous eater. His hand stole to the plate again.

"This Ket has been placed in command by S'kal-ru," I resorted to finally, perhaps lacking the requisite air of authority in this form, but he knew I was right. "Paul-Human shares my affiliation to her and her cause. She will decide on this matter."

"You will allow me to confirm with S'kal-ru." This wasn't a question.

I gave him a quelling look. I hoped it was quelling. "If we may already be followed, does it make sense to send any communications that might be monitored?"

"But—"

"Of course we must contact S'kal-ru, Captain," I soothed. "But we will not send sensitive information unless it becomes absolutely necessary. Is that clear?"

It had taken a bit more than that, but I had talked Hubbarro into letting me send the message I wanted. Skalet was much less cooperative.

"This is not a secure link," I warned her again.

Following the lag, mere seconds as the *Quartos Ank*'s com system sent the plus translight burst carrying what I said, then retrieved the response and sorted it out, there were several words in sequence my Ketself had a bit of trouble translating, not being a species that used expletives. *A waste of very expensive technology,* I thought to myself. *But descriptive.*

"S'kal-ru," I said when that seemed all that was in the message, "we'll be there by tomorrow night. I can explain—"

"Trailing who knows what behind you."

I didn't argue.

"You're sure about Ansky," she continued.

"There is no doubt."

"Tomorrow, then, Madame Ket. *With* your friend."

Out There

HIS eyes hadn't left it. After four hours or so, he found himself blinking constantly, but Joel Largas had no intention of so much as turning his head, not even to see who belonged to the footsteps approaching him now. "Any response?" he whispered, as if that thing out there could hear him, irrationally convinced it would understand if it did.

"One," the voice belonged to Char's half-sib, Denny, a young man whose preoccupation with his future as a performance musician had been left behind with his instruments. Joel found himself lost for an instant, remembering Denny's mother—a fine starship astrogator who'd believed firmly in following one's own passions even when it meant having a son who didn't want any of what she could offer. She'd shared her confused pride with him the last time they'd renewed their temp-contract.

Her ship had been lost long before the fatal attack on Garson's World.

"Captain?"

Joel pulled himself into the present, refocusing on the blue leeched to the lifepod. They hadn't told *Anna's Best*'s captain yet. No one knew what to say. "Yes, Denny. Who was it? Are they close enough to help?"

Denny's voice contained a note of strain; he deliberately didn't look outside. "It's a Commonwealth ship—a First Contact vessel called the *Rigus.* Acting Captain Kearn. Char didn't know the name."

"First Contact? What the hell are they doing out here?" Joel didn't expect an answer and didn't wait for one. "At least they'll be armed. How soon can they be here?"

"There's some confusion about that, Captain. This Kearn wants proof we're refugees. Seems to think our distress call is some kind of trick by the Kraal Confederacy."

He hadn't thought he could laugh, but he did.

"What's so funny?"

"That's not even the right war," Joel gasped, then clamped shut his lips over what could easily become hysteria. He'd seen enough of it in others to know no one was immune. "Stay here. Let me know if anything out there changes."

He looked out the viewport one last time, wondering what they could do if anything did.

44: Cruiser Night

SKALET hadn't waited for the *Quartos Ank* to come to where she and her small fleet sat in ambush. Instead, she'd pulled out the *Trium Set* and met us on the way. While I appreciated the speed, I was less appreciative of her reaction to what had happened. Maybe I was being ephemeral, as Ersh would say, but I expected at least some compassion for what I'd been through, some grief for Ansky. *From Skalet?* I should have known better.

"Her attachments led to her ruin," Skalet repeated. "I want this to be a lesson to you, youngest. There is a difference between successfully living among a species and imagining yourself part of it."

No danger of that for you, I thought rebelliously, glancing around Skalet's quarters, with its war maps and ambush plans.

"Ansky followed the Rules. She tried to protect the Web and other intelligences from harm," I said without trying to control my temper. "Do you advise me against this?"

Her lovely voice developed a sting in return. "You fool! She did just the opposite. What precipitated the crisis on Artos if not this—this exhibition of a death?! She showed herself to aliens! Ansky broke the First Rule! *Do not reveal the web-form or abilities to those outside the Web.* It seems clear enough, youngest!"

I refused to back down. "Correct me if my memory errs, Skalet, but since no one else has died this way before, how was she to know what would happen?"

Her delicate nostrils flared, once, distorting the tattoos under her skin as though they moved of themselves. "Her concern should have been with the species as a whole, not with individuals. And it should have been with those she observed, the Articans, not this plaything she kept. A distinction you seem to blur as well." This last had a warning bite to it.

"Fine," I snapped. "Ansky should have known better than to die before our Enemy could find and eat her." *This was getting us nowhere.* I waved one hand in surrender. "Believe what you will, Skalet. I've no interest in arguing about what can't be changed. What do we do now?"

She paced away from where I crouched, then returned, her scowl gone but the deeply troubled look on her face warning me we weren't quite done scolding Esen. "First, we have to do something about your Human," she announced. "We must be rid of him before he discovers your true nature."

Ersh was fond of sharing with me the pivotal moments in the history of species, cultural events, or evolutionary changes dictating this path and no other would be taken. I knew from my own recent experiences there were also pivotal moments in the lives of individuals.

I faced one now, as I stared at my instructor, my Elder, the one whose flesh was my flesh. *How well I understood her motives.* As one in the Web, I shared them. As Esen-alit-Quar I could not.

I felt my growing separateness, my individuality, weighing like a noose around my neck. Perhaps I merely pulled on my hoobit too hard. Or perhaps I was closer than I had ever been to understanding what made Ersh so unique among us. Whether I was supposed to think in terms of species rather than persons was irrelevant. I knew what was right. "You will not threaten or harm Paul Ragem," I stated flatly, as sure of this as I was of the number of molecules in this body. "I want that quite clear between us, Skalet."

"What is clear is that you have lost your perspective, 'tween. Ersh should have kept you home for another century at least!"

Odd how calm, how controlled I felt. "You are welcome to share that with her," I shrugged. "Just make no mistake with me, my sister. Ragem is as close to me as though we were one flesh. I trust him with my life—and I owe him his."

"Just how much trust have you given this ephemeral, Esen the foolish?" Skalet's eyes suddenly widened, her face turning a ghastly white under the tattoos. "You've told him about us, haven't you!" *It never paid to underestimate Skalet.* She darted toward the door and I intercepted her, suffering a painful kick in the knee as we collided. "Out of my way!" There was nothing lovely about her voice or face now.

I cycled. *Share!* I sent. *Learn!* I demanded.

Ragem kept his face carefully neutral, but his gray eyes flicked uneasily from Skalet to me and then back again. "That's the whole story," hc finished, spreading his hands outward. "I've been helping Es track down this killer—trying to, anyway. If you won't accept our friendship as motivation enough, then believe I can't sit by and watch innocent beings slaughtered in cold blood, not if I can do something to prevent it. Who could?"

Not a particularly good question in present company, I thought, watching Skalet for her reaction. She'd been very subdued, most unSkaletlike behavior, since assimilating what I'd forced her to share: my feelings for Ragem, his actions to save me and to save Ansky. In exchange, I learned more about the results of waging war in space than I'd wanted to, but neither of us felt inclined to forbearance with the other.

"I tasted the start of all this on Picco's Moon," she said at last, looking down at her steepled fingers, long, elegant hands owing nothing to a common evolution with the Human across the table from us both. "Esen, what have you done? Have you any idea what this being Kearn may do? He is obviously someone of influence, who can convince others."

"Only to a point, S'kal-ru," Ragem offered, diplomatically keeping to the name matched to the form she wore. "So far he's had a bit of evidence to wave in front of his superiors. Not much, but sufficient to arouse curiosity. He doesn't have the reputation to carry on this hunt for Esen—for your kind—any farther if there's a setback. Frankly, I'm surprised he hasn't been recalled already."

"Shouldn't we be more concerned with the enemy than any possible threat in the future from Kearn?" I interjected, knowing Skalet only barely accepted Ragem's presence and his knowledge of us; I deemed it safer not to let her focus her attention on him too long. "He doesn't have the confidence of his crew or superiors, S'kal-ru. I expect he's going to lose what credibility he has—"

"Unless he can find something else," Skalet finished for me."This being hunting us," a quick doubtful look to Ragem before she carefully chose another word, "this predator. Is it possible we can maneuver them together? Regardless of the outcome, it could deflect attention from us."

Ragem didn't so much as flinch, although I knew he immediately thought of Tomas, and all the others he cared for on the *Rigus.* I'd forewarned him that Skalet was ruthless; still, I hadn't expected him to handle her so well. *He'd earned those alien culture specialist bars somewhere,* I reminded myself. "Would it not be much better, S'kal-ru," he suggested mildly, "if Kearn goes away safely from such a meeting, having been convinced that this menace is not the same type of being as yourselves, something he currently believes to be true."

Skalet glared at me and I rolled my eyes. *Did she think I'd tell Ragem the Enemy was one of us?* If I hadn't, she certainly wouldn't.

The Human, however, drew his own interpretation of our sudden silence. "Kearn is wrong," he half-stated, half-asked, staring at us both. "It *is* something different, isn't it?"

My "Of course!" and Skalet's "How could you think—!" overlapped into a confused muttering that obviously didn't reassure a now somewhat haggard-looking Ragem. *I could see his point.* Here he was, alone in a room with two very alien beings whose existence only he knew about, on a ship crewed by Humans who owed complete loyalty to one of us, supposedly chasing an incredibly deadly and bloodthirsty creature. A creature he suddenly suspected could be one of us.

Character builder, Ersh would call it, I acknowledged to myself, curious what he would do next.

What Ragem did was leap away from the table, stumbling backward until his shoulders hit the wall with an audible thud. From the look on his face, he was planning to stay there.

"I think I'll check on the fleet," Skalet said hastily. The

look she gave me as she scurried from the room was frankly triumphant, doubtless because she thought I was about to lose Ragem's support and have to allow her to kill him.

I really hoped not.

45: Brig Morning

SKALET knew her Humans, I had to give her that. Ragem did not take my confession that our Enemy was a web-being at all well. At least I'd been able to save his life—for now. But he wasn't happy with me.

Of course, that could have been the compromise I worked out with Skalet, namely locking Ragem in the brig until he calmed down and saw reason.

Since these were events over which I had no control and which weren't my fault, I thought it unfair of the Human to blame me. Which was the interpretation I put on his sitting on the bunk, back deliberately to me, when I tried to talk to him the next morning. The guard outside the door had already told me Ragem hadn't eaten his breakfast. I wasn't surprised. The *Trium Set*'s brig was a thoroughly tasteless affair, a metal-walled box with a bunk, sleeping pad, and a 'fresher stall in one corner for necessities. A suitable spot to repent sins, I supposed, especially in an aesthetics-driven society, but hardly a reasonable place for my friend and ally.

"It's an improvement over the dungeon," I offered, daring to sit on one end of the bunk this time. "No bugs. Better food."

No response. His shoulders stayed hunched as if to deny I was even there. This was an unfamiliar Ragem to me, one who seemed to have given up—as if his curiosity had finally repaid him with an answer he couldn't accept.

Maybe that curiosity, rather than reason, was the way to reach him now.

I cycled, folding myself almost tenderly into a slightly-built form, looking at my new hands as I curled each into a ball then opened it again, the effect like that of pale yellow flowers opening to the sun.

I pursed my three lips and began to purr, letting my subvoice slide upward into the melody, counterpointed by the thrumming of my throat. The song swept away time, swept away the brig and the concerns of those in it, swept clear all but its glory.

My body still throbbing with music, I closed my lips over the last note and looked at Ragem.

He'd turned to look at me. *How could he not?* His face wet with tears, his merely Human voice sounded like some machinery grinding when he at last spoke. "That music—it's only legend. No one has heard it—"

I had just enough mass to return to simply Ket, a form almost like home. "No one has heard it for a thousand years," I finished for him. "Yes. I know."

"A Jarsh . . ." he identified, a note of wonder in his voice; then it sharpened into incredulity. "What good is the shape of a dead species to you?"

"Dead? Perhaps. But never forgotten. This is our work," I said softly.

"Is it?" he challenged: *a definite improvement over ignoring me,* I thought. "Is that why Ansky was on Artos? Is that why Skalet follows the Confederacy? Is that why this thing is ripping apart ships?" His eyes were accusing. "Do you and your kind merely observe cultures in turmoil—or cause it? What do you hope to gain? Just information to help you impersonate other beings? I could understand that," the Human finished in a strange flat voice, "but after meeting Ansky and Skalet, well, it doesn't make sense. There's more going on, isn't there."

"Of course there is, Paul-Human," I admitted freely. "We learn far more than we'd need to simply mimic other forms. That was never the point of what we do. We learn all we can, share it among ourselves. Our goal is to preserve all we can of the accomplishments of intelligent life in case you throw yourselves away, as species after species has done, as the Articans are about to do, as your kind almost succeeding in doing mere centuries ago."

"A noble purpose," he said, eerily echoing Ersh's words to me on Picco's Moon.

"We have never done harm," I said firmly, then added: "never deliberately."

"No? Explain that to the families on Tly and other

Fringe worlds who've lost loved ones. Explain tha
kin of those slaughtered on Portula Colony." Rage
bored into mine. I found one hand straying to my hoobit, a reach for comfort he understood very well. *At least he was still talking to me.* "Esen, I've reached my limit, all right? I want the whole truth about you, your kind, and about this killer. Now."

"I know. What truth would you like first?" I said, sitting down on the bunk once more, taking a moment to arrange my skirt so my fingers could soothe themselves and so my nerves. *Time to be careful,* I thought, aware of his quickness and species' loyalty, despite his attachment to me, *truthful, but careful.*

Ragem propped himself in the corner, obviously not finding it easy to settle into a comfortable position. I eyed his bandaged arm but knew better than to remind him of the *Trium Set*'s fine med equipment a few steps down the corridor. Skalet was unlikely to let him use it unless I convinced them both our alliance could be restored. "What truth?" he sighed, eyes suddenly wistful. "Fundamental ones, Esen. Are we friends?"

The unexpected question hurt somewhere deep inside me, but I had no problem answering. "We are friends, we are one, until flesh rots and time ends," I said.

He looked relieved, a bit puzzled, but relieved. "Between friends, then. Maybe you think I'm overreacting to all this, Esen. I don't. Your kind is unbelievably powerful. The idea of you living among us, unknown, hidden, is—well, I know why Kearn has nightmares. Until now, I reassured myself by thinking I knew you, what you were like. To suddenly find out what you're really capable of: ripping through starships as though they were butter, traveling through space without a ship, wanton murder—"

"I'm not!" I denied furiously. "We're not. This Enemy isn't what we are."

"You said it was," he said as hotly. "Is it a web-being or not?"

"Yes, yes. But it's not of our Web. It's not of Ersh."

"Ersh?"

Her name from his Human lips shocked me to silence. I fought to recover my calm. This conversation was important—for both of us. "I warn you, Ragem. Never say that name in front of Skalet," I said urgently, touching his knee in emphasis.

"Why?"

In this far, I decided, aware but unafraid I was about to place all of my trust in this being. *Time to worry about Ersh's opinion of my judgment in the future, if we had one.* "Ersh is Eldest," I began, trying for the first time in my life to put into words what I knew in my flesh. "She is the origin, the First of us all. Our mother," I added, and was rewarded as comprehension lit his eyes.

"I told you there was only one of us, Paul, and that is the literal truth. Together with Ersh—Mixs, Lesy, Ansky, Skalet, and I—we are one flesh; in many ways, one being." *No longer,* my grief intruded. I pushed it aside. "We shared one another's memories and lives as the Web of Ersh; we shared the purpose she gave us." I tapped my concave chest. "We just happen to spend most of our days as you've seen us, separate and individual. Ersh binds us into more." I paused. "This thing we seek is similar in biology, but it is not of our Web. It is not us. And by its very nature, it is deadly to us and to any other life in its path."

He groped for what made sense to him, a Human. "A war?"

I shuddered. "An appetite. The Web of Ersh is intelligent, aware, bound by Rules. This being is awareness only."

I drew an unsteady breath, oddly able to share my fears with him, when I couldn't with my web-kin. "I don't know its capabilities. Neither does Skalet. I assume it can cycle into different forms, but there's been no proof of it. I do know it can find us. It can move without a ship. Something I can't do." I stopped for an instant, collecting myself. "And it can—consume—us. It desires this more than anything else. It's taken Mixs and Lesy. It will come after the rest, after me—" I couldn't finish.

Something eased between us. *Had I only needed to confess my fear to him?* I wondered. Ragem leaned forward, eyes bright. "Where did it come from?"

"We don't know." Then I added honestly, "But Ersh herself is not native to this galaxy. She remembers millennia spent traveling the void between, barely surviving the passage." I resisted the sudden flood of Ersh-memory threatening to distract me. "I think this being has made the same journey."

Ragem remembered to close his mouth, before opening it again to utter one squeak: "Millennia?"

My fingers fluttered. "You wanted the truth, Paul-Human. I offer it."

"How—how old are you?"

Finally, a being who wouldn't consider me youngest. "Five hundred standard years, plus a few. Though I feel much older after what's been happening."

I watched him total up what that meant: a life span begun when his grandparents were babies, a friend who might perhaps not be the inexperienced callow youth he'd thought. Unfortunately, I was, for my kind.

"And all that time you've been spying on other species."

I bristled at his choice of words, then relaxed as I noticed his eyes were starting to sparkle with curiosity. "Actually," I said proudly, "Kraos was my first assignment."

Ragem burst out laughing. After a second feeling affronted, I had to join him. I had no idea what the guard thought we were up to, but my hands were so sore by the time we stopped, mutually exhausted, Ragem had to knock on the door himself.

Somehow I'd convinced Ragem to trust me.

Now to convince Skalet.

Out There

DEATH stretched, tasting the solar winds, reveling in the luxury of movement without expenditure. Still, there was the concept of pleasure to consider. Perhaps it was time to feed.

There were several life-forms within this shell; none were those it lusted for, yet all flavorful in their own way. Almost as an afterthought, Death formed jaws, selecting a weaker point on the shell to assault.

Pain!

Death sprang away from the burning along its edge, the force of its movement sending the pod to smash against the side of the larger ship, cables tangling, air pouring out of fractured joints on both vessels. Alarm klaxons sounded throughout the convoy. Death ignored them, intent on escape.

Pain!

It was being chased. *Impossible!* Death almost turned to attack the starship so suddenly on its trail, then self-preservation kicked in. Death flung itself away, expending mass ruthlessly, twisting through translight in a way no mere metal-and-plas technology could mimic.

But it could follow.

46: Bridge Afternoon

THE doors vanished sometime in the night. I missed them as I padded down the corridor to the *Trium Set*'s central lift; such a harmless pleasure, running my fingers over the doorknobs and hinges. But Captain Longins had decided his ship was about to go into battle, ordering the switch to metal, blast-resistant portals throughout. Their slickness was boring, if prudent.

The warship was massive, easily ten times the size of the *Rigus*; still, I couldn't get lost. Skalet-memory gave me complete schematics, something I didn't bother explaining to the helpful crewman directing me to the bridge. *Late, not lost,* I thought, hurrying a little more.

Skalet had allowed Ragem out of the brig and into the med facilities, reluctantly and after what amounted to shouting and other undignified behavior on my part, but didn't extend the Human an invitation to join her and her officers at this strategy meeting. Fair enough, but I'd delayed in order to make sure Ragem, waiting in his cabin, had the other half of the com device I carried in my pouch, easily requisitioned with the right codes from Skalet-memory. *Not really eavesdropping,* I'd eased my conscience, *merely saving the effort of repeating all that might be said.*

The lift was empty. I ordered it to the bridge, waited for the servo to confirm my right to do so, then was swiftly whooshed downward to the core of the ship. The bridge, the vital engines and grav units, as well as firing controls, were all located as far within the physical protection of the *Trium Set*'s bulk as possible. As a helpless passenger about to be dragged to war, my Ketself couldn't help but approve.

"There you are, Madame Ket," Skalet's rich voice carried not the slightest hint of impatience, but I could see from the replacement of the beverages and other ceremonial accoutrements by maps and pads of scribbles I was later than I'd thought.

"This Ket apologizes for any delay, S'kal-ru-Kraal," I panted, rushing up to the remaining seat.

"We didn't delay," she purred. "Admiral Mocktap? This is Nimal-Ket, a valued associate of mine, connected by affiliations of tenth degree reliability."

The admiral, an older Kraal whose extensive tattoos had been etched in white to show against her dark skin, looked surprised but didn't hesitate to rise slightly in her chair—a feat I appreciated from experience—and bow in my direction. Tenth degree reliability put me closer in Skalet's counsel than this woman, her commander-in-chief, a declaration that, while true, definitely put me uncomfortably in the Kraal spotlight. I would have liked to glare at my web-kin, but settled for returning the bow and taking a seat. Captain Hubbar-ro of the *Quartos Ank* leaned back with a grin, as ready to bask in my newly revealed status as it worried Longins of the *Trium Set.*

"Madame Ket," the admiral said, gesturing to the maps scattered over the table. "We have been discussing the best strategy to use when we engage this biological weapon."

Biological weapon? Skalet hadn't shared this part of her plan with me yet. I glanced at her and received a sardonically raised brow. True, she'd had to call it something the Kraal military would find interesting. "This Ket is not an expert in such matters, Mocktap-Kraal, but I will give you what assistance I can."

"What did the Commonwealth ship try against it?" this from Captain Longins of the *Trium Set.*

"There was no contact while this Ket was on the *Rigus,*" I started to explain, but was interrupted by Skalet.

"They were able to make it flee the convoy with a directed burst from their ilium guns, but there's no confirmed damage to the B.W." The Kraal nodded wisely at this, Longins making a note.

B. W.? Ersh save me from the military mind and its compulsion to abbreviate. "They've fought it? Where? When?"

"You should be on time," Skalet said in her best drillmaster voice. She raised her hand in apology, as it likely dawned on her the Kraal had no reason to expect us to have a teacher/student relationship. I was satisfied to omit it myself. "Forgive me, Madame Ket," she said more graciously. "But we had no time to spare and I wanted to bring everyone up to date. Hubbar-ro, please pass Madame Ket the messages we intercepted."

Great. Ragem would be anxiously awaiting this news and I couldn't think of any reason to read out loud. At least I could be sure of remembering all the details.

What the *Trium Set* had intercepted was a series of translight communications between a refugee convoy led by someone named Largas and the *Rigus.* Kearn, the eternal idiot, had responded to their cries for help by questioning their refugee status—I hoped Skalet found that embarrassing, though I doubted it. He hadn't so much been convinced the ships were legitimate refugees from the remains of Garson's World as he was drawn by the description of the danger Largas provided.

When I reached the line "blue, shapeless alien life, fastened like a parasite to the outside of a life pod," I looked up and met Skalet's eyes. From her grim expression, she'd been waiting for me to get there. The Kraal officers were busy discussing something in low voices and didn't pay attention to the slow nod she gave me or the way I almost dropped the pages.

So. The *Rigus* had found its monster. Small consolation that Kearn had to believe it wasn't me now—or did he? I hurried to read the rest of the flimsy plas sheets. The convoy had already lost two ships. The *Rigus* had rushed to engage the monster, succeeding in scaring it off at least, though Kearn's boast to the convoy was that they'd seriously injured the creature and sent it running for cover. He planned to follow and destroy it.

The last intercepted message was from the convoy, asking the *Rigus* to delay the chase and provide medical aid. The action against the creature had left several dead and injured, as well as one of the larger ships unable to sustain translight without repairs. I crumbled the mass of plas in my fingers, feeling strangely numb.

"Do you have a position, S'kal-ru-Kraal?" I asked.

Skalet waved to a crewwoman standing nearby. She switched on an image projector, setting the display to hover above the cluttered table. The captains and admiral stopped their discussion to watch with keen interest.

"The *Rigus* sustained no damage and is now chasing the—biological weapon?" I continued, not for confirmation but for Ragem's sake, making sure I sat so the com device in my pouch wasn't buried in the folds of my skirt.

"As far as we know, Madame, Ket," affirmed Mocktap. "She's fast. I'm astonished, in fact, that the B.W. is capable of such speed."

So was I, I thought, then realized it wasn't surprise I felt, but envy.

"Here's the situation, current to one hour ago Standard." Skalet manipulated the controls, creating an intestinelike curl of yellow winding its way through the upper third of the stars floating in the image's volume. "The Kraal Confederacy," she identified. I didn't bother mentioning several of the systems she blithely included would dispute her claim. Ephemeral border squabbles were hardly the issue here.

An irregular line of red appeared, spreading to encompass a vast sweep along the far side from me. "The Fringe, with Tly—" this a spleenlike shape, one tip wrapped within a coil of the Confederacy, the rest extending almost to the Fringe along its longest side, "Inhaven and her so-called colonies," a smattering of purple nestled against Tly space, filling the space between it and the Fringe, "Garson's World," a glowing white dot tucked down and below Tly and Inhaven. A dot without life.

To safely travel from Garson's World to their ally, Inhaven, or any of her colonies, the refugees our Enemy had attacked would have to take the long way around. Tly space would be closed to them. The Confederacy too risky. The blockade was something they'd likely planned to deal with when they arrived in Inhaven territory. I thought it probable they'd be allowed through without incident. The destruction of Garson's World had been as much a shock to the Tly people as it had been to any outside observers.

The convoy had passed close to Artos. *No help for them there.* "The Commonwealth?" I asked Skalet softly, forgetting where I was at the moment. She hesitated, then understood what I was thinking and added that political and economic unit to the map.

It wouldn't all fit, of course. The Commonwealth was immense, stretching back from the bulge encompassing the

Confederacy to the limits of Skalet's image, a span made from thousands of worlds, hundreds of species, dozens of minor groupings and territories. It was an alliance at once impressive and safely ineffective. The Commonwealth didn't exist as a government as the Confederacy was to its worlds; instead, it was an agreement to peaceful commerce and exploration. As I studied the map, it dawned on me that the ephemerals had created a web of their own, a concept I'd never considered before. A shame such agreements never seemed to last more than a few of their short lifespans.

However, my point was taken by the Kraal. "The refugees followed the Commonwealth boundary," Longins noted. "The B.W. joined them somewhere past the Jeopardy Nebula."

Skalet overlaid the route of our Enemy, as best we knew it. "It's been steering clear of the uninhabited regions. Was this avoidance deliberate, or has it been following the shipping lanes?"

"Both," I suggested, thinking of its appetite.

"So where will it go now?"

Skalet toned down the political map to barely visible pastels. She was right, I thought, since our Enemy didn't care for such markers either. Instead, she emphasized shipping patterns and inhabited worlds.

There were perhaps three directions it might take from Artos, depending on how seriously it took the pursuit of the *Rigus*—and how long that pursuit lasted. Translight travel had to cost it, a toll I assumed our Enemy would collect from any intelligent life it encountered. So any of those three routes would suit its needs. My stomach churned as though I were Lanivarian again.

One route intersected the fanlike spread of drones Skalet had launched days earlier. I was impressed by her foresight. Another led straight to the nearest curve of Kraal space, surely another lure to the creature as it hunted Skalet. The third lay toward Artos, its probable next target.

Except that Ansky was no longer there. And the *Rigus* was in the way.

"Excellent. It will come to us. We should be able to sit here and wait," Skalet concluded triumphantly. I wrapped my fingers around my hoobit and looked steadily at the last of my web-sisters, wondering if I would ever understand how she could be so delighted to be the bait in a trap.

I certainly wasn't.

Ragem had his own concerns over Skalet's plan, concerns I saw in the grim set of his mouth when I returned to his cabin. First, though, he read over the messages for himself; somehow I'd neglected to return them to Skalet.

When he finished, he shook his head. "I don't suppose. No. Forget it."

I ran my fingers along Ragem's forehead; it didn't erase the frown etched in place. "What am I to forget, Paul-Human?" I asked.

He folded the messages and tucked them in a pocket. I supposed that meant I wasn't going to return them to Skalet. "I just wondered if S'kal-ru still had that signaling device of mine."

"So you could contact the *Rigus*?" I guessed. "She destroyed it the moment it was found. And I doubt she'd let either of us at the *Trium Set*'s com equipment." The cabin was quite delightful to my Ket senses; I'd explored its furnishings thoroughly while Ragem read the messages involving his former ship. I walked over to a particularly fine picture frame and stroked it. The painting within was done partially in colors I couldn't detect with this form; what I could see suggested a portrait. Or it could have been a bowl of fruit.

"Why do you want to contact the *Rigus* now?" I asked almost casually, though I felt nothing of the kind. "To tell Kearn the true nature of his monster?"

"Of course not!" Ragem snapped angrily, then made an effort to calm himself, rubbing a hand over his face and speaking more evenly. "Esen, if the *Rigus* follows that thing, she's going to blunder right into the Kraal fleet and its ambush. Don't you think the crew should be warned? They could help, damn it!"

He had a point. "Skalet knows all this, Paul-Human," I answered slowly. "She prefers to deal with the quantities she knows and can control. This fleet of hers may be small, five cruisers and this warship, but it is the best the Kraal have. If all goes to plan, our Enemy will be overwhelmed before the *Rigus* is even aware its prey has vanished from its scopes."

Ragem rose from his chair and came to look up at me. I wasn't surprised when he lifted his good hand to my shoulder; he was becoming distressingly physical lately. "Esen, is part of her plan to destroy the *Rigus*?" he demanded, stretching so he could look me right in the eyes.

I felt threatened both by the Human's posture and his dreadful suspicion. *Skalet planning to take the* Rigus *as well as our Enemy?* "Why would—?"

"It's an effective way to deal with Kearn, isn't it? How far would she go to protect your secrets?"

"No!" I protested, but found myself frozen in his light grip, forced to think by the passion in those gray, alien eyes. *Ersh. How well did I know Skalet, after all?* Most of my sharings with Skalet had been through Ersh; she'd always decided what I was to assimilate and what I was to learn the ephemeral way. *Was Skalet capable of murder?*

I wasn't. Ansky, Lesy, and Mixs—I believed not. *Ersh? I knew she was.* But Skalet? She'd assimilated the same purpose from Ersh, lived by the same Rules, all intended to protect and preserve intelligent life. *And hide the existence of the Web,* I added. Why at this moment did I see her, not as Web, but as Kraal, her face lit by the colors of war from her imager, eyes intent above the tattoos marking her willingness to battle for the rights of clan and family? Why did I hear her threat against Ragem?

Ragem sensed my growing doubts. He added to them: "Self-preservation, Esen. Every living thing seeks to protect itself. And she sees Kearn as a threat. What will she do when the *Rigus* wanders in range of her weapons? Tell me you don't think she'll fire."

"We revere life," I said, feeling my grasp on this form weakening and raising my temperature at once. "We cannot kill—"

"You can't," he countered, giving me a gentle shake. "What I've seen of S'kal-ru says she can and will. We have to warn the *Rigus,* Es."

"No," I said, my voice seeming to belong to someone else.

I'd disappointed him. "But—"

"She won't let us," I interrupted, certain I now contemplated such a betrayal Ersh would excise me from whatever was left of the Web. *So be it.* I knew what was right.

"We have to stop Skalet's ambush, Paul," I continued, my voice strange and grim in my own ears. "Before it's too late. We have to think of a way to sabotage her plan."

I should have remembered who was supposed to teach me subterfuge.

Out There

HUNGER.

Death forgot about its pursuer, instead beginning to search ahead on this path, knowing a greater need than it had felt for a long time.

There. Reflected radiation beamed from a shining hull, the dimpling of gravity nearby an unnecessary marker. Death rejoiced, swooping close for the kill.

The shell was empty.

Disappointment. No time to waste.

Wait! There it was: the taste, the ultimate taste it sought. In here!

Death ripped apart the tiny drone ship to find the tiny cluster of molecules. As it consumed them, along with the holder and the table on which they had rested, a message began vibrating through the remaining hull plates, the medium electromagnetism, the meaning clear.

This is where I am! Come to me if you dare!

Death accepted the challenge with an unheard roar.

Hunger!

47: Cruiser Morning

"TELL me you aren't planning to attack the *Rigus.*"

"I'm not planning to attack the *Rigus,*" Skalet said promptly, "Satisfied? Why should I?" she continued reasonably. "Not only would it upset the Commonwealth, who would rumble about economic sanctions and doubtless cost my affiliates substantial funds, but it wouldn't accomplish anything."

"You'd get rid of Kearn. He's the one chasing us."

"He's hardly the first, 'tween." She enjoyed surprising me; I could tell by the curve of her lips under the visor of her helmet. "Did you think we could live all these centuries among such curious beings and never be suspected until you blundered with this Human? If we'd killed them all, it would only have made matters worse. No, there are better ways to deflate our friend out there, Esen."

"What if I don't believe you, Skalet?" I demanded quietly, my fingers tight on the hoobit.

My web-kin slid the straps of her battle suit up over her shoulders, bouncing in place to settle the heavy equipment. "What do you think, that you and your Human can somehow sabotage my plans? You are a pair, aren't you? Don't strain yourself, youngest. My gunners have explicit instructions to leave your precious ship alone," she stopped abruptly to look at me, wide-eyed. "Unless the *Rigus* gets between us and the B.W."

Skalet was acting like some hormone-pumped Ganthor about to defend its herd. I stood to one side as she clumped across the ruined carpet of her cabin's main room to rummage in the closet. The battle suit almost doubled her mass and I had no intention of risking my toes under hers. Out came a selection of side arms.

"You aren't planning a face-to-face battle,' I said dryly. "Is this all necessary?"

"One needs to be prepared," she replied jovially. "The troops expect their officers to set an example."

Skalet's preparations, in full force the moment the drone's confirmation signal reached the *Trium Set,* included space suits for Ragem and myself. Had I been truly Ket, I'd have succumbed to hysterics almost immediately, since the suits provided for me to try for best fit required a choice between amputating my arms or legs; the Kraal on board, while being quite uniformly tall and slender, were also Human-proportioned to a fault.

Ragem, needing something to tear apart perhaps, set himself the task of modifying two suits into something that might afford my Ketself a moment's protection from vacuum. He proved adept with a microblade and sealer, despite the handicap of his injured arm. The resulting cobbled-together contraption drew smiles from passing Kraal crew, but I thanked him.

"Let's hope you don't have to test it as Nimal-Ket," Ragem declared morosely, snapping closed most of the fasteners on his own suit once I was in mine. I helped him put his arm back in the sling; he'd confessed to it easing the discomfort. "Those seals are temp at best."

I hung the gloves on my belt, unwilling to cover my hands any sooner than necessary. "I'll keep that in mind."

He glanced around. We were finally alone in the suiting room, the Kraal having left to attend their duties. "What are we going to do about the *Rigus*?"

"Skalet says she's not planning to attack the ship,' I told him. "Unless it gets between her and our Enemy."

He drove a fist into his knee. "Even if we believe her, I still say we have to do something to let the *Rigus* know!"

"I'm open to suggestion, Paul-Human."

"Madame Ket? Hom Ragem?" We looked at each other, then at the quiet, steady-eyed Kraal officer in the doorway. "I am to escort you to the bridge. S'kal-ru invites you to attend the coming battle with her.'

So much for planning, I thought with disgust. Skalet was always one step ahead of me.

* * *

She was one step ahead of our Enemy, too, it seemed, a conclusion I drew with considerable relief.

The bridge had been transformed for battle. The officers and crew in charge of operating the ship and its weaponry were suited and enclosed in force fields, each individual locked to his or her control panels. They could stay in those positions indefinitely, supplied with food, medications, and even waste disposal, allowing the *Trium Set* to keep her key functions alive under the direction of her crew even if significantly damaged.

The chairs and couches, as well as the chandeliers, were gone. In their place was a ringlike bench surrounding a much larger image projector than I'd yet seen. As we walked out of the lift, I spotted Skalet, complete in her battle suit, busy making final adjustments to the image glowing in front of her. She hadn't engaged the bench's field as yet; I assumed she was waiting for all of us to make our appearance first.

"Welcome," Skalet called out cheerfully. She was in her element. Ragem touched my fingers, an unnecessary reminder of his continued suspicions. I only hoped he continued to trust my judgment of the situation. I had no wish to see what might happen if the impulsive Human decided to try and expose Skalet's nature to her own crew. While I couldn't imagine how he could do it, I put nothing past his inventiveness.

I needn't have worried. Once Skalet brought the projector up to battle readiness. Ragem's attention was as rapt as my own. He fumbled his way into the nearest spot on the bench and I dropped beside him, pulling my feet carefully underneath. The rest of the room dimmed gradually, until all that could be seen was what floated eerily before us, the rest of the bridge made up of isolated helmets, console lights playing over visors rather than faces.

Trust the Kraal, with their love of organized mayhem, to devote so much effort and creativity to being able to watch destruction unfold.

The ambush was laid out before us as though all had the ability of the Web to exist in space without ship or suit. Distances collapsed or expanded depending on Skalet's momentary focus, a somewhat dizzying experience at first, her visor linked directly to the main display commands. Admiral Mocktap would have a similar system on her cruiser, the *Septos Pa,* but Skalet-memory was quite satisfied it wasn't as state-of-the-art as this one.

For instance, Mocktap's display would use symbols to show ship locations, and graphical displays to indicate any weaponsfire or defense. Skalet's system did away with both. Her ships were represented by exquisitely detailed images of themselves, down to the ship names and clan colors along their sides. At the moment, three cruisers, including the *Septos Pa,* lay on the surface of the lifeless moon, engines semi-cooled but ready to fire up at an instant's notice, camouflaged with the latest Kraal technology. Skalet had likely insisted on some additional precautions guaranteed to puzzle her techs, if not a fellow web-being.

Skalet drew our attention to where the other two cruisers hung in space, stationary with respect to the moon, if not the planet below. They were positioned as though guarding some treasure on the moon's surface, a subtlety I thought completely wasted on our Enemy, but Skalet had been forced to play to her admiral's view of the ambush as well as her own. Since the prize—Skalet—was supposed to be on the moon's surface, there should be guard ships nearby and in sight.

The *Trium Set* was not visible in the present view. The moon stood between us and the battle field. Skalet hadn't told me what her admiral had thought of this unusual caution on her part. *She fears it, too,* I decided to myself, applauding this rare sign of common sense in my web-kin. The *Quartos Ank,* and a deliriously happy Captain Hubbarro, had the glorious if unenviable task of relaying information around the moon between Mocktap and Skalet.

Skalet gave us a momentary look at the remainder of the system, designated Kraal 67B, an oddly dull little star with sixteen tiny planets. Only the one we circled, the third from the sun, had the mass to collect its neighbor eons ago and so possess a moon. The system's ores were unremarkable; its location was inconveniently distant from the nearest shipping lanes. In sum: a lifeless organization of spinning rock. Members of the Kraal Confederacy fought over it constantly.

There was a hum as the restraint field kicked in, sucking us further into the bench. I put one hand on the surface behind me to take some of the strain as my back tried its best to fold over in response. *Something must be about to happen.* I glowered at Skalet despite knowing full well she couldn't see me past the images.

The system-wide view began to shrink back down to specifics again, but not before Skalet had added two dots to the outside edge, one blue, the other red. The blue one preceded the red by the span of my hand, if I held it between my eyes and the image.

"The *Rigus,*" Ragem breathed in my ear.

"The Enemy," I whispered back, unsure if raising my body temperature would do anything to ease the chill in my hearts. *Would anyone notice if I cycled into the Ganthor within this suit?* I wondered. It was so much braver.

Out There

SO HUNGRY.

Death careened past barren worlds, ignoring the throb of their gravity and false promise of life. It knew only desperation, so close to starvation now it almost turned again on its pursuer, risking more pain in order to feed.

Almost.

But ahead was the ultimate life source, the feast it must have. No more subterfuge, no more delays. It would take what it needed.

There would be time later to enjoy its tormentors' flesh.

48: Cruiser Afternoon

INSYSTEM travel, apparently even for a web-being, seemed to take endless amounts of time. Ragem and I sipped liquid nutrients from bulbs passed to us by a Kraal crewman, and tried not to disturb Skalet or her busy staff with questions. When we spoke to one another, it was in quiet whispers. Gradually, as the dots grew closer, we didn't speak at all.

Admiral Mocktap's outlying cruisers, the *Unnos Ra* and the *Decium Set,* began to imperceptibly slide further apart, expanding the corridor Mocktap wanted to lure our Enemy through. Skalet-memory was confident; I, less the expert, saw no good reason it would prefer to pass between them. If I could swim through space, I'd circle around the planet and come up from underneath, taking advantage of the dark side of the moon. Still, Skalet's judgment of its movements had been accurate thus far. She believed our Enemy would be desperate, exhausted beyond whatever caution it possessed by the *Rigus'* unrelenting pursuit. *She might be right.* I felt a stirring of tainted-memory and fought back my knowledge of its hunger for our flesh.

Voices rumbled through the darkened bridge. I strained the poor ears of this form, wishing at once to be Lanivarian, but couldn't make out what was going on. "Relays from the *Quartos Ank*. The *Rigus* has spotted the two cruisers standing out from the moon," Ragem whispered to me. He paused to listen. "She's sending a repeating warning about the creature, asking for help in cutting off its escape from the system. The com-tech is asking whether to reply."

I had no trouble hearing Skalet's calm negative. The image enlarged, swooping down for an instant to check on the camouflaged ships on the moon's surface, then rushing upward to focus on the emptiness where the attack might—should come.

Ersh, I said to myself, *I really promise to behave in the future.*

Abruptly, without warning, it was within the image, a brilliant blue teardrop hurtling toward us. I couldn't believe Skalet had dared instruct the projector to represent the Enemy as that perfection—as us. *She accused Ansky of breaking the First Rule?* I thought with outrage. Beside me Ragem jumped. He knew that shape, if only as glimpses of my true self during cycling; here was confirmation, as if he needed it, of his worst fears about us.

Then I wondered what it could matter. The *Rigus'* crew, the refugees on the convoy, the Articans, the Kraal—all had or would see the real thing now. *Was it like this to them?* I asked myself. *Could they see how beautiful it was?*

Skalet's attention flashed downward; my stomach heaved in answer. Her timing was again impeccable: the hidden cruisers, led by the *Septos Pa,* were starting to rise up from the surface, accelerating every second. The detail on the image was so precise, I could make out the folded petal structures marking each of the trio of nightshades on the nearest cruiser, the latest and deadliest weapons the Kraal possessed.

They were also Skalet's last choice, requiring as they did a massive recharging of energy after each firing. If the cruisers were reduced to the nightshades, they would lose much of their maneuvering speed.

The image zeroed on the *Decium Set.* Despite whatever her captain may have thought of the nature of his target, Kraal discipline held firm. Following the plans set earlier, the *Decium Set* pulled closer to the planet, turning to train the Kraal cruiser's main weapons, electromag pulse cannons, on the approaching teardrop. Distances and trajectories were confused in this real time, false space image. Still, it looked to me as though the *Rigus,* following close behind our Enemy, would arrive dangerously within the path taken by any unspent projectiles were the *Decium Set* and its partner ship to fire anytime soon.

Apparently Ragem shared my fear. He strained as far forward as the restraint field allowed, as if to put him somehow closer to being able to warn his ship and friends. Then the *Rigus* suddenly veered, rising up and away from the coming battle as if running for her life. *She might have been.*

There was no time to feel relief. Our Enemy hadn't been distracted by the loss of its pursuer. Skalet had been right. It kept coming, aiming directly for the moon, following the drone's false directions to the letter.

Mocktap sprung the trap.

The three cruisers from the moon's surface surged upward: two, the *Octos Ank* and *Hexian Ra,* plugging the gap left between the *Unnos Ra* and *Decium Set;* the *Septos Pa* curling in behind to seal our Enemy against the side of the planet. In the imager, the enclosure looked textbook.

Nothing ever worked that way, I warned myself.

The first hint of a flaw in Skalet's trap came as four cruisers simultaneously fired their pulse cannons. The Kraal were experts. The targeting was coordinated between the ships, each positioned perfectly to avoid hitting each other, projectiles hammering outward in a blaze of energy, inertia dampers likely screaming within each ship as they compensated for the recoil. Skalet-memory provided me with a vivid recollection of the *whir-thwump* echoing in every part of the hull as the next rounds rolled down the barrels.

The image representing our Enemy disappeared in a pool of violent light and debris. It reappeared an instant later, the image updated by the sensor feeding to the *Trium Set* from the *Quartos Ank.*

Our Enemy had thinned itself to almost nothing, allowing the projectiles to pass through its mass, some colliding with each other. In the pause before the next, likely as ineffectual, rounds could be fired, it reformed itself, moving almost more quickly than the imager could relay towards the ship that hadn't fired yet, the *Septos Pa.*

Skalet shouted orders. I heard Captain Longins voice replying. There was a boil of confusion on the bridge of the *Trium Set.*

Meanwhile, the imager whirled closer to focus on the *Septos Pa.*

Perhaps Admiral Mocktap made a calculated decision to sacrifice one of her own in order to stop what now seemed a more deadly foe than expected. A debate for military historians. All we knew was what the *Quartos Ank*'s sensors passed to the imager.

The nightshades of the *Septos Pa* unfurled, their hearts glowing green then red as the energy at their core built to climax. All three discharged in sequence, a snarl and a spit of white hot radiation the imager portrayed with artistically horrifying clarity.

All three bolts missed their adroitly dodging target, carrying on unimpeded to peel open the hull of the hapless *Octos Ank.* At the same moment, without slowing, our Enemy careened straight into the *Septos Pa,* shown as a collision by the projector.

Mercifully, Skalet hadn't programmed it to show how a web-being could eat its way through metal and plas.

I reached for Ragem's hand, not needing the imager to tell me what was happening at that moment on the doomed Kraal cruiser, as our Enemy feasted.

Out There

THIS was familiar. This was safe. This was—pleasure.

Death prowled the corridors of the dying ship, feeding, renewing itself, searching.

Here! Mixs-memory recognized the purpose of the bridge of the *Septos Pa.* Idly, Death tore apart the small shell around the nearest life-form, fastidiously discarding the molecules of what had been a battle suit as it consumed the living mass.

Technology. Lesy-memory surfaced. Death cycled, shedding mass in a cloud of vapor . . .

Becoming Kraal, becoming Human. Those still alive in the room shrieked in terror, discipline lost as they fought for the nonexistent safety of the lift.

Death ignored them, using its new eyes to view the images before it, interpreting symbolic information.

Ah. The one it truly sought, its feast, was there!

Satisfaction.

49: Bridge Afternoon; Shuttle Afternoon

"GET out of here!"

If I'd thought the bridge of the *Trium Set* was bustling with activity before, I'd been wrong. Skalet hadn't wasted a second. She'd ordered the *Quartos Ank* to relay a retreat order to the remaining Kraal ships, with a caution to the *Rigus* should it be still lurking in range.

Now she was ordering the evacuation of her ship. Captain Longins looked as though he would argue, then closed his mouth, nodded once, and turned away. As he herded the crew ahead of him to the lift, I saw him fastening his suit.

The lights were up, making it more difficult to see the images still displayed. The only one that mattered was blue, bright, and heading around the moon toward us. The *Trium Set* was starting to move, but I knew Skalet was right. We couldn't outrun it.

I stayed to one side, Ragem a comforting silence nearby. Ersh knew what we thought we could accomplish, but neither of us left with the Kraal. Skalet, busy fussing over some controls or other, didn't seem to notice. I thought she might be setting a self-destruct, which really implied we should all be joining the more sensible members of the crew in the life pods.

"There," she exclaimed bitterly. "That much done. Now." She looked over at us. "I thought you were leaving."

"As are you," Ragem said firmly.

Skalet's face crinkled in a smile, stretching her tattoos. "I begin to see what you find interesting in this one, 'tween," she commented. Her strong hands reached for us and somehow she was shoving us both toward the lift.

The ship lurched. A hull breach klaxon began screaming. Skalet walked down to the main control consoles, found the right spot, and shut it off.

"Well. This does cause problems." She looked at us both, I for one trembling so hard I couldn't think.

Skalet, as usual, was never in that state. "Esen, I want you to go to Ersh." She paused and smiled again. "You *and* this Human of yours. Get to a life pod; The Kraal will pick you up. Just keep out of trouble, okay?"

"What are you going to do?" I said, dreading the answer.

"Fight. With a little help from you." With that, Skalet abandoned secrecy and caution, and broke the First Rule of our kind herself. She cycled in front of Ragem, not bothering to strip off the battle suit, rather absorbing its mass then excising the nonorganics.

I understood. Beside me, I heard the Human's gasp. *Ersh, let him accept this,* I begged silently. *It's what we are. And there's no other way.* As Skalet formed her mouth, great ragged teeth ready, I cycled into web-form. Instantly I sensed the closeness of Our Enemy, its power and strength. *And hunger!* Skalet would need her full web-mass if she hoped to battle it. I shunted all I was, all I needed to survive, to my core and offered her what I could spare. I welcomed the slicing of her teeth through me—at least this was giving, not theft.

She was done. And she was gone, ripping her way through the far bulkhead in the direction of the Other, ready to intercept it—if totally uncertain of stopping it.

Dimly, I knew I had to cycle, to hide what I was, to flee. Something touched me. Without thinking I cycled into the only form I had left to me without assimilating mass. *Thank Ersh, it had an ear.*

"Esen. Es. Are you all right? Can you hear me?" Hands touched me again, lifted. Despite the desperate urgency to escape, I felt a vast relief, as though a weight had shifted from me I hadn't known I'd carried. Ragem had just witnessed the Web at its most primal; seen us, me, as I truly was. And he accepted.

"Yssss," I managed to hiss. "Run!"

We ran. Behind us, a battle raged on and on, a battle without technology or strategy, its sole purpose survival.

Somehow Ragem got us through the corridors. When breach doors cut off the most direct route to the life pods, he was the one to remember the way to the *Trium Set*'s shuttle. Somehow he launched us into space.

It was time to run home.

Ersh!

50: Shuttle Night

I DON'T know why we didn't crash into the moon, run afoul of the *Rigus* or one of the Kraal ships, or simply become a drifting hulk far from the lanes. I wasn't in much of a state to care.

The form I'd taken on the *Trium Set,* the only one I could use after giving over half my mass to Skalet, was that of a Quebit.

I really hated being a Quebit.

Still, I thought as I puttered with a loose fitting on the rear com panel, the Quebit mentality didn't allow one to panic, fear, or even speculate about the future. And I had lots to keep my appendages occupied. This shuttle was overdue for some fine maintenance.

"Are you going to stay like this much longer, Es?" The Human had to go on one knee to talk to me. My Quebit-self was annoyed at the interruption in my work. I quelled it.

"Need msssss," I admitted.

"Mass," Ragem said quickly. "You need to increase your mass." He disappeared for a while and I gratefully went back to my repairs.

"Here." He gently pulled the wrench from my upper appendage and offered me a tray piled high with various types of food.

Obediently, I nibbled on some chocolate, a Quebit treat. "Not thisss mssss," I said when I was done, pushing the rest away. "Live msss."

My senses were marvelously tuned to fine detail and observation, so I easily detected how Ragem's face went pale, then slowly grew determined. He stood and began working feverishly at the sling holding his arm to his side. I watched, quite intrigued. *Was he feeling better?*

After the sling, off came the upper half of the space suit and the underlying shirt with a muttered expletive or two. "There. What could be easier?" he said, a funny undercurrent to the words as though he were talking more to himself than to me.

Then Ragem sat on the shuttle's carpeted floor and held out his bare arm to me. "Mass."

I extruded an extra pair of leg appendages and scurried under the nearest bench. "No msss! No msss!" I squealed in a most unQuebit-like display of near-hysteria. "No msss!"

"Look, Esen," he said, still in that odd voice. "I'm not happy about this either. But I don't think you can stay as something so—small—for long. If you need . . . if I can help you, let me."

"No msss." I hissed as firmly as possible, trying to hold my Quebit mentality on what mattered.

The light coming under the bench was cut off by his shadow as Ragem crouched to the floor to continue his argument, one cheek pressed to the carpet so he could see me. "We don't know what's happening out here," he insisted desperately. "I need you, Es. I can't work the sensors on this thing. I don't know where to go. I'm afraid to contact the *Rigus* or the Kraal—who knows if that thing can pick up the signals? There's no time to be squeamish."

Squeamish? I narrowed my vision field, magnifying my view until I could see the pores on his skin, the tiny bumps raised by the relative chill of the cabin—or reasonable fear of what he was proposing. I knew the makeup of his every cell and tissue. Perhaps, I thought, I could be surgical about this. Perhaps it would only cost Ragem an arm. *Perhaps wasn't good enough.* All I remembered said there was no such restraint when assimilating living mass. One took what the basic web-form demanded and thought about it later

"Plantssss," I hissed. *After all, it was Skalet's shuttle.*

Light again as Ragem hurried away, just as glad as I was to find another option to explore. Meantime, I let my Quebit-self worry about the corner of the carpet under the bench, removing then reinserting the holding pins to stretch it properly.

"Got some."

I scuttled out at Ragem's relieved announcement. His

arms were full of uprooted duras plants. *Dear Human.* I wouldn't need all of these; I hoped he'd left some in their pots. He placed his armload carefully on the floor by my feet, heedless of the dirt he shook over the carpet.

I sat in the midst of the fleshy plants and cycled, spreading myself like a coating over the living things, moving into the fine network of channels within the dense structure awash with nutrients and water as they tried to survive uprooting. *More of me,* I coaxed, not fighting the sensation of dulling perception and intellect. I knew it would end. *More.* This was faster than consuming and assimilating, if difficult to endure. But I dared not stay in web-form too long so near my Enemy.

The moment I restored myself to the proper mass I cycled, taking on the tried and trusted Ket form. I'd have preferred my birth shape, but we still had to travel and Ragem deserved an able partner, not one living head down in a 'fresher stall.

"Es!" I endured the embrace—at least the Human avoided stepping on my toes—as long as I could.

"Thank you, my friend," I said earnestly, tracing his smile with my fingertips. "I won't forget what you offered. Believe me."

Keeping his good arm wrapped around me, as if Ragem needed the physical contact himself, he pulled me over to the shuttle's control panel. I pressed experimentally on the sensor display pad. Skalet-memory was accurate. A screen in front of us began a scroll of symbols, the lines moving from right to left and accompanied by Kraal script.

"Ah, Paul-Human?" I began, dread crawling down my spine as I made sense of the information. "We're still beside the *Trium Set.* We aren't moving."

"What!" he lunged for the pilot's seat, hands flashing over levers and dials. "It must need a code—"

A perfect time for some Kraal excess in security measures, I thought with disgust. I snaked my long arm past him to key it in from Skalet-memory.

The shuttle began peeling away from its mother ship. I kept reading the display, interpreting it aloud for Ragem in case he wasn't as well-versed in Kraal military symbolism. "The *Quartos Ank* is still in position. She's signaling on a broad band to the remaining cruisers to attack the *Trium Set*."

And Skalet. I stared at the readout for her ship. There were no power signatures; it was apparently dead, recaptured by the moon's gravity, its orbit already decaying. The shuttle's sensors lacked the sensitivity to read any signs of life aboard, even if it could be reset to detect my kind.

That the ship was this intact told me enough. Skalet had planned to destroy it. If she had failed, it could only mean our Enemy had forestalled her.

And Skalet was dead.

"Can we go any faster?" I asked Ragem numbly, watching helplessly as the Kraal ships streaked toward us from under the moon. The Enemy might already be free of the *Trium Set* and coming after us. *Well,* I thought, *we have a variety of ways to die here.*

"I'll see what I can do," he promised, dropping into the pilot's chair and eyeing the controls. "Is there a particular course?"

"Anyway away from here," I recommended. "The cruisers are seconds from line of sight on the *Trium Set.* I don't expect they'll delay in firing."

The shuttle shook around us then steadied. "Fast as she'll go," he told me. "She's got translight, but we're too close to the moon to engage."

The display gained a host of new symbols as we moved, changing the area swept by the sensors. "I'm picking up life pods," I said. "Try not to hit any."

That surprised a chuckle out of him. "If you insist," he added.

"They're firing!" I think I shouted that, the display redlining across its width as the energy signatures behind us rose into critical ranges. "Must be the nightshades."

Odd how the display took such violence and tamed it. The symbol marking the *Trium Set* winked and was gone. No chandeliers. And no Skalet. The residual energies faded almost as quickly, some splashing down on the moon's surface to echo back as a fainter glow.

"They've destroyed the ship." I told him. "You can go to translight in two minutes."

"I'm sorry, Esen."

"If they've killed it," I replied, lost my voice, then found it again. "If it's gone, Skalet would be satisfied." I closed my eyes for an instant, my hands fumbling against the bare skin of my chest. What else had I lost? *Oh, yes,* I thought, Ket-despair welling up, *my hoobit.*

A cold ring of textured metal was pressed into my hands. I opened my eyes to stare down at the circlet Ragem had just given me, then looked back up at him.

He touched one finger politely to the hoobit. "I don't know what made me grab it, Es."

My hands trembled as I secured the leather loop around my neck and settled the hoobit properly. "This Ket is again grateful, Paul-Human," I said wearily.

Ching!

"What was that?" I definitely shouted this time, not reassured as the metallic sound was immediately followed by a succession of smaller, quieter clicks. My hearts hammered, and I expected a hull breach alarm any second. "Ragem, get into a suit!"

As he hurried to take my advice, for whatever good it would do, I stared at the sensor display. We'd hit some debris. *From what?*

According to the sensors, the life pod nearest us doubled in size briefly, then suddenly winked off the display. As I watched, another life pod began to enlarge.

A surge of energy whipped past us to consume the swelling life pod. One of the cruisers had fired on its own shipwrecked crewmates.

There could only be one explanation.

Our Enemy had survived and was systematically tearing its way through the pods. It was looking for me, as a fishercat might turn over stones in a stream to find grubs.

I leaped from my seat to take the pilot's chair. "It's after me," I explained to Ragem. "It knows I'm out here. It has Skalet's memory." I fought the tendency of my hands to shake as I searched the panel for what I wanted.

"She tòld you to get in a life pod," Ragem remembered in horror, struggling to get his injured arm into the stiff sleeve of the Kraal suit. At least it fit.

I punched the translight control, not expecting Ragem to argue we were too close to the moon.

We were far too close to something worse.

Out There

TRIUMPH!

Death assimilated, healing its wounds with new web-mass, glorying in its victory. It scoured Skalet-memory, taking what it liked: passion, ambition, a ruthlessness almost a match for its own. It would discard most as energy, instinctively keeping itself from submerging under different ideas and concepts.

Ah!

It collected itself and poured out of the ruined shell, feasting done, reeling in the delight of knowing its next morsel was so close.

One of these tiny shells harbored it.

There was a name for the taste. *Esen.*

Danger! An attack came perilously close, vaporizing the shell it had just left, sending Death tumbling for a moment. Single-mindedly, it corrected its course, driving straight for the nearest life pod, cracking it open.

Nothing but the ordinary.

Try another. And another!

Danger! A new attack, this time sending streaks of pain to shake Death from its preoccupation. Survival became the imperative.

As Death fled the vengeful ships, it unthinkingly chose the path of greatest anticipation.

Time for the Oldest.

51: Shuttle Night; Moon Morning

"DO WE have a plan?"

I worked my fingers carefully around the healing wound on Ragem's back. The bruising had already faded and the Kraal meds had done an excellent job of healing the torn flesh where the branch had impaled him. Still, there would be significant damage within the ligaments and musculature of the shoulder. I concentrated on improving the blood flow to the region, hoping it gave him some relief.

"Any plan?" Ragem repeated, his voice muffled through the folds of the blanket protecting his face from the carpet.

I looked around me, my Ketself feeling the confinement of the shuttle's walls as safety, my true self finding it a growing and brutal restriction. The Enemy could travel where it pleased. *Did I have a plan?* Only to demand Ersh teach me to fly, once I was sure she was still speaking to me. The need to reach her had grown to a steady pressure, an urgency that was more than half fear.

"None," I said, slapping him gently to indicate I was done. The Human sat up—appreciably less stiff, I noted with professional satisfaction—and reached for the heavy Kraal sweater he'd found in a set of baggage in the back of the shuttle, possibly stored there by the regular pilot. *He or she was unlikely to care,* I sighed to myself.

Both of us found the tiny ship cold. If it was a malfunction, it was beyond our knowledge to repair. I tucked myself back in a cocoon made from what had been the upholstery of the rear bench, already wearing every bit of clothing that fit me. "Do you have a plan?" I asked, more to keep him talking than because I expected Ragem to suddenly find our way to safety.

"We have a com system. Anyone you'd like to call?"

"I like being hidden, thank you," I said.

Ersh-memory surfaced without warning, whirling me back from this moment, this place. I relaxed and allowed it . . .

. . . hiding. This was the safe way, the only way. The prey had become wiser, warier, harder to catch.

Mountains shed their mass into rivers, altering the landscape where Ersh/I chose to remain. Caution was firmly in place now. Secrecy meant safety.

As mountains crumbled, thought patterns became more complex, introverted. A new concept might deserve an eon of contemplation before being accepted, assimilated within the core, nothing forgotten.

Exploration. Camouflage. There was more than mass to obtain from the prey. Ersh/I encountered the achievements of intelligence, began to seek out music, conversation, technology.

There were other sources of energy and mass. The time came when Ersh/I tracked a prey as it sang, and she/I stopped, repulsed.

Murder, whispered a brand new thought.

The new thought spread like a disease into guilt, remorse, horror. Ersh/I writhed in anguish, hiding once again as the mountains lost their snowy tops and became mere hills.

Purpose. A goal. There would be Law, Ersh/I decided. Secrecy remained the key, but there was more to survival than self. Peace was of value. Intelligence was of value.

Then it ended. Destruction rained from above. The hiding place was inadequate, torn apart, exposed. War raced past, life extinguished on a scale beyond anything Ersh/I had achieved.

Abruptly, there was no further need to hide.

Ersh/I scoured the empty planet, becoming aware of a new concept.

Waste . . .

"Es? Esen?"

I pulled myself out of Ersh's grief. "I'm okay," I assured

the Human, surely puzzled by my moment of distraction. "Just—remembering."

He offered me some sombay. "We should be in Xir System by tomorrow morning."

I laced my fingers around the cup, inhaling its moist steam, and wished futilely for something to make it taste like more than hot water. Ragem did the best he could. "Have you ever been to Picco's Moon, Paul-Human?" I asked.

He took his own drink, choosing to sit cross-legged on the floor. The shuttle's space was cramped at best, but neither of us felt inclined to complain. "Seen some vistapes. And," this with some enthusiasm, "I know some Poptians. The gems they bring back each trip are amazing."

I shook my head in wonder. *Should I tell him? No,* I decided. Making myself comfortable, I sipped once, then began: "Well, if those impressed you, my friend, let me tell you the Tumblers' legend that explains why you should only travel out of the moon's crevices when Picco looms overhead."

As I settled into a storyteller's croon, I thought with sudden longing of our destination. Not the place: Ersh, the center of my universe.

She was probably going to blame me for all that had happened, starting with Ragem and finishing with the loss of my web-sisters. I could handle that, as long as she could also save me.

I suspected it wouldn't be that easy.

•

"Very scenic," Ragem commented, looking out the left hand port of the orbit-surface transport. "The Poptians were right.'

I nodded but didn't bother joining him, too anxious for the flight to be over. Any delay seemed insufferable this close. I'd begrudged every second, even though I was the one who'd insisted on shopping on the way.

But then, I couldn't bring Ersh her first uninvited guest without paying at least some attention to appearances. Forget that we were trying to outrun a deadly, voracious predator: I was more nervous about her reaction when she met Ragem. So what if the Brill jacket and pants cost more than Ragem's yearly salary? They gave him a very necessary cultured and sophisticated look.

At the very least, Ersh might think twice before throwing something at him.

I wore a knee-length cloak of twisted fiber over the new skirt I'd bought to replace the hodgepodge of Kraal clothing we'd arrived in. That clothing, and the shuttle, were now on their way to a scrap yard on Deneb, there being a regular pickup at the Xir Prime Station. From there it had been a simple case of buying passage on the next run to Picco's Moon.

"We're almost there, Paul-Human," I said a few minutes later, knowing this route. The transport would drop us off on the flat pad before Ersh's home in the cliff. She paid for the privilege, insisting only on her guests being announced by the transport pilot. Ersh didn't likc surprises.

She undoubtedly wouldn't like the ones I was bringing.

But Ersh wasn't the one surprised. I suppose I should have known.

The transport lifted away with only a slight stirring of dust. Picco was just rising over the horizon, staining the rocks with its brilliant oranges and reds. The colored light played over the walls of Ersh's fortress home, revealing ragged holes where windows had been blasted through the rock.

I rushed ahead of Ragem, cycling as I moved into web-form, straining all my senses to find some trace of Ersh. The autos were out, but I didn't need light to reveal the destruction throughout, or to taste its source.

It was the Enemy. *Not a battle,* I realized, calming myself. Traces of it clung to the floor and ceiling. Gingerly I nibbled at the nearest bit of blue.

Rage! Cheated! Emptiness!

I chose another, fighting the urge to excise every molecule from my flesh.

It dies and would take me! Terror! I must survive! Flee!

Life was close; I felt its heat, recognized the organization of its molecules. Ragem.

I cycled into my birth-form, gladly spitting forth every trace of my Enemy.

Ragem stood in the doorway, clutching a piece of broken

table leg. "Es?" he asked; from his voice I assumed he was uncertain what he faced in the dark.

"It's me," I growled, poking my way around the room until I found the cupboard I sought. Inside it were the controls for the backup lighting systems and heat. I pulled the switch and blinked as the clean white lights erased the shadows and fought back the rusty beams reflecting from Picco.

The place was a mess. I found myself standing on Ersh's tablecloth and moved my paws. The door to her inner room was ripped from its hinges. Within, duras plants and their pots were strewn about. The secret door to her storage compartment hung open like a surprised mouth, its contents gone.

The hooks on one wall remained intact, my favorite coat still hanging where I'd left it. I lifted it from the hook and pulled it over my shoulders.

Ragem spat a phrase I'd last heard from Skalet, his face like granite. "We'd better get out of here, Esen. It could be back."

"I know," I said. "There's a com system in the closet, Paul. Why don't you recall the transport while I—" I paused, as if to go on would be to step off a precipice and plunge down the kind of cliff that had always given me nightmares.

"While you—?" Ragem prompted gently.

"There's somewhere I have to go. Please wait for me, my friend. I won't be long."

52: Moon Morning

ROCKS cry crystal tears.

This, I thought, explained why Ersh's bleak and worn mountain had become littered with diamonds in my absence. They were underfoot, piled in crevices, and made landslides that ripped light into prisms. Enough tears for a lifetime.

I nibbled on a shard the size of a Human's fist, tasting nothing but carbon. "This was a bit extreme, Ersh," I complained, quite aware there'd be no answer beyond the moaning of the evening winds.

I'd been too quick to pronounce her gone. The mountains beneath me heaved, then settled. Diamond dust sparkled around me, slow to obey Picco's gravity.

So there was still enough of her to sense my presence, perhaps even to hear me. *What good was that, with all she was—all she remembered—melded into this pile of dirt?* Grief welled up inside me until I could hardly bear it. "Why?" I shouted. I dropped to my knees and pounded my paws into the unyielding rock, leaving blood behind. "Why?"

A gentler rumbling, but nothing more. Defeated, I sucked crystal grains from my knuckles. Ersh had deserted me. Instead of running or hiding or fighting or even merely surviving, she had chosen to root herself forever into an orbiting hunk of mineral. It was the old way. And it was called death.

Had it been a difficult choice? I gathered a cold handful of diamonds and wondered. Had Ersh regretted her decision when it was too late? As her body thinned and spread within the rock—her fierce intelligence fading, solidifying—had she cried for the end of her existence?

One at a time, my tears slid down, cratering the diamond

dust. "Be safe, Ersh," I whispered to the cold breeze. "Be at peace." My voice lost itself for a moment.

There was no point staying here. I stood, pulling my coat more tightly around my neck. There really was only one thing left to tell her.

"I remember, Ersh," I howled on that mountaintop, alone as I had never been before, as I had never imagined I could be. "I will remember you. I will remember Mixs, Lesy, Ansky, and Skalet." I took a sharp breath, suddenly seeing the future as Ersh must have done. "And I will build the Web of Esen," I promised the mountain. "And that Web will remember you until the hearts of stars grow cold!"

The ground shook as if in echo. I could barely hold my footing. A crack like a wound tore open just in front of me, and I resisted the urge to jump back. *What was Ersh doing?*

All still. I waited a moment to be sure before I took a step forward and looked inside.

A flawless blue gem winked at me from its cradle of leather and disturbed stone. I threw myself down and stretched my arm into the crack, grabbing the bundle and pulling back. Instantly the crack closed.

A last gift? I raised my eyebrow at it. "Ersh, you ancient bag of dust," I said, almost comforted. "I should have known simply dying wouldn't stop you from bossing me around."

There was nothing more for me here. I stood on the mountaintop, gazing into the distance, and realized that I had to rely on myself now. There was nothing more.

In that I was wrong. I turned at the patter of footsteps from behind me. Ragem climbed the last step and came to stand at my side, his breath coming in painful little gasps as his body objected to the thinner atmosphere.

"I felt a moon quake," he panted. "It knocked some of the furnishings around, but the house is okay." He paused, looking around, then whispered: "Is she here?"

What did he think, she could hide as a rock? Since that was exactly what Ersh had done, I saved the explanation for later.

"No," I answered, tucking Ersh's gift into a pocket. "But she left something for me."

Impulsively, I licked him on one dusty cheek, rewarded

by his sudden shy smile in return. "Let's go, my friend," I said. "There's not enough air for you up here. And no reason to stay."

As I hopped back down the stairs, my paws fitting nicely into the grooves etched by centuries of feet, hooves, pads, and other treads, I knew what I had to do.

If I wanted that future I'd envisioned on Ersh's mountain, or any future, I'd have to find my Enemy before it found me.

And stop it.

53: Concourse Afternoon

"AND you can afford all this?"

I'd have thought Ragem's clothing would have been enough to convince any shopkeeper, but perhaps it was the reticent way the Human handled the credit chip—as though it might bite—that raised all four of the clerk's eyebrows.

"Check it yourself," my friend said with admirable aplomb, as if he were in the habit of buying a private yacht and requesting it be ready to lift in two hours, with all the supplies and toys available installed. The clerk, an Ervickian in its ap-morph and so definitely old enough to have seen it all and no longer find any of it amusing, took the offered card and fed it into his reader.

The eyebrows went a little higher and there was a new respect in his voice. "Anything else today, Hom Slothe?"

"Rostra sprouts," I mumbled at Ragem. "And remind him about the shrubbery."

"The ship has to contain a portable conservatory, remember," Ragem insisted. "We won't travel without some life in the place. And be sure the galley has a box of fresh rostra sprouts." The clerk didn't blink, Ragem's credit rating—under the alias Megar Slothe—obviously overcoming any doubts about the sanity of a Human and a Panacian insisting on live plants or ordering food poisonous to both species.

I was impatient and found it difficult not to swivel my head around to look over my shoulder. This was Ultari Prime, a place where just about anything could be purchased. While this made it perfect for our outfitting, it also made it a logical place for anyone to look for us.

Deal concluded, at least until we could inspect the ship for ourselves in about a standard hour, Ragem, led the way from the Ervickian's shop. Once we were several steps past the entrance, walking along the broad sidewalk, he expelled a long, soundless breath.

I clicked my upper hand in amusement. "Was it that bad?"

"I just spent—do you know how much I spent?"

This form shrugged quite eloquently. I enjoyed the gesture. "There is more." *Quite a bit more,* as I recalled, but there was no point further overwhelming Ragem. "You are of my Web; what I have is yours." I'd made sure he had his own access to the accounts Ersh had set up, my future not being completely assured at the moment.

The peripheral vision of a D'Dsellan was superb, allowing me to watch Ragem as we continued to our next destination. He seemed to find something fascinating in the brick pavement passing beneath our respective feet. "You don't have to come with me, Paul Ragem," I said quietly, not for the first time. "The ship has adequate automatics."

His eyes flashed to me, their gray almost black. "We've been through this, Es. If you're going to fight this thing, you're going to need help."

What I'm going to need is a miracle, I thought, but tucked it in a private place. Habit, since there was no other to share my flesh. The pain of my loss was distant, as if I'd somehow shunted that away too for safekeeping.

What bumped against the edge of my carapace was also in safekeeping until I had a private secure place to deal with its contents. Ersh's final legacy, wrapped and still-frozen in the cryosac, lay within a small box hanging from a strap. I trusted the thing looked of little value; there were thieves here, as well as entrepreneurs of every type. Ragem had taken to wearing a very visible biodisruptor on his hip, as well as a far less obvious pair of force blades, accepting the weaponry with an alacrity that confirmed my belief in the underlying barbaric nature of humanoids in general.

Still, he was on my side. And I knew Ragem's nature; he wore the deadly things as a bluff rather than in any hope of using them.

Our next stop. I hadn't told Ragem what we were buying here. The squealing and stamping emanating from inside the low, dark building won me an inscrutable look. "Ganthor?" Ragem wrinkled up his nose and balked in the doorway.

I tapped him on his good shoulder. "Old friends," I said, not bothering to add aloud the *I hope* part of it.

Ragem looked in vain for a sign. Unlike the other buildings along the row, each flamboyantly advertising its wares, the one before us had only a number code beside its door. "Come on," I urged him, taking the first downward step.

None of my web-kin had been able to defeat our Enemy, not even Ersh. Divorced from any emotional context, the meaning was clear: nothing in my shared memories would help me save myself. *Well, I didn't intend to die.*

Hiding had some charm. Unfortunately, hiding wouldn't stop the creature's rampage through civilized space. The battle with the Kraal convinced me it was capable of resisting the ephemerals' attacks. So I'd reached the inevitable conclusion. *I had to kill it.*

I took another of the three steps down to the entranceway, Ragem now beside me, fastidiously avoiding the appendage rail with its sticky shine.

How to kill it? How to survive? Here was part of my answer. Since nothing from before would help me, I would draw on what was only Esen's, what was unique to me and not shared by my Enemy.

Starting with a barful of unemployed Ganthor mercenaries.

Contract void, the Matriarch clicked, shaking her big head in melancholy above her bowl of beer. *Tly backing down*Conflict resolving* Bad news for the mercenaries; I couldn't help but be pleased by it.

Ragem and I perched on stools beside her, her Seconds leaning against the bar to either side. The long, low-ceilinged room was hot, dark, and the source of the truly appalling smell Ragem had noticed at street level. The noise level had dropped only briefly as we stepped inside. Clickspeak worked well enough at close range, except when the bartender arrived with new glassware and deposited it on the counter nearby with a distracting clatter. We all glared at the being each time it happened. The bartender ignored us.

Opportunity for herd, I responded using the tips of my claw against a bottle. Her nose twitched, bubbling mucus, but I couldn't supply any scent to help her. All I could offer was my credit chip.

One of the Seconds took it in between the fingers of his hand and passed it through a reader. *A well-prepared group,* I thought, even though their funds had to be running low. It hadn't been difficult to find them. Mercenaries advertised, and there were no other Ganthor herds currently in the Ultari System. Skalet-like, I found I wanted known parameters.

Another interruption as the bartender needlessly intruded to take away empties and slap down replacements. I glanced at Ragem and he nodded, "On mine, for the lot," he said to the bartender, intercepting its reach for the Matriarch's card and handing his over instead. There was a minor stampede as the Ganthor hurried to take advantage of this bounty, a stampede that broke into a shoving match as the lower seniority individuals were firmly put back in their place.

The Second restored order with a quick *!!* before conferring with the Matriarch about my credit rating. They might prefer barter, but well-traveled beings such as these had learned the value of currency. Had I been Ganthor, I'd have shared the scents of pleased expectancy and new hope that raced through the room. As it was, I tried to keep my orifices as tightly closed as practical without suffocating.

My card was returned. *Task?* the Matriarch clicked as she dipped her snout deeply into the bowl to slurp up beer, her long red tongue mopping up the foam overflowing onto the counter.

Specifics I clicked, pulling out a sheet of folded plas and handing it to her Second. *Security* I summarized vaguely enough.

Resupply necessary she clicked, curling up her hand in a gesture I knew expressed a distasteful topic.

I'd known that detail, having been present when the poor Ganthor had lost all their hardware, and had made my own preparations. *Included* I clicked, pulling out a second credit chip, this one a prepaid account with the leading arms dealer on Ultari Prime. Depending on supply and demand, it was possible the canny Ganthor could buy back the very same weaponry they'd been forced to donate to the Tly.

The Matriarch eased herself off her stool and stamped twice *!!*!!* to focus the attention of her herd. *We accept*

Ragem and I had stood at the same time. I bowed, a D'Dsellan affectation I couldn't help, then nudged Ragem. The quick-witted Human stamped his boot on the floor twice, an accomplishment beyond the soft padding of my current feet. *Confirm when supplied* I clicked on the countertop.

"Mercenaries and rostra sprouts," Ragem itemized as we headed to the shipcity, the servo aircar loaded to its capacity with our final purchases. His lips twitched.

I hugged the icy box of Ersh bits on my knees. "Ganthor are very brave," I said defensively.

"And the sprouts?" Definitely a grin now.

I didn't answer. It would spoil the mood if I told him they were for a last meal if my plan failed at any of several likely moments.

The ship wasn't exactly what we'd expected, but I was satisfied. My companion wasn't. "If this is a yacht, it's my turn to be a Quebit," Ragem had growled, obviously disappointed to find out he'd spent a fortune to buy a used intersystem taxi.

Skalet- and Mixs-memory reassured me as I went over the ship. It was old, but sound. The luxury promised by the dealer consisted of some glued-on plas panels and fairly new carpeting, all intended to disguise where rows of seats used to be, but the control panels had been updated recently. "She's translight-capable," I stated, "And holds air. That'll do."

I was more concerned that our supplies were in order. The Ervickian should have made sufficient profit on the taxi not to try and cheat us any further. *Not a good bet.* We'd have to open everything, except what we'd brought with us to the ship. I shunted the memory of the Ervickian's name into a place I could recall easily.

Ragem recovered quickly, resilient as always. I found him stroking the pilot's seat a short while later, a bemused, wondering expression on his face. "Happier?" I asked.

"It's not everyone who can afford their own starship," he said ruefully. "I should have been more grateful—"

"Grateful?" I interrupted, my worry for him, and for myself, resurfacing. "Why? This ship is to carry us to my Enemy. I can't believe I'm letting you come."

His fist struck the back of the pilot's chair hard enough to set it rocking. "Enough, Es! We've been through this." Ragem's lips were tight; the joy gone from his eyes. "And it's not your Enemy. It's mine. It's everyone's. This creature has cost me my place, my friends—let alone the murders it's committed and will commit again unless we stop it." He took a deep breath, looking at me almost accusingly. "No more talk of whether I belong here. It's not your decision."

I kept my tail from retreating between my legs with an effort, having returned to my birth-form the moment we were in the privacy of the ship. I hadn't bothered shaving or putting on more than a vest. Once we lifted, it would be back to the Ket. Ragem was amazingly adaptable, but it seemed polite to use the forms he'd already befriended. *Had I made the first new Rule for my Web?*

"Well," he said, his tone deliberately light as if to make up for the outburst and, I thought, to forestall any attempt to suggest there was a debate to continue. "We can't let her go up without a name." Ragem consulted the control panel. "Right now it's Speedy InterSys Transit No. 365."

I laughed until my tongue drooped out the corner of my jaw. "You bought her, my friend," I said when I could speak coherently again. "You name her."

Ragem's answering smile was the best thing I'd seen in days.

Out There

CHEATED! *Cheated! Cheated!*

Death flung itself through space, howling its disappointment, shuddering at the closeness of its escape.

Almost death. Almost death.

The Oldest had tried to trap it, almost succeeding. Death writhed at the memory of being lured by that exquisite taste into merging with its mountain, sinking together into lifeless rock.

Must survive!

Somehow it had pulled free. Somehow it had fled.

Never go back, it vowed. *Never never never.*

Besides, it remembered, there was more.

54: Taxi Night

RAGEM had christened our little ship the *Ahab,* citing a Botharan legend about a man who succeeded in defeating a terrible monster. I didn't bother informing him that the story was far older, Terran in fact, and involved a man cursed to follow his quarry into death. Both were possibilities.

The *Ahab* lifted from Ultari Prime only a bit behind schedule. We'd had to delay—and pay the fine—to accept an emergency shipment. The plants the Ervickian had supplied were lush, green, and healthy, but he had neglected to include the lighting fixtures to keep them that way. Ragem and I went through everything else we'd ordered to make sure there had been no other potentially fatal omissions. *I was really going to remember that being.* At least we had rostra sprouts. Six large cases of rostra sprouts.

Once the automatics were engaged, and we went translight, Ragem took the first turn to sleep. The *Ahab* did have two cabins: not quite the staterooms we'd been shown on the vistape, but comfortable and clean.

I didn't waste any time once I was alone in the control room. The com gear I'd bought had been almost as expensive as the ship herself, and was illegal tech in the Commonwealth. *Another reason to shop Ultari.* I knew how to use it, in theory. One of the problems with shared memory was a certain lack of hands-on practice. But the system looked idiot-proof.

It was also supposedly eavesdropper-proof. I composed and sent my first message, the contents of which I definitely didn't want shared. Confirmation was impossible. I had to hope the lure of revenge would be sufficient motivation.

I checked that Ragem was safely asleep before sending

my second message. He wouldn't approve. I wasn't sure I did. But I owed him a future.

Then I set up the relay to Ultari Prime. Part of the cost of this device had been the services of what was euphemistically called an information collector. From the price tag, I hoped she was the best in the business; she'd soon be the richest. I was relieved to see the data feed start immediately, dumping directly into the ship's library for sorting.

I stroked my hoobit, letting the machines work, finding an odd satisfaction in using the same ephemeral technology that threatened my secrecy to track down my Enemy. It would have to feed somewhere, sometime. And those deaths, while I couldn't prevent them, would help me find it.

Meanwhile, I had one final task to perform. I'd left this until I was alone, feeling a need for privacy; a sign of respect for Ersh that I shared this last time without an alien observer, no matter how dear to me.

Putting aside the hoobit and skirt, I opened the box that had never left my side and pulled aside the covering cryosac. There were a total of three blue gems inside; the other two having been tucked beneath the first I'd seen on Picco's Moon. I cycled ever-so-slowly, intent on making the moment last as long as I could.

Ersh taste filled my mouth.

Ragem tugged the lowermost sheet from the pile covering most of the control room deck. "Where did you say the last sighting was?" he asked, spreading his prize out on his lap.

I keyed in the request. "An empty freighter was salvaged off the Commonwealth lanes near Inhaven."

"Inhaven!" Ragem tossed aside the map he'd just found and ruffled through the others on the floor until he grunted with success. "Here it is." He frowned. "What's it doing over there?"

The maps were poor representations of the volumes we dealt with; nonetheless I thought I could see a pattern emerging. "It's avoiding the Kraal. See? There's a loop of Confederacy-patrolled space here, and over there. It's learned to be wary of their weapons."

"Why? They didn't work."

"Caution. You wouldn't pick up something hot with your bare hands, would you, Paul-Human?"

"If it avoids warships, shouldn't it avoid the Tly blockade?"

The investment in information had paid off. "The Tly have pulled back their ships, according to this," I patted the constantly humming com. We'd had to dump the incoming feed into a second storage system, but it was worth it. "And it had good—luck—in the Fringe. I think it plans to hide there, where there is intelligent life, but away from more settled, more protected areas."

"If it hides, Es . . ." Ragem's voice trailed off. I saw him look over the maps at his feet, his tongue darting over his lips as though his mouth had suddenly dried. "Where would we start to look? We can't stop it killing if we can't get ahead of it."

"We do have one advantage," I reminded him. "We know what it prefers."

"Skalet used herself as bait," he protested. "You know how well that worked. And she had a fleet of ships to defend her. We've got—" he flung his hands out wildly. "A taxi!"

"I don't have a death wish, Paul," I assured him firmly. "And I havc no intention of sitting around waiting to be eaten." *Not quite, anyway.* "I've thought of something a little less high-tech than Skalet's drones and warships."

My something came from Lesy. My web-kin had been the one to add the Modoren form to our shared memory. Included in her sharing was a year's experience as a fisher in one of the many Modoren ports on their homeworld. The Modoren were very good at capturing their prey.

"Chum?"

"That's the Human term for it," I said, trying not to sound annoyed as Ragem interrupted my mental calculations for the second time. "The boats go out and spread a mixture of organics on the surface of the water. Organics that would be tasty to the type of fish they want. The fish sense the mixture and follow the concentration gradient to where it originates."

"The boats."

"Exactly."

"And you want to do this over how many parsecs of space?" Ragem shook his head. "You might live long enough to see a result. I certainly won't."

I nudged the map closest to me with my long toes, enjoying its feathery texture if not Ragem's sensible objections.

"We—I," I corrected, "can detect even a single atom and know its likely origin. In web-form, I feel the energy flickers of electrons as they dance about their cores. If we place the chum in the right locations, our Enemy will find it soon enough."

"And then what happens?"

I kept my fingers from the hoobit; the Human was too good at interpreting the physical markers of my mental state in several forms now. "Let's get its attention first."

The *Ahab* needed five more days translight to reach Inhaven. Ragem and I could have shaved a day from the total if we'd dared cut through Tly space, but neither of us felt like taking the extra risk. The Tly were smarting under Commonwealth sanctions; however, nothing in the news reports or other information we received from Ultari suggested those sanctions were doing more than temporarily subduing the territorial pangs of the Tly.

The time was welcome. What I'd planned to do required a certain sacrifice on my part, one much easier to bear if taken slowly, although less pleasant from Ragem's viewpoint.

I was molting.

To be exact, I was in web-form and shedding excess mass as a fine blue dust, carefully freed of any memory. Ragem's task was to suck up the dust using a portable cleaner and store each bagful in the ship's cryo unit.

Every so often, I'd cycle to Ket to take a rest, Ragem would put away the cleaner, and we'd go over the latest information feeds to see if anything had changed.

Then I'd cycle back, assimilate more mass from our dwindling supply of plants, and start molting again. *It wasn't dignified,* I admitted to the Ersh part of me whenever I grew queasy or protective of my mass, but it was a vast improvement over the other ways of losing mass I'd experienced in my short life.

It also gave me time to think, or rather not to think. I needed to assimilate Ersh's last memories, her gift to me, before I tried any of the new things she'd finally decided to teach me. *If I ever did,* I thought ruefully.

She'd taught me how to fly. I dreamed about it, reliving the sensation through Ersh-memory. It was simple, once you knew how.

The only problem was the cost.

I could exit the *Ahab* right now. I could soar beside her in the glory of vacuum, diving through waves of radiation, basking in streams of light. All I'd need would be every molecule of Ragem's flesh, as well as all of the remaining plant life on board.

At least I now understood why my Enemy had been so voracious, yet had never—as far as I'd tasted—succumbed to the need to divide or die. Almost all of its victims' mass must have disappeared into the energy demands of translight travel.

I was very glad Ersh had hidden this ability from us all.

Out There

"THEY want us to stop."

"They do," Joel Largas said thoughtfully. He pulled on his lower lip and considered his daughter.

"What are you going to do about it?" Char Largas' face was pale with fury, but she kept her voice down. They were on the *Loyal*'s bridge and everyone in earshot was family. No point adding to the rumor mill. News spread translight anyway.

"Be polite and stop," he answered easily.

Her control snapped. It had been a difficult week. "What!? After what Kearn did to us?"

Joel sighed. Standing up from the captain's seat, he took Char's arm and moved her firmly toward the rear lift. There was an alcove beside it with enough privacy for a quick nap on the narrow bench or an argument. He'd prefer the nap, but from the look in her eyes, that didn't seem likely.

"The *Rigus* chased off the creature," he began. As her scowl deepened, Joel added quickly: "I know what happened to the *Best,* but do you honestly believe there was another option?"

"They deserted us!"

"And three good people died because of it. Yes. I know, daughter." When had he not been this tired, Joel thought. Lately, he felt as if all the time translight sidestepped for them had crashed down on his shoulders. "But Kearn, right or wrong, was trying to stop that thing from killing anyone else. And they came back, didn't they? We got the med treatments, all AI stuff, no argument, didn't we? Their engineer patched up the *Best.*"

Char was unconvinced, her hands remaining tight fists, her generous mouth a thin unhappy line. He knew the feeling. It was hard to let go of rage these days. It kept the body warm when hope had become elusive. But he had to believe the end was in sight. And he had to keep them believing, even when he couldn't.

"Did they say why they want us to stop the convoy?"

"They want you to transfer over. And me. Anyone who saw the creature."

Joel had expected this. The *Rigus* had vid records from one perspective; the *Loyal* didn't have scanners but her crew had been eyewitnesses, probably the only living ones available to Kearn in his hunt.

"So we make a visit, Char," he said lightly. "Let's take a shopping list, shall we?" he added, watching a reluctant grin ease the corners of her mouth. "Seems to me we've been running short on a few perishables."

"I'll get one ready," she promised, mollified. "A long one."

"We will get to Inhaven," Joel said, reaching out to almost touch her cheek. "All of us."

"Yes, sir," she said, but he feared it was for his sake and for anyone listening, not because she believed in the future anymore.

55: Taxi Afternoon; Colony Afternoon

"READY?"

"As she'll ever be," Ragem responded, one finger pressing on the control we'd jury-rigged on the panel. Neither of us were techs. I sincerely hoped Mixs-memory and Ragem's childhood model building wouldn't let us down now.

"Well?"

He gave me a harried look, then examined the panel display. "It looks as though the first bag is emptying. How much did you want to send out?"

I thought wistfully of the tiny flecks of blue me, abandoned into space like so much lint. *No way to retrieve them now.* "Just the one bag," I decided, not eager to spend another five days filling up the *Ahab*'s storage locker.

He lifted his hand from the control a short time later. "Done."

"I'll reset our course, then." The automatics on the *Ahab* let me simply punch in the new coordinates.

"Are you sure we should have done that translight? Those particles are going to have quite a kick to them when they decelerate to sublight."

"Ships pull debris with them all the time, Paul-Human," I said, standing up and stretching my long Ket arms behind my back. If I'd raised them over my head, I'd have hit the ceiling. "That's what hull shielding is for."

Ragem straightened up, too. "With luck, maybe some will hit our friend out there."

I shuddered and drew my arms back around to hug myself.

"Sorry, Es."

"No. This was my idea. I'm all right."

We had a routine of sorts. It was Ragem's turn to cook, so he walked over to the servo kitchen at the back wall: our yacht's dining room. I set an alarm to let us know when the *Ahab* reached its next chumming point and went over the latest data feed. The information was still coming in, but the lag was increasing. How much of this was due to our distance from the nearest relay and how much to my informant approaching the last of her payment, I wasn't sure.

I was sure the information was worth every credit. "There's been another attack," I announced, numbed as much by the implication that we were closing in as by the consistent violence of my Enemy. "A freighter—within a day of Inhaven's Vineland colony."

"How many on board?" Ragem said in a carefully even voice.

"Eight."

He went on working, his back to me. Maybe it was time to broach a topic I'd left safely alone up to now. "Paul-Human," I began, watching him for any reaction, "What do you want?"

"Want?" He glanced over one shoulder at me, eyes puzzled. "I'm not sure what you mean, Es."

I padded over to sit at the pull-down table near to where he was adding vegetables to one of our two pots. The other he'd labeled with a skull and crossbones for my personal use. *Human humor.* "I mean, what do you want after all this is done? One way or another."

"Oh."

This monosyllable was all he uttered for a few minutes. I crouched and fondled a board he'd made me on one of those days when I'd been less company than the furnishings in his cabin. The board had four areas, each with a different surface texture. It was a close copy of a common Ket art-form. I trailed one finger over the tips of tiny pins, valuing this latest symbol of our friendship.

Ragem passed me a plate and I put away my treasure. "What do I want?" The question was troubling him, I noticed with regret. *But it had to be asked.* "If it were a perfect universe—which it isn't—" he said with abrupt, typical honesty, "I'd like to be back on the *Rigus,* exploring new worlds and species. With you and Tomas around to liven up the place." A short pause, then he winked at me. "And Kearn reassigned somewhere—Lawrenk's got a place in mind that's waaay out there."

He wants his web restored, I thought. *I'd been right.*

"Anyway," the Human continued, a bit too briskly and with his face turned away from me. "Want and like aren't even close to where we are at the moment, are they? We've a lot to do first, my jelly-faced friend."

I didn't disagree.

I watched the display. The last of me trailed outward from the *Ahab,* adrift and alone. "That's the end of it," Ragem announced awkwardly. He knew, if couldn't comprehend, the strong attachment I felt to even these tiny insignificant bits of myself.

"Then it's time," I said. "Do you want to land her, or should I?"

Ragem looked at the automated controls, then at me. "If it's all the same to you, Esen, I think neither of us should."

"Auto it is," I agreed.

There wasn't a shipcity or spaceport to receive the *Ahab* on our chosen landing site, the very lack a reassurance that we weren't endangering other intelligent life. *The organisms coating this lush little world would just,* I thought looking at the display, *have to get out of the way.*

As landings go, ours wasn't bad. I cycled into the Lanivarian the moment I felt the ship's gravity switch off. Ragem was already in motion, pulling on the hooded suit I'd bought for him.

"Could you have found anything more conspicuous for me to wear?" he complained again.

True, the suit fabric was gaudy enough to use as evening wear in a Denebian saloon. Its dark surface might conceivably blend in to some underbrush, if it didn't flash with its own light every so often. Such was the nature of a sensoscreen. "Do you want me to check it again?" I asked him.

The hood nodded.

I cycled into web-form. *Perfect.* To my web senses, Ragem was gone. The screen and its power outlay were right before me, but felt painful to even examine closely.

"Good," I said, cycling back after snatching a bit of mass from one of the few remaining plants. There were lots more outside.

Which was why I had decided to make my stand on Inhaven's latest colony, Ag-colony 413, a project abandoned during the recent escalation of the dispute with the Tly since there hadn't been any major investment in time or effort here for Inhaven to protect. We had carefully spread our chum lines leading to this world from six directions; the concentration gradients would peak here, in the system, as every particle obeyed the dictates of velocity we'd given it and continued on its course until crashing into atmosphere or rock. If I'd wanted to paint an immense sign advertising my presence, I couldn't have done better.

There could be no time, or days until my Enemy tasted the trail and came to me. *But it would come,* I knew.

If there was any justice, maybe we'd have enough time to prepare.

Out There

SAFE at last. No pursuers, no energy weapons, no tricks.

Death flung itself past yet another uninhabited system. There were living things, but no life-forms worthy of its hunger.

Ah! A shell. It took up the chase, reveling in how its quarry tried in vain to twist and evade. Death gathered itself for the kill, ready to rip out the softness hidden within—

What was this?

Death stopped, senses aflame. The shell, ignored, accelerated out of reach, its occupants escaping with a tale to use at the next barside gathering.

Death tasted.

Death *knew.*

56: Colony Night

"I AM not, I repeat, not, going to sleep in this."

"Yes, you are." I couldn't believe this was going to be the failing point of all my plans. *Stupid Human!*

"You wear it, then!"

"I don't need it!"

"Says who!"

This was ridiculous. I reached for the hood Ragem had just thrown at me, picking it up carefully from the grass. "Please, Paul. You're being unreasonable."

"Unreasonable?" the Human pulled himself up to his full height to better glare down at me, an effect spoiled by the way his hair, wet with sweat, stuck up in all directions. I tried not to twitch my nose, but he did smell. The senso-screen fabric had turned out to have one slight disadvantage as a disguise.

It was hot.

Ag-413 being a semitropical paradise and our landing at the equator hadn't helped matters.

"Esen, I'm going to pass out in this thing," he said, wilting again. "There's got to be some other way." Before I opened my mouth, Ragem shook his finger at me. "And I'm not taking off in the *Ahab.*"

I looked overhead, as if I'd be able to spot a blue projectile heading our way through the looming clouds and leafy giant ferns. "Give me your force blade," I said, shaking my head at him.

"Killing me isn't an option either,' he quipped. I gave him a look he could interpret however he liked.

The suit had been crudely sealed together from three large pieces of senso-screen. Working together, Ragem and I were able to salvage enough still-functional material to make a sort of tent. I made him crawl into his sleeping bag, then draped the odd-shaped thing over him, propping up the end over his head with some branches. "It's more comfortable," he offered.

I cycled. He was invisible to my web sense, except for his feet. It was certainly confusing to detect nothing but appendages, but not confusing enough. They resonated as Human to me.

When I told Ragem, he tucked his feet up under the fabric just to be sure. "I still don't understand why you aren't wearing one of these. You're the one it's after."

I looked upward again and didn't bother answering.

We'd made camp at the edge of an artificial clearing. Inhaven had started work here; there had been signs of experimental crops and a rudimentary road system around the crude landing area as we'd dropped down. Any buildings and machinery had been removed, an orderly evacuation rather than a rout.

I walked back and forth, sometimes dropping to all fours for old times' sake, sniffing the living messages on the night air. I'd already found what I was after, a magnificent giant fern, almost as old as I was, daunting in its mass and stillness. *Ersh,* I thought to myself, *this had better work.*

I reviewed my planning for flaws, found dozens, and decided it was a pointless exercise at best. Shivering despite the warmth of the air, I turned and trotted back to where Ragem rested. I knew by the gleam of his eyes as I approached he was no more inclined to sleep than I was. So I lay down against him, tucked my nose under his arm, and tried to be a good example.

I'd never had a nightmare before, beyond a restless worrying about cliffs, not that I remembered anyway. Ersh had explained to me once that dreams were closer to the waking mind in ephemerals and so were sometimes experienced as the truth. In us, they lodged deeper, distinguishable only in that they faded while memory remained vivid and alive.

But this had the feel of nightmare to it.

I didn't know my form. It wasn't that I had none, or that I wore some new and unassimilated shape, both were patently impossible. I simply couldn't recall anything about the thing I was.

I knew where I was, however. I was in Ersh's room, her inner sanctuary. It was intact again, the way it should be. Then, as if the recognition distorted the image, it was in ruin. I choked on dust, yet didn't know yet if I breathed air. *This couldn't be true memory,* I realized, helpless to do more than live in it.

The air cleared again. *Ersh.* There she rested, in the perfection of her web-form, a message ready to taste in the air. I tried to cycle, to be able to understand.

I couldn't. I was locked in this, this, thing!

Ersh's surface became mirror-bright. I found myself staring at Ragem's face, using his hands to touch it, to run down his body. Yet it was mine!

What was happening? What did it mean?

Suddenly, Ersh formed a mouth, with ragged sharp teeth framing it top, bottom, and sides. She advanced toward me. I screamed in horror and saw Ragem's face—my face—screaming in the reflection. I couldn't move. The mouth enlarged, bigger, bigger. It was larger than I and coming closer . . .

"Es!" Something pounded on my rib cage. "Wake up!"

I fought my way out of the lingering horror of the dream, finding myself blinking at the small handlight Ragem—properly himself—shonc between us. He was looking at me with concern. He was also a good arm's length away and from his position, it had been his foot in my ribs.

"Sorry. But you were snarling in your sleep," he explained. "Are you all right? I thought you were going to bite me."

"Keep under the screen," was all I managed to say.

Neither of us found it easy to fall back to sleep. I'd almost drifted off when Ragem said out of the darkness: "You know, you've never told me where you live."

"Where I live?" I repeated, trying to make sense of the comment.

"Well, do you live on Picco's Moon?"

Not any more, I said to myself, controlling a shiver. Ragem, seeming in the mood to hear his own voice, kept going in a slow sleepy way when I didn't reply. "The others had places of their own. Where is yours? On Lanivar?"

"It takes experience and training to live within another

species' culture," I admitted quietly. "Ersh hadn't felt I was ready."

"Oh."

The silence and the dark didn't help my thoughts. "It wouldn't have been long," I continued, almost to myself. *Another hundred years or so, at the rate I made mistakes.* "She'd likely have sent me to one of the Fringe worlds, a colony or perhaps a mining operation. There's few questions asked in new settlements. I'd have started an identity of my own, something innocuous and dull. Safe. Maybe a small import business, so I could travel without attracting any notice. To live like the others—it takes a lot of preparation to create an identity that fits into an existing society."

I paused. From the even sound of his breathing, he'd fallen asleep somewhere during my explanation. *Just as well,* I thought, settling myself to do the same if I could. *For if I survived my Enemy, my new life must start with an identity and a place secret from everyone—including my only friend.*

Out There

"YOU want us to what?"

"Hush, Char," Joel admonished his eldest. The small man across the gleaming desktop had thus far failed to impress either his offspring or himself. Funny how people seemed larger than life when you were only talking through a com link. Joel Largas was also unimpressed with the reason they were standing in the office of Acting Captain Kearn.

"Three ships. Two," Kearn temporized, his hand stealing up to rub frantically across his balding head. "That's all. Two. A short jaunt with us and you're back on course."

"And what do we get in return for these two ships and your short jaunt?" Char demanded. She was a captain in her own right, at least when the *Largas Loyal* had been one of a fleet instead of a sole survivor, and refused to be cowed by Kearn's Commonwealth uniform or his nonhuman security officer standing alertly to one side, whiskers flicking back and forth with the conversation.

Kearn looked at Joel Largas in appeal. Joel raised one eyebrow. "A fair question, Acting Captain. You're asking us to disrupt the convoy, slow it down. There's a lot of tired, hurt people on those ships and 'pods. They aren't patient with delays."

"We know, sir," the voice belonged to a tall woman, an engineering specialist if Joel read the bars on her uniform correctly. Something in her face told him this one had seen trouble in the past and had no patience for fools of any rank. He felt sorry for her on this ship.

"You're the one who came on the *Best,*" Denny said. "You patched her up in no time."

"Lawrenk Jen," she acknowledged with a nod. "My pleasure." Lawrenk had a stack of plas sheets in one hand. She held them up, as if for Kearn to notice as well as those from the *Loyal.* "These are confirmations from Inhaven, welcoming you and your families to the colony of your choice. I also have settlement vouchers for everyone in your convoy, entitling you to land and supplies once you've decided on a destination."

"We have a destination. Minas XII."

Lawrenk raised a brow at the firmness in Char's voice, then glanced at the pages in her hand. "Spectacular scenery. But you can't use these land vouchers there—"

"We aren't farmers," Denny broke in, offended as only the young could be. Joel gave his son a stern look.

But the engineer smiled broadly, understanding lighting her eyes. "Of course not. You're spacers. And Minas is the last permanent colony between the major shipping lanes and the mines of the Fringe. I'd imagine they could use their own freighter fleet."

"We think so." Joel paused and looked at Kearn, suspicious of the turn in the conversation. The man's face was too smug for comfort. "So you've taken care of our immigration. What are the conditions to this generosity? The loan of our ships?"

"No conditions." Lawrenk passed the sheets to Char, the Largas nearest to her. From Kearn's strangled gasp, Joel decided this was not in the original script. He did like this woman.

"We can offer further incentive," Kearn recovered quickly. "I think you'll be interested." He drummed his fingers on his desk. "Very interested. And I'd settle for one ship; that would do, I believe."

Joe, about to refuse any further discussion, lifted his eyes to meet Lawrenk's abruptly somber look. Something was going on. He changed his mind in that instant. He sat back down in the chair, ignoring Char's stiffening.

"I'm listening."

57: Colony Morning

THE sounds of wild, exuberant singing woke me. The sun, still below the horizon, was burnishing the bottoms of the clouds with touches of pale gold. I kept motionless as I tried to decide on the nature of the singers. Small and harmless, experience told me. *Loud enough.*

Ragem groaned beside me, flinging one arm over his head and muttering something I couldn't make out clearly. I eased myself away, pausing to pull the senso-screen more completely over him.

Dear Human, I thought, watching him settle back into a deeper sleep.

I stepped cautiously, unsure what might wake him if the singing things in the nearby fields couldn't, but not wanting to take any chances. Something inside me said this was the day. And I had preparations to make.

They didn't take long. I set the last of the signalers into the soft, moist soil, driving it in the final distance by jumping on the top twice. There were four of the devices; I hesitated only briefly before activating them all with the control on the final box.

A sullen red light glowed up at me from its surface, like the opening of an eye. I stared back, waiting. After what seemed far too long a delay, the light began to blink in a pattern. *No turning back now,* I acknowledged with a pang. I stretched my long spine, rotating each hip, remembering the same movement from another world, another me.

My first confirmation I'd set things in motion came during breakfast. Ragem wore the senso-screen as a cloak-and-hood affair—at least confusing to the Enemy, if no longer as effective as I'd planned. We were sitting in the shade of a fern, munching on ration bars, when a roar from overhead announced visitors.

"Who's that?" Ragem exclaimed, one hand shading his eyes as he stared up at the descending ship. It was going to set down right beside the *Ahab.* I took a final bite of my breakfast and got to my feet.

It wasn't the *Rigus.* I recognized the design, if not the individual vessel. Human-made. A freighter. Not particularly large as those things went, but dwarfing the *Ahab.*

Damn Kearn.

I knew what he'd done. He'd coerced some poor captain into taking the risk for him while he hung safely in orbit.

Ragem shook his head. "Of all the luck. Want to bet it's some farmers from Inhaven, checking on their crops? I'd better see what they want."

"Good idea," I said, running my tongue around my teeth and trying not to pant."I'll stay here."

He gave me an odd look. "Why?"

Figures were already emerging from the ship, heading in our direction. I took a step back. "It's safer for me," I said. "Go on. Find out what they want."

Ragem looked at the approaching trio, then back to me. "What should I say?"

I memorized the shape of his face, including the wisp of black hair the breeze tumbled over one puzzled eye. "I think you should offer to tell them the truth, my friend," I advised him, as serious as I'd ever been. "But don't sell it cheap."

"Es?" Ragem reached out to me, his face stricken. "What have you done?"

"There he is!" shouted a voice, almost too close. "Hold it!" shouted another.

"Good-bye, Paul Ragem," I said, turning and sprinting into the cover of the forest, trying not to listen to the sounds of struggle from behind as Ragem's pursuers caught him before he could follow me.

Of all my plans, this had been the hardest to do, I admitted to myself. I circled back to a vantage point where I could see what was happening.

Ragem hadn't taken kindly to being detained. He stood upright and defiant between two considerably larger Human males; I could see blood on the chin of one of them. I was relieved to see there was no animosity on their faces. The third figure, a female, was standing in front of Ragem and telling him something, emphasizing her points with waves of her hands. All three wore faded spacer coveralls and, I was thankful to see, had no weapons.

I cocked my ears to listen. The breeze carried some of what was being said to me, but I didn't dare move closer.

"—here to rescue you. Why did you hit Denny?"

"I don't need to be rescued. Who sent—" I snarled at the upwelling of happy song from overhead that drowned out the rest of Ragem's furious question.

It didn't matter. I knew the answers, or thought I did, and those I watched were in a hurry. Since Ragem didn't appear to want to be rescued, his would-be rescuers solved the problem by simply picking him up. The woman surveyed the small amount of gear we had, then picked up the senso-screen from where it had landed during Ragem's manhandling. It seemed to fascinate her; she rolled it into a bundle under her arm before following the men into the ship.

It lifted moments later. The crew must have held the engines on standby. I raised my muzzle and howled as it disappeared into the cloudy sky.

Now Ragem was safe.

Now I was truly alone.

I didn't think I'd have long to wait for my Enemy. It could have been an instinct, some unexpected carryover of web senses into the form I currently used to trot deeper into the forest. I tried to identify my feelings. *Dread,* I decided, but no fear. I had none left.

I stopped beneath my ally, the ancient fern tree, and stretched my long arms around its fibrous stalk as far as they would reach. It would have taken three of me to encompass its girth. The stalk had rows of tiny hooked spikes running up its surface, something my Ket-self would have enjoyed and my Lanivarian-self found snagged the fur of my belly.

I knew why I felt dread. If all went in my favor, I would have ensured I was the only web-being alive in this part of the universe. I, who had never killed an intelligent being, could be about to exterminate the only other member of my kind.

I rubbed my chin and side of my face against the spikes, smelling a not unpleasant vegetable muskiness as I bruised a few. There must be a stronger breeze up above. I felt an almost imperceptible motion within the fern as the immense stalk transferred its resistance to the whims of the air into the ground's solid anchorage.

My plans took whatever made me different from my kin and made those differences into weapons against my Enemy. Mixs had reacted instinctively, losing form explosively as she tried, too late, to fight. Lesy had tried to hide. Skalet had planned to meet the creature on its own terms, flesh and tooth. Ersh had tried to trick it into suicide with her.

As I released my form, cycling into web-mass, I thought my approach at least had the virtue of being different.

I was going to give it exactly what it wanted.

Out There

DEATH swam through a feast, absorbing all it could.

Not enough!

The teasing taste led it onward. Death spread itself, scooping what was before it in an ecstasy of gluttony. *Marvelous.*

There was no doubt where to find more.

There was no doubt what to do when it arrived.

Death felt like singing.

58: Colony Morning: Orbit Afternoon

IN WEB-FORM, I was terrified of the nonsentient mass touching me, overwhelmed by its sheer volume. The terror was familiar and I suppressed it.

I took a moment to savor my surroundings, listening to the throbbing heart of this planet, detecting its life as patterns of pleasing regularity and order amid the chaos of chemical reactions and change. Extending my senses outward. I could just barely detect the specks of artificial gravity and harnessed power marking ships in orbit. *Which one are you, dear friend?* I wondered to myself.

And then, I felt it. My Enemy was coming.

No time for second guessing or doubts. If I was wrong, I wouldn't live to know it. *Ersh, too short a life,* I sighed, beginning to thin myself.

The fern had a primitive internal circulatory system for so large an organism. No matter. I forced my way upward, splitting off into its hundreds of fronds, dividing myself even further to course into its tens of thousands of small leaflets. Up here, I could feel the heat from the sun, could lose myself in the complex ticktock of photosynthesis, rejoice in the harvesting of energy.

Not my purpose. Not me! I fought the fern's nature, ever-so-grudgingly turning its mass into more of me. More. More. I had to have it all.

My thoughts slowed, became almost paralyzed. It was as though they operated on a different time scale. I struggled to hold myself.

This would be a fine life, the traitorous whisper started as I reached downward and began converting the rhizomes holding the fern, holding me, to the ground. *Free of trouble or pain. Stay.*

I might have lost the battle to retain myself and my purpose then and there, if it hadn't been for gravity. I'd modified enough of the fern to make it unstable. A breeze tossed my crown of leaflets and web-mass, the force multiplied a thousandfold over my entire new body, pushing until I lost my grip on the soil and began to fall.

It took several seconds. My fronds slid between those of my intact neighbors, slowing my descent if not halting it. Three, four others—almost as large—joined me in my majestic plunge.

I didn't stay to the end. With a final effort, I pulled myself out of the mass of vegetation, all web-mass now, larger than any of my kin had become with one exception.

Ersh.

My thoughts were sluggish. *This wasn't how I was supposed to be.* There was too much. Too much.

I remembered my purpose and summoned Ersh-memory. It was time to fly.

I spent mass prodigiously, some part of me aghast at the waste, and launched myself away from the planet almost before I realized what I was doing.

The last traces of atmosphere slid away from my outer surface like condensation being wiped from a window. Suddenly I could sense all that was around me with incredible clarity. Radiation sang through my being. *If only I wasn't so large, my thoughts so heavy.*

Ships. *Shells,* corrected an old Ersh-memory, a memory tainted by hunger as well as guilt. *Friends,* I insisted.

And there was my Enemy.

She was perfection, I moaned to myself, feeling a weakening of my resolve. *How could I resist?*

My Enemy rushed toward me, broadcasting her hunger, her need. I sensed her jaws opening.

Now! a tiny part of me, a part I knew as the core of my individuality, insisted. There was one last task.

I sorted my mass, frantically collecting all that was me, all that was Ersh, Ansky, Lesy, Mixs, and Skalet into one place, my private place, that place where only I and Ersh could hoard our secrets.

Pain! Teeth ripped into my flesh, tore away a mouthful, returned to slice deeper. This was nothing like the sharing of self with my web-kin. This was violation. This was a threat to my existence.

This was what I'd hoped. I bore the pain, endured the horror of it. *Eat!* I urged silently, concentrating now on sending one memory shuddering through all there was of me.

Too large. Too much!

Ersh-memory had taught me how to reproduce, how to release my grip on excess web-mass and allow both to live. So now I relaxed my hold, spinning what would be Esen from now on away from what would be something new. Agony and relief made me dizzy. My thoughts became crystal clear again.

I answered the call of gravity, plunging down toward the planet; behind me, my Enemy radiated its continuing satisfaction, its obscene delight in every bite of what had been Esen.

Just before I touched the atmosphere, I felt something new from it: *confusion.* Too much. What to do! What to do!

I knew, but hadn't left the information behind with my other gift. I had to hurry. My Enemy could simply burn the mass away if it chose. Its need to fission, the instinct to sort itself into two or solidify, would last mere moments at best.

Down to the *Ahab.* I cycled into Ket, commanded the port to open, and ran inside. Up to the lift. *Why couldn't we pick a ship that reoriented its deck to planet gravity?* I fussed, fearing every instant of time wasted.

There, the control room. I tripped over the maps on the floor, scrambling for the com, fearing I was already too late.

I sent the message.

Out There

DEATH closed its jaws over the last morsel, satiated, content. This had been the best feeding.

Assimilate.

What was happening? *Too much!*

Pain. Fear. What is happening?

The body demands a choice; the mind must loosen its hold and permit the escape of mass, or accept the true death that beckons. Divide, or become solid, thoughtless, a rock.

I must live! Death screamed to itself. It felt selection beginning on a microscopic scale, flesh battling against flesh. *No! It is all mine!*

Preoccupied with self, Death ignored the two approaching starships.

Overwhelmed with biological imperatives, Death missed the powering of weapons, the unfolding of delicate petals almost close enough to touch, the glow of deadly energies building to release.

Obsessed with its own life, Death failed to notice the moment it ended.

59: Colony Afternoon

I'D KNOW those sleek globes and immaculate hull anywhere.

The *Rigus* touched the surface of Inhaven Ag-colony 413 like a feather, her engines shutting down immediately, the dust she'd kicked into the air washed away by an errant gust of rain-filled wind. The makeshift spaceport here was getting a fair amount of traffic these days.

I shook myself, adding my own little rainshower to the drops rolling off the ferns above me. It was almost over. The clouds were scarred with brilliant blue pockets of clear sky, the color one of so many regrets. One of those clearings had glowed hot white not so long ago. I didn't need to cycle to confirm my Enemy was gone.

Almost over, I repeated to myself, staring at the *Rigus.* No one had come out yet; her port remained sealed. I imagined Sas and his scan-techs were busy, remotes scouring the countryside. *For what?* I'd hoped Kearn would have been too intent on the web-being he could see above the planet to notice a small bit of one flying away.

I was in danger of becoming as paranoid as the Human, a fate I didn't relish. The signal to attack had come from here. Even Kearn would think to track down its source, to find out who sent it.

Forgive me if I don't wish you luck, I said to myself, more than ready for the safety of being anonymous and unknown again. I'd done the best I could, given the circumstances and my lack of expertise. The *Ahab* was registered under Ragem's alias, Megar Slothe. If Kearn or Ragem tried to trace the funds used to buy the ship, they'd soon find that the accounts were blind ones, newly created and not connected to any I might use in the future. I'd already removed or destroyed all evidence of my presence on the *Ahab*, including the com device.

Kearn would have to deal with Ragem to find out more. I sincerely hoped Ragem would use what he knew of me and my kind to bargain for his old life back, to restore his former Web. He should believe me dead along with my Enemy—safe from any further harm from Kern's searching. Knowing bureaucracy as I did, it was unlikely Ragem would be able to keep the legacy I'd given him, but I also knew Ragem valued his friendships more than physical wealth.

As did I.

I used my paw to rub the remaining drops of rain water from my face. *I wish you a long and happy life, my friend,* I thought, staring at his ship, oddly wistful.

I was exhausted, mentally and to the limits of my every molecule. But there was the issue of starting my own new life. I'd actually been optimistic enough to think about that during our journey to this world, a presumption Ersh would definitely have blamed on my youth.

First, however, I needed to leave this place. Traveling under my own power was a temptation I firmly planned to resist, knowing for myself why Ersh had so wisely forbidden that luxury to herself as well as her kin.

As if cued to the thought, the sky above the *Rigus* brightened as if a new sun had peeked through. A second spot appeared, burning its way through a cloud. I shivered with reaction, not yet believing that the final pieces might actually fall into place.

Time to sneak closer and find out for sure.

By the time I'd edged my way through the bands of shrubbery the colonies had left near the landing field, beings had disembarked from both the *Rigus* and her new neighbors, the Kraal heavy cruiser *Unnos Ra* and the *Quartos Ank*. I wasn't surprised to see the beings were all stationary.

However, Kearn was likely very surprised. I don't think he'd any reason to expect to be facing the twitching muzzles and raised weapons of a Herd of Ganthor mercenaries. I was close enough now to see the Kraal captains and their personal guards standing behind the mercenaries, the Kraal looking decidedly triumphant. My old acquaintance, Captain Hubbar-ro, was talking.

"A glorious revenge, Captain Kearn! Surely you don't plan to spoil the moment by contesting our right to this obviously abandoned world."

The Kraal were nothing if not predictable, I grinned to myself, going down on my belly to crawl closer.

The Commonwealth's man-on-the-spot definitely looked as though he wished himself anywhere but. It didn't help Kearn's confidence to be gazing up, nose to mucus-adrip muzzle, at the Matriarch's battle-scarred Second. I thought he should really have taken the time to put on a dress uniform. The Kraal were resplendent in their best, doubtless a further blow to the Human's ability to think clearly.

"This is an Inhaven colony, Captain," Kearn was blustering. I had to give him credit. "While we appreciate your assistance in destroying the Esen-monster," I lifted one lip in a snarl, changing my mind. "I hope you realize we can't allow you to simply—take over a registered, working colony of the Inhaven government."

"Working?" This from the captain of the *Unnos Ra.* "Show me a colonist, my good Captain Kearn. Show me an operational plant—or even a toilet!"

"You can't do this!" Kearn sputtered. The Ganthor's immediate *!! * sent him back a quick few steps.

"There's no need for violence, Hom Kraal," this from Sas, whose own body language was anything but pacific. "Your troops should stand down from their weapons and help us in our search."

"Search?"

Kearn wiped his face with a handkerchief and looked gratefully at his security officer. "Yes, yes," he said, gesturing beyond the *Rigus* to the abandoned *Ahab.* "We have a missing person. Someone who might be injured and need our assistance," he added sanctimoniously. I tried not to laugh.

The captain of the *Unnos Ra* nodded graciously, his mop of white hair adding to the effect. "As Temporary Administrator of this planet for the Kraal Confederacy, I willingly extend our aid to your efforts."

I had to put my paws over my muzzle to keep quiet at this. Kearn was going to have to acknowledge the Kraal claim in order to search the colony. I could see he was about to faint at the thought.

But his better sense won. After all, his monster was dead, Inhaven was only loosely part of the Commonwealth, and the mission parameters of a First Contact ship, though already thoroughly fractured by his chase after me, hardly included stepping into diplomatic or other messy negotiations over territories. Passing on responsibility was a Kearn strong point. I could almost read his mind.

It took a bit more talking before the details of the search were sorted out by all parties. The Kraal had more posturing to do, and the *Rigus* crew were not in a hurry to commit themselves in any potentially hazardous situation. The Ganthor, relieved from duty, spent the time exploring the immediate surroundings of the ships—something no one else felt obligated to stop.

I had gradually moved until I was safely downwind, having a greater respect for the Ganthor's natural abilities than for the high-tech scanners on any of the ships.

Inevitably, Kearn caved in and allowed the Kraal to command the search. I kept out of their way, watching from a safe distance as a steady stream of beings marched into the *Ahab* and out again, some carrying objects whose value in their hunt I knew would be minimal. I hope no one mistook the rostra sprouts for anything Human-edible.

It was a well-organized, if boring process. I napped at times, waiting for them to give up. The *Quartos Ank* sent out its aircar, retrieving it just before sunset. Small search parties trooped through the fields, not bothering with the forest, since there were no trails or roadways to follow. If they had, I wondered what they would have made of the vast hole I'd left, all that remained of the fern tree, its neighbors toppled to the ground.

The one piece of excitement came when Ganthor found where Ragem and I had slept, broadcasting this discovery with a volley of armsfire that sent off alarm klaxons on the *Rigus* and likely scared Kearn half to death.

The chance I'd been waiting for arrived shortly after this, the sun having finally set, and the Ganthor having been ordered back to the *Quartos Ank*. I presumed no one wanted to blunder around in the dark with a herd of trigger-happy mercs.

It wasn't a problem for me. As the herd passed my hiding place, I cycled. They stopped, nostrils flaring as they caught my scent and reacted with pleased surprise.

Come !! signaled the Matriarch, almost knocking me flat with her welcome. I had some trouble breathing as the rest of them jostled to get closest to me. The scents were overwhelmingly of welcome; Ganthor rarely exhibiting surprise at anything the cosmos threw at them. *It was a refreshing attitude.*

Once we sorted ourselves out, most of the pleasantries involving collision and a certain amount of bruising, I found myself safely tucked in the center of a mass of very content Ganthor, one with the herd. As easily as that, we marched together back to the *Unnos Ra* and boarded right under the unobservant eyes of the guard stationed at her port. Fourteen Ganthor or fifteen. The herd was its own smelly, noisy, potentially dangerous entity. No one in their right minds would argue with it.

I'd counted on that.

I took one last look at the *Rigus* before I was shoved into the ship by my herdmates.

Ephemeral memories were so short.

I hoped Ragem would remember me. *He was,* I thought with a return of overwhelming loneliness, *the only one left who could.*

60: Mountain Morning

"PUT IT in the other corner, please." I watched the Human struggle with the heavy table, but didn't offer to help. I'd tried that earlier and been thoroughly rebuffed. *Proud folks, these colonists,* I thought.

It wasn't the first time I'd noticed this since arriving on Minas XII. It was a harsh world, rich in minerals and stark beauty, torn by sandstorms at its equator and snowsqualls everywhere else. It seemed to encourage a similarly volatile attitude in those who chose to live here.

The movers departed at last, having put my furniture in approximately the right places, leaving me a ceiling-high stack of boxes to unpack at my leisure. Shipments were finally arriving on schedule, a bonus of the new freight company started by a typically entrepreneurial group of new settlers. Rumor said they were refugees from Garson's World; but on humanity's frontier, no one asked or expected specifics of your past.

One excellent reason to live here, I hummed to myself, drawn irresistibly to the window of my new home. The other reason hung overhead, patterned in the stars revealed by the midsummer's lull in storm activity. The Fringe.

I stared up at those stars, knowing what they represented. There above me was the path buried in Ersh-memory. It was the path etched in what I retained of my Enemy's past. It was the path the next invader would follow. *And maybe,* I thought, admitting myself young enough for both hope and folly, *it was the path a different type of web-being might take, a being who could be a friend.* A new idea, and one Ersh would doubtless have disapproved of. It was our way to live alone, I knew.

I had just never expected to be this alone.

I was tempted to cycle and use my web senses to seek

what might be out there, friend or foe. *Later,* I promised myself. It was my vigil, my life's work. The Web of Ersh had sought to collect and preserve the accomplishments of intelligence.

The Web of Esen, I vowed to myself, looking up at those stars, would protect what lived.

I was satisfied with my purpose. I was satisfied with my home, perched on a mountaintop the locals warned me experienced the worst possible effects of the coming winter storms. It reminded me of another mountain. *I was entitled,* I thought, *to that,* feeling a trace of familiar aloneness.

I wasn't, however, satisfied with my latest shipment. *Could no one read an order form anymore?*

"Rostra sprouts," I said for the third time to the person at the other end of the com link, a normally very helpful representative of the Largas Freight Line. "I ordered two cases of fresh rostra sprouts—prepaid!" I calmed myself. "I just want to know when you think they might arrive."

There was a sound at the other end of shuffling plas. I suspected most businesses prerecorded the sound to reassure irate customers *something* was being done. Even if it wasn't.

"Your order has been delivered, Fem Esolesy-ki. I have the record right here—"

"Well, it didn't—" I paused, cocking an ear to a buzzing from outside. "Perhaps that's it now. I'll let you know."

I hurried to the door. Sure enough, there was a delivery shuttle sitting on the pad between my porch and the abrupt beginning of the cliff that afforded me such a magnificent view, as well as a secure entrance. I found I'd lost my fear of cliff edges. *Maybe it had something to do with flying out there.*

The driver had already climbed out and was reaching into the back for a crate.

My "Come right in—" dried up and lost itself somewhere in my throat. I knew that shape . . .

Especially when it turned around and smiled at me. "Sorry I'm late," he said, eyes suspiciously bright.

"Ragem?" I realized my mouth was hanging open after the word and snapped it shut. "What—How?" This with a growl.

"When I heard the order for sprouts, I knew who it had to be." His triumphant smile faded away, replaced by something more akin to pain. "That's not true. I didn't know, Esen. All I could do was hope. I thought I'd lost you."

"You were supposed to," I whispered, but felt my tail try to wag. I spared some thought to self-preservation. "Would you get inside! Is Kearn—"

Ragem tucked the crate under one arm—healed then, I noticed—and followed me indoors. "You're safe. Kearn thinks we're both dead," he said in a ridiculously satisfied voice. He dropped the crate down on the floor and came over to take my shoulders in both hands, touching his nose to my muzzle in a quick Lanivarian-version of a hug. "Nice place you've got here."

"You are impossible!" I snarled, trying to be upset, but becoming convinced this could be the best day of my life. "I arranged for you to go back to the *Rigus*!"

Ragem ignored this, busy exploring the house. I found myself following behind, arguing to the back of his head. His dark hair had grown long enough to need a clip, I noticed. He was wearing a set of rumpled spacer coveralls. "I like this," he decided. There was a unwarranted and decidedly happy bounce to his step.

I grabbed his arm to stop him, lips curled so tightly back over my teeth I hoped the words were understandable. "I tried to give you back your friends, your family!" All I had lost, he had willingly sacrificed. *Why?*

Ragem disregarded my fangs, rubbing me gently under one ear. "I know. The Largas—great folks, by the way—explained they were sent to pick up a somewhat deranged Commonwealth officer." He pretended to frown at me. "Not a pleasant description, Es. But anyway, it didn't take a great deal of persuasion—or credits—to convince them I was quite sane, thank you, and to change their minds. It helped that our Kearn has such a gift for offending people. They told the *Rigus* they couldn't find such a person, collected their due reward for their efforts, and headed for their original destination, here, with a new member of the crew."

"Why did you come with them here?" *As cosmic coincidences went, this was a whopper.*

He turned his attention thoughtfully to my other ear.

I'd stopped snarling at some point. "You'd left the maps out, Es, one night on the *Ahab,*" he chided gently. "I guess you thought I was asleep. It didn't take rocket science to figure out that Minas was that Fringe colony you hoped to go to, if—" Ragem's voice roughened, "—if you survived battling your Enemy."

He paused. "That was the worst of it, Esen. That you pushed me away and went off to die alone."

"I wasn't planning to die," I rebutted, backing out of his hold. "And you didn't believe me dead for an instant, did you?"

The Human grinned. "Any being who can get in and out of as much trouble as you have couldn't possibly be defeated by one creature. I never doubted you." He spread out his hands. "I only doubted if I'd find you."

"Now that you have, what do you want?" I said, suddenly knowing the answer I desperately needed, but knowing it was his choice.

Ragem patted the wood trim around the fireplace. "My own room, for starters. I've got a lot of stuff in that shuttle outside."

It was much later, after we'd moved in Ragem's belongings and caught up on old news, the way friends do, that he broached the other thing he wanted. I'd been waiting for it, and it came midway through the second bottle of Inhaven wine.

"Esen, you can become any form you've assimilated, right?"

I stretched out my paw for a refill and peered over my muzzle at him. "So?"

"There's a form you might find less conspicuous and easier to live in—on Minas, at least," Ragem began. There was a charming uncertainty in his face, a combination of the wine and an unspoken hope.

"Can I be Human?" I said for him, quite aware where this was heading. After all, he'd given up friends and family to keep me company in my self-imposed exile. It was reasonable for Ragem to wonder if he had to give up his species, too. "It's not a form I do well," I went on matter-of-factly, pretending not to see the disappointment, then amused resignation on his dear face. "Mixs had the same problem," I continued. "I should tell you about the time she . . ." As I finished my story, Ragem began to laugh.

I was relieved he'd been able to accept the parameters of our friendship so easily. There would be Human companionship for him on Minas. I would make sure of it. And he would always be part of the Web of Esen. It would be enough.

Later, when he'd gone to sleep, the last bottle of wine cradled under his arm, I stood somewhat unsteadily myself and went to the mirror by the door. There, I took a deep breath then cycled into that one form, the mirror showing me the image of a young girl, perhaps not quite ten standard years of age, who gazed back at me with eyes like ancient oceans.

Ragem would never see me like this.

I stepped out on my porch, seeing the future and completely content with what I saw. We would guard this gateway together. He would show me how to enjoy life as only an ephemeral could. In return, I would share with him whatever he wished to learn of other species, possibly even satisfying his inordinate curiosity—though I somehow doubted that.

We would be together as long as he lived.

And after that, I would remember Paul Ragem, my first friend, until the hearts of stars grew cold.